MW00389335

THE CANNINGTON EPISODE

Michael Montcombroux

Canadian Cataloguing in Publication Data
Montcombroux, Michael
The Cannington Episode

ISBN 9781537537603

(Canada 9781987946031)

1. Saskatchewan. Historical. Fiction.

solitudepublishing@gmail.com

Cover G. Montcombroux
M. Montcombroux photos

In memory of Erik

Author's Note

Cannington (full name, Cannington Manor) that forms the setting of this novel was an actual place in Canada's Northwest Territories in the last decades of the nineteenth century. Today, it is a historic site, located in the south-east of the Canadian province of Saskatchewan. The settlement was founded by the Englishman, Captain Edward Pierce, as a well-heeled, upper-class colony for English gentry who wished to perpetuate the privileged lifestyle that was increasingly difficult to maintain in a rapidly-industrializing Britain. Cannington stands apart from other pioneer communities, where homesteaders strove to build a *new* and better life for themselves, in that it was a deliberate attempt to transplant an *old* English village, complete with inn, cricket pitch, fox hunt and parish church, and the social hierarchy that went with it, onto the prairies of the Canadian West.

The intricate workings of this society, as well as its success or failure, are not the focus of the novel, only the background against which the story takes place. Other than historical figures, the novel's characters are purely fictitious.
The Cannington Episode unfolds during the hot summer of 1884, a hinge-point in western history as it marks the prelude to the Northwest Rebellion that erupted into armed conflict in 1885. After the rebellion was put down by military force, the face of western Canada was forever changed through, among other things, the aggressive promotion of immigration from Europe.

Chapter 1

Empire Hotel
Regina
North West Territories

Friday, May 2, 1884

Dearest Aunt Louise,

It will come as a surprise to you to learn that a mere three days after father and I arrived in Regina, the capital of the Northwest, I am to catch a train out of the city at ten tomorrow morning. And I shall be leaving on my own to travel to a completely unknown destination, unknown to me at least. More on that in a moment.

"What is going on?" I hear you ask. A very good question, to which I know only part of the answer. I had been deliberately kept in the dark concerning the truth behind our move from Montreal to Regina. Both you and I were led to believe that the reason for us coming here was that the board of papa's bank had asked him to set up a branch in the new capital of the Northwest. I was to keep house for him. It never occurred to me to ask why papa, a senior official in the company and director of the main bank in Montreal, would be sent so far away to open a new branch. That, surely, ought to have been a role for a much younger man? But what does a girl of eighteen know about banking?

Well, I now know the truth. As you are aware, papa insisted he wanted no one to see us off at Montreal's main station. I begged him to allow my friend Millie to be there and he reluctantly agreed. My brother Julian came to help with the baggage. That was it. While father and Millie went off to buy us some fruit and chocolate to take on the train I found myself alone on the platform with Julian. It was during those ten minutes that Julian dropped his bombshell.

The story is a long one but I'll be as brief as I can. My father, the august Theodore Chesterman, was not asked to extend the bank's activities into the Northwest, after all. He has been exiled to a place the bank believes he can do no further damage. It appears dear papa had been making himself rich by investing in high-risk railroad stocks in the United States, using the bank's money, not his own. How long this had been going on, goodness knows. He was only found out when several of his ventures failed and he was unable to repay the bank its money. During an audit he was literally caught with his fingers in the till. How did Julian know all this? An uncle of one of his fellow students at Osgoode Hall law school happens to be a member of the bank's governing board. Father could have been charged with embezzlement and sent to prison, but the publicity would have reflected unfavorably on the bank's good name. Instead, they bundled him off to the far end of the country but not before seizing all his assets. Our elegant Westmount house, the furnishings, even my beloved horse, Star, everything was sold to help the bank recoup a small fraction of its losses.

I do hope you are sitting down whilst reading this, for I have another shock for you. Papa and I arrived in Regina after an incredibly long journey, first by train to Collingwood in Ontario and then by lake steamer to the American port of Milwaukee. There we took the train to St. Paul, Minnesota. Yet another train carried us north, back into Canada, to Winnipeg, capital of the province of Manitoba. After a brief stopover, we caught the Canadian Pacific across the Prairies to Regina (it's called the transcontinental but as yet it only reaches as far west as Calgary in the Alberta District).

Prior to our departure from Montreal, papa had arranged with a building contractor in Regina to construct a house for us. The wooden frame houses they build out here can be erected very quickly, and papa had been promised the house would be ready for occupancy. Yesterday, he came to my hotel room and told me to come with him. We climbed into the buggy he had hired from the livery stable. Ten minutes later we were at the edge of the city. Although Regina is the capital of the North West Territories, it was founded only a year ago, when they abandoned the original capital of Battleford in the north. The new capital consists of hastily-constructed buildings scattered like so many doll houses over the absolutely flat, treeless prairie. Our house was to have been on an appropriately-named Victoria Avenue. I say was to have been, because father brought the buggy to a halt and pointed with his whip at a pile of rough-sawn lumber standing in the middle of nowhere. That was all there was to show for our new residence. The contractor had absconded with the money father had advanced. Because of the scarcity of workmen in the capital it is impossible to get a house built this summer. Knowing now what I do about my father, the irony of the situation was not lost on me. One crook defrauded by another!

Papa will live at the hotel while he establishes his bank. Since there is nothing for me to do here, he declared it was unthinkable for me to stay. I forgot to tell you that I must be one of only a tiny handful of white women in the entire North West Territories.

There is one small exception. It appears that a hundred miles to the south-east of the capital is a settlement of some two hundred souls called Cannington Manor. It differs from the usual pioneer colonies by being composed of wealthy English families who are engaged in a unique experiment to set up a replica of an English village in the Canadian West. From what I've heard about them, they live a refined existence in elegant houses aligned along a village street. There is an inn, a church, and all the other trappings one would find in a similar village in England. Not that I have ever visited that country. Whereas the average pioneer farmer spends his days plowing the stubborn soil and planting wheat, and his wife keeps their tiny, sod-house as clean as one can, with packed-earth floors, the Cannington residents hold dinner parties, recitals, play tennis and other games, and even hunt to hounds.

It transpires that one of the more prominent of these English settlers is a distant relative of papa's. So, in short, I am about to leave for Cannington Manor, with a letter of introduction to this relative I never knew existed until yesterday evening. I know nothing about him but the name, one Alfred Addersley, whose wife is called Rosalind. Can you imagine such a thing? The journey, itself, is somewhat intimidating. I shall take the train eastward, back the way I came, as far as a small town called Moosomin. Cannington, itself, lies well south of the railroad, and it will be up to me to inquire how to get there. Naturally no one at the colony is expecting me and I have no idea what kind of a reception I shall receive.

I will write to you as soon as I arrive and give you details about my journey and my new home. Father could not say how long I will be obliged to remain in the English settlement. I have the feeling it could be as long as a year! The one thing that has buoyed my spirits during this painful transition is learning to play the lovely flute you gave me before I left. Because it belonged to your dear late husband, my Uncle Reginald, parting with such a treasured keepsake must have been difficult. But I'm sure uncle would have been happy to see his precious flute carried across the continent and played whenever an opportunity presents itself. If I found an unoccupied corner on one of the numerous trains, I would take it out and play. On the S.S. Iroquois that ferried us across the Great Lakes, I played it on deck, *even once during a fierce storm when everyone else was below being sick. Along the way I received many odd looks and even a few comments about how a flute is an unsuitable instrument for a woman, because it distorts the mouth. What rubbish! Mr. Aspinall, the flute teacher in Westmount, gave me some instruction about its care. I keep the flute well-oiled with pure linseed oil. Like that the wood has withstood the extremes of humidity on the lakes and dryness on the Prairies. I can never fully express my gratitude for your wonderful gift. I only hope I will make enough progress to be worthy of uncle's legacy.*

Your affectionate niece,
Carina

Carina reflected on the strangeness of being back on the train, just days after the same train had carried her westward to Regina. On this occasion, her departure lacked the emotion surrounding her leaving Montreal. Accompanied by her father, she walked the short distance from the hotel to the Regina station, where the train was already waiting at the platform. Without speaking, Theodore pressed a few bills into her palm and went to ensure her trunk and other items were placed in the baggage car.

She looked about her, at the locomotive taking on coal and water, at her fellow passengers, fewer of them now heading east than on the west-bound train.

Her father returned. "Everything is safely stowed. Write when you get to Cannington. I trust your Uncle Alfred will receive you warmly."

"Is he really my uncle? You said he was a distant cousin of yours. That'd make him my cousin too, wouldn't it?"

"True." Theodore pinched his lips into a tight smile. "Frankly, I'm not altogether sure about my consanguinity with the gentleman. All that matters is that you do have a family relationship to Mr. Alfred Addersley. Since, he must be about my age, it'd be civil to address him and his wife as uncle and aunt."

"What if he doesn't know about me?"

"He will. Before he and his family came to Canada a few years ago, there was a brief exchange of letters between Rosalind Addersley and your late mother, seeking information about what to expect in this country. I recall your mother telling them that conditions in Westmount, Quebec would hardly apply to a brand new settlement on the western prairies. After your mother passed away, I sent them word of her demise and a copy of the newspaper obituary. Since that time I've had no contact with them. But they'll know who you are and I'm sure will welcome you with open arms. Well-to-do English people pride themselves on being hospitable to visitors."

Their conversation was terminated by the train conductor's shout of "All aboard!"

Theodore said a few hasty words of farewell, gave his daughter a peck on the cheek and handed her up the steps of the car. He waved once she had found a seat by the window. The train had barely started moving when Carina saw him turn and stride away toward the exit. His cool indifference didn't hurt her. That's how he had behaved all her life. Journeying together to the Northwest ought to have brought them closer but it had done nothing to bridge the gulf. Rather than being slighted by his aloofness, she experienced only pity. A father to whom she ought to have looked up to had shown himself to be not only a weak, pathetic man, but also criminally corrupt. During her two-day sojourn in the territorial capital, she had come to the conclusion that he was ill-suited to cope with the new world he had been thrust into. Her only wish was that he'd find some measure of satisfaction in establishing his bank.

For most of the journey she had one corner of the train car all to herself. A few men passing down the aisle on their way to the smoking car gave her admiring looks. When this occurred she buried herself in her novel and avoided eye-contact. Evening was approaching when the train pulled into Moosomin station. By now a seasoned traveler, she stepped onto the platform and went immediately to the baggage car to make sure her luggage was off-loaded. While she was thus engaged, a uniformed railroad official she guessed must be the station agent approached.

"Good evening, ma'am. Are you being met?"

"No, I am not. Can you direct me to a hotel?"

"Just across the street, directly opposite the station, the Railway Hotel. Shall I arrange for your baggage to be sent over? On the other hand, if you're traveling on from here, we could hold it overnight in the freight shed. A porter will take your hand luggage to the hotel."

"That would be more convenient. Thank you. I'm on my way to Cannington Manor. Can you tell me how I get there from here?"

The station agent pushed back his peaked cap. "The English settlement isn't on the rail line and there's no stage service. But if you inquire at the hotel, they'll tell you if anyone from the colony is in town. If there is, they'll be sure to take you."

Carina thanked the man and walked across the unpaved street to the hotel, a two story, yellow brick building.

The hotel desk clerk greeted her.

"I'd like a room for the night."

"Please sign the register, miss." He swivelled the ledger-sized book toward her.

She wrote her name but hesitated when it came to her address. Where did she live? The hotel in Regina? No, that was absurd. Finally, she penned her former address in Westmount. No one would be any the wiser that she no longer had any connection to it. As she was writing, she was struck by the oddness of this being the first time in her life she had traveled or stayed in a hotel on her own.

The fact that she, a single woman, was checking into the hotel must have piqued the curiosity of the manager, for he emerged from a back office and introduced himself.

"Good evening, Miss...er..." He shot a sidelong glance at the register.

"Miss Chesterman. Is this your first visit to Moosomin?"

"Other than having recently past through on the westbound train, yes. I'm on my way to Cannington Manor."

"Then you're in luck. That is, if you don't mind traveling by a buckboard carrying a load of freight."

"Oh?"

"Old Norm Tucker's in town. He's heading back tomorrow morning, bright and early. I could ask him, if you like."

"Would you? I am going to Cannington to visit a relative of mine, a Mr. Alfred Addersley. Do you happen to know him?"

The manager laughed. "Do I know him? Everyone knows Alfred Addersley. He's one of the founders of the colony. And, you're doubly in luck. Norm Tucker is Mr. Addersley's stableman."

"What a coincidence! In which case, I would be grateful if you could get word to Mr. Tucker."

"Right away. If you want a bite to eat after your train journey, the dining room is through that door. Just as soon as I hear back from Tucker, I'll let you know."

Carina expressed her thanks, relieved that her travel worries had so easily been resolved.

Even with her new-found peace of mind, sleep eluded her. The air in her hotel bedroom room was stifling. She lay under a single sheet and listened to the noises from the street and thought about her bedroom in the home she had grown up in. Even during the hottest of summers the old stone and brick house remained cool. Now that she had accepted that her future lay in the Northwest, she was schooling herself to adapt to the inconveniences of a frontier region. Her comfortable existence in fashionable Westmount lay behind her and she recognized the futility of lamenting what she no longer had. Everything in the Northwest was new and different, and that, she was discovering, included the climate.

Shortly before she had retired for the night, the manager knocked on her door and informed her that Mr. Norman Tucker was willing to take her to Cannington and would be in front of the hotel at eight the next morning.

Sharp prairie light flooded the room when she awoke. Gripped by panic at the thought she had overslept, she reached for her watch. To her relief it was not yet seven. After washing in tepid water, she decided to wear her practical riding outfit, rather than a dress. She had already learned that the route to Cannington consisted of a rough trail that forded several creeks along the way.

After packing her bag, she carried it downstairs and left it in the lobby while she ate breakfast. She was ready by seven-thirty with nothing more to do but wait. She sat in an armchair with her book. As a parting gift, her friend Millie had given her a present of *Anna Karenina*, a recently translated novel by the Russian Leo Tolstoy. The very first sentence of the first chapter leapt out at her the moment she had opened the book: *Happy families are all alike; every unhappy family is unhappy in its own way.*

This could not be truer than of her own family. The word *unhappy* did not begin to describe it. When her mother was alive, the remoteness of her father mattered less. The Chesterman house was animated by a constant stream of visitors, among them leading writers, artists and musicians. Victoria Chesterman, herself a gifted musician, had envisaged a brilliant musical career for her only daughter. Inspired by the American Amy Beach, practically identical in age to Carina, who was making a name for herself as a pianist, Carina's mother sought out the best available piano teachers. All this ground to a sudden halt two years before, when Victoria Chesterman was struck down and killed by a streetcar. In an ironic twist of fate, she had been crossing Montreal's *Rue Sainte-Catherine* on her way to an interview with the dean of the Conservatory of Music.

On that day, Carina closed the lid of the drawing room Steinway and abandoned all thoughts of a musical career. Her father lacked the time, ability and interest to concern himself with his daughter's musical education. During the dark months that followed the tragedy, Carina found solace in visiting her only close relative, her widowed great-aunt Louise, whose modest house offered the comfort lacking in the vast mausoleum the Westmount mansion had become. It was the elderly Louise who rekindled Carina's love of music, with a present of her late husband's flute, a wooden Rudall

& Rose six-keyed instrument. With a few lessons, Carina began to make progress but played solely for the pleasure of making music.

Carina read in a scientific magazine about the new term *dysfunctional* to denote the unhealthy relationships that can exist within families. The term accurately described the relationship she had with her bother Julian, three years her senior. Julian had always teased her cruelly. After the loss of their mother, his taunts became even more acerbic. He even insinuated that she had been the cause of their mother's death. Worse still, now that she had grown into an attractive young woman with a head of beautiful blond hair, he made sexual innuendoes about her appearance. If they happened to pass on the stairs or if she handed him a dish at the dining table, he would touch her, yet making it seem like an accident. So blatant were his actions that she took care to keep away from him and ensure she was never alone with him in the same room. She was thankful that Julian did not accompany them west. He was to spend the summer in Montreal working in a law office before returning to his studies in the fall.

The one person with the capacity to transform the unhappy family, her father, was now disgraced and impoverished. As for herself, she was being thrown as a poor relative upon the charity of strangers. The entire wealth at her disposal was the fifty dollars her father had given her. It was doubtful any more would be forthcoming and she had no intention of asking him for further help.

The voice of the desk clerk broke into her thoughts.

"Miss Chesterman, Norm Tucker is out front."

Chapter 2

Fifteen minutes later, Carina found herself viewing the world from the high seat of a buckboard drawn by a handsome pair of chestnut mares. Beside her, gripping the reins between gnarled fingers, sat Norman Tucker, a tall, sparse man in his sixties. Behind the seat, kneeling on a cushion of horse blankets was Ellie, Tucker's fourteen-year-old granddaughter. Carina had expected them to be English, but both man and girl spoke with a Canadian accent.

From the hotel, they drove down the town's main street, lined with false-fronted stores and buildings. A woman outside a house paused from hanging laundry on a line to watch them pass. Carina waved and the woman waved back. The street soon gave way to a dirt trail and a wide vista opened before them. Unlike the flat, treeless plain surrounding Regina, the prairie here stretched into the distance in rolling waves, punctuated by clusters of willow and poplar. Once the town disappeared behind them, the landscape became devoid of any human habitation or activity, not a farm or even a fenced field in sight.

As if to compensate for her grandfather's taciturn nature, Ellie proved to be a chatterbox. The girl crept up close behind Carina and gripped the wooden back of the seat. "I love your riding outfit, Miss Chesterman,"

"Thank you."

"When the English ladies go riding they wear long skirts and ride side-saddle. They look very elegant in their velvet jackets and hats with veils. But they never travel very far dressed like that. Your outfit looks much more practical."

"I think we are in agreement on that, Ellie. Do you go to school?"

"I did till last year. I now work in the kitchen of Mr. and Mrs. Addersley's house."

"And what kind of a house does Mr. and Mrs. Addersley have?"

"Next to the Beresford brothers' mansion and Cap'n Pierce's house, it's the biggest in the village."

Tucker took his eyes off his horses for a moment. "Captain Pierce is the gentleman who founded the settlement and brought out many of the rich folk from England. He and Mr. Addersley run the Moose Mountain Trading Company store. Mr. Rodney Beresford and his brother Algernon built a big stone house close to the edge of the village. They raise some of the finest horseflesh in the territory."

For the next hour, Ellie kept up a commentary on life at Cannington Manor, from which Carina gleaned some insight into what was to be her new home, as seen, of course, through the eyes of a young servant girl.

The trail consisted of a broad track cut into the prairie sod by the passage of wagons and horses. Occasionally it skirted an area of deep ruts which suggested that at other times the conditions were wet and muddy. Carina's eye followed the brown ribbon of trail that snaked ahead over the land before disappearing into the distance. She was taken unawares when the buckboard crested a ridge and she looked down into a shallow valley that had been invisible until they were right on the rim.

Tucker grinned. "It never fails to surprise the first-time traveler. This is Pipestone Creek. We stop at the bottom to water the horses. Maybe you're ready for a break yourself, miss. I'll boil a kettle and make some tea."

"You really don't need to go to any trouble on my account, Mr. Tucker."

"It ain't no bother. We have to give the horses a good rest. After this, it's a long haul over the bald prairie with very few creeks and no drinkable lake water."

His remark *drinkable lake water* puzzled her, for along the way they had past a great many circular lakes, though some no larger than ponds. Since he was concentrating on negotiating the steep incline down to the valley floor, she didn't dare distract him with questions.

He held the horses in check as the buckboard gathered speed. When the trail flattened out the horses splashed through a shallow creek that glittered in the bright sunshine. Tucker brought the buckboard to a halt on the far side to allow the horses to drink. He then drove up onto on a grassy terrace above the level of the water. He jumped down and secured the reins to a willow bush.

Carina understood why he had selected this spot. Above them, the steeply rising south bank afforded shade from the harsh sun.

Tucker went to the back of the wagon and unpacked a canvas bucket. "Ellie, go gather some wood for the fire, will you?"

Carina climbed down, her legs stiff and her back numb. The biscuit-thin cushion absorbed some but not all of the jolting over the uneven surface. She imagined her body to be black and blue and there were still many miles to go. While the man and girl were occupied, she walked along the terrace until she was out of sight behind the thicket of willows to attend to nature.

Tucker had a fire going between two large stones, with a kettle perched at an angle on top. Ellie sat on the creek bank, dangling her bare feet in the water. Carina enjoyed the girl's companionship and appreciated her forthright manner. From her she heard for the first time about the English adherence to class distinction and guessed that the Cannington elite would frown on any over-familiarity with a domestic servant.

Tucker pointed to the lowered tailgate of the buckboard. "Miss Chesterman, there's tea for you. You'll find bread and cheese in the basket. Help yourself."

After the rest they set off again. The horses strained into their harness on the upward gradient. Both horses and humans breathed with relief when the buckboard gained the level prairie where the going was easier.

On one occasion the trail skirted a small circular lake. Tucker stopped and watered the horses. After another long stretch Carina could see the horses were thirsty and called out when she spotted another lake up ahead.

Tucker shook his head. "That's an alkaline lake. Water's not fit for drinking, neither for man nor beast."

Carina saw why when they passed it by. Along the water's edge lay a thick white crust of salt. The hours came and went. The landscape never varied. Only the jolting of the wagon reminded her that they were actually moving. In all directions the treeless plain ran to the distant horizon where it met the edge of a sky so intensely blue it hurt the eyes. Despite her effort to stay alert, her eyelids grew heavy and her chin fell forward.

She only realized that she had dozed off when the buckboard came to a jarring halt. Ahead of them lay another wide valley, this one much shallower than the Pipestone Valley. No watercourse lay at its bottom and vegetation was non-existent. Away in the distance to the south-west she could discern a shimmering violet-blue line of hills.

Tucker pointed with his chin to the valley below them, "Antler Creek. As you can see, at this time of year, it's bone dry. On the horizon that's Moose Mountain. Cannington ain't far now."

The incline down was less steep than at the Pipestone Valley. The trail zig-zagged to the dry creek bed and angled up the far side.

Carina lost count of the hours they had been traveling. She was sore from the constant bouncing over the rough surface. By the lower angle of the sun she knew evening was approaching. Ellie had fallen asleep on her bed of blankets. Her bonnet had slipped down her back and the sun danced on the highlights of the girl's tangle of dark hair.

With the shallow valley of Antler Creek behind them, the prairie landscape transformed itself yet again, from treeless plain to rolling aspen parkland with abundant grass. Carina spotted an occasional farm tucked into a fold in the land. Away in the distance she glimpsed groups of whitetail deer and pronghorn antelope.

When the buckboard next crested a bluff, Carina saw a plume of dust rising in the distance. "Do you see that, Mr. Tucker?"

The old man raised the brim of his hat and squinted into the sunlight. "That's the welcoming committee."

"Welcoming committee?"

"Captain Pierce runs a college for young gentlemen from the Old Country. He calls them his pups. They come out to Cannington to learn farming." Tucker cleared his throat spat over the side of the buckboard. "They're all from wealthy families and spend more time horseback riding, hunting, drinking and playing sports than they do studying. When they know anyone is visiting or returning to the settlement they like to ride out to form a mounted escort for the last few miles. They're in for a surprise when they discover I have a young lady on board."

"Judging from the dust cloud, there must be several riders."

"There'll be a dozen or more."

Carina straightened on the seat, unsure about the prospect of living in a small community alongside a group of unattached young Englishmen with time on their hands. Ellie hadn't mentioned them in her chatter about the English colony. Was she worried? Perhaps a few months before she might have been. Recent events coupled with having traveled more than half way across the continent had given her a new and more realistic outlook on life. She was no longer the shy girl of before but an assertive young woman who had no intention of being intimidated by anyone, least of all a troop of English horsemen.

The column drew close enough for her to make out the individual riders. Tucker had said they were from well-to-do families. Yet they did not resemble the Englishmen who had visited the Westmount house, whose demeanor had been formal to the point of affectation. These men wore a bizarre assortment of western wear, including buckskins, check shirts, red bandanas, Mexican spurs and wide-brimmed hats.

As if rehearsed, the horsemen split into two columns on meeting the buckboard and thundered past on either side. The riders waved their hats, and whooped and hollered shouts of welcome. They then wheeled back to form an escort, consisting of a small knot in front, outriders on either side, the remainder bringing up the rear. Carina saw two of them break away and head back at a mad gallop in the direction they had come, presumably to announce their imminent arrival.

Carina could have been excused in thinking that her entry to Cannington Manor had some of the trappings of visiting royalty.

Chapter 3

After a day spent traveling across the nothingness of the land, her first sight of Cannington Manor was a cluster of white-painted buildings sitting on an up-swell of prairie that sloped gently down from east to west where it connected with the trail. The houses and buildings lined a central street. It was into this street that the cavalcade turned.

Norman Tucker pointed ahead with his chin. "The Addersley residence is farther along on the right, just after the church."

As they progressed, Carina took stock of what was to be her home for the foreseeable future. The west end of the settlement was given over to playing fields, tennis courts and what appeared to be a horse racing track, complete with a raised starter's box topped with a shingled roof. Nearby, on a carefully groomed grass pitch, a game of cricket was in progress. She was vaguely familiar with the game as it was popular with the small English community in the Westmount district of Montreal. The players clad in whites halted their play to watch the buckboard and its attendant riders pass by. Along either side of the broad, unpaved street ran wooden boardwalks. On one of them, a trio of middle-aged women in stylish dresses and flowery hats waved. Unsure whether they were waving at her or the men on horseback, Carina waved back. The Moosomin hotel manager mentioned that the settlement was only a few years old. Yet it bore none of the rawness of the equally new capital, Regina. Many of the houses had fenced yards in which flowers bloomed. There were trees, too, that offered welcome shade.

They passed the church, a white clapboard structure with a bell tower surmounted by a spire bearing a wooden cross. Directly opposite was another imposing building on which hung a painted sign with *Mitre Inn* in gilt letters.

Tucker reined his team to a halt in front of a two-story wooden house set back from the street behind a picket fence. The escort remained mounted in a semicircle around the wagon. Obviously alerted to their arrival, the owner of the house waited at the front gate, beside him a woman, presumably his wife, and a girl a handful of years older than Carina. Despite the heat, the man sported a dark suit and a bright yellow, embroidered vest. The woman and girl wore somber dresses reminiscent of an earlier age in fashion.

With an agility belying his years, Norman Tucker jumped down and reached up to help Carina dismount from the high seat.

In a confidential voice he said, "That's Mr. and Mrs. Alfred Addersley and their daughter, Maud."

Addersley stepped forward, a look of surprise on his florid face. "What have we here, Tucker? I send you to town to collect a consignment of dry goods for the store and you come back with a young lady!"

Norman Tucker grinned. "Miss Chesterman, sir, a relative of yours."

"A relative?"

Carina reached into her purse. "Hello, Mr. Addersley. I am Carina Chesterman, originally from Montreal. I have here a letter of introduction from my father." She handed him the sealed envelope her father had given her.

Addersley pushed his horn-rimmed spectacles up the bridge of his long nose and read the letter. "Ah, so you are Theo's child? How interesting! I hadn't heard from him in ages. I'm sorry to learn that you were unable to stay with him in Regina. I fully understand why. The rough and ready capital is no place for a genteel young lady." He studied Carina's face for several moments, as though searching for a family resemblance. He then opened his arms and wrapped her in a bear hug. "Carina, my dear cousin, you are more than welcome to stay with us until circumstances permit you to be reunited with your father." He placed a hand in the small of her back and led her to where the woman and girl were standing. "This is my wife, Rosalind, and our daughter, Maud."

Mrs. Addersley offered her hand to Carina in a polite handshake that lacked the warmth of her husband's greeting. "Welcome to Cannington Manor, Miss Chesterman."

She said nothing more, but Carina was conscious of the woman's eyes appraising her from head to toe. Carina wondered if she had committed a social blunder in arriving in high boots, a split riding skirt and white blouse, a daring outfit compared to the more formal attire of the Addersley women.

"Thank you, Mrs. Addersley. From my first impressions, Cannington looks a delightful place."

The older woman nodded. "It has its charms. Incidentally, we always refer to it as Cannington *Manor* and would be grateful if you did too. You look terribly young to be traveling on your own. How old are you?"

"I will have my nineteenth birthday in the fall."

"The fall? You mean the autumn, I assume. At not yet nineteen you are six years younger than my daughter Maud." She looked at the girl. "Maud, say hello to our new house guest."

Maud shook hands with Carina. "Welcome, Miss Chesterman. I hope your stay will be a happy one."

Carina was about to express her thanks when Alfred Addersley cleared his throat.

"Now, now, what's all this formality about? The girl's a relative. No need for the Mr., Mrs. and Miss business."

"My father suggested I address you as uncle and aunt." Carina smiled at Maud. "And cousin, of course."

"That's fine by me," Addersley said. "Now that's settled, let's get your things unloaded and we'll get you installed. There's a room next to Maud's which will suit you." He took Norman Tucker aside and began discussing the freight the buckboard was carrying.

Having escorted the visitor to her destination, the horsemen turned their mounts and rode back down the main street, leaving a cloud of yellow dust hanging in the still evening air.

Rosalind Addersley motioned Carina to follow her into the house. "Your cousin Maud will doubtless explain about our way of life. Just let me say that because of the deplorable shortage of domestic staff in Canada, family members are unfortunately obliged to take on some of the household duties. You will be expected to do your share."

"I am more than willing to help wherever I can, Aunt Rosalind."

"I insist on punctuality at meals. We dress for dinner every evening. As a Canadian, you may be unfamiliar with the custom. A gong sounds at seven, at which time one goes to one's room to change. Another gong summons everyone to the drawing room at seven-thirty, from whence we proceed into the dining room. We have already dined this evening. If you are in need of sustenance, I am sure our cook, Mrs. Tucker, will provide you with something. One final thing, we attend Sunday services as a family. You do have suitable clothes for churchgoing, I trust."

"My wardrobe is modest but contains a couple of nice dresses."

Aunt Rosalind glanced again at Carina's knee-length riding skirt. "Good."

Carina was given a conducted tour of the house. The furnishings were different from what she was used to and she guessed they had been brought from England. Two large rooms dominated the ground floor. First, a spacious drawing room furnished with a sofa and overstuffed armchairs protected by lace antimacassars that spoke of an earlier era. Against one wall stood a massive glass-fronted china cabinet, its shelves filled with a dinner service and various porcelain figurines. What attracted Carina were the French doors that opened onto a neatly kept garden of lawns and flowerbeds. From the drawing room, double doors led into a formal dining room equipped with a heavy oak table and matching high-backed chairs that looked as though they would not be out of place in a medieval manor house. Against the walls stood tall, corniced cabinets containing linen and cutlery. Two portraits of family ancestors frowned down on the room. On the opposite wall hung a five-foot-wide oil landscape depicting storm clouds rolling down bleak English moorland to buffet a tiny thatched cottage. Although the room possessed two large windows, the overall effect was one of gloom, due in part to the heavy brocade drapery. The remaining lower floor rooms consisted of a wood-paneled breakfast room, Mr. Addersley's study, a large kitchen replete with a wood-fired cookstove and a square table whose surface was scrubbed white. Carina was shown the parlor, which seemed to be the only room that radiated joy, with its floral easy chairs, upright piano with an intricate fretwork pattern backed by red velvet. Pretty watercolors adorned the walls.

The upper floor was given over to bedrooms. The room appointed to her was referred to as the 'porch room' so named because it was directly above the front entrance. It afforded a view of the main street and the inn diagonally across the way. It might equally be called the 'nun's cell' as it was small and narrow, furnished simply with a narrow bedstead, an unpainted pine chest of drawers, a marble-topped washstand, a small desk equipped with a china candleholder and a straight-backed chair with an embroidered, padded seat. A wickerwork armchair was the only nod at luxury. Despite the austere furnishings, Carina was more than happy with her new room. At the end of the corridor was the bathroom equipped with a bath of beaten copper, so deep it reminded her of the Grand Canyon, a lithograph of which had hung in her old house.

The tour was interrupted by footsteps on the staircase. The women stood aside to allow Norman Tucker and a young man in shirtsleeves to deposit Carina's trunk in her room.

When Aunt Rosalind left, Carina washed the trail grime from her face and hands. Later, she dined alone in a corner of the kitchen on a cheese and lettuce sandwich and a glass of milk. The cook served her then disappeared to attend to other duties. After supper, since the downstairs rooms appeared to be deserted, Carina went back to her room and dressed for bed. Although weary from the long trip from the station in the prairie heat, she didn't feel like retiring immediately. She lit the candle on the desk and brought her journal up to date with an account of the train journey, the overland trek and her first impressions of Cannington Manor and its inhabitants. In one entry she speculated on the impression she, a

Canadian girl, must have made on her English relatives and wondered how long it would take her to fit in. That is, if she ever would. Her education and training instilled in her an instinct for the proper comportment in polite society. She knew, for example, how to conduct a conversation at the dinner table. Yet her first few hours in the colony convinced her that there existed a considerable gulf between the Westmount interpretation of manners and those practiced in upper-class English circles. Her only hope was that she wouldn't commit an unpardonable sin against their social code.

Even though she wrote her journal in French as a partial deterrent against prying eyes, she kept the book locked in her trunk. People of her uncle and aunt's class might well be conversant with the French language and she didn't want them or anyone else to read her thoughts expressed so openly.

Her uncle promised to show her the settlement and the tour took place after breakfast the following morning. Carina wore her second best dress and a straw hat, a more formal outfit than she would have normally chosen for walking out on a warm summer morning. Her outfit evidently met with her aunt's approval, if Carina interpreted the woman's nod and tight smile correctly. Maud, wearing a lavender dress in a style that made her look a decade older than her twenty-five years, accompanied her father and Carina.

The orientation began at the Addersley residence with the stable, coach house and other outbuildings. She was delighted to discover that her uncle owned several fine horses

"You like horses, then?"

"I love them. I was taught to ride when I was ten and had my own horse until recently."

"Indeed? I always admire a woman who knows her way around a horse. Much to my regret, my daughter rides only when obliged to. Isn't that so, Maud?"

"I can't help it, daddy, if horses make me nervous."

Addersley turned to Carina. "Perhaps some of your enthusiasm will rub off on Maud during your stay with us." He pointed his walking stick at a horse grazing along with others in the field beyond the garden. "See that mare with the black coat? That's a horse that might suit you. She's actually an American breed, a Morgan. An excellent riding horse, though, here we prefer the English hunters bred by the Beresford brothers."

"I've heard about those two gentlemen. I would be honored to be allowed to ride your Morgan."

"I'll tell Tucker to bring her in. Perhaps tomorrow you can take her for a ride. By the way, she's called Morgana, hardly an original name, I must confess."

After the frosty reception by her Aunt Rosalind, coupled with the subdued character of Maud and the somber atmosphere that pervaded the house, her Uncle Alfred's always cheerful disposition filled her with hope that her stay would have its pleasanter moments. Even when he was being serious, his eyes sparkled good-naturedly behind his old-fashioned spectacles.

The hour-long tour took them down the opposite side of the street, visiting in turn the cricket pavilion, the general store, the assembly hall, the inn, several commercial buildings, including the grist mill and the blacksmith's shop. In the latter they watched a magnificent Suffolk Punch heavy horse having a shoe replaced. On the way back they called in at the creamery. Her uncle pointed out the houses of various members of the settlement, notably that of the founder Captain Pierce.

"The present population is about two hundred and fifty. That includes the English families, their domestics, as well as some Canadian servants, such as Mr. Norman Tucker and his wife and grandchild. There are also a score or more young men enrolled in Captain Pierce's agricultural college. They were the gentlemen who greeted you upon your arrival."

Carina looked at her uncle. "Where do they stay, these young gentlemen?"

Addersley pointed to the west. "Just beyond the village outskirts lies the Beresford brothers' mansion. In due course, I'm sure you'll be invited there as the brothers are extremely sociable. They hold frequent balls and other forms of entertainment. The east wing of the house is called Bachelor Hall. It comprises single quarters for the young gentlemen who attend the agricultural college. Whilst on the subject of these single gentlemen," Her uncle halted and looked intently at her, "perhaps this is as good a time as any to offer you a word of caution."

"Caution?"

"These young fellows all come from good families but they are what one might call somewhat high-spirited." He chuckled to himself. "Not that they're bad chaps but this is the first time they've been free of the restraints of their families or their schoolmasters. They have been known to be somewhat wild. The captain, being a military man, is adept at keeping them in line. It would, however, be wise for you to emulate Maud and the other young ladies of the community by keeping your distance from them, except of course at occasions such as balls, where there are chaperons present to ensure that the proper decorum is maintained. I trust you understand. Maud will vouch for what I am saying. Isn't that so, Maud?"

Maud's face went blank, an expression Carina was beginning to recognize as the girl's habitual response to questions put to her.

After a moment of awkward silence, Maud murmured, "Yes, papa."

"Thank you, uncle, for the warning. I'll do my best to be always on my guard."

"Good, then let us conclude the grand tour with a visit to our magnificent All Saints' church."

After the brilliant sunshine, it took several moments for Carina's eyes to grow accustomed to the subdued light of the church interior. Although she had been a member of her local Westmount church, she was far from being a devoted attendee, mainly because, when her mother was alive and preparing her for a musical career, church attendance took second place to music lessons, recitals and practice times. Her father made no secret of his distaste for religion and attended services simply because, in his own words, every prominent member of the business class ought to be seen with his family in church on the Sabbath. He was equally vocal in his dismissal of the clergy as interfering busybodies.

"The church itself," Addersley explained, "was erected by our local craftsmen in three months. As you can see it's in the traditional cruciform shape, with the altar at the east end and bell tower and spire to the west. The bells, as well as the silver chalice and candle holders on the altar were presented by the Bishop of Exeter, no less. The walls are of squared logs covered by shiplap boards on the exterior and panelling inside."

"It's quite beautiful," Carina said.

"Forgive me for asking, but coming as you do from French Quebec, are you of the…er, papish persuasion?"

Carina laughed at her uncle's use of the archaic term. "No, uncle, my family attended St. Mark's Anglican church in Westmount."

She heard him give an audible sigh.

"I am so very pleased to hear that. By Anglican you obviously mean the Church of England in Canada. The rector here is a splendid chap by the name of Obadiah Featherstonehaugh. You'll meet him in due course. As a family, we attend Matins on Sundays, as well as Evensong. You will, I assume, join us."

"I promised Aunt Rosalind I would. I intend to participate as fully as I can in the life of the settlement, uncle."

"Excellent, excellent."

Maud spoke up for the first time. "Miss Chesterman, I mean, Carina, I have an extra Prayer Book you may like to use."

"That's very kind of you."

Upon exiting the church Carina thanked her uncle for the tour. "I've seen many interesting things. Is there anything I can do to help?"

A puzzled frown crossed Addersley's face. "Help? What do you mean?"

"I don't know, some sort of work, perhaps."

Again, the spectacles went higher on the nose. "I don't know how it is in your part of Canada but here in Cannington we strive to preserve the habits of the old country. That means the responsibility of young women of our class is to prepare themselves to take up their roles as society ladies and that of wives and mothers. They may engage in tennis or archery, take dancing and music lessons, even become skilled horsewomen. They often assist in housekeeping responsibilities, but the thought of paid work is beyond the pale. That pursuit is for women of the laboring class."

"Yes, of course, uncle." Carina realized that her uncle's attitude was no different from her father's when it came to women and employment. This puzzled her. She wanted to ask whether at his general store there was not a need for someone to keep the account books or perform similar duties. She decided to keep these thoughts to herself for the time being.

She became better acquainted with her cousin Maud later that day. Carina was silently amazed by the zeal with which the English settlers observed the practice of taking afternoon tea. It seemed that all work and movement in the village came to a halt at four so that the inhabitants could sit down and partake of tea and cake.

On that afternoon, both Alfred and Rosalind Addersley pleaded another engagement and after ten minutes at the tea table excused themselves, leaving Carina alone with Maud.

"How do you like living in Cannington Manor, Maud?"

"It is a very pleasant life here. Rather more difficult in winter. Keeping the house properly heated is not easy. The settlement was situated on high ground expressly to give a magnificent view over the surrounding countryside. Unfortunately, that means our wells sometimes run dry."

Beyond such details, Carina's cousin appeared reluctant to be drawn into conversation.

Carina persisted. "How do you spend your time when you are not visiting?"

"I help mother with the house. It's so hard to get servants and when we do engage a good one she's often snapped up for a wife by some homesteader in the district."

Carina noticed that Maud spoke in the same marble-like accent as her mother. Yet, when she adopted a more conversational tone, as she did once she relaxed, the accent became less pronounced.

"What about the other women in the settlement? I saw very few in Regina. People there tell me that is typical throughout the territory."

"Cannington is different. There are many women here and life is as refined as it was back in England. I hate to think what it must be like to be a pioneer woman. Everything outside the settlement is so primitive and hostile. Even towns like Moosomin. I went to Regina once and hated it."

"What about social life? Your father mentioned the community holds balls."

"We do, at various times of the year. I attend but I don't dance."

Carina wanted to ask why but refrained. It was a miracle she had gotten her cousin to open up as much as she had.

Maud gave a weak smile. "Other than that, I devote much of my time to the church as a member of the Women's Auxiliary. You are more than welcome to join. Right now we are embroidering altar cloths. And you'll enjoy meeting the rector. Mr. Featherstonehaugh is such a sympathetic gentleman."

"I'll give it careful consideration. There's tennis, too, I hear."

"I don't play, though several evenings a week during the summer months the younger set get together and play. I'm sure you'd fit in. You appear to be quite athletic in your physique."

"And cricket."

"That's for the gentlemen only, of course. Occasionally, the men challenge the ladies to a match. The gentlemen are exceedingly gallant. They give the cricket bats to the women, while they use broomsticks. It's jolly good fun."

"Do you take part?"

Maud gave a hearty laugh. "I did once. In the last such match they made me the umpire, which was hilarious since I haven't a clue about the rules."

After her conversation with Maud, Carina was convinced that the woman must have suffered some disappointment in life, perhaps an unhappy love affair that resulted in her being withdrawn and still unmarried. She hoped that she could encourage her to be more outgoing, for she found the aura of sadness surrounding the woman disturbing in one so young. Carina surmised that under that austere exterior there beat a passionate heart.

Carina explored the large garden at the rear of the house. Because of the heat the lawn had dried out to a drab brown and many of the flowers were withered. A tall caragana hedge protected the garden from the prevailing west wind and appeared largely unaffected by the lack of moisture. She also took a walk on her own in the village and took a second look at the landmarks her uncle had pointed out. Several new buildings were in different stages of construction, but the settlement lacked the frenzy she had seen in the capital. Here reigned a bucolic peace and quiet.

During her brief stay in Regina she had read in the *Leader* newspaper of the threat of armed uprising in the territory by disgruntled Métis settlers and native tribes. Yet there was no evidence of anxiety in the capital. The prospect of violent rebellion seemed even more remote in Cannington.

In the early evening, when the heat of the day had subsided, she took her flute and went to the bottom of the garden, where a wrought iron bench stood next to an aspen, the height of which suggested it predated the house and the settlement itself. In that secluded spot she devoted half an hour to practice.

She was sitting, lost in thought, when she saw Ellie approach.

"Miss Chesterman, the missus asked me to tell you it's time to dress for dinner."

"Thank you, Ellie. I'll go up to my room."

The girl's eyes fell to the flute in Carina's lap. "You play lovely, miss. I wish I could do that."

"I've only just begun to learn the flute. Would you like to try it?"

"That would be wonderful but Mrs. A wouldn't approve."

"Why not?"

"Cos you're a lady and I'm just a domestic servant."

Carina was about to say that made no difference, even though she knew the answer, when a woman's voice sounded from the house.

"Ellie!"

Ellie lifted her head. "That's my grandma calling. I'm supposed to be helping prepare dinner."

Carina watched the girl sprint back to the house before following at a more leisurely pace. She was growing fond of Ellie for her simple grace, her beautiful dark eyes and lively intelligence.

For dinner, Carina wore her burgundy red satin dress with the ruffled hem. Back in the house, when deciding what clothes to pack and what to give away, due to the lack of luggage space, she hesitated including the dress because of its formality. She had been under the impression that elaborate outfits would not be suited for the frontier. Now, surrounded by Englishwomen wearing the latest in European fashions, she was beginning to think that she may have misjudged the situation. Yet, how could she have known that such a place as Cannington Manor existed as a speck of polite society in the middle of the wilderness?

She need not have worried. At the foot of the stairs, she was met by her aunt, smiling at her.

"Carina, you look positively radiant in that dress."

"Thank you, aunt."

Rosalind Addersley, herself, wore a black lace dress adorned with sequins. "Carina, I see you are not wearing jewelry. I can lend you some of mine if you omitted to bring any."

"That's very kind of you. I rarely wear any, except perhaps for a simple necklace to attend a ball."

"Well, you do have youth and beauty on your side, but wearing jewels is the mark of a lady. By the bye, if you need anything altering or even a new dress run up, we have a skilled seamstress here in the village. Her name is Mrs. Ripley. She is a widow and a Canadian, but is extremely skilled. Her house is the last one past the grist mill on the north side of the high street."

"That's useful to know. Thank you."

"Come into the drawing room and have a glass of fruit punch before we dine. I'll have my husband introduce you to this evening's dinner guests."

Chapter 4

Cannington Manor, North West Territories
Sunday, May 11, 1884

Dear Millie,

When I last wrote to you papa and I had just arrived in the capital only to find out no house was waiting for us, as planned. I was about to leave Regina to stay with distant relatives in an English colony a hundred miles away. Well, I am now safely ensconced in Cannington Manor, which is like a small corner of England dropped into the middle of the Canadian Prairies, just like in a fairy tale.

It was father's decision for me to come here. I could have easily found something useful to do in Regina. I saw in the newspaper that they were wanting a reporter. I'm confident I could have done the job. When I hinted at it, father became quite angry and said no daughter of his was going to work as a journalist. I have been in Cannington now for a week and am gradually getting accustomed to the quirky ways of the English. Mind you, everyone is very kind, especially my Uncle Alfred, but day-to-day life is governed by a complex set of unwritten rules that can be daunting to an outsider. If you think Westmount society is stuffy it's nothing compared to Cannington Manor. The other day I committed an unpardonable blunder when I cut up the food on my dinner plate and ate with my fork in my right hand.

I noticed the other people at the table were using both knife and fork, even balancing their peas on the back of their forks!

All of that is trivial compared to my other news.

You will recall me telling you how, a week or so before my departure, I was out riding along the bridle paths on the wooded slopes of Mont Royal and came across a gentleman having difficulty with his horse. It was on that steep section that joins up with the end of the street where I used to live. A man (a handsome man too!) was attempting, without much success, to remove a pebble from under one of the shoes of his horse. I stopped and lent him the clasp knife I always carry in my saddlebag. We got talking and he introduced himself as a Mr. Dillon Granger. I got nothing more from him other than his name and the admission he was not from the area. His horse was hired from the livery stable at the base of Mount Royal. Yet, for some strange reason I had the distinct impression he knew who I was and where I lived.

Amid the bustle surrounding our departure I put the encounter out of my mind, but you will never guess what. I met him again! This time on the S.S. Iroquois, the lake steamer from Collingwood, Ontario to Milwaukee. Wasn't that the oddest of coincidences? We were one day out, leaving Georgian Bay and entering the much larger Lake Huron, when a bad storm blew up. Virtually everyone became seasick. Father was in a bad state. I had only been on a boat once before in my life, when my mother took Julian and me on a day excursion on the St. Lawrence. Yet, for some reason I was among the

handful of passengers unaffected by the pitching of
the vessel. Meal times were farcical the way we had to
hang on to our plates and cups.

The storm eventually died down and
shipboard life slowly began to fall back into its
regular routine. I spent my time on deck to escape
the lingering smell of sickness below. The lake was
still running high and I loved to stand on the
foredeck and watch the waves crashing against the
ship. While I was thus engaged I heard someone call
my name. When I looked round I saw none other
than Mr. Granger himself beckoning to me. He
shouted that I was putting myself in danger on the
exposed deck. I retreated to the shelter of the lifeboats
just as a bigger than usual wave sent water sloshing
over the very spot I had been standing on moments
before. Naturally, I was grateful to the gentleman for
saving me from being swept overboard. We got
talking and he surprised me by saying he too was
traveling to Regina, in the North West Territories.

That might have been the end of it, but that
same evening I was returning to my cabin after
taking some soup to my father who was still unwell,
when I bumped into Mr. Granger yet again. He asked
me if I would like to listen to some music. When I
said yes (there was not much to do in the evening.
The ship's lighting was too poor to even read by), Mr.
Granger and I crept down to the steerage section.
That's where the poorest people travel. They may be
poor but they know how to have fun. We entered a
low-ceilinged saloon dimly lit by just a few electric
bulbs. A wild dance was in progress! We stood next to
a band consisting of two fiddles, a man playing a

flute a bit like mine, and a girl with a hand-held
drum. It was music like I've never heard before. The
rhythm was so infectious it got my feet tapping.
Before I knew what was happening I was dancing.
Yes, dancing with my mysterious Mr. Granger! This
was nothing like the sedate waltzes, minuets and
cotillions of our society balls. It was all crazy jigs,
reels and hornpipes, with boots pounding the wooden
floor and skirts whirling. Everyone was laughing
and having a great time.

     The crush of dancers moved counter-clockwise
around the room. Just as Mr. Granger and I came up
to the foot of the stairs, I heard this angry shout,
"Carina!" I looked round and saw my father
glowering at me. I will not tire you with what dear
papa had to say, merely that he was not altogether
overjoyed at finding his well-brought up daughter
down with the common people and in the arms of a
stranger. He ordered me to my cabin and later came
and spoke to me in the severest of tones. For the
remainder of the voyage I was obliged to spend my
time in the upper deck saloon reserved for ladies.
Needless to say, I saw nothing more of Mr. Granger
for the last of the journey. I believe the incident
aboard the steamer was in part behind father's
decision to send me (his wayward daughter!) here to
Cannington, where I would be properly chaperoned.

     We have a formal dinner every evening with
several guests in attendance (anyone who passes
through the settlement invariably gets invited to the
Addersleys). Often, the table conversation is
crashingly dull. Two evenings ago I was tardy in
getting dressed and by the time I went downstairs,

everybody had gone into the dining room. I slid into my seat the foot of the table, looked up and saw, seated at my uncle's right - you guessed it - my Mr. Granger. To my utter surprise he was dressed in the splendid scarlet uniform of a sergeant in the North-West Mounted Police, all brass buttons and gold braid! Needless to say I was speechless and not a little confused.

The house was extremely hot and stuffy and as soon as I could I escaped into the garden. I was standing on the lawn admiring the last of the sunset when Mr. (Sergeant) Granger came out of the house. Because we were on our own I asked him for an explanation. If I were to give you all the details this already long letter would be even longer. So I shall be brief. Suffice to say that my dear papa had gotten himself into an awkward situation at his bank, which is why he was sent to Regina. It transpires that a board member tipped off the Mounted Police and they sent Sgt. Granger to Montreal to find out about their newest immigrant to the Northwest. The sergeant had been keeping an eye on papa when I first met him, and again on the lake steamer. Upon his return to Regina, Sgt. Granger resumed his normal duties. I learned that he was in Cannington to investigate reports of criminals smuggling illicit liquor across the border from the United States.

I have a good reason to be pleased to be away from the capital. On the evening before my departure, father and I dined at the house of one of Regina's business leaders, a gentleman by the name of Mr. Niven DeQuincy. Seemingly, this gentleman and father have commercial dealings in common.

Mr. DeQuincy is a man of some forty-five years and is an American. I took an instant dislike to him! He had a manner of speaking that made my flesh creep. To make matters worse, he is, according to papa, unattached and looking for a wife. Father went so far as to hint that now that I have turned eighteen I ought to think of marriage and was of the opinion that Mr. DeQuincy would make an ideal husband. Can you believe it? All this upon my first meeting the fellow! I have no idea how long papa had known this Niven DeQuincy. I told papa quite firmly that I would sooner join a nunnery than accept a proposal from the reptilian Mr. DeQuincy!

So, as you can see, Millie, dear, my life is far from dull. I do wish you could come out for the summer but realize that your dear mama wants you to go to France with her. Maybe next year.

With all my warmest regards,
Your constant friend
Carina

Chapter 5

Over the ensuing days, Carina settled into the life of the community and made several useful connections, not least with Mrs. Ripley, the dressmaker. She also improved her ability to navigate the finely-tuned social structure. What she suspected on her very first day in the colony proved correct, that the English, her aunt and uncle included, saw her as someone not quite of their class. Whilst everyone treated her with courtesy, she noticed they would occasionally prefix their sentences with 'As a Canadian, you...' as if wishing to emphasize the difference between the old world and the new. She found it amusing that, despite their upper class snobbery, they were still eager to learn everything about the Westmount society she had come from. She likened it to the curiosity one primitive tribe living on a desert island might have on hearing of the existence of a similar tribe on another island some distance away.

None of this gave her grounds to be concerned. She had no desire to be anything more than a temporary guest at Cannington and took care to express her genuine gratitude for their hospitality. The routine of the women consisted of a seemingly endless round of visiting. Each English lady had her day when she was *at home* and received guests between certain hours in the afternoon. A similar practice existed in Carina's Westmount but was not followed with quite the same rigor. In an effort to blend in, Carina joined her aunt and Maud on their round of visits, until she decided she had had enough of teacups and trivial conversation and politely excused herself.

Her contact with the Cannington inhabitants other than the well-off English was altogether different. This group consisted of craftsmen, workers and domestic servants many of whom had accompanied the moneyed gentry from the Old Country or had been lured over by promises of a better life. Whether they had found a better life in the Northwest she had no way of knowing. Without exception, they displayed deference to their betters on whom their livelihoods depended. Then there were the Canadian-born inhabitants, those like Ellie and her grandfather and grandmother, who tended to laugh at the stuffy manners of the English. Canadians were not accustomed to obey and were a people entirely free from subservience to rank and wealth, a people intolerant therefore of condescension. Ellie soon became Carina's main source of information about what was really happening in the village.

Once when Carina was in the garden, Ellie came out to hang a basket of laundry. Carina asked her what she knew about Sergeant Dillon Granger.

"Sergeant Granger is a really fine man," the girl said. "He passes through quite often. Always stays at the Mitre. I think he fancies you, 'cos when he was here I caught him sending admiring glances in your direction several times."

Carina laughed. "I don't believe he *fancies me* any more than he does any other lady. All men have roving eyes. You'll find that out for yourself when you get older."

Ellie let out a long sigh and pinned a nightshirt to the line. "Ah, miss, you're so different from the Cannington ladies. None of them would talk like that to me."

"Are there many visitors to Cannington?"

"There's always a stream of folk coming to the house. There's a joke in the village that if you stand long enough on Mr. Addersley's front step you'll meet everyone who's anyone in the territory."

"We've had the visit from the mounted police. Who next can we expect?"

"I've heard that Mr. Fenn is in the area. Now, he's a rum one he is. But a nice man, all the same."

"Mr. Fenn?"

"His name is Mr. Ogden Fenn. He's a scientist type gent. A botanist. Spends his life out on the prairie on his own with just his mules for company. I've seen him on his hands and knees, not moving for half an hour, inspecting a plant or an ant hill. "

"Your Mr. Fenn sounds like a character."

"You can't mistake him when you meet him. He dresses in raggedy clothes and has one of those long beards I remember seeing in a picture book at Sunday school."

"You mean like an Old Testament prophet?"

"That's right."

"From what you say, I think I may enjoy meeting this Mr. Fenn."

One activity Carina participated in to the full was tennis. Every evening, other than Sundays, after the heat of the day had abated, young Canningtonians, female as well as male, gathered at the courts on the edge of the settlement. Carina was a skilled player and had even received coaching in the game while at school. As a result she was a sought after partner in doubles matches. It was through this sport that she became well acquainted with the younger set, whom she found less rigid in their social attitudes. This included her dealings with some of Captain Pierce's bachelor pups she had been cautioned against. Expecting to have to beat off the young men with her racquet, she was surprised how well-mannered they were. From listening to their conversation she formed the opinion that they were more interested in horseback riding, shooting game and playing cricket than pursuing hapless maidens, as she had been led to believe.

A few older ladies and gentlemen attended the matches as unofficial chaperones but rarely participated in the game. One exception was a Mr. Percy Lansdowne-Coutts, a man of about fifty years, a former army officer, so she heard, having served in India. Captain Pierce employed him to oversee his agricultural college.

Carina's greatest moment of pleasure came when she first took Morgana for a ride. Her uncle led her to the tack room to pick out a saddle.

"I'd prefer a standard saddle rather than a side-saddle," she said.

Alfred looked at her in surprise. Any sternness was quickly replaced by a mischievous smile. "Would you now? I thought you were spirited lass the first time I saw you. My saddles are of the

English style. I expect you'd prefer a western saddle. That's what people in Canada seem to use."

"If that's possible."

"I'll get you one from the store. Or, rather, I'll take you there and you can choose the saddle you'd like to use."

"Uncle, that's kind of you!"

"You realize that my wife and many of the other Cannington citizens are going to be mortified when they see a lady riding cross saddle. In England it's considered rather common for a woman not to be mounted side saddle. There, only farm girls and gypsy women ride with their legs on either side of the horse."

"I'm sorry to disappoint you."

Alfred waved a hand. "You don't disappoint me. The times are changing. Young women are doing things today that would shock their grandmothers. Here in Cannington, however, those changes are barely noticeable. We prefer to stick to the old ways. I'm not sure that is a good thing or whether it's even possible to arrest the march of time. Perhaps it's not even wise."

Alfred Addersley was true to his word. After lunch, he took Carina down the street to his Moose Mountain Trading Company general store and, when they returned, he was carrying a finer saddle than the one she had owned in Westmount. Meanwhile, Mr. Tucker, on Alfred's orders, had brought the mare into the stable yard and groomed her with brush and curry comb until her coat shone.

Carina changed into her riding habit. Later, under her uncle's watchful eye as he sat astride a chestnut hunter she estimated must be more than sixteen hands high, she put her boot toe in the stirrup and swung her leg over Morgana's back.

"We'll ride out to the racecourse," her uncle said. "I want to see how you handle yourself on a horse before letting you loose to roam."

Carina began by walking her horse a short distance up and down in front of the house. Passersby stopped to look. She acknowledged them with a smile, knowing that their dinner table topic of conversation would doubtless be how that audacious Canadian girl was riding like a man. What scandalous behavior!

In Morgana, Carina had a fine mount. The mare possessed a gentle disposition and steady movement. She was a joy to ride and responded positively to Carina's commands. On horseback for the first time since leaving her Quebec home, Carina was filled with a sense of being at ease with her surroundings.

She and her uncle made one circuit together around the oval track. Upon returning to the starter's box, he ordered her to continue for another round, while he watched. For the first half she held her horse to a steady canter. For the remainder, she gave Morgana free rein. Her steed took the tight bend at the head of the track at a gallop before quickening the pace even more in the final stretch. She passed her uncle at full speed.

Her breath came in short gasps when she wheeled and rejoined her uncle.

"Bravo, young lady! You exhibit an excellent degree of horsewomanship, remarkable in one so young. You have my permission to ride wherever your fancy takes you. Of course, you ought to be accompanied by another lady but I don't know of anyone who would be willing to do so. Cannington ladies decline to climb on the back of a horse when the temperature is elevated as it is during this unusually hot weather."

"Thank you, uncle. I shall be fine on my own."

"Now, any number of Captain Pierce's young fellows would volunteer to ride with you but that would not be seemly. An attractive young woman accompanied by a troop of men? No, no." He laughed at the absurdity of the picture.

They rode back to the house at a brisk walk. At the stable they dismounted and handed their horses over to Tucker.

For the short walk across the stable yard, her uncle took her arm and tucked it under his own. "You know, I do believe you are going to do well in the West. Any girl who rides the way you do is obviously suited to this new country. By the way, I said you were free to ride wherever you want but I strongly recommend you restrict yourself for the time being to the stretch of country between the settlement and Moose Mountain. Of course, it is a mountain in name only. The correct terminology is an escarpment. There's a delightful lake there you might enjoy exploring. South of the escarpment it's completely featureless prairie. Once you get out of sight of Moose Mountain it would be easy to become disorientated."

"Thank you for the advice. I will be very careful."

Carina's riding outfit, ideal for the moderate climate of the East, was too heavy for the hot prairie summer. She visited Mrs. Ripley and had her make up two outfits in lighter cloth than the one Carina had brought with her.

The June days had lengthened until the sun appeared to hang in the western sky late into the evening. Carina and Morgana soon bonded. The mare needed no guiding, as she seemed to know instinctively the wishes of her youthful rider. Carina spent two or three hours every day exploring the environs of the village and the wooded slopes of the escarpment. In the saddle, with the breeze blowing through her hair that spilled from beneath her Stetson, Carina regained a semblance of the happiness she had lost when her former life had come crashing down.

Captain Pierce, she found out on the few occasions she met him, was a man of conflicting views. In spite of having settled in the West, he took a dim view of everything Canadian and voiced his displeasure at attempts by his fellow English to fraternize with the Canadian inhabitants of the village and the local homesteaders. This negativism also extended to the considerable number of unpedigreed Britons employed as domestics and manual workers. Members of the latter category were referred to disparagingly as *drones*, and yet were generally the industrious and progressive members of the community.

Carina wrote in her journal:

Cannington, Saturday, May 24, 1884
This afternoon, upon returning from my ride, my aunt came out of the house to meet me.

"Carina, do get changed, Captain Pierce and his wife have invited us for tea."

My guess was that the colony's leader desired to become better acquainted with me - the Canadian girl in their midst.

I went to my room and washed off the trail dust and changed into something suitable. I settled on my finest tea dress, pinned my hair into a fashionable couronne and wore my best hat and gloves for the occasion. When I was ready, my aunt, Maud and I walked the short distance to the Pierce residence. We took tea in a pleasant, airy room at the rear of the house. French doors stood open giving us a view of the lawn surrounded by rose bushes, not yet in bloom. Like ours, the lawn was dusty brown, rather than green.

Other than an elderly Englishwoman who proved to be profoundly deaf and used a brass ear trumpet to follow the conversation, we were the only guests of Captain and Mrs. Pierce.

Our hostess served tea in bone china cups and offered everyone slices of Battenberg cake, with its cross-section displaying a distinctive two-by-two check pattern alternately colored pink and yellow and the whole confection held together by apricot jam and covered in thin marzipan. The cake is named in honor of the marriage of Princess Victoria, a granddaughter of Queen Victoria to Prince Louis of Battenberg earlier this year. I'm sure the regal gentleman was moved to have a gateau named after him.

Part way through the visit, the captain sat on the edge of his armchair and scrutinized me through a monocle wedged in his right eye. "Well, my gal, settling into Cannington Manor, are you, eh?"

"Yes, thank you, sir. Very well, indeed. Everyone has been extremely kind."

"Missing your old home in Montreal, I imagine."

"I lived there all my life. So it's natural it will be a while before I get used to the change."

"You were born in Canada, then?"

"Yes."

"Tell me, what nationality do you consider yourself to be?"

"Why Canadian, sir," I replied. At this, I saw the man's upper lip curl.

Then in a voice I can only describe as scornful, he said, "You can't be Canadian." He emphasized the word Canadian. "Where was your father born?"

His question puzzled me. "He was born in England."

"Then you're English, like the rest of us. I say, just because someone was unfortunate to be born in a stable, it wouldn't mean he was a horse, would it, now?" He accompanied this statement with a laugh.

I struggled to keep a straight face at what I considered the sheer absurdity of the man's logic.

Either Captain Pierce was in a talkative mood or else he was just trying to impress me, for he discoursed at length about how he founded the settlement and how he had convinced the dominion government to grant him a large contiguous block of land in a region that was not yet open for settlement. Normally, homesteaders receive a relatively small parcel of land. My aunt and Maud must have heard it all before. He seemed bent on justifying the existence of Cannington, saying, "A certain stamp of Englishman is, by moving here, able to continue to enjoy a life that is becoming increasingly difficult without large means at home. A

*gentleman with modest tastes can find healthy
occupation out of doors and get as much shooting as he
wants. So long as his farming covers covers his expense,
that's all a fellow needs."*

*At least, the good captain left me in no doubt as
to his views on life and society.*

Carina was aided in her exploration of the area of Moose
Mountain by one of her uncle's business associates, a man called
Paul Fripp, who besides being the owner of the successful
Cannington flour mill was also building a resort on the edge of a
large lake, named Fish Lake, that lay at the base of the north slope
of the escarpment. Mr. Fripp was an Englishman but had not come
across from England with Captain Pierce and his party. Instead, he
had arrived in the district a decade earlier and attempted to establish
himself on a homestead.

Mr. Fripp was delighted to show his visitor around the
construction site busy with carpenters and men with wheelbarrows.
Through conversations with him she came to realize the man
possessed a wealth of information about the region and its history
and was more than happy to share it with her.

"Mr. Fripp, the other day when I was up near the top of the
escarpment, on the south side, I came across what appeared to be a
huge circle marked out by large stones. They were covered by moss
and lichen and looked as though they've been in that position for a
long time."

"What you found is a centuries-old, Indian medicine wheel.
Its function, so it's believed, was to regulate the migration patterns
of the tribes by calculating the vernal equinox and summer solstice
back in the days when the native people were truly nomadic, before
the demise of the plains bison. Legend has it the Indians consider
the Moose Mountain area sacred."

"I've read about the bison. It must have been an
impressive sight to see them in herds of thousands. Such a shame
they're gone."

"That's a sentiment echoed by the Indian. His way of life depended on them. Without the bison the native tribes are dying of starvation. If you search a few hundred feet below the medicine wheel you'll find a sandy terrace with the remains of Indian sun beds."

"Sun beds?"

"They're shallow, grave-like pits in which a man might lie and look up at the sun and imagine himself divine. It was all part of their religion."

Carina went home with a head full of information. Questions, too, but very few answers. After changing in her room, she went downstairs and met her uncle on his way up.

"Ah, there you are, Carina. I was on my way to invite you come outside to meet a most interesting gentleman. Mr. Ogden Fenn has arrived in the settlement."

Chapter 6

Carina followed her uncle out of the house. When Ellie described Mr. Ogden Fenn as having the appearance of a figure from the Old Testament, she was not exaggerating. Pulled up in the main street was an ancient wagon with weathered canvas stretched over wooden hoops. Five mules were harnessed to it and standing next to the lead animal was a man with a flowing beard. His loose-fitting garments fluttered in the breeze like a robe.

Her uncle advanced with his hand outstretched. "Mr. Fenn, what a pleasure to see you again. It's so good of you to pay us a visit."

Fenn replied in a soft voice, "Mr. Addersley, I always enjoy my visits to your hospitable community."

Alfred introduced Carina, and when she stepped forward to shake his hand she was impressed by the lively gleam of intelligence in the man's pale blue eyes. Although the beard and his odd attire made him appear old, Carina guessed he was no more than forty years of age.

That evening, Ogden Fenn, dressed in a clean but threadbare suit, was among her uncle's dinner guests. Carina sat opposite him at the table and was able to observe at close hand the strangest person she had met since coming to the Northwest, or ever. Westmount did not lend itself to eccentricity.

Also present was Mr. Featherstonehaugh, the rector. After the reverend gentleman said grace and the meal was under way, Alfred Addersley initiated the conversation by questioning Mr. Fenn.

"Well, Ogden, what have you been up to since we last saw you?"

"I spent the winter in the new settlement of Calgary. I wanted to talk to the ranchers about the changes the railway was bringing to their operations. As soon as the snow melted I hurried back to complete my scientific field work on the southern prairies."

"And that field work consists of what?"

"The complete classification of the flora and fauna of the region, together with accurate readings of soil moisture and precipitation rates."

"Hasn't that already been done by Palliser and others?"

"True, the Eighteen-fifty-seven expedition led by Captain John Palliser collected meticulous geological and magnetic data as well as studies of the area's natural history. What is more, it determined that the southern Canadian Plains were too arid to sustain agriculture. Those findings have recently been disputed."

"By whom?"

"By that damn charlatan, John Macoun, that's who."

The clergyman choked on a spoonful of soup and reached for his table napkin to stifle his cough. Carina assumed he wasn't used to the more forthright manner of some of the dinner guests she had come to accept as the norm in the Addersley household.

With a wicked gleam in his eye, Fenn glanced at the clergyman. "Pardon me, sir. I didn't mean to upset you."

Alfred prodded his spectacles back up the bridge of his nose. "What have you against this fellow Macoun?"

Before he could reply, a gentleman named Wardlaw spoke up. "I remember John Macoun coming through here a few years ago. He struck me as a very entertaining gentleman, an Ulsterman, I believe."

Ogden Fenn nodded. "True enough, John Macoun is a personable fellow but he's no scientist, even if he likes to be called the Professor. He collects phenomenal quantities of specimens, both plants and animals, but spends hardly any time documenting and classifying them. I'm sorry to say his summer field trips over the prairies are not much more than haphazard sweeps through a region to gather whatever he chances upon. I'm sure you'll agree that that is poor science."

"He *is* the official dominion botanist," another guest said.

"And for that reason the government listens to him. Mr. Macoun harbors some dangerous ideas."

Alfred jabbed the air with a finger. "Ogden, surely, you're overstating the case?"

Carina noticed the look of determination on Ogden Fenn's face.

"Permit me," Fenn said, "to try the patience of the table while I justify my position."

Alfred laughed. "Go ahead, old chap. We're just at the end of the soup course. There's still the main course, the dessert and the cheese to come, not to mention the coffee and liqueurs. Lots of time to expound your scientific theories."

"When it comes to our friend Macoun, it's not so much science as politics. The man's a fanatical Tory supporter and an Orangeman to boot. He tells the government what they want to hear. How could they not love him? But let me say something about the Palliser Expedition. Captain Palliser, himself was a trained naturalist and his members were scientists of the highest caliber. James Hector was a geologist and naturalist, Eugène Bourgeau, a fine botanist, Thomas Blakeston a magnetic observer in possession of the very latest equipment. Then we have John W. Sullivan, a fine mathematician and sextant observer. Anyone who has navigated the prairie knows what an asset a man like that would be. The work they did was extremely thorough and precise. A whole region of the southern plains is named the Palliser Triangle because the expedition determined on solid scientific evidence that it was too dry for agriculture."

Alfred Addersley leaned in. "Then why didn't their findings settle the matter once and for all?"

The conversation halted while Mrs. Tucker and Ellie brought in the main course, consisting of roast prairie chicken, accompanied by baked potatoes and steamed carrots.

Once everyone was served, Fenn resumed his discourse. "The answer to your very pertinent question is because Captain Palliser submitted the general report of his expedition to the British Colonial Office in 1862. Remember, this was five years before Canadian confederation, but it was at the height of the American

Civil War, which featured hugely in the politics of Canada and England at the time. For this reason the expedition report received only muted attention. About the same time, another survey made by Henry Youle Hind, although less scientific, came to much the same conclusion and warned about luring hapless immigrants to the infertile southern Prairies."

Carina ventured a question. "Mr. Fenn, why was Mr. Macoun so successful at changing the prevailing view of the dry Prairies?"

"The main reason was government worries over the previous policy of directing settlement to the north. They feared it would leave the southern prairies along the border open for annexation by the Americans. In addition, the railroad company realized that the original surveyed route across the northern plains involved crossing countless river valleys. Bridges are expensive and take time to build. John Macoun comes along and spreads the word that the previous expeditions of Palliser and Hind got it wrong, that the southern plains were, after all, fertile and not the desert everyone thought them to be. Unfortunately, Macoun's visits coincided with the wettest years in more than a century. Not surprisingly, he spoke in glowing terms of an agricultural Eden with ample soil moisture. He harangued both the government and the CPR. Overnight, the railroad's chief engineer, Mr. Sanford Fleming's meticulously planned northern route was abandoned. They telegraphed the construction crew at the head of steel to change direction. The line that was to cross the Red River at Selkirk, north of the present city of Winnipeg, made an abrupt change of direction and proceeded south to cross the Red at Winnipeg. That dog's leg change of direction of the rail line is still there for everyone to witness."

"That's a fascinating account, Mr. Fenn," Mr. Wardlaw said.

"Of course, the CPR made no objection to the change of plan. Because there was already considerable settlement in the northern plains in anticipation of the rail line, the company made no secret of its preference to push through unsettled territory so they could dictate both the location and the size of the new towns. And maximize their own profit."

"You make a very convincing case, Mr. Fenn," Mr. Featherstonehaugh said. "May I venture to suggest you may be overstating the negative influence of this gentleman, Mr. Macoun?"

Unperturbed, Fenn responded in a level voice. "That's a reasonable charge, sir, but I am not alone in my opposition to the influence of the man. Last year, Macoun's own superior, Mr. Lindsey Alexander Russell, the Deputy Minister of the Interior, in Ottawa, called him a good botanist but a fool outside of that. Many scientists, Hind among them, challenged Macoun's assertions because they know that large areas of the Northwest are unfit for agriculture, because of lack of precipitation. It's Macoun's contagious enthusiasm that has influenced policy. Why, he even maintains that settlers require no assistance during the pioneering stage. He is singlehandedly undermining the dominion government's homesteading policy."

"What I fail to understand," Alfred said, "is why you are continuing your scientific studies. Surely, the die is cast. The line is built through the south as far as the Rockies. If it's all a mistake, as you claim, what can be done about it?"

Ogden Fenn leaned back on his chair. "I appreciate that you folk here in Cannington stand to benefit from the present situation. All you need is a spur to be built down from the main line at Moosomin and your future is assured. The government fondly believes their grant of a homestead of one hundred and sixty acres, a quarter section, is sufficient for a settler to create a profitable farm. That's fine in the eastern parts of the country and in the province of Manitoba. In Cannington you have ample water, but the amount of available water decreases dramatically the farther west and south you go. On dry land, no one can make a living from so few acres, no matter how industrious they are."

Alfred nodded his agreement. "I'm still not sure what you hope to achieve."

"I have concluded my field studies that have been progressing now over several summers. When I'm finished, in a few weeks time, I intend to go to Regina to complete the report I am working on. I already have the promise of support from the *Leader* newspaper editor, Mr. Nicholas Flood Davin, with respect to publication. My aim is to open the government's eyes to the problem of western settlement and have them halt the publicity that is luring European immigrants to the southern regions."

"Where would you have them go, these new settlers? Once the tide begins it will be impossible to stem the flow."

"The government should revert to the original policy and settle homesteaders in the northern parkland."

"What, with no railway?"

"There is already talk of building a grand trunk line through the north. Let's not forget, the CPR's primarily goal has been to link British Columbia with the rest of Canada not settle the Prairies. It was that promise that brought British Columbia into the Confederation."

"Your views are likely to make you enemies, Ogden. There are a lot of people who have invested heavily in the present scheme of things."

"If one speaks out, one is sure to make enemies, no matter what your views. There's always someone who believes their toes are being trodden on."

Fenn's remark was followed by a lull in the conversation, the silence being broken by Mrs. Teague changing the subject, "This is a delightful chicken dish, Mrs. Addersley. I shall have to get the recipe from your cook."

The remainder of the dinner conversation centered on the safer topics of weather, the price of wheat and a question to Ogden Fenn as to his choice of mules rather than horses for his wagon.

"Simple, mules know how to look after themselves better than horses when the going gets tough and food's scarce."

As was the custom, when the meal was over the ladies retired to the drawing room and the gentlemen remained at the the table. Mrs. Tucker and Ellie were on hand to serve the coffee and tea. There was nothing for Carina to do other than retire with the ladies. Carina quickly grew weary of feminine conversation, which consisted of the perennial complaint as to the near impossibility of hiring and retaining domestic servants.

At the earliest moment, she excused herself and went into the parlor to read the novel she brought down from her room.

She had not read more than a couple of pages when the door opened and Ogden Fenn entered.

"Hello, young lady, do you mind if I share your refuge?"

She closed her book and smiled at the scientific gentleman. "Not at all, Mr. Fenn."

"The dining room is filling up with cigar smoke and so too are my lungs. I'm used to pristine prairie air and take badly to tobacco smoke."

"I found what you were saying about prairie settlement enlightening."

"I could see you were following closely. Women, I regret to say, usually don't trouble their pretty heads with such matters."

"The West appears on the brink of considerable change. I wasn't fully aware of that before."

"You are right. Last year, the DLS surveyed more than twenty-seven million acres for subdivision into homesteads. That's a lot of land."

"The DLS?"

"Dominion Land Survey, the government agency for deciding who goes where and on how much land."

"You appear to have a deep understanding of these plains."

"I've spent more than twenty years in these parts. I've seen the changes. Science, too, is changing to adapt to the new challenges. In 1866, a German physician-philosopher by the name of Ernst Haekel coined a new term. He cobbled together two Greek roots, *oikos*, meaning household, and *ologie*, which means the study of, to describe a new way to approach life science. It's closer to thinking of nature as in interdependent network. He based his ideas on Mr. Charles Darwin's discovery that organisms are shaped by the environment in which they evolve. Herr Haekel described his new endeavor as *ecology* or the study of natural selection in action. The essence of life, he claimed, lay not in a static display of specimens in a collector's cabinet but in the wonderfully tangled web of interconnections in the field." Fenn chuckled to himself. "I realize that sounds more like poetry than science."

"I have always had an interest in science but I've never heard it described in those terms before."

"If you care to pay a visit to my camp, which I use as a base for my scientific studies, I'll show you more wondrous things about this land other people describe as desolate."

"I would like to do that. Where is your camp?"

"Abut two hours south and west from Cannington. Go due south from the settlement. Keep the Moose Mountain escarpment to your right, to the west, that is. You'll eventually leave the trees behind and find yourself on open prairie. When you reach the buffalo rubbing stone, change direction to the south-west and you'll easily find your way to my camp. There are hoof and wheel tracks to guide you."

"I have no idea what a rubbing stone is, Mr. Fenn. How will I recognize it?"

"You can't miss it. It's a massive granite boulder taller than a standing man on the perfectly flat plain. The rock was deposited there some ten thousand years ago by the retreating glaciers. The plains buffalo used it to rub themselves and rid their hides of parasites. There are several such boulders scattered over the prairies, with paths leading up to them from miles away. They now sit in deep rounded depressions, the result of generations of animals working their way around them."

"There is one problem. How do I know that I'm heading due south and then south-west? I've heard it's easy to become lost when there's no marked trail."

"Do you have a watch?"

Carina reached into her dress pocket, drew out a man's slim pocket watch and showed it to Fenn. "This used to belong to my maternal grandfather. I always carry it with me."

"A fine looking timepiece it is too. You can use it as a compass." He took the watch from her. "Hold it in the palm of your hand like this and point the hour hand at the sun. Run an imaginary line between the hour hand and twelve o' clock. That line points directly south. Once you know that it's simple to calculate southwest. If you'd care to visit, do so the day after tomorrow. I'll be at my camp."

The next day, Carina succeeded in persuading her cousin Maud to come with her. At first the young woman refused with the excuses it was too hot, that she didn't enjoy riding, that the empty landscape frightened her and that they could be attacked by wolves or coyotes, or even Indians.

Carina countered each objection with patient reasoning. "I checked the barometer in the hall. The pressure is falling. That means it might be cloudy and therefore not as hot as it has been. I spoke to your father and he's agreed to let us use the democrat. I know how to drive. I have Mr. Fenn's assurance there is nothing to be frightened of on the open prairie. And there's never been a credible account of wolves or coyotes attacking humans. As for Indian attack, I understand that is extremely remote in these parts."

"Very well. You seem determined to go. I suppose it's only proper that I keep you company."

Before the planned expedition to visit Ogden Fenn's camp, her uncle came into the dining room and handed Carina an envelope.

"The mail carrier arrived. This is for you."

Her first thought was that letter was from her father. She had written to him upon her arrival in Cannington but had as yet received no reply. That gave her no reason to be concerned, as she assumed he was too busy with bank business to write. When she examined the envelope she saw the address was not in her father's handwriting but Millie's.

She tore open the envelope.

My Dearest Carina,

My news will come as a surprise to you. I am not going with my mother to Paris, after all. The reasons are too complicated to summarize in this hasty note. I will explain later in person. Yes, that is right! I have every intention of coming out to visit you in your new home in Cannington Manor. That is if it is convenient. If I hear back from you with a positive answer and I hope I do, I shall come at the end of the month, which is when mama leaves for Europe. She has arranged for me to accompany a clergyman and his wife. They are a Mr. and Mrs. Kennedy, who are traveling west to visit a mission school in the diocese of Qu'Appelle (I think that is how you spell it!) not far from Regina. I am so thrilled at the prospect of seeing you again. Do write back and say yes I can come.

    Your ever faithful friend,
    Millie

All this time, her uncle kept his eyes on her. "Not bad news I trust."

Taken aback by the new development, Carina was momentarily lost for words. "Oh, no, no, uncle. Just a bit of a surprise, that's all. A very close school friend of mine was to have gone with her mother to spend the summer in France. She writes to say there's been a change in plan and she wants to come to the Northwest to visit me."

"Well, that's something to be joyful about, isn't it?"

"Yes, but…"

"But what? Your friend can come and visit you here. You know we keep an open house. All and sundry are welcome."

"You mean that? She won't be imposing? I already feel I am."

Alfred dismissed her concerns with a wave of his hand. "What rubbish you speak, girl. You are certainly not imposing on anyone. We would be delighted to have your friend stay. What's her name?"

"Millie. Millie Vanderhagen."

"Sounds Dutch."

"She's American. Her mother, Mrs. Vanderhagen is a well-known actress in Montreal. Millie was in my class at school. We've known each other for several years."

Alfred rubbed his chin. "Daughter of an actress, indeed! When does Miss Vanderhagen intend to travel out here?"

"She wants to set out at the end of the month but would like to hear from me as soon as possible."

"Well, then, sit yourself down this minute and pen Miss Millie a reply. The mailman is returning to Moosomin this afternoon. Go to my study. You'll find paper and envelopes in the top drawer of my desk."

Carina wrote to tell Millie the changes that had occurred and that she was welcome to come to Cannington. She included directions of where to get off the train and asked for her date of arrival so that she could be met.

From earlier discussions with her uncle, Carina now knew there was a quicker way to travel to the Northwest than the route she and her father had taken. Their journey by train to Collingwood, lake steamer to Milwaukee then train to St. Paul, Minnesota, and another train north to Winnipeg was the least expensive option but the slowest. She surmised that had been a deliberate choice by a bank reluctant to lavish travel expenses on an employee that had swindled them out of thousands of dollars. The all-American but more costly route involved train from Montreal south of the Great Lakes to Chicago and on to St. Paul and thence to Winnipeg and the CPR. This route reduced the journey to a matter of days and rendered it unnecessary to stop in hotels along the way. Carina passed this information on to Millie in her letter, which she then sealed and gave to her uncle for mailing.

A smile came to her lips when she thought of Millie coming to Cannington. Her own arrival had caused something of a stir and her Canadian mode of dress had ruffled a few English feathers. How the settlement's stuffy elite would react to the vivacious and exuberant Millie Vanderhagen gave rise to some interesting speculation. Although the same age as her, Millie revelled in coquettish behavior and fashion. If that wasn't volatile enough, her being American and an actress' daughter was certain to create a stir in the starchly English colony.

Chapter 7

Carina's brief conversations with Ogden Fenn deepened her appreciation of the natural world and in the prairie landscape in particular. Yet her intention to visit Fenn at his camp to see first hand the work he was doing was met with disapproval by her Aunt Rosalind.

"Canadian ladies, it appears, care little about their reputations. Whilst I hold Mr. Fenn in the highest regard, it would compromise a lady's reputation were you and my daughter to pay a single gentleman a visit at his quarters, no matter if his quarters happen to be a tent." Rosalind sniffed. "However, since my husband has already given his approval to this outing, there is nothing I can do to prevent it."

Early the following morning, Carina and Maud stood by as Norman Tucker prepared the democrat. When Carina asked if she could use Morgana, Tucker shook his head.

"Morgana's a good horse but she's not been trained as a driver. Cyrus, here, is a solid Cleveland Bay with plenty of stamina. He'll get you there and back just fine. He's gentle and obeys well. That's important in a carriage horse."

"Thank you, Mr. Tucker. I understand."

From the gleaming black lacquer on the body and the absence of trail dust on the wheel spokes, Carina guessed she was one of the first to use the two-seater. This was confirmed when Tucker told her it had been brought from Moosomin station two months before on one of the Trading Company's freight wagons and that it had sat in the coach house ever since. The Addersleys were not given to driving much in the summer heat. It was therefore with some trepidation that she climbed onto the dimpled leather seat. Even though she would be driving she still wore her riding skirt, preferring that to matching Maud's ankle-length dress complete with petticoats.

"I'm unused to getting out of bed at five-thirty in the morning," Maud said.

"You can doze as I drive."

Maud let Tucker hand her up next to Carina.

"Are you going to manage, Miss Carina?" he asked.

"I'm sure I will. And thank your wife for the picnic lunch she's provided."

"I've put a keg of water behind the seat, an' a canvas bucket to water the horse. Just take it easy. It's going to be another scorcher of a day."

Carina nodded her thanks and slapped the reins to set the carriage in motion.

At that hour few Canningtonians were about, only some laborers digging the foundations for a new house. The men stopped work to stare at the two young women as they drove past. Carina heeded Fenn's instructions and headed due south, keeping the Moose Mountain escarpment to her right.

Maud presented an anxious face to Carina. "You know where we're going, I hope."

"Mr. Fenn said we're to look out for a very large boulder."

Maud gave an anxious laugh. "A boulder! I don't find that very reassuring. That's like looking for a needle in a haystack. One could easily get lost out here."

Carina admitted silently that her companion was right. Without landmarks to act as a guide, it was not much different to being in a boat on an open sea. Eager to sight the boulder, she scanned the prairie in front of her. Once, she stopped and used her watch to reassure herself they were traveling in the right direction.

Carina breathed easier when she saw in the distance the dark shape of the massive marker stone. When they drew level with it she reined in the horse.

Maud remained on the seat while Carina watered the horse.

"Maud, hold onto the reins, will you? The horse is not likely to move but it's best to be careful." While the horse slaked its thirst, Carina circled the towering boulder and ran her hand over its rounded sides worn smooth by generations of animals. Before rejoining Maud, she stared into the distance and marveled at the heat mirage that gave the impression the horizon floated above a shimmering lake.

Nearly an hour later Carina pointed ahead. "There's the camp!"

Ogden Fenn had pitched his two tents at the edge of a low bluff, which may have been formed in ancient times by the meander of a long-vanished creek.

As they arrived, Fenn came out of one of the tents and waved his hat. He wore the same shabby clothes as before but his manners were faultless. "Miss Addersley, Miss Chesterman, welcome. I am indeed honored among men to have two beautiful young ladies visit my humble encampment. I have just made a fresh pot of coffee. May I offer you some?"

"Yes, please," Maud said.

Carina looked around her. The camp consisted of the two wall tents, each some twelve feet long by six feet wide with pine poles supporting the ridges. The sun had bleached the canvas white. One of the tents was the living tent, for she spied the foot of a camp bed through the open flap. It possessed an awning that cast a rectangle of shade on the ground in front. Nearby, stood Fenn's wagon, which, from the faded lettering on the canvas stretched over the hoops, proved to be a former United States Army freight wagon. In places the wheels and body still bore traces of the standard military colors, red and Prussian blue. Picketed some distance away were his five mules. A blackened coffee pot sat on the edge of a smoking fire. A ring of stones prevented any embers from accidentally catching fire to the surrounding withered grass.

"We've brought along a picnic lunch. We can all share it."

While Carina helped Maud set the lunch items on a folding table beneath the awning, Fenn went to the wagon and brought back, of all things, a dining-room chair with a faded maroon velvet seat and an elaborately-carved backrest.

"I have my folding campaign chair, which one of you may use. Some time ago on one of my peregrinations, I came across this fine specimen of a chair in an abandoned farmhouse and thought it might come in useful on the rare occasions I receive guests, such as today."

"And what will you sit on, Mr. Fenn?"

"I have a wooden crate in the tent to use as a stool. As I said, my camp is simple." He eyed the contents of picnic hamper the young women had brought. "Pork pie, fresh tomatoes and cucumbers, the latter no doubt from Mr. Addersley's company greenhouse. I am truly being spoiled."

Fenn poured coffee into red enamel mugs, then entered the tent and brought out a packing crate. He produced a can of condensed milk and punctured it with a knife blade. Maud was offered the elegant chair and the three of them sat down to lunch.

Carina motioned to the campfire. "I imagine you're obliged to carry firewood with you." Then with a smile, she added, "That must be difficult. There are next to no trees in these parts."

"I always have some wood in the wagon but often I just use buffalo chips."

Maud looked at him over her coffee mug. "Buffalo chips?"

"The dung dropped by the Plains bison. Although the animals have long since disappeared their droppings remain, everywhere. It has dried into hard lumps which burn like charcoal with no offensive odor."

Maud pressed together the corners of her mouth.

At that moment, a gopher pushed its head out from a hole at the corner of the tent, doubtless curious as to the noise in its otherwise peaceful environment. Having decided that the presence of three humans posed no threat, the small animal scurried past the table on its way to the longer grass at the edge of the camp. When she saw the creature a few feet from the hem of her dress, Maud uttered a scream and lifted her feet.

Fenn placed a reassuring hand on Maud's arm. "Miss Addersley, it's only a harmless prairie gopher."

Maud cautiously replaced her feet on the ground and the meal continued.

"How long have you been out here, Mr. Fenn?" Carina asked.

"At this particular spot, about three weeks. Every year for the past five years I've lived in various locations on the prairie to conduct my scientific work, which, as I mentioned before, has reached a conclusion."

"You obviously have a great love for the plains."

He made a sweep with his hand. "I do. Yet you might question why. When you look out over this billiard table expanse of land, what is there? Contrary to popular belief, the mixed grass prairie, which comprises the majority of the Canadian portion of the Great Plains, is rarely entirely flat but rolls away in all directions, billowing off to the horizon in wave after wave. More like the ocean than a terrestrial landscape. In places, in the deeper folds, some timber hides along with carpets of flowers. Other than the few trees, the occasional pronghorn antelopes were the only living creatures. The buffalo herds have now vanished, never to return, like the glaciers that once covered this part of the continent."

During this conversation, Maud nibbled one of the small cakes from the picnic hamper and stared off into the distance, not sharing Carina's enthusiasm for what the scientist had to say.

"There's something sad about the loss of the bison," Carina said. She glanced at the books and papers Fenn had stacked to one side to make room on the table. Her eye fell on a well-thumbed Bible. "May I ask if you are a religious man, Mr. Fenn?

Fenn chuckled. "You may find it strange that a man of science also reads the Good Book. You are a very perceptive young lady. You may be aware that thanks to Mr. Charles Darwin, great changes are taking place in our understanding of the natural world. Many of these developments also challenge our long-held religious beliefs."

On hearing this, Maud shifted uncomfortably on her chair.

"You refer to his theory of evolution," Carina said.

"That and the whole way we see nature. I'm afraid it's not as neatly ordered as we've been led to believe." He reached over and picked up the Bible. "However, I am one of those few scientists who still cling to some of the old ways. Call it nostalgia, if you like, but not everything can be explained by the laws of chemistry and physics. Sometimes this book gives us a mysterious and poetical glimpse at the way forward."

Maud put down what remained of her cake and, with renewed attention, fixed her eyes on Fenn.

He flipped open the tattered Bible. "Take for example what the Book of Ezekiel says." The scientist cleared his throat and in a rich baritone voices read: "*And the hand of the Lord was there upon me, and he said unto me, Arise, go forth into the plain, and I will there talk with thee.* Well, as a man of science, I certainly don't expect to hear a voice coming from a cloud. Yet one could argue it's the hand of God that undulates the prairie grasses. Perhaps, too, it's the divine breath that blows as a hot wind across a dry alkaline lake. In winter, we may hear the voice of God in the hiss of a ground blizzard. Who knows? What is important is that the message is always the same: what the white man is doing in this still-pristine land is wrong, terribly wrong."

After Fenn stopped talking there was a lull in the conversation.

Then Carina asked, "What, if anything, can be done about it?"

"By me? One man against the combined might of the government, the railroad companies, and the land speculators? Not a lot. That doesn't mean I can't try."

"You say that what people call progress is wrong."

Fenn nodded. "I'm not the first to say these southern plains are not suitable for settlement. They're too drought-prone to sustain agriculture.

"Yet the Cannington farmers appear to be prospering."

"Cannington is like an oasis in the desert. Thanks to the Moose Mountain escarpment water is plentiful. That is not typical of the majority of the land in the west. With all due respect to Miss Maud and her family, the members of the English colony don't have to rely on making a living from farming. They brought wealth with them."

"You say your work has been to try to prevent a tragedy from happening. What do you mean by that?"

"When I heard of the plans to build the transcontinental railroad across the south, rather than across the wetter northern plains, I just had to speak out against the sacrilege being perpetrated in the name of progress. Only half the line has been built, the part that runs in a straight line across the plains. Men are at work on pushing the tracks through the mountains. This railroad is only the first of many. At one time the only sound was the thunder of great herds of bison. Now it's the whistle of steam locomotives. Homesteads and ranches are taking over the traditional hunting grounds of the Plains Indians. In his wake the white man has brought disease and starvation. Because I have acquired a deep knowledge of the region I cannot stand idly by and do nothing."

The discussion drifted to lighter topics while they finished their lunch. Fenn then invited his guests to view his scientific work housed in the second tent. Inside were two trestle tables laden with glass jars, cases and specimen boxes.

Fenn pointed to a tray of glass containers filled with earth, each one labelled and identified in neat script. "I've made a thorough examination of the various soil types across the plains, as well as putting together a collection of the grasses and forbs."

Maud looked up from a case containing insect specimens. "Forbs?"

"Any herbaceous plant that is not a grass."

"By now you must have answered every question concerning the natural history of the area," Carina said.

Fenn combed his fingers through his beard and smiled. "A great many but many more remain. In my journeying back and forth over the plains, one question kept gnawing at my brain. Why grass? It was as though when God moved west, he ran suddenly out of trees."

"Why, then, are there no trees?"

"I think I've found the answer. These plains are the result of the same primal forces that elsewhere on the continent raised the land into lofty mountains and gouged the deep canyons. The scientific explanation for this treeless region lies with the wind."

Maud, who had been pacing back and forth in the tent's confined space, came and stood beside Carina. "The wind? How on earth can the wind be responsible for the lack of trees?"

Fenn, with the patience of a born teacher, replied, "In prehistorical times, this part of North America was covered by a great icecap. When the climate changed and the glaciers retreated, they left behind the underlying rock ground into into a fine dust, which the winds swept up into huge dust storms. Eventually, the dust settled on the ground in thick layers. Geologists, those who study rock formations, call the soil resulting from this dust layer *loess*. It's a German word for loose. This aeolian soil was ideal for the growth of grasses."

"But not trees?"

"Oh, yes, trees also grew well on it. But rainfall on the prairies is sparse and the water quickly drains away. The trees couldn't adapt to the parched conditions and died out."

Maud didn't appear convinced. "Other parts of the country have winds and dry conditions. Yet the trees seem to have adapted."

"On the prairies the grassland has a powerful ally, against which the trees cannot hold their own. And that is fire. The Indian calls the fires that periodically sweep across the plains the Red Buffalo." Fenn gave a laugh and added, "The farmers and ranchers have other names for it. When fire rages over the land the trees are quickly destroyed. As do the grasses, everything burns, but grasses are quick to spring back. They have deep penetrating roots which permit the plants to throw up new stems and leaves to take advantage of the burnt-over soil and draw nourishment from the ashes left behind."

Beside the soil samples on the table lay a flat metal box with rounded corners and a carrying strap. The object sat on top of a plant press

Carina pointed to them. "Is this the equipment you use to collect your plants?"

"Yes, my vasculum and my field press. Over the years I've amassed a plant collection running to several thousand specimens." He picked up a white card on which a grass plant had been meticulously glued to show off its roots, leaves and flowering head. "This is an example of needle and thread grass, *Hesperostipa comata*, perhaps the commonest of the prairie grasses."

"With those curly stems and leaves one can see where it got its name from."

"What you call a stem is actually an awn, a long spike attached to the seed. That's the needle part. If you were to look at the awn under a lens you'd find that it is tightly twisted. When the seed drops to the ground and becomes moist, the awn unwinds and actually drills the seed into the ground."

"Nature is truly incredible."

"To prove how this plant is ideally suited to the prairies, it has a fine line of what are called hinge cells on the upper surface of its leaves. Under extremely dry conditions these cells contract and cause the leaf to roll up to prevent the loss of precious moisture. Also, the grass has no need to waste its energy on showy flowers or alluring scent, for it is wind pollinated." He picked up another specimen card. "This is wheat grass, one of the more adaptable plants. It's not related to the wheat grown for flour but is so named because the seed head resembles that of wheat. You notice how slender and fragile it appears. Yet even the strongest windstorm is not strong enough to break it."

"Is that because the stem is very tough?"

"Yes. I have examined the stem under my microscope and found it's hollow. The stem and the leaves contain silicon, a mineral we usually associate with rocks."

"Is that why a blade of grass can sometimes cut your finger if you're not careful?"

"It's the silicon what gives the leaves that glossy appearance. You're familiar with bamboo. It has so much silicon in it gardeners use the dry stems to use as supports for plants like tomatoes."

"I'm beginning to understand why you find plants so fascinating."

Fenn smiled at his guests. "Now you see why the grasses flourish here and not trees. They don't form wooden trunks and branches. A grass plant lives freely, one year at a time, and nourishes the animals that roam the surface. When it dies it enriches the black soil below. My fear is that when the grassland has gone it will be lost forever. All our wonderful machines won't be able to restore it. Nothing will be able to transport us to where it has vanished." Fenn looked into Carina's eyes. "We're living at the end of an era, Miss Chesterman. When I lie in my tent awake at night I can hear the prairie wilderness all around me saying farewell. The birds and animals know it."

Carina and Maud spent another hour at the camp. Carina did most of the talking. Maud fanned herself and gave every impression of wanting to be far away from the lonely spot on the open prairie.

Mindful of her debt to Maud for making it possible for her to visit the scientist, Carina thought it prudent not to prolong the visit. Fenn walked them to the democrat and hitched up the gelding, which had been picketed and allowed to graze alongside the mules.

"Miss Chesterman, I'm impressed by your remarkable understanding of scientific matters. You'd make a fine scientist were you to take up a study of the subject."

"Thank you, Mr. Fenn. I'm not sure that would be possible, except as an amateur. As you know there're many obstacles in the path of women seeking a higher education."

"Alas, that is true. We'll have another opportunity to discuss topics of scientific interest. I'll be in the settlement again shortly. Mr. Addersley has graciously invited me to attend the Cannington races next week. Frankly, horse racing is not a passion of mine but I enjoy having the opportunity to mingle with society for a while." He gave a laugh. "You've probably come to the realization that the nature of my work turns me into a hermit for much of the year."

After an exchange of pleasantries, the two women said goodbye to Fenn and set out for Cannington. On the return leg of the journey Maud was unusually talkative.

"Mr. Fenn is, indeed, an odd character. What he says is interesting enough but I fail to see the purpose of the work he's doing. I assume it's important to study and preserve the prairie flora and fauna. I have a cousin in England, a clergyman, who is also an avid botanist and has written a book on the subject. When I visited his vicarage he took great pride in showing me his herbarium containing some beautiful wildflowers. But collecting grasses? Surely, grass is grass, nothing more?"

"I'm sure Mr. Fenn could provide you with a cogent explanation of the many varieties of grasses."

"I was heartened to find that he read the Bible. I wish more scientific gentlemen would do likewise, rather than attack religious ideas. If they continue in that manner, we'll have nothing left to believe in."

The return journey passed without incident. It was early evening when Carina and Maud reached the Addersley residence. Maud quickly got down and went into the house. Norman Tucker came from the stable and took the reins from Carina. Rather than follow Maud indoors, Carina stretched her cramped muscles by walking along the boardwalk as far as the tennis courts at the west edge of the settlement. On the courts, a group men and women with whom she was friendly were playing mixed doubles. One of the players interrupted his game and came over to her. He wore a white open-necked shirt and was sweating profusely.

"Miss Chesterman, would you care to join us? We all admire your killer backhand stroke."

"Thank you for the compliment, Mr. Brewer. I fear my reputation has outstripped my skill at the game. I must decline on this occasion. Miss Addersley and I have just taken a long drive in the country and with this heat I must confess to being weary."

"I understand. It is deuced hot. Perhaps tomorrow, then. We look forward to your participation."

"I'll do my best to come and play."

Mr. Brewer rejoined his partners and Carina strolled back to the house. She was drawing level with the church when, out of the corner of her eye, she saw a man come from the Mitre Inn and head diagonally across the street to intercept her. When he came closer, she turned and found herself face to face with her brother Julian.

Chapter 8

Mrs. Sybil Halliday surveyed the scene from the train window as the west-bound Canadian Pacific drew into Regina station. Her auburn hair and sensuous figure would have attracted attention in any situation. That she was traveling on her own made her arrival doubly remarkable.

She had been warned not to expect paved streets or brick and stone houses. The primitive prairie settlements the train had passed through after leaving the province of Manitoba, together with the tediously long halt in the small town of Moosomin, had given her a foretaste of what to expect in the Northwest.

Despite this, her first sight of the territorial capital came as a shock. The town resembled a joke perpetrated by a drunken stage designer. Wooden buildings, many still unpainted, and in a hodgepodge of styles, dotted the landscape. Tents large and small occupied the gaps between some of the buildings. From what she could see of the streets, they appeared to be not much more than strips of dirt choked with the dust thrown up by the bustling cart and wagon traffic. Not a tree or a patch of green alleviated the uniform drabness. To make matters worse, the entire scene shimmered under a sun that blazed down out of a blue sky swept clean of even the smallest vestige of cloud.

A male passenger at the next window echoed her thoughts. "Not that impressive for the chief city of a vast territory, wouldn't you agree, ma'am?"

Sybil expressed her disdain by tugging down the corners of her mouth. "I'd hate to live in such a place. I'm thankful I am simply passing through."

"I come from Brandon, Manitoba, and I read in the paper that the wife of Canada's governor-general named this place Regina after her mother, Queen Victoria. The reporter suggested Golgotha would've been a more appropriate name. I can see why now."

The train shuddered to a clanging halt and released of a cloud of steam. Sybil took out an embroidered handkerchief and mopped the sheen of perspiration from her forehead. She brought down her hand luggage from the overhead rack before joining the line of passengers waiting to disembark.

Her original intention, to stay in Regina only long enough to eat a meal in the station restaurant before traveling on to Calgary, had seen a change of plan. This was the result of a chance conversation in the dining car with a certain Mr. Harris, a Regina grain merchant returning from a business trip to Toronto. Because of the crush of diners she had been obliged to share a table with the gentleman.

Sybil didn't find Mr. Harris' conversation overly stimulating, consisting as it did of complaints over the extra paperwork he had to complete to conform to government regulations. But the man was talkative and Sybil found it simpler to let him talk and to listen quietly. At some point between the dessert and the coffee, the merchant mentioned a name that galvanized her attention. She put down her cup so hard that she spilled some coffee into the saucer. "Forgive me for interrupting, Mr. Harris. Would you mind repeating the name of this gentleman you were speaking to?"

Harris leaned forward, obviously flattered by Sybil's attention. "Mr. DeQuincy, he's one of the leading businessmen in the new capital. I was in conversation with him a couple of days before I left for the East. He recommended we establish a chamber of commerce to fight the imposition of tariffs imposed on goods to and from the Northwest. And I replied—"

"Do you happen to know the gentleman's first name?"

"He's Mr. Niven DeQuincy, a real go-getter, perhaps the richest man in the Northwest. Why do you ask? Do you know him?"

"Is he American?"

"As a matter of fact, he is but we don't hold that against him." He chuckled at his own joke.

Just then a steward approached. "Sir and madam, I hate to press you but if you are finished your meal, would you kindly vacate your table? We have a great many passengers waiting to be served."

Sybil folded her napkin and got to her feet. She offered her hand to her table partner. "So nice to have met you, Mr. Harris. Perhaps I shall have the pleasure of dining with you again before you reach your destination." With her brain swirling with the information she had received from the unwitting Harris, she walked back along the swaying train to her seat. If, Harris was right, and her old friend and sometimes adversary Niven DeQuincy was now established in Regina, it necessitated an alteration to her itinerary.

She had considered sending DeQuincy a cable from the next station along the line. On reflection, she decided not to. An element of surprise would be to her advantage.

The train conductor touched the peak of his cap. "Stopover in Regina is about three hours, ma'am. There's a hotel opposite the station, if you wish to rest in comfort."

"Thank you. I've changed my mind about continuing to Calgary. I'll be breaking my journey here. Would you please arrange for my trunk to be sent over to the hotel?"

"Certainly, ma'am. I'll see to it immediately."

Sybil crossed the street, taking care to lift her skirt to avoid the piles of horse droppings. There was no doorman at the hotel entrance so she opened the door herself. A clerk lazed on his stool behind the counter, in front of which stood a man in a dark suit.

"Good day, madam. Welcome to the Empire Hotel. I'm the manager, Mr. Wagstaff, at your service. Is your husband joining you?"

Sybil shot him a withering look. "I'm traveling on my own, thank you very much. I'd like the best room you have."

"Forgive my mistake, madam. It's not often we have an unaccompanied lady as a guest."

"Well, you have one now. Show me to the room. I trust a hot bath is available."

"Most certainly, ma'am. Please follow me." Manager Wagstaff led the way up the wide staircase. On the first landing, he opened a door and stood aside to let his guest enter.

"This is our finest suite, Mrs...?"

"Mrs. Halliday." Sybil nodded her approval. By Eastern standards, the room was small and plainly furnished. It reflected the general newness of the hotel itself but it was clean and well lit by two windows overlooking the street.

Wagstaff followed her in. "That door leads to your personal bathroom. I'm sure you'll find everything to your liking."

Sybil rewarded him with a smile that revealed pearl white teeth. "Thank you, Mr. Wagstaff. I'm sure I'll be quite comfortable."

"May I inquire how long madam will be staying with us?"

"That is yet to be determined."

"When you descend to the lobby, please sign the hotel register." The manager gave an exaggerated bow and left the room, closing the door behind him.

She consulted her watch and decided the day was too far advanced to put her new plan into effect. It would keep until morning. Some ten minutes later two men arrived at her door panting under the weight of her steamer trunk.

"Place it at the foot of the bed, please." She handed them a generous tip.

That night she slept soundly for the first time since starting her journey.

The next morning, before going to the dining room for breakfast, she approached the front desk. The clerk smiled in anticipation.

"I wish to send a cable."

The clerk produced a pad of blank forms and a pen. "Simply write your message and its recipient, ma'am, and I'll be more than happy to take it over to the station telegraph office."

Once the task was dealt with, Sybil went to the dining room where she breakfasted on coffee and toast. A few minutes after nine, she knocked on the manager's office door.

The door opened and Wagstaff appeared, a frown on his round face. "Mrs. Halliday, good morning. Nothing's wrong, I hope."

Without an explanation, Sybil brushed past him into the office.

Wagstaff closed the door. "Do sit down." He pulled forward a chair.

"Thank you, I'd prefer to stand." Sybil lowered her voice to a confidential tone. "Mr. Wagstaff, I have a favor to ask of you."

At the realization that she was not there to make a complaint, Wagstaff's features melted into a broad smile. "A favor? I'd be happy to help in any way I can, dear lady."

"I wish to contact a certain gentleman, who, I have reason to believe, is a prominent resident of this city." When she saw the manager raise his eyebrows, she added, "It concerns a deeply personal matter."

Whatever suspicions Wagstaff may have harbored over the sudden arrival in his hotel of an attractive, unaccompanied woman in her mid-forties vanished. "You have no need to divulge anything you don't wish to, ma'am. As I said, I am here to assist you. What is the name of the gentleman in question?"

"His name is Mr. Niven DeQuincy. Have you heard of him?"

The manager slapped his thigh. "Niven DeQuincy! Not only have I heard of him, I am on first name terms with the gentleman. We are both members of the Assiniboia Club."

"Which is what?"

"The Assiniboia Club is an exclusive society of gentlemen engaged in commerce. Mr. DeQuincy, by virtue of his importance, is the club's president."

"How very interesting! Do you know how I might get in touch with Mr. DeQuincy?"

"If you were to write a note to him, I will ensure he gets it with the least amount of delay. Please avail yourself of the writing materials on my desk."

While she wrote, the manager stood with his back to her at the window. He appeared to sense when she had finished, for he turned and faced her just as she was sealing the envelope.

"Mr. Wagstaff, as an additional favor, I would ask you to keep this matter completely confidential. Please do not mention my name to anyone."

"But, of course. Just as you wish."

"I have invited Mr. DeQuincy to meet me here at the hotel. I want it to be a surprise for him. Consequently, I have not told him who I am. Simply inform him that this letter is from a lady of his acquaintance. Will you promise me that?"

Wagstaff gave every indication of being delighted to be part of an intrigue involving an alluring woman. "Certainly, madam. Trust me, I shall exercise the utmost discretion on your behalf."

A knock came on on her door an hour later. "Madam," Wagstaff said, "I regret to inform you that Mr. DeQuincy is presently out of town but will be back in two days. However, I personally placed your letter on his desk and his Métis housekeeper promised that she would tell her master of it immediately upon his return."

Sybil's initial reaction to the news was one of irritation, but after Wagstaff left she began to think how she could turn the delay to her advantage. To ensure she'd create a favorable impression, she unpacked her entire wardrobe and decided to wear a different outfit every day of her stay in the capital.

It took only a day to win over the manager. Wagstaff confessed to being surprised to see her walk through the entrance door of his hotel. "Men here are usually unattached. If they are married, they've left their wives behind in the East while they try to establish themselves. As for unaccompanied women, I can count the number on the fingers of one hand. Naturally, I am referring to respectable ladies like yourself. We had a young woman, a girl, really, arrive recently with her father. She must have hated it here, because she left on the very next train east."

"There must be more women than what you report, surely?"

"Some servant girls and the occasional washerwoman. A number of businessmen and store owners have brought their wives out. Our lieutenant governor, the Honorable Edgar Dewdney, is here with his lady. Then we have a businesswoman, Mrs. Eloise

Trephine, who owns Madame Trephine's Emporium on Albert Street. Of course, there are wives of settlers passing through on their way to join their husbands on newly established homesteads."

"Is that all?"

"A smile then crossed Wagstaff's lips. "A handful of white women are in town. They are what one might call…"

"Ladies of easy virtue?"

The manager's smile widened. "Madam Halliday, I can tell you are a lady with experience of the world. May I offer you a drink? I have a bottle of the finest French cognac in my cabinet."

"I rarely partake of spirits and never in the middle of the day, but I appreciate you do things differently in this part of the country."

"Then, you will?"

"A small glass, with a splash of water."

Wagstaff took a bottle and two glasses from the cabinet and poured the drinks. He handed one to Sybil. "Here's to your health, ma'am." He drained his glass. "Excuse me for being forward, Mrs. Halliday, may I ask what brings you out here?"

"Here, as in Regina?"

"Well, yes, and the Northwest in general."

"I am on my way to Calgary in the Alberta District to visit an old acquaintance, an English aristocrat by the name of Lord Cottesmere. The gentleman owns the Eagle Ranch south of Calgary. You may have heard of it."

"Everyone knows of the Eagle Ranch. It's famous for its size. They employ over a hundred ranch hands. And you're a friend of his lordship! It's not often we have the honor of receiving such a distinguished guest. There is some ranching in this part of the territories but nothing on so grand a scale as in the Alberta District. And you broke your journey to call on your friend Mr. DeQuincy. He is a fortunate gentleman, indeed, to have such a beautiful friend."

"You flatter me, Mr. Wagstaff."

During her wait, Sybil put her time to good use. She visited Madame Trephine's Emporium where she purchased three pairs of silk stockings and six pairs of lace gloves. The quality and quantity of goods on offer surprised her in a place that boasted so few women. While in the store, she encountered two other women, a Mrs. MacPherson, the wife of one of the town's two doctors, and a Miss Scranton, the spinster sister of Edward Scranton, the secretary of the territorial council. Miss Scranton kept house for her brother. Both women were some ten years older than Sybil. This lucky encounter earned her an invitation to call upon Mrs. MacPherson that same afternoon. It was in her parlor that she was introduced to three other women who, along with Miss Scranton, made up what she guessed must be the elite of Regina's female society. Sybil found herself welcomed with open arms. The ladies complimented her on her flair for fashion and admired her American outlook that brought a breath of excitement to an otherwise dull and dusty Canadian frontier city.

Her prestige was further enhanced when they found out she was an acquaintance of the vaunted Mr. Niven DeQuincy. What really confirmed her position as something of a celebrity among the upper echelon of Regina's society was the letter she received from Lord Cottesmere bearing his family coat of arms and confirming that a warm welcome awaited her at the Eagle Ranch 'whenever her other obligations permitted.'

It was not just the Regina ladies who were enraptured by the sudden appearance in their midst of the vivacious Sybil Halliday. The husbands, too, found her irresistible, particularly her talent for dressing with just the right amount of skin on display. So as not to antagonize the wives, Sybil ensured she didn't overly exploit this aspect of her appearance. Consequently, she treated the men with a firmness that bordered on the strict, which, not surprisingly, made her all the more attractive to the male eye.

At a dinner party Sybil suspected was thrown mainly because of her, she found herself seated next to Mr. Scranton, who was so severely short-sighted that when he spoke to her he brought his face to within inches of hers.

"You can have no idea how much we admire your good friend Niven DeQuincy," he said. "His philanthropy and business acumen will for sure earn him the honor of being considered one of Regina's founding fathers."

This piqued Sybil's curiosity, as it did not sound like the Niven DeQuincy she knew. "Really, Mr. Scranton?"

"He is presently financing a scheme to dam Wascana Creek – that's the miserable excuse for a waterway that runs along the southern edge of the Regina townsite – in order to create an artificial lake. When completed, this body of water will not only provide the capital with a much-needed source of water but will give the town a pleasing aspect."

"How noble of him!"

"Not content with that, he is the main backer of the proposed Qu'Appelle, Long Lake and Saskatchewan Railroad, a line which will open up the lands to the north of the city."

Scranton laughed, and Sybil pulled back just in time to avoid being hit by a droplet of spit.

"Yes, indeed," Secretary Scranton continued, "DeQuincy is a man of means. Why, I'd go so far as to say that very few goods are bought and sold or land changes hands without some profit accruing to a DeQuincy company."

Sybil listened with a growing realization that her chance encounter on the train with Harris was turning out to be the greatest piece of luck to befall her since leaving Boston. She could hardly wait to meet the reincarnation of the Niven DeQuincy of old.

Once launched on his praises for DeQuincy, Scranton showed no sign of stopping. "If, as you say, you have been out of touch with Mr. DeQuincy, you'll be filled with admiration for this remarkable gentleman. Under the recent Dominion Lands Act, Mr. DeQuincy's colonization company has taken up several extensive tracts of land north of the twenty-four-mile railway belt at a meager two dollars an acre. Once he's brought in enough settlers to occupy these homesteads, for an appropriate fee, his company will receive a rebate from the government of a dollar an acre."

"One dollar? That doesn't sound like a lot of money."

"But, madam, you must understand that the amount of land in question runs to more than sixty-four thousand acres between here and the foothills of the Rockies. Only a man with DeQuincy's business skill could have foreseen the potential of such a scheme."

Sybil's mind began to drift as she listened to Scranton rattle on about debenture stocks and overland cargo rates. Like Niven, she too was developing a scheme. Hers centered on DeQuincy's newly-acquired ability to repay the kindness she had shown him in the past. Only, as yet, Mr. Niven DeQuincy was unaware of it.

Chapter 9

Carina came to an abrupt halt on the boardwalk and stared at her brother. He wore a linen jacket, light brown plus fours and sported a straw boater. Despite the heat, he appeared at ease.

"Julian! What on earth are you doing here? I thought—

"Hello, sis, pleased to see me? You thought I was still in Montreal?" He gave a broad smile.

"Why, yes, you said you were working for a law firm for the summer."

"Three days into my temporary job I couldn't stand being shut up all day in a musty old office in the company of even mustier old barristers. I quit and decided to come out West and see what you and the guvnor were up to. I got to Regina only to find you had flown the coop."

"The house father was expecting hadn't been built. The contractor absconded with the money."

"So I heard. You can't trust anyone these days. The world is full of crooks. I decided to come and pay you a curtesy call. Father is following in a few days."

"He's coming here?"

"Yes, and he's bringing with him a gentleman who hopes to be your suitor."

"What are you talking about?"

"Pa introduced me to a man called DeQuincy. I understand you've met him."

"Mr. Niven DeQuincy?"

"Yep, that's him."

"He's coming to Cannington Manor! He's a dreadful man!"

Julian shrugged. "I don't give a tinker's cuss what you think of him. He's the leading businessman in the capital and he's been good enough to offer me employment."

"You mean you're working for Mr. DeQuincy?"

"As of a couple of days ago."

"Doing what?"

"To start with, just learning the ropes. Then I'm going to be in charge of overseeing deliveries."

"Deliveries of what?"

"His land settlement company places homesteaders on farms and supplies them with tools and seeds, everything they need to get established."

"Isn't being a delivery boy a bit of climb down from being a lawyer?"

"Don't talk rubbish. I'll be responsible for ensuring deliveries are made in an accurate and timely manner. Maybe I'm just not cut out to be a lawyer. I reckon I can make just as much money working for a man like Niven. Father seems to agree with me."

"You're already on first name terms with Mr. DeQuincy?"

"Niven and I hit it off on our very first meeting. We get along fine." Julian stepped onto the boardwalk and slipped his arm around Carina's waist. "Enough talk. Aren't you going to give your favorite older brother a welcoming kiss?"

Carina wrenched herself free and strode toward the house. "Julian, you don't behave like a proper brother. Your behavior makes me feel uncomfortable."

Julian laughed and fell into step beside her. "That's my Carina, ever the strong-headed bitch! By the way, I've already met our so-called uncle and aunt, and Cousin Maud. Nice people."

They reached the house. Julian opened the garden gate and stood aside to let his sister enter. "Do you like it here?"

"In Cannington or here at Uncle Alfred's?"

"Both."

"I appreciate what the people of Cannington are doing to try to establish a gracious way of life in the Northwest. Uncle Alfred and Aunt Rosalind are hospitable in offering me a place to live until papa gets established in Regina. I'm grateful to them for that."

Julian adopted a confidential tone. "Don't expect anything to happen in Regina any time soon."

"What to happen?"

"Getting established. The old man's bank is not flourishing."

"Why is that?"

"Niven tells me business is in the doldrums. Wheat prices are low. A drought has taken a bite out of business. And settlers are not moving into the area in the number people expected. Plus I think the scandal back in Montreal has taken a toll on the old man's health."

"That may be true. I didn't think he was looking well."

"That's why he's counting on you."

"On me! What can I do?"

"Help him solve his financial problems."

"As ever, Julian, you talk in riddles."

"No riddle, my lovely. He expects you to marry Niven DeQuincy."

"He did hint at that when I was in Regina. But it's absurd."

"Not as absurd as you think. How many options do you think a girl like you with no fortune to her name has available? You can't live forever on the charity of distant relatives. Father is making no move to acquire a house in the capital. Besides, he's unlikely to be able to support you, even if he did. What will you do?"

Carina halted and glared at her brother. "What will I do? Get a job, that's what I'll do. If father thinks he can marry me off to Mr. DeQuincy or some other man simply to ease his financial woes, he's sadly underestimated his daughter. I'm sure Mr. DeQuincy is an honorable gentleman but I have not the slightest interest in him."

Julian grinned. "My sister's still as fucking stubborn as she always was."

"Your manner of speaking disgusts me." She hurried into the house.

That evening's dinner at the Addersley residence was solely a family affair, with Julian in the guest of honor's chair to Alfred

Addersley's right. Carina's gratitude to the Addersleys was genuine enough, but she found it difficult to think of Mr. and Mrs. Addersley and their daughter Maud as family. Such was the tenuous link between her and her cousins. As much as she detested Julian's vulgar language, she had to agree with him that her options were few. She couldn't stay in Cannington for ever. There was no question of returning to Westmount or Montreal. What to do? Go to Regina and find work? In the male-dominated Northwest, perhaps that would not be easy to do.

***

"Mrs. Halliday, Mr. DeQuincy is downstairs."

Mr. Wagstaff hovered at her hotel room door, flushed and out of breath. He gave the impression that he was relishing this long-awaited encounter as much she was.

Sybil smiled her thanks. She already knew of DeQuincy's return. Not an hour before, she had heard a locomotive's whistle and bell, and from her window observed the bustle of activity that always accompanies a train arrival. Among the crowd of passengers streaming out of the station, a familiar figure stepped onto the boardwalk and climbed into a waiting two-wheeled open carriage. As it passed beneath her hotel window, she obtained a good look at the man she had not seen in five years.

For the manager's benefit, she feigned surprise. "That's good news, Mr. Wagstaff. Thank you. I'll be right down."

"If you so wish, you may use my office for your meeting. I'll ensure you are not disturbed."

"That's kind of you. And am I correct in thinking he still doesn't know who he's to meet?"

The manager placed his right hand over his heart. "Rest assured, madam, that the matter has been dealt with with the utmost discretion on my part. Mr. DeQuincy is expecting to meet an unnamed lady. That is all."

"Bid the gentleman wait until I finish dressing." Sybil saw the manager's gaze hover over her figure as if taking a mental inventory of what more was needed. For the occasion she had put on a peacock-blue dress with a contrasting, ruffled, black underskirt.

Over the course of her short stay she had taken the measure of the slightly pompous hotel manager and a conspiratorial familiarity had developed between them. When he remained standing at her door, she asked, "Does my appearance meet with your approval, Mr. Wagstaff?"

The man's jaw sagged. His face reddened and he tugged at his starched collar. "Uh? Oh, yes, Mrs. Halliday. You look absolutely…er, ah…" He struggled to find the appropriate word.

Sybil enjoyed the man's confusion. "Absolutely what, Mr. Wagstaff? Absolutely hideous? Absolutely outrageous? Stunning? Captivating?"

Wagstaff swallowed hard. "Yes, yes, absolutely captivating, indeed."

"Mr. Wagstaff, please, go tell Mr. DeQuincy the lady he's expecting will be down shortly."

Wagstaff regained his composure. "Yes, of course. And if there's any way I can be of further service to you, please let me know."

Sybil thanked him and closed the door. She looked at her appearance in the long mirror. Some minutes later she took the stairs down to the lobby. Wagstaff was nowhere in sight but she guessed he must be lurking close by. Without knocking, Sybil opened the office door strode in.

DeQuincy stood at the window, his back to her. She noticed that his former raffish style of dress had given way to a more sober appearance. He must have heard her enter but didn't immediately turn from the window, which suggested to Sybil that he attached next to no importance to the prospect of meeting a mystery woman in Regina.

"Hello, Niven! Long time no see."

At the sound of her voice he spun round. She derived pleasure watching the color drain from his face.

"Sybil! What the hell are you doing here?"

"What kind of a greeting is that? I stopped off expressly to see you. We have some unfinished business to attend to. Don't you remember?"

A nerve twitched in his forehead as he struggled to maintain an even voice.

"What d'you mean, you *stopped off*?"

"I am on my way to the Alberta District as a guest of the Eagle Ranch. I have a personal invitation from its owner, Lord Cottesmere, a real English aristocrat."

DeQuincy raised his eyebrows. "Since you seem to have friends in high places, why waste your time coming to see me? Besides, how did you know I was here?"

"I have spies everywhere. You didn't think you could hide from me forever, did you? The continent may be huge but word gets about."

DeQuincy closed the distance between them. When he next spoke, his tone was less defensive but his face remained stern, his lips unsmiling. "I ain't hiding from anyone."

"No? I could name a certain U.S. Marshal who would be interested in knowing your whereabouts."

"This is Canada. American law doesn't apply here. Besides, all that shit is behind me. I've built a new life for myself in the Northwest."

"Well, that's wonderful to hear. I'm happy for you." Sybil's voice hardened. "But you've done it at my expense. You cleaned me out and left me with not a penny to my name."

"What do you mean? Old man Halliday must have bequeathed you his fortune. And your...business venture among the city's upper crust seemed to be thriving."

"Aubrey bequeathed me nothing but a load of bad debt, which is why I opened my emporium."

"Is that what you called it? I don't understand. Aubrey Halliday was Boston's wealthiest merchant. He had to be worth a cool million or more."

"That's what it might have looked like to the outside world. My late husband was a secret gambler. Unbeknownst to me he frittered away his money at the card table. That ten thousand dollars he loaned you could not be covered and I was stuck with repaying it."

Niven glanced round the room. "Does that hotel manager keep any liquor in here?"

Sybil motioned with her fan toward a lacquer cabinet. "I happen to know that Mr. Wagstaff keeps a good selection of spirits in there. "I take brandy with a splash of water in it."

Niven opened the cabinet and poured the drinks.

"Okay, so your husband was careless with his money, but you were raking in cash on your own, you and your young lady assistants."

"I was doing well enough until the the city fathers, goaded by a clutch of hypocritical hellfire preachers, decided their city needed purifying. They put pressure on the chief of police and overnight I was out of business."

"What did you do?"

"What could I do? I moved north to Canada, but with no capital I couldn't re-establish myself."

Niven frowned at her before draining his his glass. "Don't tell me you intend to set up shop here in Regina?"

Her silvery laugh rippled around the manager's office. She took her time answering. "This town is too small and too backward for my liking. No, I was on my way west to Calgary."

"Calgary! If you think this place is the end of the world, you're in for a shock, my darling. I've been there. Calgary is no more than a collection of tents and shacks. Before the railroad arrived, no one knew which side of the Bow River the Canadian Pacific station would be located. Consequently, no one dared build anything permanent. They still haven't, even though the line went through twelve months ago."

"Calgary may be like that now. In a few years it will rival any metropolis in the territory. The ranches in the district are huge and boast magnificent houses. I know. Lord Cottesmere showed me photographs of his ranch house. It would rival any New England mansion."

"In which case, don't let me stop you. There's a train to Calgary this very evening."

"You can't get rid of me that easily."

"You want money? I can write you a check right now."

Sybil shook her head. "You don't seem to understand. You can't buy me off with some quick cash."

"Okay, what more do you want?"

"In the short time I've been in this city, awaiting your return, I've met a number of its leading citizens. It seems that everyone holds you in the highest esteem. You even rub shoulders with the territorial governor himself."

"For your information, he's called a lieutenant governor here in Canada."

"Indeed? Thank you for putting me straight on the matter. Here's what I want. I intend to remain here for an undetermined length of time, during which you, in your exalted position, will acknowledge me as an old family friend and a wealthy widow. *Widow* is accurate, the wealthy part isn't. No one needs to know that."

Niven grunted. "Then what?"

"Once I am integrated into their social circle, into which I've already made some progress on my own, you and I will make a trip farther west to the Alberta District. Your good standing will ensure that I will have similar success out there.

"Why me when you have this Lord whatever-his-name-is to look after you?"

"Lord Cottesmere is a useless old fool."

"Even old fools have their uses."

"Not this one. He's a broken down alcoholic in the advanced stage of syphilis. The pathetic wretch has retired to his ranch to die. Despite the aristocratic name, he's not going to be of much help to me."

"What if I refuse these crazy demands of yours?"

Sybil gave an exaggerated shrug. "Then, you'd leave me with no alternative. I'm sure you have provided these good people with a carefully laundered account of your background. They might be interested in hearing the unabridged version. I ran into the editor of the city newspaper the other day, a certain Mr. Flood Davin. Do you know him?"

"Of course, I do. He won't believe you. Nor will anyone else. It would just be your word against mine."

"Mr. Flood Davin and I get along very well." Sybil smiled. "As a newspaper man, he's always looking for stories. I could give him some useful leads. You know how reporters like to muckrake."

"This is insane. You're trying to blackmail me."

"No, Niven, let's not call it blackmail. I simply want you to redress the wrong you did me back in Boston. Life has not been easy for me. On the other hand, it looks like you've done well for yourself."

"Everything I have here is due to my own hard work and perseverance. I am a respectable man of commerce. And you're making things difficult."

"That was not my intention." Sybil pouted with just the right amount of coquettishness for a woman who knows she has the upper hand. "All I need is a modicum of cooperation from you."

"You're too clever for words, Sybil. You have me over a barrel."

"Is it a deal?"

"I guess it has to be."

That evening, Niven and Sybil dined together at his house. By then Niven had recovered from the shock of finding his past intruding into his new life. His mind was already at work on a scheme to contain the damage Sybil could inflict on his reputation. When the meal was over they sat on the shady veranda and drank coffee and liqueurs. Niven smoked a cheroot.

Sybil wrinkled her nose. "You still smoke those hideous American cigars?"

Niven flicked off the ash. "One of my few indulgences."

"I suppose a man of your importance wields considerable authority."

"You had better believe it."

"Isn't it a case of big fish, small pond?"

Niven laughed. "Today, a small pond. Tomorrow, a huge ocean. The Northwest has a big future ahead of it. By the way, I must inform you I am thinking of getting married." He waited for Sybil's reaction.

Sybil raised a finely curved eyebrow. "I thought you already were. The woman's name escapes me."

"Then I shan't remind you. That was a long time ago and in the States. Besides, I have lost contact with her."

Sybil shrugged. "Mind you, being married never seemed to crimp your style."

"You never complained."

"Legally, it'd still be bigamy."

"This is Canada and the frontier. No one needs to know. You're not going to say anything are you? You're already blackmailing me over the other matter and I'm doing everything to please you, like taking you to Cannington."

"Excuse me. I don't understand."

"Cannington Manor is where the lucky girl is living."

"Girl?"

"Her father tells me she's going on nineteen."

Sybil shrugged. "What's a twenty-odd-year difference? What's she called?"

"Carina, Carina Chesterman. Her father is a banker here in the capital. I have his blessing."

"And, this Miss Chesterman has accepted your proposal of marriage?"

"She knows nothing about it yet. We only met once, briefly at dinner. Hence my visit to Cannington."

Sybil stared at him for several long minutes. "You haven't changed one bit, Niven. Still the same arrogant bastard. You want me along to give my approval. Is that it?"

"I don't give a fig for your approval. No, a woman with your persuasive skills might help me overcome any resistance on the part of the young miss."

"What's she like?"

"Pretty, blond, a good figure, but..."

"But, what?"

"She strikes me as being headstrong and too damned independent for her own good."

"I thought you liked spirited women?"

"Her father said she could be difficult."

Sybil pursed her lips. "Are you sure she's the kind of bride you want?"

"Why do you ask? You're not jealous because you think I should be marrying you?"

Sybil leaned back and laughed. "We could never get married. People like us end up killing each other. No, I just have difficulty picturing you, a man of mature years, with a wife young enough to be your daughter."

"Out here, finding a bride is not easy."

"What do you mean?"

"The pool of eligible females in the Northwest is mighty shallow. And I'm too busy to travel east to find someone."

"Where is this Cannington place?"

"A couple of days from here. We leave in the morning. The father, Theo Chesterman, will be with us. I'd better warn you, the gentleman is not in the best of health. Another word of caution. Cannington Manor is a colony of well-heeled English folk. They like other people with class."

"I can play the part of a lady when I want to."

"Yes, I know. But, like me, you're American. The Brits have no love for Americans. They've never gotten over losing their thirteen colonies."

Chapter 10

Cannington, Tuesday, June 3, 1884

Over the past few days, I have been doing all I can to keep my distance from Julian. I find him so offensive. However, tonight was surely the worst evening of my stay here. The day started well enough. First, I rode out to Fish Lake. It's so peaceful there. Mr. Fripp proudly showed me the progress being made on the resort he's building. On my return in the late afternoon, I encountered none other than Mr. Ogden Fenn in the street.

"Mr. Fenn," I said, "what a pleasure to meet you again!"

Mr. Fenn looked at me from behind those funny horn-rimmed spectacles he wears. As usual he was all smiles. He said he had found our conversation the other day so stimulating that he wanted to come to Cannington without delay. He was also here for the horse races. I asked if he was camped nearby.

"No, no. whenever I visit, the Beresford brothers insist I stay with them in the annexe they call Bachelor Hall. It's extremely comfortable. My mules receive the royal treatment too, being allowed to graze on some lush grass in one of the many paddocks."

Another surprise came when I heard my name called from across the street. I looked and saw father standing in the doorway of the Mitre Inn. Mr. Fenn bid me goodbye and said we'd talk again later. My uncle had invited him to dinner.

I was taken aback at father's appearance. He seemed to have shrunk in his clothes. I asked him if he was unwell.

He answered in his typical gruff manner. "Of course not, girl. Don't worry about me, I'm fine. Too much work lately and not enough sun. I hope to correct that over the next few days."

Before I could say anything, a woman appeared behind him. Right away, I saw she was not a Cannington woman. No one here dresses in peacock blue or has deep auburn hair.

She held her arms out wide. "So, Mr. Chesterman, this is the lovely daughter you've been telling me so much about. And you weren't exaggerating. She's a beauty!"

I saw father shift uncomfortably from one foot to the other. He cleared his throat and, in a voice that made it plain he'd prefer to be a thousand miles away, introduced me. "Carina, I'd like you to meet Mrs. Sybil Halliday. Mrs. Halliday is a friend of a business acquaintance of mine. You may remember meeting Mr. Niven DeQuincy in Regina before you left. Mrs. Halliday, this is my daughter, Carina."

I held out my hand. The woman not only took it (in both hers) but she pulled me to her and kissed my cheek. In the process I was engulfed by an aura of heady perfume. I noticed that her fingernails were painted carmine. I had never seen a lady of good society with painted nails. So I was nonplussed what to make of this exotic creature. But, strangely enough, she had an outgoing manner that made me feel at ease. Also, she talked all the time. I must remember to tell Millie about her next time I write. What made my spirits sink was when she said Mr. DeQuincy was also in Cannington and that she, my father and Mr. DeQuincy were dining at my uncle's the same evening.

At the sound of the gong, I went down to the drawing room. Sure enough, that DeQuincy fellow was there. He must have seen me enter but because of the crowd of people, he remained talking to my aunt on the other side of the room. During the wait to go into the dining room sherry was served. I never touch it. To me it tastes like turpentine!

I was seated between Mr. Fenn and, yet another surprise, Sergeant Dillon Granger! I expressed my delight, for he's a very pleasant gentleman.

He grinned at me and answered, "The pleasure is all mine."

I reminded him that because we first met in Westmount he was one of my few links to my old home.

"You must find quite a contrast between there and here."

"Cannington does have a few of the same qualities. Other than that, you are correct. Sometimes I feel I'm living on another planet."

He lowered his voice to a whisper. "There are many in this settlement who think the whole of Canada belongs to another planet - a very uncivilized one."

Up to this point in the dinner everything was fine. I was happy to see my sergeant again and I always enjoy talking to Mr. Fenn. So what went wrong? I put the blame on Mr. DeQuincy. He was sitting diagonally across from me. Mrs. Halliday, fortunately, was tucked away on my side of the table to my uncle's right. It was the acrimonious exchanges DeQuincy initiated, first with Sergeant Granger and then with Mr. Fenn that ruined the evening.

In a taunting tone, DeQuincy said to Sergeant Granger, "Sergeant, as a representative of the only armed force of law and order in the Northwest, don't you feel you're overwhelmed by the threat of violence posed by the half-breeds and their full-blood cohorts?"

Sergeant Granger, to his credit, remained calm in the face of the man's belligerence. "The North-West Mounted Police has always been able to handle whatever situation arises, sir."

At that DeQuincy gave a vulgar snort. "Handle the situation! How many men have you got in total?"

Still in a level voice, the officer replied, "The Force currently consists of some five hundred and fifty-seven men, with sixty-eight at Fort Macleod, sixty-six in Calgary, nineteen in Edmonton, one hundred and three in Battleford and ninety-six at the Regina depot. The rest are in scattered detachments, which includes two troopers here in Cannington."

I admired the precision of his answer.

DeQuincy then rapped his knuckles on the tablecloth. "Just as I thought. A miserable handful of police officers to cover an area as large as Europe! You're telling us that number will be strong enough to put down a half-breed rebellion and contain several Indian tribes on the warpath?"

"It's not for me, Mr. DeQuincy, to make any such claim," Sergeant Granger said.

DeQuincy sat back in his chair. "Of course not. One can't expect a mere non-commissioned officer to do anything but follow orders."

Uncle Alfred looked at DeQuincy. "May we inquire, sir, as to what you recommend be done, were you to be in command? It would be instructive to have an American perspective on the matter."

"The first thing would be to bring in a sizable armed force. Military, not police. Four regiments of regular mounted troops, equipped in a similar manner to the United States Cavalry, backed up by units of infantry, would effectively put an end to this simmering rebellion. That would allow honest businessmen like myself to engage in commerce without fear and trepidation. At present, prospective immigrants are being scared off by the reports of unrest. I have said as much to the government in Ottawa. Are they listening? No they damn well are not."

Uncle Alfred coughed into his fist. "Sir, I would be grateful to you if you would moderate your language. There are ladies present."

"Excuse me, Mr. Addersley. It was not my intention to offend anyone, least of all the ladies. I merely feel that the powers-that-be are walking blindfolded into a crisis."

"I would agree that there is some cause for alarm."

Undeterred by his host's reprimand, DeQuincy then pointed his finger at Mr. Fenn. I can't begin to describe the torrent of invective he poured on the poor man's head. Everyone at the table was aghast. He accused the scientist of singlehandedly attempting to thwart the government's attempts to settle the southern plains, when more eminent scientists than he had already proved beyond a doubt that the region was suitable for agriculture. Like Sergeant Granger before him, Mr. Fenn remained as calm as could be expected, given the provocation. My uncle was at his wit's end, for DeQuincy's angry outburst shut out all other conversation around the table.

I excused myself as soon as I could and went to the kitchen to help Ellie with the dishes. Ellie's a bright girl and obviously overheard what had transpired in the

*dining room. "He's a bad'un," she said, meaning
DeQuincy.*

I think she may be right.

After helping in the kitchen, Carina went up to her room, rather than rejoining the dinner guests, many of whom drifted into the garden to take in the cool evening air. After some time, the sounds of departing guests filtered up from below. She went to the window to watch them go into the fading light. As if out of nowhere came raised voices. She looked down and saw Ogden Fenn standing close to the house on the flagged walk, engaged in an acrimonious argument with DeQuincy, who had positioned himself at front gate, as if to prevent Fenn's escape.

DeQuincy appeared determined to have the last word in the exchange. He used the same aggressive manner as at the dinner table. "I read that you opposed the government's decision to bring the rail line through the south. Who the hell gave you the right to question those elected to develop this country?"

In contrast to his opponent's emotional outburst, Fenn maintained the reasoned logic of a man of science. "Every citizen has the right to question a government's actions. First, I spoke up because they were about to make a big mistake by changing the route of the rail line from the north to the south. They had been badly advised by Mr. John Macoun, who is really no scientist. If you question my opinion, take a look beyond the limits of this well-watered spot and you'll see things differently. This year, for the third year running, the West is in the grip of a severe drought."

"Hah, that means nothing! Droughts are common. Would you have the railroad company tear up the goddam tracks?"

"Of course not. But it's not too late to prevent further settlement. It may take a generation or two before the full effects of the arid conditions take hold, before the aquifers run low and the soil becomes depleted. But that will happen."

"I guess this report you're writing is intended to change the government's mind, correct?"

"I can but try."

DeQuincy stood aside to let Fenn pass. "Be warned, Mr. Fenn, be warned. You're treading on the toes of a lot of powerful people with your crackpot notions."

Ogden Fenn walked away and was soon swallowed up by the darkness. DeQuincy said something to those who had witnessed the argument but not taken part. Carina could not make out his words.

One thing she had noticed about her English hosts that when faced with an unpleasant incident, they later acted as though it never happened. She was not surprised next morning that her uncle behaved in his habitual, jovial manner. A couple of days later, he mentioned that Ogden Fenn had stopped in at the store on his way out of the settlement.

"He's left?" Carina asked. "Where's he gone?"

Her uncle shrugged. "Back to his old campsite, I assume."

The news of Ogden Fenn's sudden departure hardened her attitude toward DeQuincy, whose attack the evening of the dinner had been unprovoked. She was incensed that Fenn had been insulted for conducting valuable scientific research. On a personal level, the man had been deprived of some well-earned relaxation at the Cannington Races he had been looking forward to. She, in turn, had been deprived of further discussions with him on topics she found fascinating.

To take her mind off the unpleasantness, she took a walk to view the preparations for the races. The entire area around the racecourse had been transformed into a canvas city. Laid out in orderly rows were tents of every conceivable design from one-man bivouacs to more grandiose structures. Behind the tents and separated by a stretch of grass was a scattering of Indian teepees. Everywhere were horses, some tethered on picket lines, others in temporary corrals. Ahead of her on the boardwalk she saw two men surveying the scene. Only when she came close did she realize one of them was Sergeant Granger. He was not wearing his distinctive scarlet. Instead, dressed in a blue shirt, brown cord breeches and wearing a slouch hat, he could have passed for a ranch hand. The only indication that he was a police officer was the brown leather belt and service revolver. Canadian civilians in the Northwest did not carry side arms.

Dillon doffed his hat when she approached. "Good day, Miss Chesterman."

"Sergeant Granger, I didn't recognize you at first. I'm used to seeing you in uniform."

Dillon laughed. "I wasn't in uniform when we first met."

"Perhaps we could forget about that time."

He grinned and replied, "Very well, ma'am. By the way, this is my sidekick, Trooper Durkin."

The officer nodded and touched the brim of his hat. He looked at Dillon. "Sarge, I'll take a stroll across to make sure our native friends are keeping their noses clean."

Carina waited a few moments then asked, "Sergeant Granger, may I ask if my father is aware the police were keeping him under surveillance before his arrival in the territories?"

"I don't think so and I didn't tell him. I have met him a number of times since then, both here and in Regina and he's made no allusion to having seen me before, neither in Montreal nor on board the lake steamer."

"In the company of his daughter on a dance floor, I might add."

Dillon grinned. "I thought you didn't want to talk about what happened prior to your arrival."

"You're right. I don't. If you'll pardon my curiosity, how long have you been in the Northwest?"

"Seven years."

"And all of that time in the mounted police?"

"I joined four years after the force was founded in Seventy-three."

She saw his eyes focus on something behind her. To her dismay, Mr. Niven DeQuincy was walking toward them. Sergeant Granger replaced his hat and excused himself. Carina wanted to grasp his arm and beg him to take her with him, so much did she dread the thought of being alone with DeQuincy. But he had seen her. She had nowhere to hide.

"Miss Chesterman or, since your father and I are on such close terms, may I address you as Carina? Such a pretty name for the prettiest of women."

Carina cringed under his cloying words. "I am quite indifferent, sir, as to how you address me. Our acquaintance will, of necessity, be of short duration. Father tells me you and he are returning to Regina in a few days."

"That's true. You and I will have the pleasure of each other's company later, in August, when lieutenant governor Dewdney holds his annual territorial council meeting. To celebrate the event he throws a magnificent ball. Your father wants you in attendance."

"He never mentioned anything about a ball to me."

"Perhaps not. Your father is a man of the moment. He has no time for things past and gives precious little thought to the future."

She made no reply, DeQuincy leaned closer. She caught the stale smell of liquor on his breath and the hint of cigar smoke.

He lowered his voice. "Why are you avoiding me?"

"Avoiding you?"

"That's what I said. Ever since I arrived I've noticed you take great care to remove yourself whenever I show up. Like the other evening at dinner. As soon as you could, you excused yourself and left. When I did have an opportunity to speak to you, I received a few curt words by way of a reply. I can tell when a girl is evading me."

Carina was tempted to make some bland excuse for her actions or even deny that she had been avoiding him. She was surprised, therefore, when her anger over the man's treatment of Ogden Fenn and his rudeness to Sergeant Granger came to the surface and gave her courage. As recently as a month or so ago, in her old life, she would never have considered standing up to a man like DeQuincy.

"Mr. DeQuincy, you're correct. I find your presence disconcerting."

With a startled look on his face, he took a step back. "Well, now, you're a girl who speaks her mind! And, why, pray, do you wish to shun my company? "

"My father has intimated to me that you have openly expressed your intention of marrying me. Considering we are strangers, I find that presumptuous and arrogant in the extreme."

DeQuincy regained his composure. "It's not presumptuous in the least for a gentleman to seek the approval of a young woman's father on the subject of marriage."

"However, that would normally take place only after the gentleman and lady were well acquainted, which we are not, and that they are mutually compatible, which we are certainly not."

DeQuincy grinned. "This is the Northwest frontier, sweetheart. Your fancy Eastern conventions don't apply here."

"Since you asked for an explanation for my motives, I must add that your general rudeness repulses me."

"You surprise me. When was I ever rude to you?"

"Your very way of speaking borders on rudeness, as does your unwarranted familiarity. Then, there is your rudeness to others, such as Mr. Ogden Fenn."

DeQuincy guffawed. "Your Mr. Ogden Fenn is a crazy old buzzard, poking his nose into matters that don't concern him. I might have spoken forcefully to him but that's the only way to get through his thick skull."

"Mr. Fenn is an extremely intelligent gentleman."

DeQuincy again laughed. "Clearly, our opinions differ." All humor drained from his voice when he added, "You may soon find yourself welcoming an offer of marriage from me."

"I fail to see what kind of situation that might be. I know my father values you as a business associate, and you are employing my brother Julian for the summer before he returns to his law studies. That's of concern to them alone. I am under no obligation to you. So, if you'll excuse me, I have other things to attend to." With that, she walked away, all the time feeling his eyes on her back.

Chapter 11

At lunch Carina remarked on the frenzy of activity at the racecourse.

Maud pressed her for more details. "I'd love to see what's happening, myself. Would you come with me this afternoon?"

Carina weighed the chances of running into DeQuincy again and decided it unlikely. Even if they met the man, he would not say anything to her in the company of Maud. "If you'd like to go, I'm more than happy to come with you."

She and Maud set off down the street. To remove any possible friction between her and her cousin, for Carina sensed Maud's disapproval of her western riding skirt, she wore a dress and carried a parasol.

Maud was in a talkative mood. "Every year at the races we get hordes of people from far and wide. Father is pleased because it means extra business for his company. Personally, I don't care for it, as it upsets the tranquility we enjoy here."

On the boardwalk they met Mr. Featherstonehaugh, walking in the opposite direction toward the church.

The churchman clasped his hands. "My, my! Two angelic nymphs dressed in white, what a welcome sight for weary eyes! Good day, Miss Addersley and to you, too, Miss Chesterman."

Carina responded with a tight smile. She detested the man, not in the way she detested DeQuincy, but because of the clergyman's unctuous and condescending manner. Disconcerting, too, was the way his eyes seemed to undress her. He didn't look at Maud in the same way.

Maud dropped a curtsy and appeared to melt under his smile. "Hello, Mr. Featherstonehaugh, I've been dying to tell you how much I enjoyed your sermon last Sunday on the temptations of the flesh. Such a pertinent topic when one sees such profligacy all around one."

Carina wondered what kind of profligacy Maud was alluding to. Was there an aspect of Cannington society she had yet to encounter?

Mr. Featherstonehaugh inclined his head in acknowledgement. "It's comforting to know that my words fell on such fertile ground. I wish more members of my congregation were as attentive as you, Miss Addersley." He consulted his watch. "Now, if you'll excuse me, ladies, I've an appointment with a young couple wishing to arrange for their banns to be published."

Maud stepped back. "I realize how busy you are, sir. Goodbye."

Featherstonehaugh took the path leading to the church door. The two women continued down the street. Maud linked arms with Carina, which surprised Carina, for her cousin, hitherto, had made few overt gestures of friendship.

"Mr. Featherstonehaugh is such a wonderful man, so caring and so deeply pious."

"He's not very old, is he?"

"Twenty-nine, three years older than me. Some time ago one of the ladies in the altar guild learned, purely by accident, his date of birth. We held a tea party in his honor. I believe he was quite touched."

"Married?"

"No, a bachelor."

"Then, why don't you marry him?"

Maud stopped dead in her tracks and faced Carina. "I'd like nothing better but the gentleman hasn't proposed. In fact, he scarcely pays me any attention. I honestly believe he only stopped to talk because you were there." Maud let out a long breath. "That's how it is in polite English society, the man has to ask. Surely, that's the same with you in eastern Canada, isn't it?"

Carina nodded. "Though, I have friends back in Montreal who didn't go so far as to *ask* the man of their choice to marry them but did engage in what one might call some serious coaching."

"Good lord! And it worked?"

"Those friends are now happily married, each with a brood of children."

Maud resumed walking. "That might work in elsewhere in Canada, but not here. Mr. Featherstonehaugh is immersed in his ecclesiastical duties. He probably hasn't given a thought to marrying."

"I'd venture to say that the gentleman has probably given a great deal of thought about the opposite sex. You need to attract his attention."

"Oh, but I do. I sit in the very front pew at services. He knows I hang on his every word."

"Maud, do you consider me a friend as well as being your cousin?"

Maud squeezed Carina's arm. "I have come to regard you as a very dear friend. You are some years my junior but you seem to know so much more about the world than I do."

"Then you wouldn't be offended if I offered some suggestions as to how you can pique Mr. Featherstonehaugh's interest, over and above listening to his Sunday sermons?"

"I wouldn't be offended in the least. I've never had anyone I could speak to regarding personal matters before."

"If you are serious about wanting to attract the gentleman, you need to take a long hard look in the mirror, firstly at your clothes."

"My clothes?"

"Your dresses and other outfits are certainly of the highest quality, but they reflect the tastes of an older generation."

"Really? Mama always compliments me on my appearance."

"With due respect to your mother, her views are of a past era. Times and fashions have changed."

"I do admire the way you dress. I must tell you that mama and several of the Cannington ladies consider your mode of dress rather provocative."

Carina hid her smile. "If you wish to make the most of your youth and natural beauty, give serious consideration to the changes taking place in women's fashions."

"I recently read an article in *The Woman's Home Journal* about the reforms in ladies clothing. I'm not sure I fully understand what is meant by *artistic dress*."

"It is all the rage back in Westmount among progressive women."

"What does it entail?"

"The rejection of highly structured and heavily trimmed fashion in favor of beautiful materials and simplicity of design. Hoop skirts, bustles, and above all corsets, are out."

"Not wear a corset! I have worn one since I was eight, just like every other lady I know. Don't tell me you don't."

"Place your hand on my waist and tell me if you feel any whalebone stays."

Maud did as Carina instructed. "Good gracious! You have a slim waist but no corset. Did you never wear one?"

"I was made to when I attended Miss Dalton's Academy for Girls. The school not only valued mental accomplishments but also placed high importance on figure training so that we would graduate as fashionable young ladies. The first item of dress attended to was our stays. Those I had from home were taken away and another pair, smaller in the waist and more heavily boned, was substituted. I was not allowed to remove them during the day, no matter how painful they were and no matter how they restricted my movements. I was also instructed not to remove them at night, but since I was a day girl, they weren't able to enforce the rule. My mother wore a corset tight enough to grasp the figure, but not so tight as to nearly cut it in two, like my school stays. She made no fuss when I ripped them off the moment I came back from school. They were awful. I couldn't bend down or even sit comfortably on account of the stiff whalebones."

"That's very similar to my experience. Only, I wore mine day and night, removing them just twice a week for bathing. Mother used to tighten them a bit more each day until my waist was as narrow as it is now. I did suffer perfect torture, especially in the evening after having eaten dinner. When did you give up wearing stays?"

"Several months before I finished school. I'd leave them at home whenever I thought I could get away with it, particularly on the days we had athletics."

"Mama says a tiny waist is epitome of fashion and is only attainable by tight lacing. That is what attracts a gentleman's admiration."

"I'm afraid that notion is wrong. Many men shudder when they see an unnaturally slim waist and realize it's been achieved through a garment that virtually cripples the woman."

"How, then, do you maintain your trim figure?"

"Through daily exercise and being careful what I eat."

Maud fell silent for several minutes during which time they reached the racetrack. Before surveying the feverish activity taking place in front of them, Maud looked Carina in the eye. "You're telling me that a gentleman is not drawn to a woman with a narrow waist?"

"Doubtless, some are. More and more, men find tight lacing inconsistent with beauty. What is more telling is that they've found out that tight-laced women suffer headaches, shortness of breath and other ailments. And above all they tend to exhibit an irritable temper. What kind of man wants to have a life companion like that?"

"What kind, indeed? I do believe you are correct."

"Give it a try. As the saying goes, you have only your stays to lose."

Maud laughed. "Tomorrow morning, I am going to pay a visit to Mrs. Ripley. I heard she has just received a new shipment of very fine cloth. Would you care to come with me?"

"I'd be happy to, Maud."

While they were watching the activity, a group of horsemen rode by, led by Mr. Percy Lansdowne-Coutts. He acknowledged the two women by touching peak of his cap with his riding crop, for he wore an English-style riding cap rather than a brimmed hat. The man might as well have been saluting a stone statue for all the warmth there was in his greeting. Maud responded with a wave. Carina simply nodded

The racetrack was no makeshift affair but a properly laid out oval course measuring two furlongs in length. A white post and rail fence lined the two sides of the track. Close to where Carina and Maud stood was the starter's box, elevated on posts some ten or twelve feet above the track, with windows and a shingled roof. A steep set of stairs led to the upper platform. The tent encampment filled the grassy space at the farther end of the track. Near the track workmen were erecting a large frame tent.

Carina pointed to them. "What's that for?"

"It's for the Cannington Agricultural Society's annual fair. It's always held in conjunction with the races."

"Two events in one, that's exciting!"

"I'm happy when it's all over."

**

Sybil removed the pins and threw her hat on the sofa of her hotel room. "This is the craziest town I've ever found myself in."

Niven sat back in his chair. "Sybil, don't exaggerate. You've been in some weird places in your time."

Sybil gave him an impatient stare. "Cannington Manor caps the lot. This afternoon I was invited to take tea with some of the ladies."

"What's wrong with that? They're a sociable bunch."

"For one thing, at first, I could hardly figure out what they were saying, even though they spoke English. It was all 'Good gracious me, this' and 'I say, how positively quaint, that.' The way the women stared at me you'd think I had gone there barefoot with straw in my hair."

Niven laughed. "I told you they'd look down their aristocratic noses at you, because you're American."

"I don't think they looked down at me. They asked me about life in Boston and I must have shocked them with my stories."

"How do you know they were shocked?"

"Some blushed. Others declared how hot the parlor had become."

"You're a like a breath of fresh air through their stuffy corridors."

"I saw you in conversation with the charming Miss Chesterman."

"The stubborn bitch!"

"Do I deduce that your marriage plans have run into a snag?"

"Not really. These are early days. She hasn't yet grasped the precariousness of her situation."

"What do you mean?"

"The girl can't stay here for ever. She doesn't fit in. Sooner or later she'll outstay her welcome with her English relatives."

"She was supposed to keep house for her father in the capital."

"Her father is a sick man. The poor guy might not last the year."

Sybil's eyes glittered. "Is that when you step in to offer your hand? With her father a banker you're in line for a fat dowry."

DeQuincy laughed. "You joke! The Chestermans were once well off. Now, Theo is skint. His bank is going nowhere because he's too ill to make it work."

"Why would you want to marry a penniless woman?"

"I've no need to marry money. The girl is young and pretty. That's good enough. I want an attractive wife to consolidate my position in society. Here in Cannington, I'm viewed as an American upstart. But Cannington is just a freak show, a bunch of English toffs pretending they're still back in the Old Country, with their hunting and shooting and their stupid dinner parties. In the capital people look up to me. I create jobs, make land available, and provide settlers with the means of making a living. Even the governor treats me as an equal."

"Who would have known that a former Mississippi riverboat gambler could rise to such prominence?"

"Always ready to deflate a fella's ego, aren't you? Mr. Halliday must have led a happy life."

"Mr. Halliday died a very happy man. It's too bad he couldn't have taken himself off earlier. By the way, the hotel proprietor stopped me in the lobby this morning when I was coming from the dining room."

"What did he want?"

"He was concerned that you had been seen entering my room, like you are now."

"He accused you of engaging in some dubious trade?"

"On the contrary, he went to great pains to assure me he held me in the highest regard but was worried what his other patrons would think."

"How did you convince him you were as pure as the driven snow?"

"I said you and I were brother and sister."

"You did what?"

"Don't be so naïve. People are very quick to think the worst when they see a handsome gentleman like you traveling in company of an attractive, younger widow. And these English, I've found, are prudish beyond belief. You see, I was protecting your reputation as much as mine. And that's essential considering how important a personage you say you are."

"Tell me, does being your brother give me the right to wander into your room any time I feel like it?"

"You're being mule-headed, today. No, of course it doesn't. I informed the manager that I'd been feeling feverish and that I summoned you to attend to me."

"Attend to you, what the hell's that supposed to mean?"

"I said that before you entered the world of commerce and became a millionaire you had trained as a humble country doctor. I was simply seeking your medical expertise."

"God, woman! Are you nuts? If word gets out that I'm a fucking doctor, I might be called to deliver a baby or remove gall stones."

Sybil's lips curled into a slow smile. "I'm sure that would pose few difficulties to a man of your self-proclaimed talents."

Niven ran his fingers through his hair. "I'll be glad to get out of this place. First I run into that idiot Ogden Fenn, and now everybody's going to call on me to perform surgery, thanks to you."

Sybil smoothed the creases from her skirt. "You always did have a way of over-dramatizing things, Niven. You have nothing to worry about from me. I asked the manager to keep our conversation confidential, saying you were an extremely sensitive gentleman. Of course he agreed. Men love playing the confidant to a beautiful woman. How serious a threat is Mr. Fenn? You and he had a furious argument the other evening."

"How serious? Have you ever been stung by a hornet? If you have you'll know that something small and insignificant can inflict a lot of discomfort, but it's not life threatening. That's Fenn for you. He is a lone voice but he could stir up trouble. What with the drought and depressed wheat prices in Canada, immigrants are choosing to head to the United States rather than the Northwest. If he publishes his scientific findings, like he says he's going to, it might tip the scales further against settlement. If that happens, businessmen like me are going to get stung."

"I can see why you are angry with him."

"If I thought he could be sidetracked, I'd get you to use your charm to distract him and preventing him from writing his book."

"I'm not overly enthusiastic about that prospect. I doubt if Mr. Ogden Fenn has had a bath in six months."

"You have nothing to worry about on that score. He's married to his science. I'd be willing to bet the man has zero interest in women."

"How long are you remaining in this Little England?"

"I'll take in a couple of days of the races and then head back to Regina. I think I have to get Theo Chesterman to a doctor, a real one. And we can only do that in the capital."

"Why the compassion all of a sudden?"

"He and I have business dealings that will only work if he's still alive. Besides, he's my number one ally in my bid to win over the lovely Miss Chesterman."

"I plan remaining here in Cannington a while longer."

"I thought you hated the place?"

"That's beside the point. I've heard that your Miss Chesterman is expecting the arrival of a close friend, a pretty girl who is of American origin."

"And you want to meet her, is that it?"

"You know me. I'm always eager to offer my assistance to help a young woman get on in society."

"Do whatever you want, so long as you don't upset my bride-to-be."

"By the way, I've run out of money. I hadn't anticipated an extended stay."

"I'll give you some cash and I'll pay your hotel here until the end of the month."

"Niven, how can I thank you? You are generosity itself."

***

Two of the young men from Captain Pierce's agricultural school, as well as the principal, Mr. Lansdowne-Coutts, were the guests that evening, making it an unbalanced dinner table, with more men than women. Carina was repulsed by the grim-faced Lansdowne-Coutts. When they came face to face in the drawing room, he nodded and made no other greeting.

A voice sounded behind her. "Good evening, my adorable sister, looking as ravishing as ever."

"Julian, how's father? I haven't seen him since this morning."

Her brother shrugged. "As well as can be expected. He finds this heat intolerable. As I do. When will it end?"

"Is he coming to dinner?"

"He went to bed early. He already ate at the hotel."

"I'm worried about him. He ought to see a doctor."

"We're returning to Regina in a few days. I imagine he intends to consult a physician then."

Carina let the dinner table conversation flow past her. The talk focused on which horses and riders were to run, in what order, and who was to judge the livestock. She was relieved when the few ladies present rose and retired to the drawing room. As soon as she could, Carina went into the garden. The sun had long since set and, although there was still a band of light low against the western sky, stars shone bright. She tried to remember the names of the various constellations.

So absorbed was she in her star gazing that she failed to hear the approach of cushioned footsteps across the lawn.

"What the hell are you doing?"

Startled, Carina spun round. "Oh, it's you! You scared me."

Julian laughed. "I didn't mean to."

"I was looking at the stars. There are so many out tonight." For a moment she appeared oblivious to the fact he had placed an arm about her waist. "Why aren't you still in the dining room with the other gentlemen?"

"They're a bunch of old fuddy duddies talking endlessly about things that don't interest me."

Carina slipped out from under his unwelcome touch and walked a few paces away. She was never at ease talking to her brother but she couldn't turn her back on him and return to the house without appearing unnecessarily rude. He continued to look at her intently.

After a minute or two of silence, and without any preamble, he said, "Do you recall the time I saw you naked? You must have been all of ten at the time."

"What a curious question. Yes, I remember. I had forgotten to lock the bathroom door and you barged in knowing full well I was there taking a bath. It was very inconsiderate of you."

Julian laughed in the vulgar manner Carina detested.

"You were just a scrawny kid then. But you've grown into a lovely young woman. You know that, don't you?"

"What's the purpose of this line of conversation?"

Her brother closed the gap between them, and before she could distance herself, his two hands gripped her waist. "I wanted to express my admiration for my attractive sister. I'm sort of ashamed by the way I've treated her in the past."

She tried to free herself but he held her tight. "I'm happy to hear that. Your behavior toward me has not always been kind."

Julian hung his head in a gesture of mock remorse. "Can you find it in your heart to forgive me?"

"You are my brother. I suppose I can't hate you forever."

"So, you actually hate me?"

118 - Michael Montcombroux

"At times, yes. It seemed that after I reached the age of thirteen or fourteen, you used to go out of your way to be mean to me. I could recite a litany of the instances when you played nasty tricks on me, such as spoiling my birthday parties, spreading false stories about me among my friends, speaking in a vulgar way to me, as though to purposely upset me. I could go on."

"I agree, I acted like a real shit. I'd like to make it up to you."

"Make it up to me? What do you mean?"

"Like this, for a start." Julian slid his hands down to cup her buttocks.

Carina gave a shriek. "Julian!"

"Make less racket, you silly girl. I only want to show my affection. Let me come to your room tonight."

Carina struggled to free herself but Julian gripped her tighter. "Let me go. I can't believe what you're proposing. You're my brother!"

"That needn't be an obstacle. Brothers and sisters have often made love through the ages. Think of Tamar and her brother in the Bible."

"Amnon forced himself on his sister, Tamar. He raped her. Perhaps you need to re-read the story. It's in Second Samuel, if I'm not mistaken."

"Who cares? I've been with a woman. I know you'd enjoy it. I also know how to take precautions so there would be no consequences."

"Julian, you're obscene. I find all this talk disgusting Take your hands off me."

Her brother guffawed. Instead of removing his hands he pulled her closer. In desperation she raised her right leg and razed the heel of her court shoe down his shin as forcefully as she could. Julian grunted in pain and his grip loosened. Carina seized the opportunity and broke away. He lunged at her but she was too fast for him. She lifted her skirts and darted across the grass to the kitchen door. Inside, she paused to catch her breath, leaning her back against the closed door.

Ellie, who had just set a tray laden with a coffee pot and cups and saucers on the kitchen table, looked up at her with the eyes of a startled doe. "Miss Carina, what's the matter?"

Carina waited until her heart stopped pounding. She shook her head. "Nothing, Ellie, nothing. I thought I saw something in the dark that frightened me, but it was probably just a passing animal."

Ellie made no reply. From the look in the girl's dark eyes, Carina knew that she knew. Ellie was no fool and must have seen Julian on his way into the garden. Carina straightened her dress and walked calmly to the door leading to the main corridor. She hoped she wouldn't meet anyone before she could reach the stairs. Through the half open dining-room door, she saw the men seated around the table, cigars and glasses of port in hand. The door to the drawing room was still shut. Carina took a deep breath and ran up the stairs. Once in the sanctuary of her own room she turned the key in the lock.

Chapter 12

Carina lay on her bed and tried to make sense of what had transpired in the garden. The sound of men's laughter drifted up from the dining room. Later, she heard voices in the entrance hall below as the guests took their leave. She remained motionless until the house fell silent and everyone had gone to their rooms. Only then did she get off the bed and cross to the window. Before her lay a scene of complete tranquility, breathtaking in its quiet beauty. The moon had risen over the sleeping settlement. The lighter roofs of the houses contrasted with the ink-dark shadows of the trees. Two of the upper windows of the inn were lit.

She struck a match and lit the candle. Seated at her writing table, she reached for her journal.

Cannington, Tuesday, June 17, 1884

Was I to blame for what happened this evening? Was it the way I dressed? My summer dress with a low neck? Perhaps I was wrong to go into the darkened garden on my own. Or, was it something I said that encouraged him to think I might welcome that kind of an advance from a brother? Perhaps I was at fault but somehow I doubt it. For as long as I can remember, Julian has always made crude comments. When I was growing up he would take every opportunity to be physical, pretending it was play. But it wasn't. Tonight was merely the culmination of years of an unhealthy relationship between us. Ours is truly a dysfunctional family.

I don't believe I was to blame. I didn't lure him into the garden. I didn't make him put his hands on me. He was the aggressor. I was the victim.

I would like to tell someone what had happened. But who? Father would be logical person but he is too sick for me to place this burden on him. Uncle Alfred? As nice a man as he is, I have the suspicion he would listen with great patience then tell me to keep quiet about it. Young men are like that, he'd say. They have needs and those needs need an outlet. I happened to be convenient. Convenient! He'd emphasize the importance of remaining silent to protect the family and the settlement from any hint of scandal. The English place great importance on that.

Of course, I could always report the matter to the police. I have a police officer here in Cannington at the moment. I'm sure he would lend me a sympathetic ear. But did Julian commit a crime? I don't believe making an indecent proposal is, in itself, a crime. What if he had been successful in forcing himself on me? That would have been a crime. It'd have been incest too. Was incest a crime between two adults? Does it matter? I couldn't imagine laying myself open to scandal. I'd be obliged to leave the settlement, and where would I go? How could I support myself?

Yet once a woman decides to keep quiet and say nothing about such an incident, it's the same as admitting you're guilty. Keeping quiet has the dubious advantage of not needing to do anything. No need to upset the family or tell anyone. You can keep it bottled up inside you and avoid any further shame. In a warped kind of way it's easier to put it behind you and pretend nothing happened.

That's not right, though. Julian deserves to be punished for his lewd behavior. But I can't do anything about it. Perhaps, he knows this and that's why he made his advance. He is, after all, a student of law.

Until this evening, I had naively, looked upon the world as a friendly place. True, the loss of mother was a cruel blow, but it didn't shake my belief in the goodness of people. The actions of my brother have changed that. I remember being moved by a poem I studied in my last year at school. It was written by the English poet, Matthew Arnold, and was called Dover Beach. I memorized it and the teacher asked me to recite it in front of the class. The last few lines touch me even now.

...the world, which seems
To lie before us like a land of dreams,
So various, so beautiful, so new,
Hath really neither joy, nor love, nor light
Nor certitude, nor peace, nor help for pains,
And we are here as on a darkling plain
Swept with confused alarms of struggle and
flight,
Where ignorant armies clash by night.

The garden incident brought home to Carina the somber realization that she was alone, utterly alone. Her father had always been a stranger to her and now, in failing health, he was even more distant, not that she could ever see herself confiding in him. For one fleeting moment this evening, she thought that Julian might be on verge of reforming himself by admitting to his previous behavior and asking forgiveness. Yet that had been only a sham, a cruel ploy to seduce her. She wanted nothing more to do with him. Her uncle and aunt were well meaning, but they were too far removed from her. Alfred, ever the gentleman, treated her with the utmost courtesy, as he did everyone else. Her aunt, whilst keeping a smile on her lips, frequently dropped hints that Carina's stay with them was only transitory. Beyond that, she had no one. Millie was due to arrive soon and she was a good friend, but that was all, a friend.

The once proud Chesterman family had in a short space of time, crumbled to dust. She was reminded of something else she had read, this time from Sophocles' *Antigone*:

"Blest are those whose days have not tasted evil. For when a house has once been shaken by the gods, no form of ruin is lacking."

After a night punctuated by nightmarish dreams, in which she was being pursued through a dark forest, she awoke to the sound of drums. Drums! Curious, she jumped out of bed, dressed and went downstairs. Dawn had broken, but at that hour no one else in the house was astir. She put her head out of the side door, the one marked *Tradesman's Entrance*. Long shadows stretched across the adjoining meadow. Although there was no sign of movement anywhere, the drumming continued. She determined it came from the native encampment by the racecourse. Pausing only long enough to fetch her hat from the hallstand, she left the house.

Minutes later, she was following the bridle path that skirted the churchyard and looped across an open field to approach the racecourse from the south side. By now the drumming had fallen into a steady cadence. As she came closer, she saw native men wearing traditional headdress dancing in a wide circle. Five or six others were striking a large drum resting horizontally on logs of wood. The group beat out a steady, hypnotic rhythm. Seated outside the circle were small groups of women, some holding their children. In tune with the drumming, they called out to the dancers.

Then, as abruptly as it had begun, the drumming stopped and with it the dancing. The men retired to one of the larger teepees and the women rose to tend the smoking fires. Carina was about to return to the house when she saw a man, a white man, walking across the racetrack toward the big teepee. Her interest was sparked when she saw that the man was her brother. So purposeful was his stride that he failed to notice her in the shadow of a clump of willows.

She wondered what Julian was up to. From the little she knew about his work for DeQuincy, she understood he had dealings with white homesteaders and farmers. He had made no mention of being in contact with the native people.

Julian stopped to speak to the two men guarding the entrance to the teepee. After some discussion, the men motioned him inside. Carina looked for a way to eavesdrop on his conversation but realized it was impossible to approach without being seen. Instead, she stepped back into the willows and kept watch. Some ten minutes elapsed before Julian and the natives emerged. The fact that they were all smiling and laughing suggested Julian was on good terms with them.

Julian retraced the path he had come. Had he not been so deep in thought he would have seen his sister observing him from thirty feet away. As much as she wanted to ask him what he was up to, she remained in hiding. Besides, talking to Julian was not something she wanted to do after his indecent advances.

Only when he disappeared from view did she move from the trees and return home, her mind filled with anxiety. She had the suspicion there was more to Mr. Niven DeQuincy than the successful businessman he made himself out to be. His association with her father and now her brother was cause for concern.

Then there was the wider question of how serious were the storm clouds gathering over the Northwest. She was aware that life in Cannington existed within an artificial bubble, cut off from the rest of the country. These well-to-do Englishmen and their ladies carried on their rituals in complete oblivion as to what was happening elsewhere. News of unrest among the Métis buffalo hunters, illegal whiskey shipments, and Ogden Fenn's scientific arguments against wholesale settlement, all contributed to her belief that some kind of crisis was brewing. How typical that the pressing concern for the inhabitants of Cannington Manor was the forthcoming week of horse racing and the agricultural fair!

On entering the house she met Ellie carrying a tray from the breakfast room.

The girl gave a mischievous smile. "Miss Carina, have you seen Miss Maud?"

"When I left to go for a walk, no one was up. Why?"

"Because when she came down for breakfast she looked like a new woman."

"Do you mind explaining what you mean?"

"Miss Maud looks quite different."

"Different in what way?"

"A real lady. She's wearing a new dress that…"

"That what?"

The girl lowered her gaze for a moment. "That shows off her figure in a way I've not noticed before. She's suddenly become quite striking. She's done her hair in a style I've only seen when I sometimes snuck a look inside one of Mrs. Addersley's ladies' magazines."

Carina tried not to smile at the realization that her advice to Maud must have borne fruit. "Where is Miss Addersley now?"

"She went back upstairs. She was hoping to speak to you. I believe she'd like you to accompany her to the races and the fair."

"You seem to know everything that happens in this house, in the entire settlement, even."

The girl's dark eyes widened. "Honest, all I do is listen to what folk are saying." The girl tilted her head in the direction of the breakfast room "Everyone's already eaten and the table's been cleared. Can I get you some breakfast?"

"That's kind of you, Ellie. I'd love some coffee and toast. I'll eat in the kitchen."

Carina took a seat at the deal table. Among the dishes on the tray that Ellie had set down was a copy of the Regina *Leader* newspaper. It was a week old, which was customary, considering the snail-like pace of mail service to the settlement. She unfolded the paper and read the headline: *Métis Agitator Returns from Exile in United States. Fears Deepen of Armed Rebellion.* She was unable to read the accompanying article, for at that moment Maud appeared in the open doorway.

"Ah, there you are, Carina! I was hoping you'd be free so that we could go to the races together."

"I'd be happy to. May I say how nice you look?"

Maud blushed. "Thank you. I did as you suggested. I'm having Mrs. Ripley make up some new dresses for me. This is the first one. Do you like it?"

"I do. It suits you perfectly."

Maud sat beside Carina and whispered, "I left my corset in its drawer. I feel, how shall I say, quite liberated. I hope people won't consider me a brazen hussy."

"Don't worry, Maud, you're a long way from being brazen or a hussy. Besides, brazen has more to do with how one acts than how one dresses. You always behave like a perfect lady."

Maud squirmed under the compliment. Carina couldn't help but agree with Ellie's candid assessment of how striking Maud looked. "It's just possible Mr. Featherstonehaugh might change his tune once he sets eyes on you."

Maud sat back on her chair. "You know, Carina, I'm not sure I care anymore what the reverend gentleman thinks."

"No?"

"No. I'm beginning to see him for what he is, a rather pompous man, obsessed with himself alone."

Carina stifled a laugh. "I'll go upstairs and change. Since you're the height of elegance this morning, I feel it's incumbent on me to to wear something better than this plain cotton dress."

"Please finish your coffee."

"When I come down."

In order to reassure Maud, now that she had encouraged her to change her appearance, Carina put on her best walking dress, selected her newest shoes and wore the broad-brimmed hat she had brought from Montreal. When she was satisfied with her appearance in the small mirror in her room, she rejoined Maud downstairs.

Her cousin scrutinized her from head to toe. "No matter what I do, I don't think I'll ever have your flair for style. You always seem to get it just right."

Carina squeezed her cousin's gloved hand, a reminder to put on her own gloves. "You are doing very well, Maud. Too bad there's no photographic studio in town. We could have your picture taken just to prove to you how attractive you look."

"True, there's no professional photographer in the settlement. However, Mr. Lansdowne-Coutts is a very talented amateur. People often request he take their picture."

"Is that so? No matter, I'd prefer not to ask Mr. Lansdowne-Coutts."

"Why is that?"

"I don't know. There's just something about him that makes me feel uncomfortable."

"Come to think of it, I do find he's a bit snippy around women. Perhaps because he's a former military man."

Carina did not think that had anything to do with his manner, but she said nothing. She put on her gloves and followed Maud out of the house. On the boardwalk, Maud slipped her hand into the crook of Carina's arm. "Carina, dear, I am so glad you came to Cannington. You have done so much to enrich my life."

"Why me? There are plenty of other young women in the settlement."

"None like you. You have such an original turn of mind. It takes my breath away. The way you dress, the fact that you are at ease on the back of a horse, that you speak up for what you consider right, all that is so different from what I'm used to."

Carina was tempted to explain that the main reason for any independence of character she might display was through necessity. For the past several years she had been forced to stand on her own feet. The lack of a mother, an absent father and a bully of a brother did that to a girl. She refrained from saying anything, as this was not the moment to reveal details of her past. That Maud was willing to shed her aura of prim spinsterism was enough for the moment.

"I don't know how keen you are on the races," Maud said. "For me, there is only one I really want to see. The start is at ten-thirty. Five of the Beresfords' horses are running. They are such magnificent animals. It's such a thrill to see them run."

Carina took her watch from her dress pocket. "We won't have long to wait."

"Then, at eleven I have to help judge the flower show."

"Are there are enough flowers in Cannington to judge?"

"You'd be amazed. Quite a few of the families have very fine flower beds. They have to have the seeds sent out from England and start them in glasshouses. Unfortunately, many of the varieties don't take to the climate out here."

"We'll watch the ten-thirty race. I'll then accompany you to the flower tent and return when your judging is complete,"

Chapter 13

Today got off to an odd start, what with the drumming, then seeing Julian engaged in some mysterious conversation with the natives in the teepee. I'll probably never know what all that was about, for I don't wish to speak to him again.

Later, Maud and I walked to the racetrack. I couldn't help but notice she was the recipient of several admiring glances. I can't say I blame the gentlemen as it seems that all of a sudden Maud has blossomed into an attractive young lady.

There was no prior indication that events would take such a bizarre turn. With so many visitors the settlement had a festive air. Some had brought their horses to take part in the races, others their livestock to show in the fair, and many more had come just to enjoy the spectacle. This was remarkable, considering how remote everything is out here.

Maud and I found a good spot close to the start line from which to watch the race, races, actually, as we had to watch several before they ran the one Maud especially wanted to see. Secretly, I believe the reason for wanting to watch that particular race was because the jockeys were the young men from the agricultural college and before the race they showed off their mounts (and themselves!) by parading in front of the spectators. I noticed they chose to mill about where Maud and I were standing by the rail. Many of the gentlemen saluted us by doffing their caps. Maud reveled in the attention, the saucy girl!

The starter fired his pistol and the race began. I love horses but have never taken much interest in racing, believing it to be cruel to the animals. Mother refused to attend the races held in Montreal, because she was of the opinion that horse racing appealed to the vulgar element of society. Which is not true. It's called the sport of kings. Everyone in our social circle used to attend, and the women were as enthusiastic as the men, because it was yet another occasion to display their finery. The real reason, I suspect, was that mother didn't want anything to distract me from my musical studies.

Seeing a race close up was exciting and we had an unobstructed view. It was a long race, too. The riders had to make four complete circuits of the track. When the horses thundered past we did get smothered in the cloud of dust thrown up by the hooves. The crowd cheered madly. It was impossible not to get caught up in the emotion.

On the third round, one of the horses stumbled right in front of us. Horse and rider went down taking two other horses with them. I had to physically restrain Maud from rushing out to help the riders. Fortunately, no horses or riders were hurt. Well, maybe the gentlemen's pride was somewhat bruised.

When it was all over, Maud was flushed with excitement in a way I had not seen before.

"That was wonderful," she said. "Judging flowers is now going to be tame in comparison."

I walked with her to the big tent which housed the flower show. It was crowded inside, too crowded for my liking after the crush beside the racetrack. I told Maud I'd return in half an hour. I needed to breathe some fresh air. I wandered around, going nowhere in particular. The races were over for the morning and attention had shifted to the agricultural fair. I found myself back where Maud and I had been standing, close to the starter's box. I had my back to the track and was watching a dozen sleek dairy cows being judged. The judges wore long white coats and black bowler hats, which, my uncle said was how they did such things in England. The impeccably-groomed animals were led by their handlers into the sawdust ring. The crowd of spectators sat on tiered benches. Because all the seats were taken, several young men and boys had perched themselves on the top rail of the adjacent corral containing the animals up next for judging, which happened to be six or seven lively young bulls.

I was watching the proceedings with only half an eye, as I was lost in thought, about my father's health, among other things. For the duration of his stay in Cannington, father had remained in his room at the inn. On the occasions I had gone to visit him he waved me away, as he had done on the steamer when he was in his cabin ill because of the storm. Now his condition was more serious. He had a dry rasping cough, which even to my untrained ear suggested a serious condition.

My attention was attracted by a voice over a megaphone announcing the winners of the judging. The audience clapped. The men balanced on the rail stood and cheered. The temporary corral was clearly not built to withstand such a strain and, amid yells from those perched on it, the structure swayed madly before crashing down, spilling the men and boys into the spectators. For a brief moment, as if not believing their good fortune, the bulls stared at the large gap that had opened up in their enclosure. Then pandemonium broke loose. The animals charged through the opening, scattering the crowd before them like a flock of panicked chickens. The orderly line of dairy cows broke free of their attendants and ran in all directions, pursued by the bulls. I saw several men and women bowled over by the animals, though the bulls were too interested in the cows to attempt to gore any humans.

Rampaging cattle are dangerous and everyone ran in search of the nearest available shelter. I saw people run into the flower tent but they were not out of danger there, as several cows squeezed through the tent door after them. Nor was I immune. A particularly mean-eyed bull came charging in my direction. I lifted my skirt and made a dash toward the rail fence bordering the racetrack. In retrospect, I would not have been safe even there, as the fence consisted of one rail intended a track marker rather than a real barrier.

Just then I heard someone call out "Miss Chesterman, this way!" I looked and saw Sergeant Granger waving to me. I ran to him and he took my hand and half-dragged me to the foot of the stairs leading up to the starter's box. He pushed me in front of him and we scrambled up the steep, narrow steps. On the upper platform, I leaned over the balustrade gasping for breath.

When I had recovered, I looked at my rescuer and we both burst out laughing. "Thank you, sergeant. For one horrible moment I thought I was going to be trampled by that angry bull."

For the next several minutes we stood shoulder to shoulder, observing the scene below. Gradually the chaos subsided. A handful of stalwart gentlemen arrived on horseback and lassoed the bulls. They then tethered them to the corral posts left standing. Deprived of their male

paramours, the dairy cows resumed their docile
behavior and allowed themselves to be rounded up.
From what we could see, and this was borne out later,
no one was seriously injured beyond a few scrapes and
bruises. The biggest casualties were some ruined ladies'
dresses and torn gentlemen's suits.

The bulls incident put paid to the agricultural
fair for the day. The officials also cancelled the races
scheduled for the afternoon. Sgt. Granger walked with
me to the flower tent because I was eager to find Maud.
The tent was empty. All the tables were overturned and
the ground was strewn with broken vases. The lovingly
arranged bouquets were trampled into the turf by the
passage of hooves. Fortunately, Maud and her fellow
judges had made their selection of prize winners before
the stampede. As for Maud, she escaped unharmed out
of the rear of the tent.

Sergeant Granger kindly accompanied me home,
for which I was very grateful.

If that wasn't enough to contend with for one
day, what followed later in the evening ended the day
on a sour note. The Cannington ladies put on informal
refreshments in the assembly hall. I wasn't that eager to
go but Maud wanted to and asked me to accompany her.

Upon our arrival at the hall, Maud was
immediately mobbed by a clutch of ladies who wanted to
commiserate with her over the floral mayhem. I took my
cup of tea and dainty sandwich on a plate to one corner
of the room, where I thought I'd be out of the way and
not have to speak to anyone. I was sadly mistaken.
Before I knew what was happening I was confronted by
Mr. DeQuincy, glowering at me in much the same way
as that bull, earlier. I looked around for an escape route

but I was hemmed in by tables and people engaged in conversation.

DeQuincy shocked me by accusing me of unladylike behavior by running to safety with a common police officer. He said, "You actually allowed yourself to be manhandled by the fellow."

"Sergeant Granger saved me from being attacked by a raging bull. Beside, sir, what concern is it of yours?"

The man adjusted his celluloid collar (I detest celluloid collars!) and replied, "Because your devoted father is temporarily indisposed, I feel it my duty on his behalf to watch out for the virtue of his only daughter."

Those words made me extremely angry. "That's very presumptuous of you, Mr. DeQuincy. I am no longer a schoolgirl requiring a chaperon, and you are certainly not my guardian. Sergeant Granger did the right thing. He would have helped any woman in similar circumstances, or a man, for that matter."

DeQuincy ignored what I said but continued in the same vein. "If that wasn't bad enough, when you mounted the steps to the Starter's box, it was reported to me that you lifted the hem of your dress so high your legs were on show. Then, you were seen standing on the platform with the gentleman in question, even laughing and exchanging pleasantries with him. You appear to have paid scant heed to your reputation."

"When those animals ran amok, I think there were many ladies who gave more thought to life and limb than to any sense of decorum. Several of the men didn't act in the most honorable fashion, either. I saw one fine gentleman push a lady out of the way in his haste to find safe refuge."

Again, DeQuincy did not respond to what I said. Instead, he continued lecturing me in that sneering tone of his. "Not tomorrow but the evening after, they are throwing a ball to mark the end of race week. It is also a send-off to Captain Pierce and other Cannington notables, who are off to Ottawa to try to convince the government and the railroad company to build a branch line to the settlement."

I demanded to know why he was telling me this and what had that to do with me. He had the temerity to reply, "Your father has expressed his wish that you allow me to be your escort for the evening and that you dance with me and no one else."

At this my jaw dropped. "What arrogance!" I set down my cup and saucer on a nearby table and glared at the infuriating man. "I will do no such thing." With that I brushed past him and joined Maud on the other side of the room.

Chapter 14

Carina was so incensed by DeQuincy's remarks that during the time leading up to the ball she took pains to avoid the slightest possibility of an encounter with him. She achieved this partly by keeping company with the Cannington ladies and, when not attending the races, going for long rides in the vicinity of Moose Mountain.

After lunch of the day on which the summer ball was to be held, Ellie handed Carina a folded piece of notepaper.

"What's this, Ellie?"

"That Mr. DeQuincy fella asked me to give it to you."

Carina unfolded the paper. Written in a scrawling hand was a curt message to say that the writer, Mr. Niven DeQuincy, wished to call on her at two o'clock that afternoon to discuss, among other things, arrangements for the ball that evening.

"The gentleman asked me to take him your reply."

Carina crumpled the paper into a ball and thrust it into the pocket of her skirt. "Tell him that I do not wish to meet with him…that I am not at home."

Ellie nodded. From the set of the girl's lips, Carina guessed that DeQuincy had not made a favorable impression on her, either.

"Could you please ask your grandfather if he would kindly saddle Morgana for me?"

A smile lit up Ellie's pretty face. "I'll tell him right away."

By the time Carina had changed into her riding habit, her mount was saddled and waiting for her in the bright sunshine. Although Carina was quite capable of climbing unaided onto a horse, she let old Mr. Tucker help her up, because she guessed he had a soft spot for her.

At that moment Ellie appeared. "Miss Carina, hold on! Here's your canteen. I filled it with ice-cold well water."

Tucker chuckled. "With this heat, it'll be more like warm tea when the lady comes to drink it." He patted the horse's neck and looked up at Carina. "Don't forget to water your horse every time you stop. I reckon you must know where the springs are, by now."

"We'll be all right. I have no intention of straying beyond the slopes of the escarpment, where water is plentiful."

She waved farewell and touched her heels to Morgana's flank. To avoid the chance of being seen on the main street, she detoured through the meadow behind her uncle's house and gave the racetrack and fairground a wide berth. The festivities had settled back to normal after the previous day's debacle. A crowd thronged the exhibition grounds and horses and riders were preparing for the first race. Without encountering anyone, she reached the trail to Moose Mountain on the west side of the settlement close to the drive leading to the Beresford mansion.

Just as she was passing, she was met by half a dozen of Captain Pierce's pups dressed in white trousers, blazers and straw boaters.

"Miss Chesterman," one man called out, "you're not attending this afternoon's races?"

"Too hectic for my liking. I decided to spend the afternoon exploring on horseback."

"On your own? Any one of us gentlemen would be delighted and honored to saddle up and accompany you."

"That's very kind of you, but I'm perfectly content with my own company."

The men laughed. "Well, enjoy your ride. We hope to see you at this evening's ball. We're already squabbling among ourselves as to who'll get to dance with you first."

Carina bid them goodbye and continued on her way. The bachelors resumed their promenade toward the settlement.

A wave of anger swept over her at being forced to avoid the afternoon's activities. Yes, the bustling crowd could be annoying at times but the influx of visitors had temporarily brought a cosmopolitan touch to the normally staid English colony. One man alone had spoilt the enjoyment for her.

All traces of anger evaporated when she looked at the sun-drenched plain that rolled away in all directions. She had always been amazed by nature's soothing effect. There was something about having the breeze in her hair that quickly put human affairs into perspective. In a day or two, DeQuincy would be gone from Cannington and she could forget about him. As for the ball that evening, she was unsure whether to attend or not. If she did, it would be on her own. Maud, in spite of her earlier misgivings, announced that she would be escorted by Mr. Featherstonehaugh.

Carina traversed the now familiar trails on the slopes above Fish Lake. She eventually found herself at the base of the southern edge of the escarpment. At this point, the scattered birch and aspen poplar gave way to bald prairie. To one side a spring bubbled out of the stony earth, formed a tiny creek which after a short distance disappeared underground. She dismounted and let Morgana drink her fill. At the same time she refilled her water canteen.

In her haste to leave the house she had forgotten her watch and could only estimate the time. From the angle of the sun and by its progression toward the west she guessed it was mid-afternoon. It would take her just over an hour to return home. That would certainly oblige her to change and attend the ball. DeQuincy would be there and if she ignored him he'd be sure to make a scene. The only way to ensure that did not happen was by avoiding the ball altogether.

But where to go? The thought of retracing her steps over the Moose Mountain trails didn't appeal to her. It was too hot to sit in the shade of the trees and wait for evening. She thought of visiting Mr. Ogden Fenn. His camp was not far, less than an hour's ride to the south-west. His sudden departure from the settlement gave her reason to believe something had happened to make him leave so abruptly. Without a doubt, that 'something' was the verbal attack he had suffered from Niven DeQuincy. Because of this she was reluctant to call on him unannounced. Besides, he may have already decamped and be on his way to Regina, as he intended.

On an impulse she headed onto the open prairie. She remembered Ogden Fenn telling her about a series of teepee rings to be found due south of the Buffalo rubbing stone. He described the rings as being field stones arranged in circles of twelve or fourteen feet in diameter. The native tribes used them to weigh down the edges of their buffalo hide teepees. When the tribes lived their traditional nomadic life, they left the stones in situ to be used over again when they next came through the region. According to Fenn, many of the tent rings dated back several millennia.

Such an excursion would make for a satisfying day's ride. First she must reach the rubbing stone. From there she'd ride south for an hour to the teepee rings before riding back the same way. Upon returning to the stone, it was no trouble to find the well-marked trail back to the settlement. By that time, dusk would be approaching. All of Cannington society would be at the assembly hall and she could get to her uncle's house unobserved. She would feed and water Morgana and let her loose in the paddock. Ellie might have left some supper on the kitchen table, if not she was capable of finding something in the pantry. By the time the ball ended she'd be in bed. Next morning, she'd offer some excuse for missing the event.

With no difficulty the found the giant boulder and rode round it several times to examine the trench cut by the hooves of long-vanished buffalo. Before setting out over the level plain, she noted the position of the sun and by estimation pointed her horse to the south. Fully aware of how easy it would be to become lost on this tractless ocean of land, she inwardly cursed her stupidity for forgetting her watch.

From the parched earth her horse's hooves kicked up dust, which hung like smoke in the still air. In many places the earth was devoid of vegetation. What grass there was appeared brown and withered. Carina took care not to push her horse but let the mare find her own pace, only giving the occasional tug on the reins to keep heading in the right direction. That direction became more and more arbitrary, for everything looked the same no matter what direction one looked. All around her the world had been reduced to an unbroken expanse of flat land that stretched to meet the edge of a perfect dome of sky. She found it exhilarating to be in a totally featureless landscape, where she and her horse were the only vertical elements in an otherwise horizontal world.

After estimating she had been riding for sixty minutes she shielded her eyes to try to locate the elusive stone circles. Usually, as the prairie day wore on, the temperature would slacken. Not today. Even with the sun beginning to dip toward the west the air remained as oppressive as at midday. Carina wondered if it was an indication of a storm. Yet, the sky was clear, save for a slim bank of cloud low on the northern horizon.

The heat may have been why she became drowsy. She was jerked fully awake when her horse came to an abrupt halt. Without warning Morgana reared up and Carina saved herself from falling only by gripping the mare's flanks with her knees. She looked down and saw a few feet ahead the coiled form of a prairie rattlesnake. Prairie rattlers were not large as snakes go but she had read that its bite could be deadly to man or animal. Ogden Fenn had assured her that rattlesnakes were not unduly aggressive but may attack if threatened.

The dun-colored reptile that blended perfectly with its surroundings lifted its triangular head. Its forked tongue flickered, probing the air. It began to uncoil. Carina estimated the reptile to be some three feet in length. All of this occurred in a matter of seconds. Before she could take action, the snake lunged. The mare leapt forward over the creature and broke into a gallop. It was several hundred yards farther on before Carina was able to bring her horse under control.

She dismounted and, holding the reins firmly in one hand, examined the horse's legs and chest but found no trace of a wound. Relieved, Carina climbed back into the saddle. After a few minutes of rest, Morgana's breathing relaxed.

The incident with the snake threw Carina's careful navigation awry. There was still no sign of the teepee rings, and she was no longer confident that she was heading due south. When she had discussed the problem of prairie travel with Ogden Fenn, he had advised her that if she became disorientated, to stop and retrace her own tracks until she reached familiar ground. This is what she now attempted to do.

She abandoned all idea of finding the historical rings and altered direction to keep the sun to her left. This meant she would be heading back the way she had come. The band of cloud to the north had elongated toward the east and no longer served as an indicator. To get back to Cannington she must first locate the rubbing stone marker. By now the sun sat lower in the sky than she expected and she estimated that no more than a small handful of hours of daylight remained.

Her reasoning dictated she would soon see the dark mass of Moose Mountain. But she didn't. After riding for what she guessed must be another hour, she reined in her horse and scanned the horizon. To her dismay, it seemed as though she had not moved at all. Everywhere, the same empty landscape stretched unbroken into the distance. Nature appeared to be playing tricks on her. She lost all track of time. The first signs of darkness were present in the east. What had started out as a leisurely outing was now becoming a race against approaching night.

She supressed the panic gnawing at her insides. Morgana shook her bridle and whinnied, as if to say she shared Carina's growing fatigue and anxiety. Both horse and rider were suffering the effects of dehydration. Even though it meant losing precious minutes, Carina dismounted, took a few sips from the canteen, then poured the rest into her hat and offered it to the mare.

Carina resumed the saddle and determined that her only course of action was to keep riding until she came across the boulder or the Cannington trail. If the worst came to the worst, she would keep heading north. Like that she would pick up the lights of Cannington.

Navigating the open plain in daylight was difficult, at night, it was nearly impossible. She thought of finding a grassy hollow and waiting until daybreak, for prairie summer nights are short. But the thought of sharing her bed with a rattlesnake was enough to reject the idea. As if to reinforce her sense of isolation and vulnerability a lone coyote howled close by, its plaintive cry answered by its mate off in the distance.

Without her becoming aware of it, darkness closed in around her. The only assurance she had that she was traveling northward was the narrow strip of light still illuminating the western sky to her left. Soon, even that disappeared and the darkness was complete. The moon was down. A diffused haze, arguably from that cloud bank she had seen earlier, covered the sky and annulled any hope she had of being able to navigate by the stars. She wished she had a dog with her. Dogs can find their way home in darkness or a raging blizzard, a sixth sense that horses, despite their intelligence lacked.

She thought about the people at Cannington and realized there was no chance of immediate help from that quarter. Her absence would have been noted at the ball but her aunt and uncle would assume she had been tired on returning from her ride and chosen to remain home. The ball would extend into the early hours. Only at breakfast would the family become aware that her room was empty, her bed unslept in.

To conserve energy she held Morgana to a steady walk, a wise decision as the ground contained gopher holes, a constant hazard in the dark. By now she had lost all notion of direction and could only hope she was moving north. No wind blew to help her find her way.

Periodically, she strained her eyes to scan the horizon marked by the faintest gradation of tone from the dark sky above. Failure to see any light from the settlement etched away her self-confidence.

She estimated that more than an hour had elapsed since nightfall. Now, a gentle breeze had picked up and carried with it the scent of wildflowers. Could that indicate she was nearing Moose Mountain? How could she tell when all about her was inky-dark?

When her morale was about to reach its lowest ebb, her pulse quickened. In the distance, a few degrees to the west, she imagined she saw a fleeting pinprick of light. She rubbed her eyes, wondering if her brain was becoming addled. She stared again, straining to focus on the place where she had seen the light. When she saw nothing more, she concluded it must have been the twinkle of a faint star low on the horizon. Yet, a few seconds later it reappeared, not at all bright, just a speck, but very definitely a light, not a star. A tug on the reins and she altered course toward it.

She doubted it came from the settlement, because it was one solitary light, with no other lights beside it. It may be an isolated homesteader's dwelling like the ones she had seen in the district around Cannington. Humble or not, it offered safety, it spelled an end to her ordeal.

Chapter 15

To say that Sybil Halliday's entrance to the Cannington Summer Ball created a stir would be an understatement. Until now, her presence in the settlement had gone partly unnoticed, mainly on account of the large influx of other visitors. On one occasion, she had taken afternoon tea with a group of English ladies and, on another, Maud Addersley invited her to accompany her to a meeting of the vestry women's guild. In the company of Niven DeQuincy she had dined twice at the Addersleys. This evening, however, was the first time she had attended a formal gathering, the kind that Cannington was noted for, and it vexed her that she was obliged to attend it without a male escort.

Floral garlands, colored streamers and paper lanterns decorated the assembly hall. Light from a hundred lamps gleamed on bare shoulders, reflected off the women's hair and bejeweled necks. An observer would be dazzled by the sea of starched shirtfronts and women's satin gowns.

Sybil's arrival coincided with a lull between dances, the time when people drifted into groups and engaged in small talk and the consumption of fruit punch fortified by some unnamed spirit or other.

Confronted by the scene, an outsider, particularly a woman on her own, would have been intimidated. Sybil, who surveyed the room from beneath the wide arch leading into the main hall, suffered no such inhibitions. She caught sight of the familiar face of Alfred Addersley at the end of the room and, raising her skirt just high enough to show off an alluring pair of heeled button boots, advanced with a purposeful step across the dance floor.

A mere three paces was all it took to silence the chatter. Sybil was conscious of being the cynosure of every eye in the hall. She was well aware of the contrast between her attire and that of the other women. White or peach were the dominant hues. A small number of older women wore black bombazine. Sybil's bustled gown, the one made for her by a French couturier in New Orleans, was of sumptuous, viridian silk. The startling compliment of green dress and the up-swept auburn hair captured the attention of the men, young and old, and clearly earned her the enmity of every woman present.

Ever the gentleman, Alfred Addersley stepped forward to meet her. He took her proffered hand and bowed.

"Mrs. Halliday, what a delightful surprise to see you here, and alone! When I spoke to Mr. DeQuincy, he informed me that, regrettably, he would be unable to attend our ball. Something to do with last minute business, which I found surprising, since everyone he could do business with is here at the ball."

Unfazed by the implied rebuke for breach of etiquette, Sybil smiled. "Mr. DeQuincy conducts himself in ways known only to him. If the truth were known, I think he is resting before his early departure tomorrow."

"Ah, yes, of course. He's accompanying Captain Pierce's party to Moosomin station, from whence he will take the train back to Regina. But are you not leaving, too?"

"I am so impressed by your charming settlement that I've decided to delay my departure for a few days."

"You do us a great compliment, madam. Yet, now that the races and the agricultural fair are over, I fear Cannington will be somewhat a dull place for you. The only exciting events will be cricket matches and tennis parties, perhaps not to your American tastes."

Sybil agitated her fan, not out of any affectation but because the air in the assembly rooms was heavy and hot. "Please don't worry on my account, Mr. Addersley. I will be content to enjoy the civilized atmosphere you and your fellow countrymen have created in the midst of a wilderness."

"That's good of you to say so. We have striven hard to replicate here on the Canadian Prairie the genteel life many of us enjoyed in the Old Country."

Sybil made a sweeping gesture with her fan to encompass the elegantly dressed men and women. "I'd say you've succeed. Never in my wildest dreams did I expect to find such refinement on the frontier."

"My wife and I would be honored if, for the rest of your stay, you would accept to be a guest in our house."

"Mr. Addersley, that is kind of you, sir!"

"Mrs. Addersley will make the necessary arrangements to have your effects brought over from the inn."

Just then, the small orchestra struck up a waltz. Addersley excused himself and went over to where his wife was standing. Sybil spied several men who appeared to be summoning the courage to ask her to dance with them. She was not ready to be rough-handled by perspiring young bucks, even if they were well-dressed. She walked over to where Maud Addersley was sitting on her own.

"Miss Addersley, why aren't you dancing with one of those handsome young gentlemen?"

The girl looked up with annoyance written on her pretty face. "I am actually in the company of Mr. Featherstonehaugh."

Sybil made a pretend show of looking about her. "And where, pray, is your ecclesiastical escort?"

Maud pointed a gloved finger to the far end of the room. "Quarter of an hour ago he went to fetch two glasses of punch. I fear he has been waylaid by someone, maybe one of his parishioners wishing to discuss church matters."

"You look lonely here on your own. Would you like me to sit with you until your beau returns?"

Maud's cheeks flushed. "Mrs. Halliday, Mr. Featherstonehaugh is not my *beau*." She patted the chair beside her. "But please sit down. I would love to talk to you."

Under Maud's watchful eye, Sybil sat and arranged her skirts. She noticed the young woman examining her. "Do you like the dress?"

In a flustered voice, Maud replied, "Please forgive me, Mrs. Halliday, I didn't mean to be rude."

Sybil laid a hand on the girl's thigh. "That's quite all right, my sweet. A woman is allowed to look at another woman. It's not the same as a man staring at a woman, is it?"

"I'm fascinated by your bustle. I read that they are back in style. We haven't adopted them here. Because of the lack of servants, we're obliged to perform duties normally done by domestics. Plain skirts are far more convenient."

"I understand. You're quite correct. The bustle is making a comeback in fashion, but they are much more comfortable to wear than the earlier ones. Mine is the very latest. It's called the *Phantom* and it's made up of steel wires that pivot when the wearer sits down. You may have remarked how effortlessly I seated myself. The wires spring back into place when I stand up." In order to demonstrate, Sybil got to her feet then quickly resumed sitting.

"That is wonderful. I do so admire you, Mrs. Halliday."

"I fear that the fashion for bustles is going to end up looking ridiculous. I read that in three years' time to mark the Golden Jubilee of your gracious monarch Victoria they are going to bring out a bustle that incorporates a music box that will play *God Save the Queen* when the wearer sits down,"

Maud burst out laughing. "That is carrying things to the extreme."

Sybil brought her face closer to the young woman's. "Excuse my boldness but I notice a change in you. I haven't been in the settlement long, but when I first arrived, I thought you dressed in an overly sober style for one so young. How old are you?"

"Twenty-six."

"I thought so, quite young. You appear to be undergoing a transformation right before my very eyes. I am reminded of a beautiful butterfly emerging from its chrysalis."

Maud gave a nervous laugh. "Please stop, Mrs. Halliday, you're making me blush."

Sybil ran the backs of her fingers up the creamy smoothness of Maud's bare arm. "Tell me, my dear, had it anything to do with the influence of the attractive Miss Carina Chesterman?"

148 - Michael Montcombroux

Maud lowered her eyes and for a moment appeared intent on adjusting her lace gloves. She faced Sybil. "As a matter of fact, Miss Chesterman did make a few suggestions about my dress and appearance. She has a keen eye for detail."

"And where is Miss Chesterman this evening? I don't see her anywhere."

"She went out riding this afternoon and hoped to be back in time for the start of the ball. I can only assume she misjudged the hour and by the time she did make it back it was too late."

"A pity. The two of you make a lovely pair."

"Mrs. Halliday, may I ask you a rather personal question?"

"Fire away, my dear. I warn you, if it's too personal, you may not get an answer."

"You came to Cannington with Mr. DeQuincy, but what about Mr. Halliday? Are you a widow?"

Sybil's laugh revealed her even white teeth. "Mr. Niven DeQuincy and I are just good friends. We go back a long way. As for Mr. Halliday, he's dead, keeled over at his desk more than five years ago."

Maud brought her hand to her mouth. "I'm so terribly sorry, Mrs. Halliday. I had no intention of stirring painful memories for you."

Sybil took Maud's hand and dragged it over to her lap, effectively making the girl her prisoner. "Relax, my dear girl. Frankly, these days, I much prefer the company of my own sex. Men can be so infuriating. Tell me, since Miss Chesterman has helped you become more worldly, would you allow me to take you a few steps farther down the path of emancipation?"

"What do you mean, Mrs. Halliday?"

"You've heard the expression Death is the Great Leveller. Well, death is also a great liberator, too. I'm not the first woman to discover that losing a husband can sometimes be an experience akin to being let out of prison."

"Good gracious! I never thought of it like that."

"Married women have virtually no freedom. But as a widow, I am able to go where I like, dress as I wish and make friends with whomever I choose. No man tells me what I must or must not do."

Maud made no effort to reclaim her hand. She sat, mesmerized by the words and the closeness of the attractive older woman. "All the same, you must miss your late husband terribly. I know I would in a similar situation."

"You wouldn't if your husband came home drunk and beat you. That is, except when he didn't come home at all because he was sharing the bed of some cheap whore he'd picked up in the vaudeville theater bar."

Maud wrenched her hand free. "Really? Is that what Mr.–?"

"That and a whole lot more." Sybil sensed a presence behind her.

"Good evening, Mrs. Halliday. I thank you for keeping Miss Maud company whilst I was otherwise engaged."

Sybil looked round at Mr. Featherstonehaugh. "Sir, you are extremely remiss for leaving Miss Addersley on her own for so long. The poor child had to fight off the attentions of half a dozen gentlemen. That is why I offered my protection."

Seemingly, caught off guard by Sybil's forthright remark, the churchman stammered, "I-I had intended to be absent just long enough to fetch two glasses of punch."

Sybil gave him a critical look. "And where, sir, are these two glasses of punch?"

Confusion distorted the man's features. "I was so distracted I must have completely forgotten what I went for."

Maud stood up. "Mr. Featherstonehaugh, why don't you sit down and I shall get us some refreshment?"

The clergyman took the seat vacated by Maud. His pained expression suggested he'd sooner be anywhere except left alone with Sybil. The man's thin lips quavered when he looked at her. He was clearly troubled by Sybil's forthright manner and by the proximity of such unabashed sensuality.

After regaining a modicum of composure, he said, "You must be coming to the end of your visit to Cannington, Mrs. Halliday."

"And why do you say that, Mr. Featherstonehaugh?"

"Yesterday, I happened to meet your…er, gentleman companion, Mr. DeQuincy, in the street. He mentioned that he was about to return to Regina."

"So he is. Myself, I have plans to remain here a while longer."

The man's smile faded. "Oh, really?"

"As a house guest of the Addersleys."

Featherstonehaugh ran a boney finger along the side of his nose. "Indeed, is that so?"

Maud reappeared carrying a small silver tray with three glasses of punch. "I brought a glass for you too, Mrs. Halliday."

"That's so kind of you. I'll take mine and leave you two lovebirds on your own. We mustn't forget the saying, two's company, three's a crowd." She patted the back of Maud's hand. "We'll have a further opportunity to talk, you and I." Sybil took a glass from the tray and, with a nod to Mr. Featherstonehaugh, walked away.

She had not gone more than a few steps when she came face to face with a stocky man with a broad smile on his face.

"Mrs. Halliday, we have been introduced before but there were so many gentlemen monopolizing your attention I never had the pleasure of conversing with you."

Before replying, Sybil took a sip of punch and studied the man over the rim of her glass. He was fresh-faced like the brash young men of Captain Pierce's agricultural college, but older, in his early forties, she guessed. "I have been introduced to so many people in my short stay here, sir, that I'm afraid I can't remember your name."

"That's quite understandable, madam. My name is Rodney Beresford. Along with my brother Algernon I own the large house on the outskirts of town. It's called Inglesbury but people refer to it as simply the Beresford place. "

"Ah, yes, you're the horse people."

"We do indeed breed horses. The North-West Mounted rely on us exclusively for their remounts."

"I have no eye for horseflesh, but I recall seeing some of your horses at the races. Fine-looking animals."

"May I be so bold as to offer you an invitation to visit Inglesbury? We are by default a gentleman's establishment but we thoroughly enjoy having lady visitors. Regrettably, visits by members of the fair sex, particularly those of your beauty and elegance, are few and far between. If you would grace us with your presence one afternoon, we would be flattered."

"That is kind of you, Mr. Beresford. I would be delighted to accept your invitation. One snag: my traveling companion, Mr. Niven DeQuincy – whom I trust you've met – is leaving in the morning. He has to return to take care of his business in Regina. I believe it might shock the residents of the settlement if I attended your bachelors' lair unaccompanied, even though I am, perfectly capable of taking care of myself."

Beresford's face creased in a broad smile. "Of course, we must not offend society's sensibilities." He looked about the room. "What about that young fellow in your party? What's his name again?"

"Mr. Julian Chesterman? He's probably returning with Mr. DeQuincy. Besides, I couldn't ask him to accompany me. With the difference in our ages, it would have every appearance of a mother and son visit." Sybil motioned toward Maud, presently preoccupied in listening to Mr. Featherstonehaugh. "I'm sure Miss Maud Addersley would agree to come with me. If not, perhaps Miss Carina Chesterman would fill the role."

"Why not all three of you?"

"I shall ask the girls."

"Then, it's settled. Sometime in the next few days send me word when it would be convenient for you to visit and I'll roll out the red carpet for you. My older brother Algernon, of course, is leaving with the captain in the morning for Ottawa. But I will be on hand to welcome you. I have much to show you. Our stable buildings rival any in the East or in England, for that matter. And the house itself is unlike anything you'll find this side of the province of Ontario."

Sybil laughed. "The red carpet will not be necessary."

"I'll make a point in telling the bachelors they must be on their best behavior – no smoking or racy language while you ladies are present."

"I hope I won't intimidate them."

Rodney grinned. "It'd do them good to be intimidated. Sometimes, they can get out of hand. Mind you, a woman of your character would have no trouble keeping them in line."

"How? With a horsewhip?"

"That would certainly work. Though, a whip would be wasted on them." He came closer and adopted a confidential voice. "Yes, indeed, that would be an absolute waste. But madam could use one on me any time she chose." He smiled a knowing smile.

Sybil gave him a long, searching look. "Is that part of the invitation? If it is I couldn't possibly bring along those two innocent young ladies for fear of corrupting them."

"We could always arrange for a second invitation, for you, alone. How about that?"

"That's something to consider. I understand Englishmen have a penchant for the kind of activity you mention. Is it because you are whipped as boys at school?"

Rodney idly scratched his ear. "Dunno, it may have something to do with it. Naturally, I'd make it worth your while, dear lady."

Sybil tapped his wrist with her folded fan. "You're a very wicked man, Mr. Beresford. It's something to consider, but we have to become better acquainted. I absolutely refuse to whip a total stranger."

Rodney gave a bow. "Perfectly understandable. If madam's dance card is not full, could I crave the honor of the next waltz?"

"I wasn't aware we ladies were to come with dance cards. Nonetheless, I'd love to dance with such a handsome gentleman."

Chapter 16

I feel the need to make a record of the horrific events of last evening, not because they might fade from my memory, for that is never going to happen, but because they might become distorted by all the frenzy that is currently taking place.

When I saw that pinpoint of light on the darkened prairie I thought my ordeal was about to end. I didn't know then that a far worse ordeal was about to begin.

There was no way of gauging how far away the light was. The Prairies, like the ocean, have a way of playing tricks on the eye. A light could be as near as hundred yards or as distant as ten miles.

I urged Morgana forward as fast as humanely possible. The poor animal, I knew, was tired and thirsty. The heat of the day had taken its toll. Even though the air cooled slightly after sunset, it was still stifling. Much to my consternation, instead of becoming brighter as we closed the distance between us and it, the light appeared to grow fainter. I worried that perhaps it came from a lantern on a moving carriage, which was speeding away faster than I could keep up. My only comfort was that, if it were so, the carriage would be on a well-marked trail and that even if the light disappeared altogether, I would soon stumble on the trail and it would lead me back home. The thought then struck me as foolish. A carriage has bright lights in the front not at the back.

The light had to come from some other source. But why
was it fading?

I lost track of how long I rode toward that light.
It seemed like forever. I became aware that the night
was no longer pitch black. I looked behind me and saw
that the moon had risen, just a half moon but giving
enough light to see where I was going, which was a relief
as my greatest fear until then was that Morgana would
step in a hole and stumble.

The light was still visible but faint. It was then
something strange happened. One minute the light
seemed as far away as ever, the next it was right in
front of me and the mystery was solved. A short
distance away was a campfire. The light had diminished
because the fire had burned itself to glowing embers.

I then realized I had veered toward the west and
stumbled upon Mr. Fenn's camp. I knew it was his. On
the other side of the fire I could make out the pale
rectangles of his two tents. Beyond it stood his
unmistakable covered wagon.

Without knowing why, the scene appeared
unnatural. Something was wrong. I saw no sign of Mr.
Fenn but reasoned at that hour he would be abed.
Despite that, I was filled with growing unease. Morgana
came to a halt. She shook her bridle as though sensing
something amiss. Her ears stood erect and she shied
away when I urged her on.

I dismounted and led the horse. When I came close
to the fire I saw on the ground between me and the
dying embers of the fire a shape that proved to be a
saddle with a folded blanket on it. Next to it was a
cooking pot and a tin cup.

An audible gasp escaped my lips when I saw,
lying between the saddle and the campfire, the form of a

man. He lay on his side with his face pressed to the earth.

I dropped the reins and ran forward. In a shaking voice, I called out, "Mr. Fenn!" The figure didn't move. He was in a grotesquely twisted position, with his legs bent under him at an awkward angle. One arm lay outstretched toward the remains of the fire.

Instinctively, I bent down and touched the man's upper arm. That was all it took for him to roll over onto his back. I shrank away. It was Mr. Fenn, all right. He was dead. Where his face ought to have been was a mass of bloody flesh like the hollowed inside of a melon.

All this took just a matter of seconds, far less time than it does to describe it. I stifled the urge to scream, for I knew the poor man had been murdered, and whoever had committed the crime might well be lurking close by in the darkness. I could have been in mortal danger.

Fortunately, Morgana had not budged from where I dismounted. Trembling with combined shock and fear I climbed back up into the saddle. The mare wheeled and galloped from the nightmarish scene. After some fifty yards I reined in to a brisk pace to conserve energy. At any moment I expected a shot or the sound of pursuing hoof beats behind me but nothing came.

I thought I knew the trail from Mr. Fenn's camp back to the settlement, but in the dark and given my distressed state I must wavered from it. I never did find the granite boulder landmark. At one point I came too close to an alkaline marsh. Morgana suddenly sank to her knees and I slipped out of the saddle and landed face down in the water. Luckily, I kept hold of the reins. With difficulty, I was able to get to my feet and lead the horse back to firm ground, but not before I was caked in foul-smelling slime. In the process I lost my hat. My wet hair stuck to my muddy face, my clothes to my body.

By a pure miracle I picked up the trail again. In spite of the warm night I shivered in my sodden clothes. In my mind I kept replaying those moments by the campfire. The image of the body, the destroyed face of the man I once knew. I still feared that the murderer might be pursuing me in the darkness.

My spirits rose when in the distance I saw what proved to be the lights of Cannington. I wondered if anyone knew I had failed to return. Perhaps a search party was out that moment looking for me? Then I remembered the ball.

My progress toward the the settlement and safety was painfully slow. When at last I reached the main street, it was deserted. A blaze of light shone from the assembly hall windows. The strains of music came from the open doors.

I halted in front of the hall and half-fell to the ground. The poor animal stood there, head hanging, too tired to move another step. To tell the truth, I didn't know what I was doing. In my dishevelled condition I ought to have gone straight home not blundered into the midst of an elegant ball. But the prospect of entering a dark, empty house terrified me. What if I was being followed?

I staggered into the hall and advanced as far as the arch opening onto the dance floor. A waltz was in progress. I have this picture in my mind of a room full of swirling dresses and the absurd notion that in my delirious state I was in some kind of warped fairy tale and had stumbled into an enchanted ballroom.

For several long moments nothing happened. The dancers swept by me in time to the music. No one noticed the muddy apparition hovering on the edge of the circle of light. I recognized Maud in the arms of Mr. Featherstonehaugh. She caught sight of me and came to an abrupt halt. A look of horror filled her face. She then lifted her hands to her face and screamed.

Within seconds I was surrounded by a crowd of people.

"What on earth has happened?" a man asked.

"Mr. Fenn..." I blurted out. "Mr. Fenn has been murdered."

What happened next is too confusing for me to remember accurately. I heard someone shout an order to fetch the police. My uncle elbowed through the crowd and put his arms around me. Someone else pressed a glass into my hand. I drank but immediately spat the liquid out, for the drink contained spirit and what I needed was plain water. Strong hands picked me up and carried me out of the hall and down the street to the house. I remember pleading with those around me to take care of Morgana. It was no exaggeration that I owed my life to that horse.

Maud and my aunt helped me change out of my wet clothes and I washed off the worst of the dirt. Sergeant Granger arrived and asked to speak to me. Despite my bone-numbing fatigue, I wanted to tell my story.

He listened in silence while I related how I had miscalculated the hour and was returning in the dark and came upon the grisly scene at Mr. Fenn's camp. I saw no reason to mention that I had become hopelessly lost. No matter what the circumstances, a girl needs to preserve some sense of pride. To confess my stupidity might have prompted my uncle to curb my freedom. Sergeant Granger pressed me for details. Had I heard a shot? No. Had I seen anyone? No. Did I touch anything at the scene, other than turn the body over? No.

Sergeant Granger thanked me and said I needed a good night's rest.

I went to bed and, out of sheer exhaustion, fell into a fitful sleep punctuated by nightmares of being stalked by a shadowy figure. Through it all I kept seeing Mr. Fenn's mutilated face.

I was grateful that Maud sat by my bed and held my hand when I awoke trembling and perspiring with terror.

Chapter 17

Carina's first act after getting dressed next morning was to go outside to see how Morgana had fared. Norman Tucker had put the horse in the stable, given her plenty of water, a generous allowance of oats and a thorough grooming. The mare looked none the worse for the previous evening's ordeal. Carina pressed her face against the animal's sleek neck and whispered how grateful she was. The mare responded with a gentle whinny.

On returning to the house, Carina found Sergeant Granger in the living room in conversation with her uncle. He cut an impressive figure clad in what Carina by now recognized as his official undress uniform, consisting of scarlet jacket, with a blue collar and gold braid edging and hussar-style crow's foot near the cuffs. He wore dark-blue pants and black riding boots.

Dillon turned as she entered. "Good morning, Miss Chesterman. I know you must be still in shock but it would help us greatly if you would answer a few questions."

"You have the use of my study," her uncle said. "I'll get Ellie to bring you some coffee."

Carina sat on a straight-backed chair at the corner of her uncle's mahogany ormolu desk. She expected Dillon to occupy the high-backed leather chair behind the desk. Instead, he pulled up a similar chair to hers and sat facing her.

"Why would someone want to kill such a harmless man like Ogden Fenn?"

Dillon paused, his lips pressed together. "That is what I'm hoping to find out. Despite people calling this Canada's wild frontier, the principal crimes we have to deal with are liquor violations not murders."

A knock on the door and a sad-faced Ellie entered with a tray. "Shall I put the coffee on the desk, miss?"

"Yes, please. I'll move my uncle's papers."

The girl gave Carina a searching, melancholy look before leaving the room. Carina poured the coffee and handed a cup to Dillon, which he balanced on his knee.

He cleared his throat. "I know this will be hard for you but could you go over again what occurred last evening leading up to and immediately following the discovery of the body? You gave me a very good account last night. I am hoping that now you've had some rest the picture may be clearer."

"I doubt if there's more to add. The events are so burned into my memory."

When she finished relating her story once more, Dillon asked, "Did you at any time hear or sense the presence of anyone in or near the camp?"

"There was no sound at all, other than the mules snuffling the grass. Of course, in my imagination I feared the killer was still there, lurking in the shadows. That's why I rode away as fast as I could."

"You said you turned the body over."

"At first I thought he must be ill, perhaps had fallen and hurt himself. Murder was the last thing on my mind."

"Do you remember how the body felt?"

"You mean, was it still warm?"

"Yes, and whether it was stiff."

"It didn't take much effort to turn him over. Mr. Fenn was not a very big man. I hardly did more than lay my hand on him. The way the body was positioned, it just flopped over when I touched it. That's when I saw the awful hole where his face had been. I was seized with panic at that point and I don't remember whether the body was warm or not. It couldn't have been stiff or it probably wouldn't have rolled over the way it did."

"You knew immediately it was Mr. Fenn."

"I'd visited his camp before. I knew it was his from the tents and the wagon. Even without seeing his face I recognized him from the rather worn clothes he always wore. Mr. Fenn was not one to worry about his appearance."

Dillon paused to drink from his cup, and then looked at her. "Are you all right?"

His suddenly personal tone and the solicitous nature of the question surprised her.

"I think I am. However, when I close my eyes, I have this horrible feeling that the person who killed Mr. Fenn is coming after me."

Dillon nodded. "That's understandable. Yet, you've nothing to fear. I doubt if the killer hung around after committing the act. You're perfectly safe."

"I keep telling myself that."

"You must have stumbled on Mr. Fenn's body very soon after his death. Rigor mortis obviously hadn't set in."

"Just how long does it take for a body to become stiff with rigor mortis?"

"It can vary. Three to four hours is about normal. Can you say how long it took for you to reach the campsite from first seeing the light from the fire?"

Carina brushed back her hair. "I must confess I was somewhat disorientated by the time I caught sight of that light."

"Disorientated?"

"I hate to admit this but I'd foolishly strayed onto the open prairie and lost my bearings, not that there are many bearings to lose. As you know, landmarks are few and far between."

"True."

"My horse was exhausted and I guess we were both suffering from thirst. Dehydration does strange things to the mind."

"So, you'd gotten lost?"

Carina gave a tight smile. "I was well and truly lost. Seeing that faint light in the distance was a godsend, or so I thought then."

"Are you able to give me a rough estimate how long it took to reach it?"

"Perhaps one hour. It seemed like a lifetime."

Carina looked away for a moment, distracted. She tried to read the titles of her uncle's books in the case behind the desk.

"From what you say about rigor mortis, Mr. Fenn could have been killed, then, up to three hours prior to my arrival on the scene?"

"Yes, but let's not forget one vital detail. You said the campfire was just about burned through by the time you came upon it. Was it a big fire?"

"No, not really. Mr. Fenn had to carry his own firewood. So he never built an extravagant fire. He must have simply used it to prepare his dinner. There was a cooking pot beside it. He didn't need a fire for warmth. You know how stifling hot it was last evening."

"Even an average-sized fire would be visible for several miles over flat prairie. But it wouldn't burn for very long. It must have been at its brightest when you first spotted it. Within an hour it was out. During that space of time Ogden Fenn was shot. Before reaching the camp you heard nothing that could have been a gunshot? Sounds travel a long way at night, especially when there isn't much wind."

"What wind there was came from behind me, from the south." She shook her head. "I'm certain I heard nothing. Mind you, my poor horse was coughing and making wheezing sounds, and there was the usual jingle of harness and squeak of leather, not to mention to thud of hooves on dry ground. But I doubt that'd have been enough to mask the sharp crack of a firearm. He was shot, wasn't he?"

"From behind, with a high-powered rifle. The bullet entered the back of his head." Dillon placed a finger at the top of his own neck to demonstrate. "When it exited at the front it tore open that gaping wound you witnessed. Sorry to dwell on the unpleasant details."

Carina lowered her eyes. "Then, the murderer could well have still been close by when I found the body. That frightens me still."

"You didn't actually witness the murder. So the killer had no motive to be concerned about you and still hasn't. Our preliminary investigation rules out robbery as a motive. Nothing of Mr. Fenn's possessions was touched. That is, as far as we can tell.

It's unlikely the perpetrator was still at the campsite when you came across it. Logic suggests he would have wanted to put as much distance as possible between himself and the crime scene."

"I can understand that the motive was probably not robbery. No one could imagine that Mr. Fenn possessed anything of great value, beyond a few scientific instruments. I doubt he carried much money with him."

After a few moments of silence, Dillon asked, "Ogden Fenn was a fairly frequent visitor to Cannington. Did he have any enemies that you are aware of?"

"As you know I haven't been in the settlement very long. There are others here who have known Mr. Fenn much longer."

"True, but you did have some lengthy conversations with the gentleman and you are one of the few to have been invited to visit his camp. I understand that wasn't an honor he extended to very many people."

"I went there with Miss Maud Addersley."

"I have spoken to Miss Addersley." A fleeting smile crossed Dillon's lips. "The young lady was not able to tell me much about our scientist friend."

"If I were to mention a name, I suppose that would immediately bring suspicion down on that person's head. Is that not so?" She was thinking about DeQuincy. Yet, no matter how much she detested the man she couldn't imagine him creeping up in the dark on Ogden Fenn and shooting him in the head.

"Not necessarily. I want to find out what drives a man to murder an innocent person in cold blood. One can be a police officer without worrying too much about who did what to whom and why. But some of us, and I'm one of them, want to know what makes a person tick. One has to get beyond the obvious. So, anything you can tell me, no matter how trivial it seems, may help me get to the bottom of this gruesome crime."

"The only time I ever heard Mr. Fenn raise his voice was in a heated discussion with Mr. DeQuincy. They were both guests at a dinner my uncle gave not long ago. Do you remember it?"

"Yes, I remember the occasion."

"There were harsh words spoken at the dinner table. Later, when Mr. Fenn was leaving the house, he was accosted by Mr. DeQuincy. Another argument took place outside the front door. My bedroom is right above and I couldn't help but overhear the exchange."

"Did Mr. DeQuincy utter any threats against Mr. Fenn?"

"I don't recall him uttering physical threats. Mr. DeQuincy was certainly abusive toward him."

"How well do you know this Mr. DeQuincy gentleman?"

"Not that well. I first met him, briefly, in Regina. As you know, my father is a banker and apparently he and Mr. DeQuincy have business dealings in common, the exact nature of which I have no knowledge. My father tells me nothing about his professional affairs."

"Did Mr. Fenn explain to you the nature of the scientific work he was engaged in?"

"Yes, he did. I'm interested in science and I believe that was why he invited me to visit his camp. Miss Addersley accompanied me. He showed us the plant specimens and soil samples he'd collected. He had copious field notes on everything, from the numbers and species of the birds and animals he'd observed to detailed records of temperatures and precipitation."

"Did Mr. Fenn explain what he intended to do with this wealth of information?"

"I think you know the answer to that question. At that dinner he told us he planned to go to Regina and write a comprehensive report on his findings. When he left the settlement, I was under the impression that he had already left for the capital."

"Mr. Fenn left Cannington following his altercation with Mr. DeQuincy. Isn't that correct?"

"He didn't leave immediately. It was two days after the encounter with Mr. DeQuincy. I was angry at Mr. DeQuincy because his stupid argument ruined Mr. Fenn's well-deserved break from his work. He was looking forward to the races and the fair, which were about to get underway."

"Did you express that sentiment to Mr. DeQuincy?"

Carina shook her head. "Why would I? Mr. DeQuincy and I are not on the best of terms."

"May I ask why?"

"Encouraged by my father, the gentleman has it in his head that I should be his bride."

Dillon raised an eyebrow, "That doesn't sit well with you, I gather."

"Marriage is not a priority for me, and certainly not with a much older man like Mr. DeQuincy. However, this is off topic. My connection with him has no bearing on this terrible crime."

"Perhaps not. Did Mr. Fenn give you more information about why he wanted to write this report of his?"

"Mr. Fenn was a remarkable man who lived close to nature. I have the impression that something of the earth's fierce simplicity had seeped into his bones and into his soul. He was passionate about the Prairies and was convinced the government's actions were going to ruin the land. He wanted to point out the error of their ways in opening up the land for farming. He said he could prove it was unsuitable and that the government had been misled by earlier studies. The rail line had already been laid but he believed it was not too late to prevent wholesale settlement in a region too arid to support intensive agriculture. He made no secret of his views. You heard him express those same opinions over dinner that evening."

A short silence followed.

Dillon grinned. "You sound pretty passionate yourself, Miss Chesterman. Mr. DeQuincy, of course, did not appear convinced by the man's theories."

"Do you think he was motivated to murder Mr. Fenn over them?"

"Having an argument with someone is not in itself sufficient evidence to lead to an accusation of murder. Whoever killed Mr. Fenn had to have a strong motive. Mr. DeQuincy, undeniably, had an interest in not having this report see the light of day, but maybe he was not alone."

"Have you spoken to Mr. DeQuincy?"

"No, he's left the settlement. Before dawn this morning, he joined Captain Pierce and his delegation on their way to the train station at Moosomin. Your father went with them."

"And my brother?"

"Mr. Julian Chesterman was not among the party."

Carina thought it odd, particularly given the trauma she had experienced, that her father had made no attempt to see her before he left, no matter the early hour. She excused him because his health wasn't good and his thoughts must have been on seeing a doctor. That Julian had chosen to remain in the settlement puzzled her, particularly since he was in the employ of Mr. DeQuincy.

"One final question. It would assist my inquiry if, this afternoon, you would agree to come down to Mr. Fenn's campsite and show us on the ground how the events unfolded. Would you be willing?"

Carina's eyes widened. "I'm not sure I want to revisit that terrible place."

Dillon rose and surprised her by placing placed a reassuring hand on her shoulder. "There's nothing to be frightened of, Miss Chesterman. I've had the deceased removed. At this moment the body is on its way to Broadview on the Canadian Pacific line. There's a police doctor there who will perform an examination of the body."

Carina grimaced. "I don't envy him his task. Given these temperatures, a corpse will quickly be in a sorry state."

"The wagon stopped in Cannington on its way north. The remains have been packed in ice from the settlement's ice house. That will help. It would be of great assistance if you would agree to come to the campsite."

"My horse is too fatigued. I wouldn't want to further stress the poor animal."

"That's no problem. I'll put a police horse at your disposal. Unless you'd prefer to make the trip by wagon."

"I'd sooner ride." She gave a weak smile. "I imagine that with a Mounted Police escort I will not be in any danger."

Dillon removed his hand. "That's settled. I'll call on you at one o' clock."

Chapter 18

Carina was watching from the drawing room window when, with unnerving punctuality, Sergeant Granger, accompanied by four officers dismounted in front of the house at one o'clock that same afternoon. An officer she recognized as Trooper Durkin held the reins of the saddle horse intended for her.

Ellie answered the door and ushered Dillon into the room where Carina was waiting, dressed in a fresh riding outfit.

Dillon held his hat to his chest and gave her a curt bow. Ellie hovered by the open door, her eyes fixed on the handsome young police sergeant.

"I'm glad to see you didn't have a change of heart, Miss Chesterman."

"It's important to bring whoever committed this awful crime to justice. I'm willing to do anything that might help."

"Good. I have a horse for you. Shall we go?"

On the way out, Carina plucked her straw hat from the hallstand.

Trooper Durkin handed her the reins of the black gelding.

Carina took a moment to admire the horse.

"He came from the Beresford stables right here in Cannington, ma'am." Durkin held the stirrup to assist her into the saddle.

The four officers were, like Dillon, resplendent in their scarlet. She wondered whether this display was for her benefit and also to reassure the residents of Cannington. The murder of Ogden Fenn, a man to whom they had often offered hospitality, had sent shockwaves through the close-knit community.

Conscious of the admiring looks from the officers, Carina swung her leg over the horse's back. Once settled in the deep saddle, she smiled at Dillon. "Sergeant, I didn't realize the mounted police possessed such comfortable saddles."

"It wasn't always like that. In the old days, we used British Army saddles but they proved unsatisfactory. They slipped from side to side on rough terrain and the steel buckles and stirrups rusted easily. The powers-that-be finally saw the light and issued us these California saddles."

Dillon gave a hand signal and the party set off, he and Carina in the lead, Durkin and another officer bringing up the rear and two men acting as outriders. Carina swivelled in the saddle and saw Ellie at the gate, staring after them. She waved and the girl waved back.

The day was cooler than it had been for a week and they were able to maintain a brisk lope without overheating the horses. Other than Dillon asking her if she was comfortable with the pace, they rode in silence. Carina was amazed at how soon they reached the buffalo rubbing stone. Here they dismounted and allowed the horses to rest and drink.

Dillon offered Carina his water canteen. "Apart from removing the body of the victim, everything at the camp has been left untouched. When we get there, I would be grateful if you would show me from which direction you approached and what you were able to see in the dark."

Carina nodded her agreement. With a growing sense of unease, the thought of reliving the previous evening's episode filled her with dread. When they set off again, they followed the wheel marks leading south-west across the prairie. Carina became aware that her fellow riders had closed in around her, until she was riding stirrup to stirrup with Dillon and the outrider. She wondered if this was on Dillon's orders to dissuade her from having second thoughts and breaking away to gallop back home.

She was tempted to say that such precautions were unnecessary. She was as eager as they to unravel the mystery surrounding the murder. Still, she took comfort from the proximity of the law. Her mind was still troubled by the irrational fear that the murderer could be lurking nearby.

Dillon ordered a halt at a hundred yards distance from the camp. Carina jumped down and watched in mute admiration the efficiency with which the men hammered iron pins into the ground and ran a picket line between them. The horses were then unsaddled and tethered to the line. Dillon gathered his men about him and spent several minutes giving them orders. The officers then dispersed.

He walked over to Carina. "Miss Chesterman, I realize things must appear very different to you in the daylight but can you indicate how you approached the camp?"

"Yes, of course. If we walk over to the remains of the campfire, I can backtrack from there."

All that was left of the fire was a blackened patch of ashes ringed with flat stones. She shuddered when her eyes fell on the spot where Ogden Fenn's body had been. Ants swarmed over a dark patch she realized was dried blood. The saddle with its folded blanket that Fenn had been using as a backrest sat where she had first seen it.

"Why do you think Mr. Fenn had a saddle with him?" she asked. "His only animals were the mules which hauled his wagon. I never saw him with a horse and I doubt he rode the mules."

Dillon shrugged. "Who knows? Maybe he used to own a horse. Maybe he rode a horse when he wasn't doing his field work. Mules were more suited to his purpose in the field."

Satisfied with Dillon's reasoning, she drew an imaginary line with her hand. "When I approached, the saddle was directly between me and the fire. I must have arrived this way."

"From the same direction as the shooter."

"How do you determine that?"

"Fenn must have been sitting with his back against the saddle. The cooking pot is empty. He probably had just finished his supper. Folk like to sit and contemplate the flickering flames of a campfire. That's what he must have been doing when the assassin came up from behind. Because of the darkness, the shooter had only one option. He had to line up his victim's head with the fire so that it was silhouetted against the light. There was a moon but not bright enough to enable him to shoot from any other angle."

172 - Michael Montcombroux

"Yes, the light was so weak it wasn't until I was close did I see Mr. Fenn's body, which, at first, I took to be a shadow."

At that moment a shout went up from one of the officers searching the perimeter of the camp. "Sarge, over here!"

"Excuse me, it looks like they've found something. I'll be back in a moment." He strode across to the two officers, one of whom was crouching looking down at the earth.

Left on her own, Carina walked back along the killer's line of sight, counting her paces as she went. At twenty paces she stopped and looked back. She could see the saddle but not where the fire had been. Directly in line with the saddle was the entrance flap of Fenn's sleeping tent. She now used that as a guide.

At fifty paces she stopped to work the stiffness from her neck. Despite scrutinizing the ground in front of her, she had found no trace that anyone had been there. This came as no surprise. Not even the hoof marks of her own horse were visible. She tested the surface with the toe of her boot. The prairie sod, elsewhere so deep and springy, here was shrivelled to a scattering of wiry grasses imprisoned in a hard pan of brown dirt.

Dillon was still in conversation with his men. The three of them were on hands and knees. Carina gave a mental shrug. At least, they were having more success than she was. Undeterred, she continued for another fifty paces. Still nothing. If, as Dillon calculated, the shooter had approached this way, there was no sign he had been there.

She gave up hope of finding anything. But on her return to the campsite, her eye caught a metallic glint in a sparse clump of needle and thread grass just to her right. She looked down and saw a shiny brass cartridge case. The temptation to snatch it up was great but she had the presence of mind to leave the evidence undisturbed. She saw that Dillon finished talking to his men and was standing by the campfire, looking in her direction.

She waved for him to join her.

When he drew close she smiled and pointed to the ground. "Take a look."

"Now, that's interesting." He examined the cartridge case without touching it. "You must have the eyes of a hawk to spot it lying in the grass like that."

"I must have walked right over it on my way out. On the way back, the sun reflected off the brass."

Dillon brought his face closer to the casing. "It hasn't lain here long. The brass isn't weathered." He took a stubby pencil from his tunic pocket and with it picked up the cartridge case. "I do believe, Miss Chesterman, that you may well have found the empty casing from the shot that killed Mr. Fenn."

"It was sheer luck."

"Plus some clever thinking." Dillon cupped a hand to his mouth. "Trooper Durkin, bring one of the men. Oh, yes, and we'll need the surveyor's half-chain."

The two officers arrived and Dillon showed them the find. "Our keen-eyed Miss Chesterman discovered the most valuable piece of evidence so far."

Durkin smiled at Carina and nodded. He was an older man, sporting a thick walrus mustache and a dour expression on his tanned face. The trooper rubbed his bristled chin. "What d'you reckon, Sarge?"

Dillon decided it was no longer necessary to balance the item on the end of the pencil and took it between the finger and thumb of his left hand. "At first I thought it was a .45-70 – government ammunition – or a .45-75 like the police Winchester carbines, but given the length of the casing it's probably the larger .45-90. What do you think?"

Durkin took the casing. ".45-90 for sure. That narrows the field to just a few makes of rifles."

"Snider-Enfields are common but they have a .577 bore. The likely candidate is a Sharps."

Mystified by the terminology, Carina listened with interest. "I know nothing of firearms but is there a way to match this casing to the rifle that the murderer used?"

Dillon grinned. "In theory, yes. In practice, impossible."

"Why in theory?"

174 - Michael Montcombroux

"Three or four years ago, a Scottish doctor by the name of Henry Foulds, who happened to be working in a hospital in Tokyo, Japan, demonstrated that the fingers leave invisible marks on objects they touch, particularly those with smooth surfaces, such as glass or metal."

"Like on this cartridge?"

Dillon held up the spent casing. "Yes. Everyone leaves a different pattern of marks. Dr. Foulds used his knowledge to prove that a man accused of theft didn't commit the crime because his fingerprints, as they are called, were not the ones found at the scene of the robbery."

"How interesting, but proving someone didn't commit the crime is not quite the same as finding the real culprit."

"That's true. As yet this science of fingerprints hasn't advanced enough to help police officers like us solve crimes."

"Then, finding this cartridge doesn't help much?"

"Not so, ma'am." Durkin took the casing and laid it in his open palm. "Whoever was carrying it, reloaded his own ammunition. Look here." He pointed to the base of the casing. "It has a white metal primer. That's the round bit in the center with the dimple in it caused by the firing pin. The primer ignites the powder in the cartridge. Self-loaders use white metal. Factory rounds have brass primers, the same as the case color."

"What does that prove?" Carina asked.

"That the shooter probably does a lot of hunting and takes great care to improve the accuracy of his firearm."

"I'm afraid this is all too technical for me to understand."

"Keen hunters will buy a box of factory-loaded ammunition and fire off all the rounds at a target. The chamber of one rifle, although machined to the same bore, will have a slight variation to another rifle of the same make and caliber. Therefore, each chamber is unique. When the hunter fires off all those rounds, the brass cases mold themselves to the exact dimension of the chamber of his particular rifle. It's called fire forming. It improves the efficiency of the rifle by preventing the gas from escaping back between the sides of the cartridge casing and the chamber. He then reloads the ammunition himself and the result is a rifle that is extremely accurate. What is more, these enthusiasts often ream out the chambers themselves to make them slightly larger, then fire-form the ammunition. Like that the rifle is more accurate and takes a more powerful round. This casing will fit the weapon used in the murder but will probably not fit another rifle of the same make and model."

"Now that we have the casing, all we have to do is find the gun that it fits."

Dillon smiled at her. "That's easier said than done." He took the empty casing from Durkin. "One useful detail is that the murder weapon appears to have a slight fault in the firing pin." He pointed to the indent in the middle of the primer. "Normally, when the firing pin strikes the end cap, it punches a perfectly round impression. See how this particular firearm leaves an irregular, teardrop indent. The firing pin must have been damaged in the past but since the defect didn't affect the rifle's accuracy, the owner left it as is, rather than have the firing pin replaced."

Carina took a closer look at the base of the cartridge case. "Does that mean that every time the rifle is fired it leaves this characteristic mark on the casings?"

"Correct."

"That's interesting. Though, as you say, finding the gun it came from might be next to impossible."

Dillon shielded his eyes and looked toward the camp. "In the meantime, we have to try to reconstruct how the assassin went about his business. Assuming he fired from this spot, we need to measure the distance to the saddle against which Mr. Fenn was sitting."

Carina squinted into the sunshine. "It must be at least fifty yards. Do you believe the man would have been able to hit his target in the dark?"

Durkin nodded. "In the hands of a marksman, the Sharps rifle, if it was a Sharps, would be deadly accurate at this range, so long as he had his victim's head silhouetted against the light of the fire."

"We're making a thorough search of the area," Dillon said. "But it looks like the killer fired only a single shot. Our preliminary examination shows just one bullet wound on the victim, but I'll wait for the doctor's report. There is one problem that undermines our hypothesis. You said that there was just a light wind, Miss Chesterman."

"Yes, a light southerly breeze."

"The killer would have arrived on horseback. How is it that Mr. Fenn failed to hear him approach? How could the shooter have crept up to within fifty yards without alerting his victim?"

"You do know that Mr. Fenn was profoundly deaf?"

"No, I didn't. When I attended the dinner party where he was also a guest, I didn't notice he had any difficulty engaging in the conversation."

"That was because he was an expert lip-reader."

"Indeed!"

"I found that out afterwards when he came into the parlor after dinner. He said he needed to get away from the gentlemen's cigar smoke, because it irritated his lungs. We sat and talked and he asked me to turn toward the lamplight so that he could read my lips. This was confirmed later when Miss Addersley and I visited his camp. In our conversation he watched our lips and understood everything."

"Thank you for sharing that information. It suggests that whoever committed the crime knew the victim was deaf and would have used the knowledge to his advantage."

Carina and Dillon walked back to the tents while Durkin and his fellow troopers marked the spot where the cartridge casing had been found and set about measuring the precise distance to the saddle.

"May I ask what your men found?"

"This." Dillon took an envelope from his pocket and tipped the contents into his palm.

"A cigar stub."

"It's actually a cheroot."

"I wouldn't know the difference."

"Unlike cigars, cheroots have both ends cut square. This one has been smoked just recently."

"You can rule out it belonging to Mr. Fenn. As I just mentioned, he couldn't tolerate tobacco smoke."

"What is interesting is this is a type of cigar not available in the territories. Generally speaking, cheroots are more popular in the United Sates."

A chill ran down Carina's spine when she thought about the significance of Dillon's remark.

Dillon appeared to have read her mind. "I'm afraid suspicion falls heavily on your acquaintance, Mr. DeQuincy. When I finish my investigation here I'll be going to Regina to interview the gentleman."

Dillon walked over to where his officers were combing the ground. Carina thought about her brother and his work for DeQuincy.

Dillon rejoined her and led her over to the tents. "I have no reason to believe the perpetrator went inside. Nothing appears disturbed. Since you're familiar with the work Fenn was doing, could you take a look and tell me if you think anything is missing?"

He pulled aside the flap of the tent containing Fenn's scientific material and allowed her to enter. Inside, the air was stifling. Carina ran her eyes over the tables lined up against each wall, and over the boxes and cases of collected specimens.

She pointed to the stack of well-used notebooks. "In these are details of the fieldwork Mr. Fenn collected. Some of them go back several years. And over here…" She opened a manila folder and removed a thick wad of of notepaper, each page filled with Fenn's meticulous handwriting, "is the first draft of his report."

"Does it look to you that anything's been touched?"

"Everything appears the same as it was when I visited. Mr. Fenn was not the tidiest of gentlemen in his personal life but was well organized when it came to his scientific work. Every notebook entry bears the date and location of when and where the information was gathered. Each specimen is labeled. Everything is ordered. When he took something out to show us, he replaced it where it came from."

Carina looked at Dillon. "If, as you say, Mr. DeQuincy is a possible suspect because Mr. Fenn's research had the power to damage his business interests, surely he would have wanted to destroy the scientific evidence? Yet everything appears be here."

"Maybe he was in the process of doing just that when he was disturbed by the arrival of a possible witness to his crime."

Carina put her hand to her mouth. The fear she had experienced on discovering Fenn's body came flooding back. "Then he might have been standing in the tent doorway watching me!"

"He could well have been."

"Surely, he'd have done something."

"He may have thought it unnecessary. By all accounts, you didn't hang around. You climbed on your horse and rode off, which was the only sane thing to have done. It's not as if you saw the perpetrator and would be able to identify him."

"I shudder to think what might have happened if I had stumbled on the camp earlier."

"Don't dwell on what might have happened. It isn't good for your peace of mind. My guess is the killer didn't bother with the tents or any of Fenn's possessions." Dillon picked up a notebook from the pile. "To Mr. Fenn this research meant a lot, but to anyone else it's just a jumble of figures, scientific names and pages of writing. That the killer ignored these papers does weaken the case against Mr. DeQuincy but he's still our prime suspect."

Carina pulled back the tent flap. "I find it unbearably hot in here. Unless you have further questions, I need fresh air."

Dillon followed her out, "I've seen all I need to for the moment. And I'm grateful for your help. While my men continue the search of the area I'll take you back to the settlement."

"Thank you. By the way, what happened to Mr. Fenn's mules? They were here last night. I heard them."

"We took them to Cannington. Rodney Beresford generously offered to care for them until this business is cleared up."

"I feel terribly saddened by this whole business. Mr. Fenn was a remarkable man."

Chapter 19

Upon finding that Mrs. Sybil Halliday had moved into the house and now occupied the bedroom opposite hers, Carina became even more anxious. Although she harbored a secret admiration for the way the woman flaunted convention in matters of dress and behavior, she found Mrs. Halliday's connection with the now-suspect Niven DeQuincy troubling in the extreme. On top of that, she didn't understand why the woman remained in Cannington when she was more of an outsider than Carina herself.

The morning after her visit to the scene of the crime, Carina came across Mrs. Halliday and Maud on their way to the drawing room. Sybil's face lit up.

"Miss Chesterman, you've been out riding. I would have thought you'd never want to climb back in the saddle, not after your ordeal."

"Good morning, Mrs. Halliday. I wanted to ensure that my horse had suffered no ill effects."

"And did it?"

"None whatsoever. She's the best horse I've ever ridden."

"I do so admire you. You are a fearless horsewoman. And you look striking in that outfit. Don't you agree, Miss Addersley?"

Maud inclined her head and smiled. "My cousin puts me to shame. I have never been very confident on the back of a horse."

"If you'll excuse me, I must go and change."

"Please come and join us when you're done."

A short while later, she entered the drawing room. Sybil stood and grasped Carina's hand between both hers. "My heart goes out to you, my dear. I can't begin to imagine what you must have gone through after finding that poor fellow's body. What an awful thing to happen!"

Carina wasn't sure whether Mrs. Halliday was referring to finding the body or the actual murder itself. She didn't ask for clarification as she wished not to dwell on the tragedy nor discuss it with the woman. She was relieved when Sybil let go of her hand to offer her coffee.

"The kitchen maid brought us fresh pot just moments ago. What's the girl's name?"

"She's called Ellie."

"Such a sweet young thing, though I thought she was looking sad."

"Like many of us she's upset by this terrible crime. Ellie knew Mr. Fenn quite well."

"Of course. This is such a tight community."

"I understand you have decided to prolong your stay in Cannington, Mrs. Halliday."

"As I may have mentioned before, my reason for coming to the Northwest is to visit an old friend in the Alberta District but am in no hurry. Mind you, I didn't bargain on being caught up in a murder investigation. One of those mounted police officers questioned *me* for half an hour yesterday. Did he imagine I jumped on a horse and shot the poor man? Mind you, I've wanted to kill a man on more than one occasion. If I were to act on my impulses, I would take off my shoe and beat him over the head while he was in a drunken stupor. Like that there would be no mystery for them to solve."

Carina and Maud exchanged blank looks. Neither she nor her cousin knew what to make of Mrs. Halliday's brash manner. Carina wanted to escape but thought it best not to leave Maud alone with the woman.

Sybil took a sip from her cup. "This afternoon, after luncheon, the younger Mr. Beresford has invited the three of us to pay him a visit. His house is exceedingly fine and I am eager to see inside it. Miss Maud has agreed to come with me. I do hope you are free to accompany us, Miss Chesterman."

Carina hesitated. It was the imploring expression on Maud's sad face that swayed her. "Very well, Mrs. Halliday, I've nothing planned for this afternoon. I'd be willing to accompany you both."

Sybil clapped her hands. "That's wonderful!"

Carina became aware, as if for the first time, of the array of rings on the woman's fingers.

"Mr. Addersley has kindly put his buggy at our disposal," Sybil said. "Mr. Tucker was to have driven us but that would have meant being cramped on the seat. Now, if you were to drive, it would be much more convenient. I've heard you are a remarkably capable driver."

"I could do that."

"Splendid! I wish I had half your talent. And, by the way, Mr. Rodney Beresford insisted the visit be informal. We have no need to dress elaborately."

Carina laughed. "That's good because my wardrobe doesn't extend too far into the formal."

Since business kept Alfred Addersley at his store over the noon hour, luncheon was an all female occasion. Neither Carina nor Maud spoke much during the meal, mainly because Sybil and Rosalind Addersley dominated the conversation with a discussion of the contrast in English and American dress fashions. Although interested, Carina chose not to join in out of fear of prolonging the meal. As for Maud, she rarely expressed her views in the presence of her mother.

For the outing, Carina wore a plain cotton skirt, a functional shirtwaist blouse and a straw boater. When she went back indoors, she was forced to suppress her smile. Sybil's notion of informal was a magenta brocade dress. Her only concession to practicality was that the outfit lacked a bustle. Maud wore a beige linen walking dress. From the ease in which the girl moved, Carina could tell she had given up wearing a corset. As if to compensate for the young women's absence of stays, Sybil gave the impression relying on the contribution of one entire blue whale.

Tucker helped Sybil up onto buggy seat. Carina climbed in next and picked up the reins. Maud had no problem taking her seat under Tucker's watchful eye. The two young women on their own could have easily covered the mile and a quarter on foot, but Carina guessed Sybil was not much of a walker, and because of that refrained from suggesting they dispense with the buggy.

They reached the drive entrance and entered between stone gateposts, each bearing a bronze griffin. As a reminder of the newness of the settlement, the poplar saplings planted on either side of the drive were no more than head high. Carina tried to picture how it would like be in years to come to drive under a continuous green canopy.

Mr. Rodney Beresford stood waiting to greet them on the mansion steps. Her uncle had described him as 'your typical English country squire,' which was of no help as she had no idea what an English squire looked like. He wore twill riding breeches and high-topped brown boots. In defiance of the midday heat, he sported a yellow brocade vest and a checkered tweed jacket. At his throat was knotted a sky-blue foulard.

The sight of his dashing appearance brought words of approval to Sybil's lips. "My, what a handsome figure he cuts!"

For once, Carina had to agree with her, even though the gentleman looked a trifle absurd.

"Ladies, you do me a great honor by visiting my humble abode. It's not every day the house is graced by three beautiful members of the fair sex." He motioned to a young man standing near by. "Bertie will you take care of the ladies' horse and conveyance?"

While the young fellow held the bridle, Rodney Beresford handed the women down.

He held on to Carina's hand a shade longer than he had done the others. "Miss Chesterman, you have my deepest sympathy for the unpleasant experience you recently endured. I do, however, admire your resilience and your skill." He gestured to the buggy being led away. "Not many young women are capable of handling a horse and carriage."

"We're all so very proud of her," Sybil said.

Rodney rubbed his hands together. "Well, I intend to offer you a conducted tour of Inglesbury, the establishment I jointly own with my brother Algernon, who, I'm sure would love to be here to welcome you."

"Then, lead on, sir," Sybil said, "We will follow in your footsteps."

"I'll leave the main house for last. I have ordered tea to be served when we have finished the tour. Let's start with the stables. Please don't hesitate to ask any questions you may have. I have to warn you," and at this he chuckled, "Inglesbury is exclusively a male domain. To the more refined feminine eye, the furnishings may appear somewhat outlandish."

At one end of the gravel courtyard stood the stables, its interior refreshingly cool and dim after the outside glare and heat.

"All the horses are presently out in their paddocks. I'd like to draw your attention to the stalls. They are lined with Honduran mahogany especially imported by the architect. You'll note that above each stall is affixed a brass plate engraved with the name of its equine occupant. We brought stone masons and carpenters from England to build this and the other buildings. Construction is a mixture of limestone, carried by rail and ox-cart from the province of Manitoba, and local blue stone. The bunkhouse for the workers, which I will point out presently, is the exception. It is built from undressed fieldstone."

Sybil was so effusive in her admiration of everything that Carina deemed it unnecessary to add her comments. She did, however, ask where the lumber other than the mahogany had come from. As she anticipated, the source was the slopes of Moose Mountain and produced by Cannington's own sawmill.

When they exited the stables, Rodney led the way along a paved walk skirting the east wing of the house. "This part of the house provides accommodation for the young gentlemen attending the captain's school, and for staff members. Perhaps it's best if we omit it from our tour. Suffice to say the upper floor comprises bachelor rooms and ablutions. The lower floor is given over to a dining hall and a communal recreation room. Let's proceed to the paddocks at the rear of the house."

The enclosures, each one surrounded by a white post and rail fence, contained sleek, long-legged horses. Carina paused to watch a chestnut mare rolling on its back on the dusty earth.

Beresford stood beside her. "As a horsewoman, Miss Chesterman, you will doubtless be aware that the mark of a good horse is one that can roll completely over, and then stand up without skipping beat."

"Which is what she's doing."

"Penelope is one of our finest broodmares."

"What are these other buildings?" Sybil asked.

"The small house over there is the foreman's residence. The others are for storage, the usual kind of appendages one finds on a ranch. Inglesbury, after all, sits on two thousand six hundred acres. It is one of the largest in the Northwest, exceeded only by the Bell Ranch near Regina and the government research farm at Indian Head on the Canadian Pacific line."

They circled the house and came back to the gravelled yard at the front. The yard was equipped with a hitching rail and a mounting block. No flower beds or other ornaments adorned the area. The house's male occupants obviously lacked interest in things decorative.

Beresford gave a wide flourish. "So, we've seen the exterior, the stables and other outbuildings. We come now, dear ladies, to the *pièce de résistance*, as our French cousins would say, of the entire estate, namely, the house itself. As you can see it has a fine mansard roof. The tiles were brought here all the way from eastern Canada. As you can see, the big rooms at the front of the house have bay windows. Shall we go in?"

He held open the oak front door. Carina followed Maud and Sybil into the spacious vestibule. It was not lost on her the way Rodney Beresford's eyes dropped to watch the ruffle of Sybil's skirt brush over the toes of his high-polished boots. This man seemed to derive pleasure from even a cursory contact with a woman.

The tour then took them from the sunlit living room with its carved marble fireplace and gilt-framed paintings depicting English hunting scenes, through the dining room furnished with a long refectory table and chairs with padded seats. Brightly-patterned Turkish carpets were scattered over the dark-stained plank floors. One room that Beresford called the smoking room was furnished with dimpled leather armchairs and a matching sofa covered with a leopard skin. African trophies in the form of oval shields and slender assegais adorned the walls.

Beresford saw Carina eyeing them. "Our younger brother, Basil, sent them home while on military service during the recent Zulu Campaigns."

Carina was about to inquire about the fate of the younger brother but Rodney was already striding toward the next room down the broad passageway. He pointed to the closed door. "This is the gun room. I hardly imagine it is of much interest to you ladies."

He was about to walk on when Carina spoke up. "Mr. Beresford, you invited us to see your house. Don't you think we ought to be allowed to see everything? Perhaps we don't need to see the young gentlemen's quarters but you could show us your gun room."

A smile creased the man's features. "Why, of course, Miss Chesterman. I'm honored that you wish me to show you our fine collection." He opened the door and stepped aside to allow the women to enter. "As you can see, we own a considerable number of guns."

Carina took in the contents of the room: guns in glass-fronted cabinets, guns standing upright in wall racks and more guns on the table in the center of the room. "Mr. Beresford, you have enough here to equip a small army."

Their host laughed. "Indeed, that is what it may look like. Yet each gun has a specific purpose." He opened one the glass cabinets. "These, for example, are doubled-barrelled shotguns for fowling. They belonged to my father. Some of them are over sixty years old. Excellent London-made guns by renowned firms such as

Purdey and Holland, and today worth a small fortune. The names may not mean much to you but to a collector…"

Carina, standing next to a rack of guns, asked, "And these..?"

Beresford smiled. "These are an altogether different kettle of fish. Large caliber rifles for hunting big game like deer and moose. We also use them for long-range, competitive target shooting, which has become a popular sport in recent years." He tapped the stock of one of the firearms. "This for example, is a Sharps single-shot rifle."

Carina tried to conceal her excitement at hearing the familiar name. "A Sharps? As you can imagine, sir, I'm completely ignorant concerning firearms but I'm eager to learn, as are my companions. Could you tell us something about this particular gun?"

"I'd be delighted to, Miss Chesterman." Flattered that a woman possessed more than a cursory interest in his treasured guns, he warmed to his subject. "In the world of firearms, the name Sharps is one to be reckoned with. Mr. Christian Sharps, who died some years ago, designed a series of guns that have helped shape the history of North America, notably, during the American Civil War. Personally, I tend to favor British arms but have to admit that the Sharps sporting rifle is unparalleled for its precision. You may have heard the expression *a sharpshooter* for one who is a skilled marksman. The term comes, of course, from the name of this rifle."

"May I hold it?"

Beresford took the gun from the rack. "I must warn you that you'll find it heavy."

Carina accepted it both hands and immediately her arms sagged under its weight. "You're right. It is heavy. How can anyone hold it steady enough to fire?"

"It does take practice. In the hands of an experienced hunter this rifle is deadly accurate at three hundred yards, even at longer ranges."

She ran her eyes over the long, octagonal barrel and the smooth wooden stock. Knowing it was probably a firearm similar to the one in her hands that had killed Ogden Fenn gave it particular, if sinister, significance. "How does it work?"

"Do you mean how does one load and fire it?"

She laughed. "Yes, I suppose that's what I mean."

Rodney pointed to the curved brass lever that formed the trigger guard. "Take hold of that and push it down. Yes, like that. The rifle has what they call a falling block mechanism. You see how the center part of the breech drops down to expose the chamber at the base of the barrel? To fire the rifle, you would insert a round into the breech and close it by pulling the lever back up. Yes, like that. As you see, that action raises the block again and seals the breech. Now cock the hammer by pulling it back with your thumb."

Carina did as she was instructed, only, she found it next to impossible to pull back the hammer with her thumb alone. "This isn't easy, sir."

"You have small hands. A man would find it easier." He reached over and pulled the hammer into its raised firing position.

"Why, if it fires only a single shot does it have two triggers?"

"Ah, now, that's part of the secret of its extreme accuracy. It has what is called a doubleset trigger. When squeezed, the rear trigger sets the forward 'hair' trigger so that it requires only the lightest pressure to release the hammer. That allows for improved trigger control and less chance of pulling the rifle off its target when you fire."

"I see." Carina handed back the rifle. Rodney lowered the hammer and replaced the gun on the rack.

"Are all those Sharps rifles?"

"Yes, all ten of them."

"There are only nine here." Carina placed her fingers in the empty slot in the rack. "It's a pity one is missing. The collection looks incomplete."

Rodney frowned, visibly irritated that he had failed to notice the vacant space at the end of the rack. "We allow the young gentlemen from the agricultural school to borrow the guns. They do enjoy their sport. I insist that all firearms be brought back to the gun room at the end of the day. I can only surmise that some negligent fellow forgot to do so and still has it in his room."

"May I see the ammunition the Sharps rifle uses?"

"The ammunition?" Rodney looked surprised. "Certainly. I must say, you are an exceptional young lady. I have never had a member of the opposite sex show such interest in the contents of this room." He leaned in and lowered his voice to a whisper. "Then, again, I've heard that you are not one of those typical women whose mind ranges no further than frilly clothes and teacups." He pulled open a drawer and took out a tin box. "These are the cartridges the Sharps take. They are point-four-five of an inch in caliber and take ninety grains of black powder, which makes them one of the more powerful rounds available." He took out a cartridge and handed it to her.

She looked down at the object and was immediately transported back to Ogden Fenn's campsite. She imagined she could hear again the voices of Sergeant Granger and Trooper Durkin explaining the intricacies of firearms and the ammunition that goes into them. On that occasion, she held a spent casing. The one nestled in her palm was a live round, heavy with powder and with a blunt-nosed lead bullet at its tip. Slowly, she turned the cartridge over and looked at its base. A shudder ran down her spine when she saw that the primer cap, as yet unmarred by a firing pin, was of white metal, identical to the found casing.

Chapter 20

Cannington, Sunday, July 20, 1884

The family members, Mrs. Halliday included, are at church. I have the house to myself. What luxury! Immediately they left I took my flute to the bottom of the garden and spent half an hour practicing. In one of the two books of music I managed to bring with me, I found a charming flute sonata by Michel Blavet called La Dedale. I read that Monsieur Blavet was considered the finest flute player in eighteenth century France. What I like about his work is that he wrote many pieces expressly for amateurs. And, being self-taught on the flute, I consider myself very much an amateur. This is a piece I want to learn thoroughly.

The music helped take my my mind off the recent unpleasantness. Frequently at night I lie awake thinking about what happened. Somewhere out there walking free is the person who committed the horrible crime. Sgt. Granger suspects it was Mr. DeQuincy because he stands to benefit from the death of the scientist.

As much as I dislike Mr. DeQuincy, a truly detestable character, I question whether he could be the perpetrator. Any one of those Sharps rifles in the Beresfords' gun room might have been the murder weapon. Also, the Beresfords reload their own cartridges in the manner Trooper Durkin explained. The cartridges in that box had white metal primers like the one I found on the ground. But what does that prove? That DeQuincy got his hands on a Sharps? I somehow

doubt it, because someone would have seen him. I asked
Mr. Beresford if other people owned Sharps rifles. He
said such rifles were not uncommon, but if anything,
homesteaders favor Winchester carbines or smaller
caliber, less powerful, single-shot rifles. He showed me a
Winchester. It's a repeating rifle with a shorter barrel,
practical to carry on horseback or under the seat of a
wagon but definitely not the weapon that killed Mr.
Fenn.

Just because Mr. Beresford and his brother own
several, I don't think for a moment either of the two men
committed the crime. The brothers were favorably
disposed to Mr. Fenn and gave him lodging when he
visited. The gentlemen scholars of Bachelor Hall have
access to the guns but why would they commit murder?
On the drive back from the visit I asked Mrs. Halliday if
Mr. DeQuincy was a sportsman. She said he made no
secret of his preference for city over the country and
would sooner spend an afternoon at the card table than
out killing wildlife. None of this definitively rules him
out as the murderer of a man he hated. Frankly, I don't
believe he possesses the skill to handle such a precision
weapon (and in the dark, too).

So, if Mr. DeQuincy didn't do it, who did? Only
time will tell. I've full confidence that the North-West
Mounted Police will find the culprit.

I must confess that much of the luster has worn
off Cannington Manor and I'm not adverse to the idea of
moving. But where? Regina? Julian says father has not
acquired a house and still lodges at the hotel. Even if he
had, I no longer relish the thought of living under the
same roof as him.

On a brighter note, I received a letter from Millie.
She'll be arriving soon. Had a long talk with Uncle

Alfred about fetching her from the station. Uncle said he'd dispatch Mr. Tucker with the buckboard for her, like he had done for me. I protested saying that Millie was my friend and I ought to be at the station to meet her. The buckboard was unnecessary as Millie would be be traveling light, with only enough for a short stay. After much discussion, he agreed to let me have the democrat but that he didn't think it was right that I drive there on my own. He suggested that Julian could accompany me. I recoiled at the thought of finding myself alone on the open prairie with him, and convinced uncle that I had to drive myself as this was necessary to help me restore my shaken self-confidence. Besides, the democrat seats two only.

Now that the distraction of the races and the agricultural fair are over, Cannington's social life has resumed its regular routine, with tennis games, cricket matches, dinner parties and musical recitals. It amazes me how these English can exhibit such gaiety with the unsolved murder of Ogden Fenn hanging over them.

Because of my outsider status, I avoid many of the dinner invitations. Naturally, I attend those here at the house. At the dinner two evenings ago, after we had finished eating, the guests were in a jovial mood.

Mr. Paul Fripp got to his feet, swaying slightly. I had noticed his enthusiasm for the bottle of my uncle's best Beaujolais that had circulated the table. Nonetheless, he's a likeable gentleman. He called for silence and said, "I say, ladies and gents, rather than we men being our usual boorish selves and sending the ladies into the drawing room, how about we all go into the parlor and gather around the piano?"

His proposal was met with applause.

Seth Teague then spoke up, "All very fine, old chap, but our regular pianist is not with us this evening. Where is she?"

"Maud retired to her room early," replied Aunt Rosalind. "She was suffering from a headache."

A collective groan met her words. To my horror, I suddenly found all eyes fixed on me.

Fripp beamed. "Miss Chesterman, I've heard you are a talented musician. Would you take Miss Maud's place on the piano stool?"

Alarmed at having been put on the spot, I protested, "But, Mr. Fripp, I play the flute or, rather, I am learning to play the flute."

At this, Uncle Alfred spoke up. "Come, come, my dear girl. Don't hide your light under a bushel. When your father was here he boasted how you had been destined for a concert career as a pianist."

"I haven't touched a piano in ages. I'm completely out of practice."

"No matter. We won't hold it against you if you bang out a few duff notes."

Fripp waved his arm like a general commanding his troops. "Then, that's settled. Everyone to the parlor. To quote Mr. Shakespeare's Lady Macbeth when she dismissed her guests: Stand not upon the order of your going, but go!"

Amid shrill laughter I was practically frog-marched into the parlor and deposited at the piano. I'm not exaggerating when I say I was overcome with panic. I hadn't touched the ivory keys since mother's death.

Mr. Fripp called for silence. "Since this jolly musical idea started with me, I volunteer to start the singing."

He leafed through the pile of sheet music on top of the piano and stuck a well-thumbed copy of Come Into the Garden, Maud in front of me. I wasn't familiar with it but guessed it's a popular parlor song in England. I had a few brief moments to look over the score while Mr. Fripp drank from his glass. To my amazement, my fingers instinctively went to the correct notes. I was in luck. Mr. Fripp had a fine tenor voice and he knew how to carry the tune, which made it easier to accompany him. A glance at the next page of the music showed the song had no less than eleven verses to it! I gasped thinking that I'd collapse before I could finish. To my delight, my vocalist sang an abridged version, less than one third the length of the original. The room erupted in wild clapping when the song ended.

After that, it was one song after another, solos, duets, some beautifully rendered, two or three completely massacred. All my anxiety evaporated, and as long as I had the written score in front of me on the music rest, I could play them.

I went to bed later that evening aware that a spell had been broken. I had fallen in love again with the piano.

The regular tennis matches brightened Carina's day. She looked forward to the late afternoon when Cannington's young people gathered at the courts to play friendly games. Carina even even persuaded Maud to come with her, and after some initial hesitation, the formerly shy young woman became as enthusiastic as Carina herself. One evening Carina was walking home alone, Maud having gone to visit a sick friend, when she heard an unwelcome voice behind her.

Julian caught up with her on the boardwalk. "Sis, you've been keeping yourself to yourself lately. What's wrong? You don't want to talk to me?"

Carina quickened her pace but Julian kept up with her.

"Are you surprised?."

"What the fuck are you talking about?"

"Must you use such disgusting language?"

"Okay, but tell me, why the bee in your bonnet?"

"If you've already forgotten how you behaved outrageously it's not up to me to remind you. Anyhow, why are you still in the settlement? I thought you were working for Mr. DeQuincy."

"I am. Niven has given me the task of overseeing some shipments in this part of the territory. That's quite a responsibility, given the size of the area."

"Business mustn't be booming. You don't appear to be run off your feet."

"Cut out the sarcasm. Right now there's a lull. In a week or so things are going to be humming and will remain so through the fall."

"Then, you're not planning to return to your law studies?"

"Law school can wait. This is far more exciting."

"Father is going to be disappointed."

"Pa approves of me working for Niven. That man is putting his stamp on the Northwest. Why, he could even be the next lieutenant governor. It pains me to tell you that Niven was disappointed in you."

Carina glared at her brother. "Since when was I supposed to live up to that man's expectations? On the subject of Mr. DeQuincy, it pains me to tell you that I find him highly obnoxious. I don't care how successful a businessman he is, I have not the slightest interest in him. It was insulting of him to talk to me about marriage, when I scarcely know the man."

"Father, too, is disappointed."

"This conversation is ridiculous. If Mr. DeQuincy is looking for a wife, I would recommend he asks Mrs. Halliday. They seem to get along together. Besides, they're closer in age."

"You're going to regret being such a stubborn bitch."

"Keep your insults to yourself." At that, Carina broke into a run toward the house, leaving Julian on the boardwalk.

Upon reaching the house, she went straight to her room. Just as she was opening her door, she heard sounds coming from the room opposite, Sybil's room. Carina paused on her threshold. She made out Sybil's voice and Maud's. She heard Maud's excited laughter. Carina shrugged and pushed her door shut behind her. A few minutes later, a knock came on her door. She opened it and found Ellie clutching a letter in her hand.

"Miss Carina, while you were out the mail driver arrived. Among the letters he delivered is this one for you."

"Thank you, Ellie." Carina took the letter. She looked at the girl who possessed the air of a frightened doe. "Ellie, dear, you seem to have lost that sparkle I loved so much. You're upset because of Mr. Fenn, aren't you?"

The girl looked down at her feet, and then raised her head to meet Carina's eyes. "Nothing like this has ever happened before. I'm scared."

Carina wrapped her arms around the willowy fourteen-year-old and gave her a hug. "I know it's terribly sad but there is no need to be frightened. No one is going to hurt you."

A weak smile formed on Ellie's lips. "You're so kind, miss. I do wish I could be strong like you."

Carina laughed. "If the truth be known I'm not that strong. I just refuse to be cowed by the tragedy. They'll find out who killed Mr. Fenn and justice will be done. In the meantime we have to be brave." She kissed the girl's cheek.

Ellie brightened up. "I'll try. Thanks."

After the girl left, Carina went to the window. From the handwriting she knew the letter was was from her Aunt Louise. She tore open the envelope. It alarmed her to see that her aunt's usually elegant cursive script wavered across the page in a spidery hand.

Westmount

My Dearest Niece,

Do not be alarmed when I write to say this may be the last time you hear from me. My health has deteriorated in recent weeks and I wanted to reach out to you one last time before I grow too weak to write. My doctor tells me I have no disease or other ailment that he can treat with the many pills the apothecary has available these days. No, he says, simply, that my earthly stay is coming to a close and soon it will be time to go.

It seems like an age, darling Carina, since the day you said goodbye and departed for the Northwest. I treasure every one of your letters you have lovingly written. I am so glad that your new life is to your liking and that your father is succeeding in his bank. That your dear brother Julian is spending some time in the West must be a blessing for you.

Please do not worry about me, and on no account think of coming back to Westmount. You have nothing to keep you here and I am well taken care of.

I wish you health and happiness and may you live as long and as rich a life as I have had. Do not grieve for me when I am gone. Simply keep me in your thoughts. Someone, I know not who, said if you think often of the departed they are still with you.

Yours affectionately,

Louise

Carina held the letter limply in the fingers of her right hand. From her window she idly watched a wagon carrying a load of hay trundle up the street. She had the strange sensation that the last few remnants of her former life were fading away. Soon, nothing would be left except memories. The eventual loss of her Aunt Louise would come as a shock, as she had been a fixture in her life for as long as she could remember. Her father, too, may not have long to live. She had no way of knowing the nature or the seriousness of his illness but feared the prognosis was not good. She had disowned her brother. For all practical reasons, she was alone. And like everyone without a family for help and guidance, she must summon the strength to forge her own way in the world.

Already the germ of an idea was forming in her mind. In an article in the Regina *Leader*, the editor had bemoaned the lack of culture in the capital city of the Northwest. No theater, no literary society, no recital hall or opera house existed to counter balance Regina's materialistic preoccupation with trade and commerce.

Since it was plain she had outstayed her welcome in the Addersley household, there was an imperative need to find a new home. Even if her Aunt Rosalind had a change of heart, Carina knew she didn't belong in the English settlement, with its rigid class structure, its devotion to teas and petty amusements. The presumption of entitlement, of superiority, and the vacuousness of Cannington society were alien to her. If she had to choose, she'd prefer the company of Ellie, with all her youthful simplicity. She harbored no bitterness toward anyone and she was grateful for the kindness she had received. She loved having the opportunity to ride in beautiful surroundings, and she admired the bold attempt to create a life of refinement in the middle of the wilderness. She just couldn't see herself making her home among these people.

After Millie's visit was over she would quietly announce her departure, go to Regina and find lodgings. To support herself she would offer music lessons, even though that meant starvation wages. For the foreseeable future there would not be many children or young adults desiring tuition. No matter, she'd persevere and, inspired by the optimism expressed by the *Leader*'s editor, she'd succeed. If she didn't, at least she would fail on her own terms.

The sense of relief at having reached a decision revived her spirits. She went to her writing desk and penned a letter to her Aunt Louise. With luck she would be able to give it to the mail driver before he left on his return trip to Moosomin.

Chapter 21

Two days after the visit to the Beresford mansion Carina saw a curricle come to a halt in front of the house. Only the Beresfords owned such a sporty rig, yellow lacquered and drawn by two milk white horses. Carina recognized the driver as Bertrand Lee, one of Captain Pierce's pups. She hadn't long to wait for an explanation for the curricle's appearance. Sybil left the house by the side door and climbed, unaided, into the carriage. Her attire piqued Carina's curiosity. The normally colorful Mrs. Halliday today was dressed in black, but nothing like somber style favored by the Cannington matrons. The front of the dress was daringly cut away to reveal a froth of black silk petticoats and a generous expanse of gleaming black stocking. A black dotted veil draped over the brim of a plumed hat hid her face. Despite the night-dark appearance, only the naive would assume that Mrs. Sybil Halliday was on her way to a funeral.

With consummate skill, Bertie, as he was called, swung the horses round in a tight arc and set off back down the street at a brisk pace.

Carina happened to be at the foot of the stairs later in the afternoon when Sybil returned to the house. The woman carried her hat in her hand and her auburn hair fell in disarray.

"Hello, Mrs. Halliday, such a beautiful day. Did you enjoy your drive?"

At first taken aback, Sybil quickly recovered her composure. She reached out an ungloved hand and caressed Carina's cheek. "Simply wonderful, my dear, simply wonderful. Next time, you might care join me." Without another word she swept past Carina and went up to her room.

The yellow curricle made an appearance on several subsequent occasions, always at the same early-afternoon hour. Carina assumed that Sybil and Mr. Rodney Beresford had formed an attachment, the nature of which she decided she'd rather not know. Along with this observation, she noticed that Maud, who rarely left the house, now absented herself in the afternoons. Carina wondered whether Maud had taken to accompanying Sybil to the Beresford mansion. Neither Maud nor Mrs. Halliday gave any hint of how each spent their afternoons.

Carina began to devour the *Leader,* the newspaper which was more than a week old by the time it arrived in the settlement. Not surprisingly, the Ogden Fenn murder featured prominently on its front page. A reporter had come to the settlement to interview anyone who was willing to talk. The journalist had pressed Carina for details of how she found the victim. She gave a factual account of her involvement but kept her opinions to herself. The published story was heavy on sensationalism and light on accuracy. The writer had no qualms in blaming the murder on the current instability and offered it as proof that law and order was disintegrating.

Not everything in the paper was depressing. Inspiring was the account of a certain Thomas Stevens who had set out from San Francisco on the morning of April 22, 1884 to travel across the United States. What made the story unusual was that Mr. Stevens was traveling by bicycle. He had purchased a 50-inch 'Standard,' sometimes called a penny-farthing, packed the handlebar bag with socks, a spare shirt, a raincoat that doubled as a tent, and a bulldog revolver. The gentleman followed the old California trail eastward across the mountains and plains, astonishing the Indians and any white men he encountered along the way. He was now in the eastern states and was expected to arrive in Boston in early August. There was also talk that he intended to take a steamer to Europe and continue bicycling around the globe.

Carina made plans to travel to Moosomin on the day prior to Millie's arrival. She would overnight in the hotel in order to meet the morning train. On the departure day, before dawn, Carina helped Norman Tucker harness Cyrus, the Cleveland Bay, to the democrat. Ellie begged to be allowed to go along but Carina reluctantly had to refuse on the grounds that the buggy had room for only one passenger and the driver. True, she, Sybil and Maud had used the democrat to drive to the Beresfords' but that had been just over a mile. On this trip, the space behind the seat would be taken up by Millie's luggage and Carina's overnight bag. Carina considered this unfortunate as she'd have welcomed the girl's company on the long trek to Moosomin station.

The journey was the reverse of the one she had made on first coming to Cannington. She remembered the best stopping places where the water was potable. One major difference between this and the earlier trip was the condition of the terrain. Weeks of drought had taken its toll. On either side of the trail stretched an unbroken expanse of desiccated brown grass. Even the verdant Pipestone valley, where they had halted for lunch, was now parched, the creek reduced to a muddy trickle. After a short respite, the intense heat had returned with a vengeance.

She worried that Millie would think she had descended to one of the lower levels of Dante's *Inferno*.

Carina had a feeling of triumph when she arrived unscathed in the town of Moosomin. She handed Cyrus and the democrat into the care of the groom at the livery stable, took her bag and walked the short distance to the station hotel. After luxuriating in a bath and changing from her riding habit into a skirt and linen blouse, she went into the dining room, where the patrons at the tables were all men. She needed no reminder that white women, particularly if traveling alone, were a rarity in the Northwest.

After eating, she stretched her legs with a walk to the edge of town to watch the sun set over the prairie. Back at the hotel she went to her room and prepared for bed. For an hour or more she lay on the uneven mattress and stared up at the ceiling. On the journey, the driving had occupied her every minute. Now free of that responsibility, she could let her mind wander. This was the first time she had spent a night away from the settlement. For all its creature comforts and the emphasis on games and sports, life in Cannington was not without its cares. The murder had only served to heighten that latent anxiety.

For the first time in weeks, she fell into a sleep untroubled by dreams.

At dawn next morning she rose and crossed the street to the station to await the westbound train. She shared the platform with a mixed bag of humanity. Huddled in the meager shade afforded by the station canopy stood a knot of men, women and children. They talked among themselves in a language unfamiliar to her. From their appearance, the men in dusty coveralls, the women in homespun skirts and brightly-colored headscarves, she assumed they were immigrants on their way to take up homesteads. Also in the crowd were several young men, whose features were tanned from the sun. The bundles of tools at their feet suggested they were construction workers by trade, traveling between assignments. She wondered why her father could not have hired them to build his house, but that was immaterial now. There were men dressed in city clothes, either government officials or commercial travelers. One older man was accompanied by a stern-faced woman, who scowled at Carina with unabashed disapproval. When she caught Carina looking back at her she hastily averted her eyes.

At that moment the station agent came from his office with an announcement. "Sorry to disappoint you, folks, but the westbound train is held up ten miles out. Rails buckled in the heat. The section boss is asking for a dozen volunteers to help the section crew fix the track."

The young workers immediately gathered round him. After some discussion, they were joined by some of the immigrant men. Under the agent's direction, they manhandled a handcar onto the rails and piled aboard. Four men pumped the crank handles, sending the cart trundling down the line toward the site of the blockage.

Carina approached the railway official. "How long will the delay be?"

He pulled a glum face. "You're looking at a couple of hours, ma'am, before the track gets repaired and another forty minutes after that for the train to get here."

"I'll wait at the hotel."

"A good idea. I'll send word across when the train is about due."

The hotel offered no respite from the heat, but being able to stretch out on a sofa in the public lounge and read her book was preferable to standing in the crowded train station.

Later in the morning a boy thrust his head around the door and informed her that the train would be arriving in fifteen minutes. Back on the platform, Carina shielded her eyes and spotted the locomotive's smoke in the distance. It took many more minutes before the train reached the station. Then, with a body as black as Erebus and a cone of noon-day light at its head, the locomotive thundered into the station and screeched to a halt. The previously static tableau of waiting figures came to life and pressed forward. Doors swung open and perspiring passengers disembarked.

Carina searched for her friend's face. After the initial surge, the crowd thinned and she saw Millie emerge through a cloud a steam.

Millie caught sight of Carina and waved.

Carina ran to embrace her. "Millie, it's wonderful to see you again! You look great."

Millie laughed. "I don't feel great. It was so hot in that train, I feel like a leaf of boiled cabbage. And look, I'm covered in soot!"

Carina laughed. "No matter, you're here finally."

Millie stepped back and examined Carina from head to toe. "In that outfit, I could see you packing a six-shooter." She glanced around at the simple prairie station. "How can you live out here? I feel I've dropped off the edge of the world."

"Don't worry. You'll like Cannington. It's only a few months since we said goodbye but in that time you've seem to have grown. How was the rest of the journey?"

"I traveled with Mr. and Mrs. Kennedy. He's a Presbyterian minister. On the journey, several nice gentlemen stopped to talk to me but Mr. Kennedy has such a forbidding air about him it made even the boldest gentleman beat a hasty retreat. It was rather funny, really. I must say goodbye to the Kennedys before the train leaves."

"You have time while the locomotive takes on water. Go and say your farewell, I'll ensure your things are taken from the baggage car."

Chapter 22

The dilemma facing Carina was whether to set out immediately for Cannington or wait until the following morning. The train's delayed arrival thwarted plans for an early start on the journey. The prospect of spending another night in a stuffy hotel room with its lumpy beds decided the issue for her.

That meant arriving in the settlement long after dark but that didn't discourage her. The Cannington trail was well marked by the passage of wagons and horses and the moon was full. Traveling at night had the advantage that the air was cooler.

Before they left town, the hotel kitchen obligingly supplied a basket of sandwiches and pastries to keep hunger at bay. One worry stemmed from something the livery stableman said as she was driving off, which was to warn her to be on the lookout for grass fires.

Once they were clear of the town, Carina scanned the horizon in all directions and saw nothing but sun-drenched prairie. At first, Millie was full of questions, questions about the land, about Cannington and Carina's new life in the Northwest. Gradually, fatigue overcame her and she lapsed into silence before drifting off into a doze.

After one of the rest stops, Millie was again alert and asked how long it would be before they reached Cannington.

Carina motioned with her chin. "See that low ridge on the horizon? When we reach that point, the land begins to slope toward the south. We cross a dry creek and from there it's no more than five hours to the settlement."

Millie shielded her eyes and stared at what seemed like a thin band of dark cloud low on the eastern horizon. "Is that a storm blowing up?"

Carina tried to sound calm. Her earlier concern over the liveryman's warning had given way to the somber recognition that the fire threat was real. For some time she had monitored the sky and was forced to admit that the cloud was smoke, and that it grew more menacing the farther south they traveled.

To reassure herself as much as her friend, she said, "Even if it advances this way, we'll be in no danger. Once we make it past the dry creek, the bare earth will act as act as a firebreak."

Millie pouted her lips. "I don't like the look of it one bit."

An hour later the desired southerly ridge appeared no closer. Yet, there was no ignoring the advance of the fire. A hot southerly wind had arisen, carrying with it the smell of burning grass and fine particles of ash. The horse, too, sensed the danger and adopted a skittish gait that Carina struggled to control. She looked at the pall of smoke and then at the trail ahead to try to gauge if she could reach the creek before the fire closed in. By her estimate they still had time to outflank the flames.

All this changed some half hour later. To their left and advancing faster than a man could walk, lay an ominous bank of fire. It stretched across the prairie from horizon to horizon. Even from the distance Carina heard the steady roar as the flames devoured everything in their path. Wisps of smoldering grass, carried upward by the heated air began to rain down from a dark sky.

Millie hugged her lace shawl about her and shrank back on the seat. "Carina, I am scared."

Carina made no reply but brought the buggy to a halt.

Millie clutched Carina's arm. "Why have we stopped?"

"There's a rider coming this way, at a gallop." Carina pointed at the approaching figure, at times obscured by smoke and distorted by waves of heat.

To meet the rider, Carina urged her reluctant Cyrus forward but the horse flattened his ears and refused to budge. Moments later, the oncoming horse and rider burst through the smoke and came to a halt alongside the democrat.

Carina's jaw dropped. "Sergeant Granger!"

Dillon, drenched with sweat, waved his arm, "Quick, turn the buggy around! The trail ahead is blocked. If you don't get out of here fast you'll be trapped." With that he grasped Cyrus' bridle and pulled the horse in a tight circle until the buggy was facing the way it had come. He then shouted at Carina. "Get going and don't stop until I give the order. I'll ride with you."

This time her horse needed no encouragement and broke into a mad gallop back along the trail. Dillon spurred his mount and kept pace with the democrat. They kept this up until Dillon reined in his horse to a steady lope. Carina followed suit.

When they put some distance between them and the fire, Dillon commanded Carina to stop at a point where a line of long-dead cottonwoods intersected the trail. Carina looked about her and saw, a short distance away, a small lake no bigger than a duck pond.

She motioned to it. "How is it I never noticed that before?"

Dillon laughed. "Easy to miss if you're focused on driving."

"Why is this spot safer than any other from the fire?"

The sergeant dismounted and dragged his boot toe over the blackened ground. "Because it has been already burnt over earlier this summer."

The only green was a ring of bulrushes bordering the pond. She kept the reins in one hand and jumped down. "This may is not be an auspicious moment, but I'd like to introduce my friend, Miss Millicent Vanderhagen. She is visiting Cannington for a few weeks. Millie, this is Sergeant Granger of the North-West Mounted Police."

Dillon removed his hat and offered Millie his hand to help her down. "Pleased to make your acquaintance, miss."

Millie, who had been showing signs of panic as the fire closed in, straightened her skirt and brushed back a loose curl of dark hair. "Thank you, sergeant, for your timely intervention. I believe Miss Chesterman and I are exceedingly fortunate you arrived when you did."

Carina watched with mixed emotions as the bank of flame rolled across to where she had previously been stopped. "What do we do now, sergeant, wait for the fire to pass and then continue on our way?"

Dillon nodded. "By morning it'll be safe enough to drive over the burnt out section."

"Morning! Not before?"

"The ground remains hot long after a grass fire has moved on, too hot for the horses' hooves. And too hot for the rubber tires on your fancy new democrat."

Millie looked alarmed. "What do we do, then? Just stand here?"

"No, we take refuge over there, ma'am." He gestured toward what at first glance appeared to be a mound of earth.

Carina gasped. The bump in the earth was, on closer scrutiny, a simple shelter. Its front side contained a low door and a small window, now badly cracked. A corroded stove pipe that could easily be mistaken for a dead branch protruded from one corner. "That's something else I hadn't noticed. What is it, a hut?"

"This is what's left of an early pioneer homestead of a family of Icelanders. The simple dwelling is what they call a *kofi*, which means a hut or temporary shelter, but can also mean an old run-down shack. Take your pick. The family intended to live in it until they had enough money to build a real house. That never happened. Their luck ran out."

He walked over to the *kofi*. Carina and Millie followed.

"Nothing very grand, as you can see. They dug a rectangular pit a few feet deep and used the sod to build up low walls along the edges. Over the top they laid a roof of poplar poles covered with more sod. Unfortunately, the poor souls chose one of the driest parts of the country during the driest of years to try their luck."

"Is the water in that lake alkaline or is it fit for human consumption?"

"Fortunately for us, the water is drinkable. In fact, I'll take the horses over to it. They've earned it."

Carina and Millie stood by and watched Dillon unharness the gelding, unsaddle his own mount and lead both horses to the water's edge.

"I'm sorry your first day had to be like this," Carina said.

Millie gave a good-humored smile. "I suppose being trapped half a day in a stalled train, getting roasted alive in a fire and now about to spend the night in this deluxe prairie guesthouse are everyday occurrences out here in the West."

"You'll find Cannington is quite civilized in comparison."

"I hope we make it that far."

Dillon tethered the horses where they could graze along the edge of the water.

"Sergeant, what happened to the original homesteaders?"

"Take a walk over by the trees and you'll find out." Without further explanation he busied himself putting order into the jumble of harnesses,

Millie glanced at Carina. "What do you think he means?"

"I don't know. Let's find out."

Carina led the way over what she assumed must have been the yard of the homestead. Off to one side was a rusty water pump, missing its handle. "There's your answer." She pointed to the foot of the remnant of a stout cottonwood tree, now gnarled and broken.

"Oh, my goodness!" Mille brought her hand to her mouth.

A few feet away stood three wooden crosses, one large and two smaller ones on either side of it. All three leaned at crazy angles.

Millie sank to her heels to examine them. "There are inscriptions but too weathered to read. I wonder how the people died."

Carina imagined the graves belonged to the pioneer wife and her two small children, who had met an untimely death. Millie stood up and slipped her hand under Carina's arm. In a somber mood they walked back to the democrat. Dillon had finished his task.

"Sergeant," Carina said, "I have to thank you for coming to our aid. I hate to think what would have happened had you not come along at that time."

Dillon acknowledged her thanks by touching the brim of his hat. "Let's see if we can make you as comfortable as possible for the duration of your enforced wait. Take a look at the accommodation."

Millie looked at the *kofi* then back at Carina. "He doesn't expect us to sleep in *there*, does he?"

"It might be better than bedding down on in the dirt. On the subject of dirt, I am afraid your beautiful dress is badly soiled because of the dust and the ash from the fire."

Millie brushed a hand over her sleeve. "It doesn't matter. I've almost outgrown this outfit, anyway."

Dillon forced the door open with a sharp kick or two. The doorway was no more than four feet high. After some urging the door swung inward on protesting hinges. He stooped and put his head through the door "A bit musty for having been closed up for so long. Otherwise, it's clean and dry. Be careful when you enter. There's a drop to the floor but you'll find some wooden steps." He then crawled into the tiny structure.

Millie shrugged at Carina. "May as well go in." She copied Dillon's mode of entry, helped by the set of rickety steps. Carina followed. The three of them stood on the packed earth floor. Light filtered in through the dusty window panes. Carina and Millie were able to stand upright but Dillon was obliged to bend his head to avoid hitting the roof timbers.

"I can't believe a family actually lived in this cramped space." Carina looked up and saw the roots of the grass sod that formed the roof.

"At least the place would have been cozy in winter." Dillon examined the tin stove. "Whatever furniture the dwelling originally contained has long since disappeared, possibly scavenged by other homesteaders or passing travelers. They left the stove, because it's rusted beyond use. Over the years many a wayfarer has found shelter here. Over in the corner someone has put together a mattress of willow twigs covered with hay."

Carina tested the makeshift bed. "It's surprisingly soft and springy."

Millie looked unconvinced. To Dillon she said, "Are you sure there are no snakes or other creepy crawlies in here?"

Dillon grinned. "I guarantee your rest won't be troubled by animals."

They climbed back out and Dillon went to collect wood for a fire.

Millie grinned. "Carina, is he the police officer you told me about in your letters?"

Carina decided this wasn't the time to talk about the murder investigation discuss further her earlier meetings with Sergeant Granger. Instead, she replied, "Indeed he is. And he is a frequent visitor to Cannington. The North-West Mounted Police have a small detachment there."

Millie stared at Dillon returning with an armful of branches. Without taking her eyes off him, she said, "Isn't it exiting to be rescued by such a handsome gentleman of the law? Nothing like this ever happened to me back home."

Carina raised her eyebrows. "*Rescued* is perhaps not the right word. Even if he hadn't arrived when he did, the fire would have forced us back. We wouldn't have found this place, though."

Millie laughed. "You mean the rabbit burrow? By the way, where is he going to sleep? Not…"

"No, not with us in the burrow." Mimicking an English accent and expressing mock indignation, Carina added, "My dear, things may have become primitive all of a sudden, but we Cannington ladies do have standards to maintain." In a normal tone, she said, "When he and his troopers are out on patrol, they just bed down on the ground."

Dillon dropped his bundle of firewood. "I have some coffee in my saddlebag."

"And we have food left over from our packed lunch."

"Then we can dine in style. I'll light the fire."

Carina admired the skill with which he quickly kindled a small fire between two stones. He produced a military-issue mess tin and filled it with water fetched in the canvas bucket the democrat carried. Between them they had enough tin cups.

The meal was frugal but no one complained. Carina was heartened that Millie, once over her initial dismay, treated the situation as an adventure. The fact that Millie flirted with Dillon came as no surprise. Millie had always behaved that way.

After eating, Carina took her half-finished mug and climbed onto the roof of the sod house. She thought of making a pun of the *coffee* in her cup and the *kofi* under her feet, but let it pass. From her modest vantage point she saw that the fire had receded into the distance. Dillon was right that the surrounding area was still too dangerous to cross. Patches of grass glowed red in the fading light. In places, smoke spiralled upward from the charred ground.

Millie got to her feet. "I've had an exhausting day. That bed of twigs looks tempting."

Carina handed her the horse blanket from the democrat. "I'll join you later."

Millie disappeared through the dwarf-sized door. Carina was glad Dillon kept the fire going, not for heat, for the evening was still warm, but because of the reassuring comfort of the flickering light. Millie's small trunk had been pressed into use as a seat. Carina sat and stared into the flames. Dillon placed his saddle on the opposite side and used it as a backrest, which she found unsettling. That was how Ogden Fenn had been sitting the night of his murder.

To dispel the morbid thoughts she said, "Tell me, sergeant, it was no coincidence that you just happened to to be on the trail, was it?"

Dillon stretched out his long legs. He didn't answer immediately. Then with a laugh, he said, "I was in the detachment office writing my report on the Fenn murder when Trooper Durkin burst in. He had just come off patrol and reported seeing a fire. Barring a wind change, it was going to cut across the Moosomin trail. Mr. Addersley mentioned you'd gone to fetch your friend."

"And you rode out especially to warn me?"

A burning stick fell from the fire. Dillon gingerly picked it up and tossed it back into the fire. "When people are in danger, it's my duty to do something about it."

"First the murder and now the grass fire. Am I becoming a woman dogged by misfortune?"

214 - Michael Montcombroux

"The murder had nothing to do with you. You just happened to be in the wrong place at the wrong time. As for the fire, we can chalk it up to a certain lack of experience. You probably never came across one before."

"That's true."

"The next time you'll know what precautions to take, namely heeding warnings. I presume someone told you in Moosomin."

"Yes, sergeant, and I consider myself duly reprimanded. I ought not to have continued, with the fire bearing down on the trail."

Dillon merely grinned. He picked the mess tin from the edge of the fire and poured out the last of the coffee into their cups.

"It's not that long since Cannington was established, is it?" she said.

"I remember when the site was merely a sea of prairie grasses. I was in the area when Captain Pierce first came out to appraise the land. He wanted me to show him where there was good water and grazing and where the high ground was. He very much wanted to find a place with a view."

"You've seen the settlement grow from nothing."

"Indeed."

"What is your opinion of Cannington Manor?

"Since you are related to one of the leading members of the Cannington community, my opinion is best left unspoken."

Carina gave a quick laugh. "Mr. Addersley, whom I call my Uncle Alfred, is really my father's distant cousin. I'm a complete outsider, and they never let me forget it. You obviously know the settlement better than anyone. I'd like to know what you think."

"I wouldn't want to hurt your sensitivities."

"I'm not quite sure what you mean, sergeant. My sensitivities won't be hurt, I promise you. Besides, it won't be long before I'll be leaving Cannington."

"Really, leaving to go where?"

"Possibly, Regina, though nothing's settled yet. Give me your candid opinion of these people."

"Individually, they are extremely kind and hospitable."

"I'd agree. They've made me welcome."

"Cannington Manor is an experiment, one that I believe is doomed to failure."

"Why do you say that?"

Dillon adopted a more informal tone of voice. "You have to realize that the majority of immigrants to this country come with few possessions and not much money. They're seeking a new life. Many are escaping religious persecution or economic hardship. Our English friends, on the other hand, are on the whole wealthy and are certainly not persecuted. They come not to make a fresh start but to perpetuate their old way of life. They want to impose the social order they enjoyed in England onto a new land."

"And by social order, you mean their privileged way of life?"

"Yes, one based on wealth and entitlement. They want to foist their English class structure on the workers they employ and on the homesteaders around them. I read somewhere that they view themselves as an outpost of imperial Britain, connected to the mother country by invisible silken threads. They fail to realize that Canadians are a people entirely free from subservience to rank and wealth. They're intolerant of condescension."

"You believe the English are condescending?"

"Surely, you've seen it for yourself? You just said they never let you forget you're Canadian, with the implication that being Canadian is inferior to being British. Please don't misunderstand me. I don't mean to condemn the good folk of Cannington. I too have always been treated with respect and hospitality. I admire how they try to bring refinement to a rough frontier. Where else in the Northwest can you find people who enjoy summer picnics, card parties and amateur theatricals? Why I predict that their way of life cannot be sustained is because they put more emphasis on leisure pursuits than on farming. Admittedly, they have produced excellent crops of wheat. Last year, flour from their mill won a gold prize at the Chicago Fair, of all places. Their livestock and horses are among the finest in the region. They imported their foundation breeding stock directly from England.

The problem is that they haven't succeeded in adapting to the harsh conditions of the Canadian prairies."

"What about Captain Pierce's agricultural college? Surely that will produce young farmers who understand the conditions?"

"They farm the way they farmed in the Old Country, and that's what they teach in their college. Not that there is much teaching or learning happening. Those young gentleman pupils spend more time hunting and playing cricket than studying farming. It's only Captain Pierce's firm discipline that keeps them in line. So far, the colony has been lucky. The crops have been good and the profits high. But, as you're aware, we're in the midst of a drought. Yields are low. To make matters worse, wheat prices have plummeted."

"You seem to have made a comprehensive assessment of the Cannington settlers."

"I'm sorry if I spoke out of turn. I mean no disrespect to your relatives there. And I wish them well. I'd like to see them prosper. Cannington isn't the only English colony of its kind on the continent. There's another like it at a place called Runnymede in Ohio, in the United States."

"Is it thriving?"

"It did for a while. Now, it is all but abandoned, for many of the same reasons that Cannington may end not succeeding."

"Because of the failure to adapt?"

"That and the resentment of the Americans to the often over-bearing English."

Carina smiled. "I appreciate your candor. I share your sentiments but I haven't been there long enough to see the broader picture. Captain Pierce and some of the other community leaders are currently in Ottawa to petition the government to build a rail line to the settlement. Surely, that will ensure its survival?"

"If they succeed in getting their spur. Right now, the government has many pressing issues on their plate."

"You mean like the uprising everyone is talking about?"

"Yes. The Métis and the Indian tribes are stirring up trouble. There are other problems, too. Among them low immigration due to drought, killing frosts and social insecurity. The decline in wheat prices is discouraging the government to invest in railroad expansion. All this, however, is only the opinion of a humble police sergeant. I could be quite wrong."

Darkness closed in, which made the fire seem all the brighter.

After a few minutes of silence, Carina asked, "You went to Regina to interview Mr. DeQuincy?"

Dillon nodded. "Yes."

"May I ask what he said?"

"Before I answer that question, let me say I showed the cigar butt we found at the Fenn campsite to the owner of the tobacconist store in Regina. He confirmed it was a cheroot of American manufacture. What's more, he stocks that brand on the specific request of our Mr. DeQuincy."

"How interesting! But that doesn't prove it was Mr. DeQuincy who dropped it."

"That is pretty much what Mr. DeQuincy said to me. In fact, he laughed in my face and said that unless I had some solid evidence against him, I'd best keep out of his way. He even threatened to take legal action against the police for casting a shadow on his good name. The man does enjoy considerable esteem among the business community and with the territorial lieutenant governor."

"Do I take it, then, that you've made no great progress into Mr. Fenn's murder?"

"You could say that, Miss Chesterman."

"You do still have the empty case from the gun that killed the poor man."

"The police armorer confirmed that there was a high probability it was fired from a Sharps rifle. That doesn't help much, unless we can put our hands on the actual weapon and trace that weapon to an actual owner. We would then have to prove it was that person who used it to commit the murder. That's a tall order."

Carina was tempted to tell him about her visit to the Beresford mansion and having been shown a whole rack of such rifles, with one missing from the gun room collection. But she kept silent out of fear that she would bring needless suspicion on the Beresfords.

The conversation changed to less weighty topics until, eventually, Carina pleaded weariness and joined Millie in the *kofi*, leaving Dillon the sole guardian of the fire.

Chapter 23

By noon the following day they were within ten miles of Cannington, with Dillon riding ahead of the democrat.

Carina looked at Millie and gave a laugh. "You may not believe it but on my arrival, a troop of young men on horseback came out to escort us the last few miles. It was quite impressive. I'm perplexed why they haven't done the same now. Everyone knows I'm returning with you, and the young men never pass up an opportunity to display their horsemanship."

When they reached the outer limits of the settlement, Dillon rode up. "I wish you a pleasant stay, Miss Vanderhagen. Goodbye, Miss Chesterman." With that, he was gone, galloping off toward the police detachment.

Carina pointed out the various landmarks to Millie as they drove up the street toward her uncle's house. She rationalized that the lack of a welcoming committee was due to summer being a busy time of year. Yet on the Cannington's main street, daily life appeared normal. The few couples on the boardwalks waved at the passing democrat. In front of the general store, men were loading a delivery wagon and the habitual knot of men, beer tankards in hand, lounged on benches by the door of the Mitre's saloon bar.

Carina swung the democrat into the Addersley stable yard. "Here we are, finally, my uncle's residence."

No sooner had she come to a halt when Norman Tucker appeared from the tack room.

"Am I glad to see you back safe an' well, Miss Carina! We were all sorely worried when word came in about that grass fire."

"We were in good hands, Mr. Tucker. Sergeant Granger met us on the trail."

"He's a good man, that sergeant."

"Mr. Tucker, I'd like you to meet my friend, Miss Millicent Vanderhagen."

Tucker raised his hat and handed Millie down from her seat. To Carina he said, "You'd better go in and talk to Mrs. A. I'll take care of the horse and deal with your effects."

Carina studied the old man's face. "Is something wrong?"

Tucker gave a non-committal clack with his tongue. "You'll soon find out."

Puzzled, Carina led the way inside. Rosalind Addersley met them in the hallway. Carina saw by the look on her aunt's face that something was not right.

"Millie, I'd like to introduce you to my Aunt Rosalind. Aunt, this is my friend Miss Millicent Vanderhagen."

Rosalind extended her hand. "Miss Vanderhagen, I am pleased to meet you. Welcome to Cannington Manor. We heard about the fire. It is, indeed, unfortunate that your journey was somewhat onerous. Since you are Carina closest friend, perhaps you'll permit me to address you as Millicent."

Millie dropped a pretty curtsy, which brought a smile to the older woman's thin lips. "By all means, do, Mrs. Addersley. Only, for as long as I can remember, I've always been known as Millie."

"Very well, Millie it shall be." Rosalind looked at Carina. "I regret to inform you that the household, as is the community itself, is currently at sixes and sevens. Your friend's visit may not be as relaxed as you would have liked."

"Aunt, what's happened?"

"Maud has run away."

Carina recoiled with an incredulous look on her face. "Maud, run away?"

"Three days ago, she took off in the company of a man."

"Gracious! What man? Mr. Featherstonehaugh?"

"No, *your* brother Julian."

"With Julian! I can't believe it. She gave no warning of intending to elope, least of all with Julian."

Rosalind gave a sigh. "Had she *eloped*, it would be less of a scandal. At least the couple would be intending to marry. My daughter can be extremely stubborn when she wants to. It is thought that the couple was heading to Regina, where she and your brother intend to live together in the same dwelling without the sanction of marriage. Mr. Addersley, aided by other gentlemen from the settlement, has gone after her."

"If Maud and Julian left three days ago, why we didn't meet them in Moosomin or pass them on the trail?"

"My husband says they must have gone due north to Broadview, which is situated farther west on the railway line. They probably chose that route because the Broadview trail is less traveled than the one to Moosomin. We know this because your brother paid a man from the Broadview livery stable to return the conveyance Mr. Julian Chesterman borrowed from the Beresfords. The liveryman said the last he saw of the pair they were on the station platform, awaiting a train going west."

Millie's eyes widened. "Why, that may have been the same train I traveled on!"

Despite Carina's many questions, her aunt was not able to give any further details. The conversation was cut short by the entrance of Tucker carrying the luggage.

Cannington, Thursday, July 31, 1884

If I thought Millie would be dismayed at finding herself plunged into the midst of the turmoil surrounding Maud's sudden taking off, I was quite wrong, just as I was wrong about the delay on the trail because of the fire. Millie confided that from the moment she stepped on the train west, she was overwhelmed by a sense of liberation. None of the hardships and setbacks along the way diminished her exhilaration of her new-found freedom. She was glad to be out from under her mother's thumb. I expressed

222 - Michael Montcombroux

surprise, saying that Mrs. Vanderhagen always seemed
like an easy-going person. Millie said friction had arisen
between her and her mother because of her mother's
frequent dinner parties, when she would invite her
theatrical friends and acquaintances to her Montreal
apartment. The mother accused Millie of flirting with
the gentlemen and complained they paid more attention
to Millie than to their hostess. Millie said, "It was very
unfair. I did nothing to encourage the attention of the
gentlemen." No, Millie, you didn't deliberately
encourage them. Flirting comes to you as naturally as
breathing. Millie mentioned that one of her mother's
female friends was extremely amorous toward her,
something that angered the mother. I've heard that
Sapphic love is not uncommon among women of the
stage. Yet another strange world!

What also surprised me was how Millie responded
when she met Sybil. Mrs. Halliday, insisting that she did
not wish to be a burden on the family at this time of
crisis, has moved back to the Mitre Inn. We still see a lot
of her, and Millie and Sybil are getting along like a
house on fire, despite the difference in their ages. Both
share a love for fine clothes in the very latest styles. In
their different ways they each possess a vivacious
beauty that attracts admiring glances from men.

Despite the turmoil over Maud, Millie's presence
in the settlement hasn't gone unnoticed. The moment
Mr. Rodney Beresford set eyes on Millie, he invited her,
along with myself and Sybil, to afternoon tea at
Inglesbury. His brother Algernon is still away in
Ottawa, so it was just the four of us in the mansion's
spacious sitting room. He sent a carriage for us (not the
sporty curricle, which is a two-seater).

It transpires that the brothers don't employ any permanent domestic staff, other than the stable hands. The men shift for themselves, and when a waiter is needed, they press one of Captain Pierce's agricultural students into service, which is quite droll. The young gentlemen, all from wealthy families, quite clearly grew up accustomed to having servants but are perfectly happy to play the part when needed. The gentlemen, however, draw the line at cleaning and dusting. Ellie and a couple of the women from the settlement go to the big house twice a week to scrub floors and generally tidy the place.

On the occasion of our visit, Sybil wore a demure white lace tea gown and an extremely wide-brimmed hat adorned with silk roses (Millie shared with me privately that such hats are now all the rage in Montreal). Mr. Beresford, as usual, was impeccably attired in a cutaway gray coat, light-blue velvet trousers and white spats over brown boots. He greeted us ladies in a courteous manner with a low bow (only an Englishman can get away with that in Canada). Naturally, Mr. Rodney insisted on showing Millie the house, though this time, we omitted the visit to the gun room.

That evening, after dinner, Millie talked about how much she had enjoyed the afternoon and how impressed she was by the Beresfords' house. She had heard about Maud and wanted me to explain what happened to her. When I gave her a summary of the events, she looked surprised and said, "I would never have expected your brother Julian to do such a thing." - proving how Julian manages to fool everyone.

Millie then asked endless questions about the 'fascinating' Sybil Halliday. I explained how Sybil, in the company of my father and Mr. DeQuincy, arrived from Regina for a visit. When the men caught the train back to the capital, Sybil chose to prolong her stay in Cannington. I didn't feel inclined to talk about the murder and only hinted that an unpleasant incident had earlier taken place. She'll find out soon enough. Nor did I express my dislike for DeQuincy. He has gone now and I hope never to see him again.

I'm not entirely thrilled that Millie has attached herself to Sybil. So much about that woman remains a disturbing mystery. Yet, I'm not the girl's chaperone. To paraphrase the Bible: Am I my sister's keeper? No, of course not. She's free to do as she sees fit.

She did amuse me a couple of days ago after a chance meeting on the street with Sergeant Granger.

Afterwards, Millie said, "You know, I think the good sergeant is in love with you."

I laughed off the notion, but she insisted, "Aren't you aware of how he looks at you with those gray eyes of his? Well, I am. Why don't you marry him, Carina, darling." (Millie calls lots of people darling, a habit picked up from her actress mother). "He's by far the handsomest man I've come across in the Northwest."

"I don't happen to be in the marriage market. Even if I were, there's one small technicality as far as Sgt. Granger is concerned. Non-commissioned officers in the North-West Mounted Police are not permitted to marry. I can't imagine Sergeant Granger would want to sacrifice a career he loves."

"What a positively medieval notion, not allowed to get married!"

Although I shrugged off Millie's suggestion, I came to realize that I am strangely attracted to the gentleman. We are only a few years difference in age, and we seem to know what the other is thinking without the need for speech. And she's right about him being handsome. But, no, not for me.

Carina's concern over Millie's attachment to Sybil heightened after seeing her sitting next to Sybil in the yellow curricle, driving off toward the Beresford mansion. This occurred two days in a row. She quizzed Millie about her Inglesbury visits.

Millie's cheeks flushed red and she stumbled over her reply. "Oh, nothing very much happened. I just sat to one side as Mrs. Halliday and Mr. Beresford just, er, talked."

"Just sat to one side? Talked? That's an odd way to spend an afternoon."

"You're not upset, are you that I went on my own with Mrs. Halliday? Sybil did wonder if you'd care to join us. Mr. Beresford is a very fine gentleman and very entertaining. I'm sure he'd be more than happy to include you in our little circle."

"I'm quite sure he is, entertaining, that is. I enjoyed my visit the other day, as well as the earlier one but I've no great desire to repeat the experience."

"Then, you don't mind if I go? Sybil is a woman with such a broad understanding of the world. I've already learned so much from her."

Carina was tempted to press her friend for a more precise account of the visits she suspected weren't entirely innocent. She didn't, because, no matter what went on in the opulent mansion on the edge of the settlement, there was nothing she could do to prevent Millie from going there. In that respect, Millie could be as obdurate as Carina herself. To banish these concerns from her mind she saddled her horse and went riding.

A few days later, she was returning from one such outing when she spotted a telltale plume of dust to the north-east that indicated someone approaching on the trail from Moosomin. Since she had time on her hands she let curiosity get the better of her and altered direction to intercept the visitors. From the dust she could tell there was more than one rider or carriage. As they drew closer, Carina saw that the party consisted of a two-horse carriage accompanied by three men on horseback. She waited and was able to recognize the occupants of the carriage as Maud and her father. One of the riders was Carina's brother Julian, looking awkwardly out of place on horseback. The other two riders were Cannington men whom she knew by sight only.

Carina touched her heels to Morgana's flanks and rode forward to meet the cavalcade. As she came level with them she wheeled and fell in beside the carriage. "Hello, uncle, hello, Maud."

Her uncle kept his attention fixed on his horses but acknowledged her with a wave of his whip. Maud smiled and mouthed a greeting before averting her gaze, but not before Carina saw the downcast expression on her face. Carina dropped back and looked across at her brother. His jaw was set in a way that made it clear he wasn't inclined to talk. From his pained expression, she guessed he must also be saddle-sore from the long ride from Moosomin. As a youth, Julian had never shown much enthusiasm for learning to ride and was obviously paying for it now.

The Cannington man on her side of the carriage smiled a greeting and saluted her by raising a gloved hand to his hat brim. Carina rode beside him in silence. In this manner they entered the settlement and rode up the main street to the Addersley house. Their passing turned several heads of the people in the street. The two Cannington riders took their leave and continued to their respective homes. The carriage, Julian and Carina entered the stable yard.

Norman Tucker took charge of the carriage horses. Julian threw himself off his horse, tied the reins to a hitching post and barked an order to Tucker before limping across the street to the Mitre Inn. Because Mr. Tucker was busy with the other horses, Carina removed Morgana's saddle and bridle. She brushed down the mare before leading her into the paddock behind the house. By the time she took her saddle and bridle to the tack room, her uncle and Maud had gathered up their bags and gone into the house.

Tucker met Carina's eyes. His weathered face creased into a grin. "Don't expect much mirth from that quarter tonight."

Carina entered the house eager to hear the news. She found her uncle and aunt in the the living room. Alfred Addersley stood in front of the empty fireplace, feet astride, hands clasped behind his back. Carina had never seen him so stern. Her aunt sat primly on the sofa, her eyes fixed on her husband. Maud was nowhere in sight. Carina assumed she had gone, or been sent, to her room. Millie was absent and Carina guessed she and Sybil had gone to the Beresfords.

Her Uncle Alfred's features softened when Carina said, "Do you wish me to leave you alone, uncle?"

"No, no, my dear, you may as well hear the sorry tale. By the way, that was most civil of you to ride out to meet us. I'm sure Maud was touched by the gesture."

Rosalind's face showed her irritation at the delay in receiving the news. "Alfred, do tell how and where you tracked down the errant pair and what transpired."

"I was correct in my assumption I'd find the pair in Regina. It was the obvious place for them to go. Young Mr. Chesterman is employed by a company in that city and must be familiar with it. The railway station agent confirmed they'd detrained in the capital, though he could furnish no other details. Fortunately, Regina is still sufficiently small to be able trace someone with not too much difficulty. After making inquiries, we, my colleagues and I, found Maud and Mr. Chesterman in a somewhat less-than-savory rooming-house overlooking the freight yards."

Aunt Rosalind clapped her hand to her mouth. "My God! Our worst fears realized. What happened next?"

"I won't trouble you with the tedious details but, after considerable discussion between myself and the young gentleman on the subject of salvaging our family's honor, Mr. Julian Chesterman agreed to marry our daughter."

Aunt Rosalind let out a low wail, reached for her handkerchief and collapsed against the back of the sofa.

Carina's spirits sank. Julian marry Maud! She couldn't see how that could lead to happiness for either of them, least of all for Maud, for whom she had developed considerable affection. She asked, "Forgive me, uncle, but was there no other alternative?"

Alfred shook his head. "I only wish there were. Maud's virtue has been severely compromised by her rash behavior. There has never been a fallen woman in the Addersley family and there never will be if I have any say in the matter. As soon as I have recovered from what was a dashed wearisome journey, I shall go and speak to Mr. Featherstonehaugh about arranging for a speedy wedding. Fortunately, although Maud and Mister Julian are related, they are sufficiently remote as cousins that the church can raise no objection. The proposed union falls outside the forbidden degrees of consanguinity."

Carina heard all she needed to hear. She went up to her room and changed out of her riding habit. The door to Maud's room remained shut and Carina thought it best to postpone any discussion with her.

Chapter 24

The tense atmosphere that pervaded the Addersley residence persisted long after Maud and her father returned. To find some respite, Carina took her book into the garden and spent an hour reading. She had not been there long when Maud came looking for her. It was the first time they been able to talk in private.

Carina put down her book and stood up. "Maud, I'm at a loss for words to express my sadness over what has happened."

Much to her surprise, Maud burst out laughing.

"Why be sad? I am going to marry your brother. You and I will be sisters-in-law as well as cousins. Isn't that exciting?"

Carina took Maud's hand and dragged her down onto the bench. "Maud, I don't think you fully understand. I'm concerned for you because I don't think you fully appreciate what kind of a man my brother is."

Maud creased her brow. "What do you mean? Julian is a wonderful man. You should be proud to have him as a brother."

"Julian has many fine qualities but he'll break your heart. For one thing, he's never been able to focus on one line of work for very long."

"He convinced papa that he has great prospects working for Mr. DeQuincy."

"He had great prospects training to be a lawyer, but he's already turned his back on law school. Earlier, he had great prospects for a career in banking, but he quit after a few months. My brother has a grasshopper mind. His attention span is restricted to what he finds interesting at the moment."

Without openly slandering Niven DeQuincy, Carina hinted that Maud's husband-to-be was in the employ of a man with dubious personal morals and questionable business ethics. She omitted that the man was a prime murder suspect as well. That might not ensure conjugal bliss. Because she could see that Maud was in thrall to Julian's charismatic charm, she didn't dwell on the negative aspects of her brother's character. To alienate Maud would achieve nothing.

"Your father says he's going to speak to Mr. Featherstonehaugh."

Maud eyes sparkled. "He already has. First thing this morning."

"And..?"

"The rector says he can obtain a special license for us from the bishop. The wedding will be held just as soon as it arrives. In just a matter of days."

Carina gave a laugh. "Just think, Mr. Featherstonehaugh was until recently on your list of eligible suitors."

"Yes, and now he's going to have to officiate at my marriage to someone else. Life is funny, isn't it?"

"Perhaps he doesn't think so."

"You'll be my bridesmaid, won't you?"

"Of course, I'd love to. Only, my wardrobe contains nothing suitable for a wedding."

"Don't worry. Your everyday clothes will do. That's what I shall be wearing. Papa said that the ceremony is going to be *severely curtailed*. Those were his actual words. No bridal gown, no elaborate decorations in the church or at the wedding breakfast, which is going to be a small affair held here at the house. He was quite blunt in saying I'd behaved no better than a harlot and that the sooner I was married the sooner I could begin the redeem myself."

"The poor man is concerned about your family's honor."

"All very nice talking about family honor. What about my happiness?"

"I'm sure he wants only what's best for you. Perhaps you'll be the steady influence Julian needs. Whatever happens, I'll always be your friend."

Maud grasped Carina's hands in both hers. "And I really value your friendship."

"Maud!" A woman's voice sounded from the house door.

Maud stood up. "That's mama. I have to go. We'll talk more later."

During her stay in Cannington, Carina had on more than one occasion remarked how quickly the English colonists resumed the regular pace of activities following a crisis. Such was the case now in the Addersley household. The family gathered around the dining table for luncheon and dinner as though nothing untoward had happened. Her Uncle Alfred soon reverted to being his old jocular self, and even Aunt Rosalind smiled as if she hadn't a care in the world. Cannington society dropped back into its customary routine of cricket matches, tennis parties and afternoon tea visits. Carina sensed this air of unreality and had to remind herself that an unsolved murder hung over the seemingly idyllic village. She saw nothing of her brother in the days leading up to the wedding, though Sybil reported, with a laugh, that she had spotted him at Inglesbury in the company of the bachelors. "Probably enjoying the last of his freedom."

Carina's previous involvement in weddings was limited to the nuptials of a few friends and friends of friends. One common feature of those events had been the frenetic activity leading up to the important day, involving the labor of a legion of dressmakers, caterers, attendants and musicians. Hours were taken up in the dispatch of hundreds of gilt-edged invitations and the writing of place cards for the wedding breakfast. Then there was the obligatory attendance at church rehearsals. None of this happened in the case of Maud's wedding. It was as if everyone had forgotten about the matter, though her uncle assured Carina that everything that needed to be done had been taken care of. The following Saturday was the selected date. Just as Maud had said, it was to be a simple ceremony at All Saints' followed by a modest reception at the Addersley residence. The guest list could hardly have been shorter, consisting of family members and a handful of close friends. Out of courtesy, Millie and Sybil were included.

Carina's unofficial role, as explained to her by Aunt Rosalind, was to stay close to the bride from the moment the girl got out of bed on Saturday until later that morning after the minister had pronounced the couple man and wife. Maud was allowed a modest bouquet of wildflowers. A vase of chrysanthemums would adorn the drawing room mantelpiece. That was the extent of the floral arrangements.

Carina was quietly amused to discover that her uncle, notwithstanding his status as one of the settlement's leaders, had misjudged his fellow countrymen with regard to their love of pomp and circumstance. Although uninvited, a large number of Cannington's inhabitants descended on the church early on Saturday morning and decorated the interior and the doorway with colorful garlands of flowers culled from their gardens. They tied white satin bows to the ends of the pews and draped streamers of daisies from the lectern and pulpit. They then informed Alfred that they had organized a more conventional wedding breakfast to be held in the assembly hall so that the entire population could attend and celebrate the nuptials. Alfred acquiesced with a shrug.

On the morning of the wedding, Carina rose early. When she was dressed she went to Maud's room and was surprised to find her cousin up and getting dressed with the assistance of Millie. Carina left them to discuss the merits of one plain dress over another and went down to breakfast, satisfied that Maud was in good hands.

At the foot of the stairs she came to an abrupt halt. The door of her uncle's study stood open. Standing with his back to her and in conversation with her uncle was the last man she expected, or desired, to meet: Niven DeQuincy.

Alfred looked over his visitor's shoulder and caught sight of her. "Ah, there you are, Carina, dear. Good morning. Please come in here a moment. Mr. DeQuincy would like a few words with you."

Effectively trapped, Carina entered the study.

DeQuincy acknowledged her with an inclination of the head. "Good day, Miss Chesterman. A pleasure to meet you again. Your father asked me to convey a message to you."

"How is he?"

"As well as can be expected. He sends his regrets that he is not well enough to make the long journey from Regina. It pains him that he is unable to be present at his son's wedding and, of course, to see you. I offered to come in his place, not that anyone can replace a father at a time like this."

"That is considerate of you, sir."

She noticed a muscle in his face twitch imperceptivity. His mission might well be to carry her father's regrets at being unable to attend the wedding but, she guessed his real motive for coming had more to do with her. She had no intention of letting down her guard. Hopefully, the presence of Sybil would be sufficient to deflect his attention. She made a mental note to warn Millie about him.

He held out his hand, clearly hoping she would place hers in it. When she didn't he thrust his hand into his trouser pocket. "I shall be staying in Cannington for a few days. If your uncle approves, we could renew our acquaintance by taking a carriage ride together? The countryside here is so beautiful at this time of year."

Alfred muttered a few words of approval.

Carina took a step backward as a way of emphasizing her remoteness from DeQuincy. "I'm sorry, Mr. DeQuincy, that is out of the question. At the moment I have a friend visiting from Montreal. I cannot neglect my responsibility to ensure her stay is as enjoyable as possible. And I am also the bride's attendant."

DeQuincy clenched his jaw but said nothing.

Carina left the two men and went into the breakfast room.

The wedding ceremony took place at eleven o' clock. Bertrand Lee stood in as Julian's best man. If Carina read the signs correctly, her brother was not moved by the general air of excitement around him. Those knitted brows and tight lips masked a sour mood. She wondered whether he was suffering jitters at being the center of so much attention or was angry because he had been forced into marrying Maud. Yet the unhappiest-looking person in the tiny church, in Carina's estimation, was the minister himself. In a voice more suited to a funeral, Mr. Featherstonehaugh intoned the ancient words of the Church of England wedding service. "Dearly beloved, we are gathered together here in the sight of God, and in the face of this congregation, to join together this man and this woman in Holy Matrimony."

With a certain dread, Carina watched her brother and Maud be united. Afterward, the newlyweds walked down the aisle and out into the sunlight. To add to the ceremony, the couple were obliged to pass beneath an arch formed by the bachelors holding aloft polo mallets. Those well-wishers unable to get into the church, stood in the grassy churchyard and applauded the happy pair.

From there, the wedding party, the guests, both those officially invited and the self-invited, covered the short distance to the assembly hall on the other side of the street.

Cannington, Saturday, August 2, 1884 (close to midnight)

An incident happened toward the close of today's wedding reception that was so disturbing I can hardly believe what I heard.

Despite my uncle's attempts to the contrary, the wedding breakfast followed a more traditional pattern, with a ceremonial cutting of a hastily-baked and decorated cake, speeches (my uncle kept his to no more than two minutes) and toasts. No one seemed to be in the least perturbed that the bride had run away and had been living under the same roof (and most likely, having been intimate) with the groom before they were legally married. My uncle and aunt's fears that the family reputation was forever tarnished appeared unfounded. Yet I'm no expert in how these English people behave in times of crisis. I've noticed before how they keep what uncle calls a 'stiff upper lip,' which is another term for stoicism. So, on the surface, things look normal but underneath, who knows? Certainly, in Westmount a similar situation would have resulted in the guilty parties being socially ostracized. Cannington, an isolated settlement, may follow a different set of rules from what might have happened in England or back East.

The dramatic event I allude to took place in the evening in the assembly rooms when things were beginning to wind down. For most of the time, Sybil had kept Mr. DeQuincy company and out of my hair, for which I was grateful. When she was preparing to leave, she found that she had left her silk shawl in the ladies' cloakroom. At that moment, Mr. DeQuincy, who was on the other side of the room in conversation with a man I didn't recognize, not someone from the settlement, turned and walked across the floor to where Sybil and I were. To avoid meeting the gentleman, I offered to fetch Sybil's shawl.

The cloakroom is a windowless room off the main hall. I was there rummaging through the pile of ladies coats and other garments draped over the back of a long sofa, when I heard DeQuincy's voice in the corridor outside the door. I was having difficulty finding Sybil's shawl and had gone behind the sofa to see if it had fallen. While thus engaged, the door opened and two men entered. They didn't see me and I had just enough time to dip down out of sight. I heard DeQuincy speaking angrily with none other than Julian!

"I don't give a shit if it's your wedding night. You saddle up a horse and get out there. I've just spoken to Gibb. He informs me the wagon train has arrived in Holsten. The drivers are waiting for their delivery instructions. That's your job. I don't want that much liquor sitting there with the mounted police snooping around. This consignment is special, ninety-percent proof, not your usual rotgut whiskey. You'll find the wagons gathered at the north end of town. I have armed guards watching the compound. To contact the drivers just ask at the hotel. One of the wagons is carrying a special cargo to be forwarded on to the Métis on the

North Saskatchewan. Give that one your careful attention. Do you understand?"

I heard Julian reply in a meek voice. "Okay, Niven, you're the boss."

"When it's all over and everything is safely delivered, you can take a few days off and enjoy your new lady. I suppose having a second pair of bare legs in the bed will knock some of the craziness out of you. Don't mess up this deal. I've not had a shipment as big or as important as this one."

I heard the scrape of a match and a minute later smelled the smoke of a cigar. Then Niven's voice again. "Send word the moment everything has gone through."

The door opened and closed. I didn't dare stand up because I didn't know if one of them was still in the room. I waited some more before looking. I was alone in the room.

In retrospect, I could have run after Julian to tell him I overheard everything and say that what he was doing was illegal. I didn't because Julian had shown no respect for me and I was sure he'd only bluster and deny everything.

After delivering Sybil her shawl, Carina made her escape from the reception hall and walked back to the house. She found Norman Tucker sitting on a bench outside the stable door, taking in the early evening air. He held his unlit pipe in his fingers.

"Well, Miss Carina, did you see your brother and Miss Maud properly hitched?"

"Yes, thank you, it all went smoothly. Tell me, Mr. Tucker, do you know of a place called Holsten?"

"Holsten? Sure, it's a settlement to the west of here. Not much of a town, though. It used to act as a staging post on the trail that comes up from the Dakota Territory before the Canadian

Pacific rail line came through. In those days, goods used to come up the Missouri by sternwheeler and then overland by ox-team from Bismarck. The place hummed with activity. Nowadays, it don't see much traffic."

"How long would it take to drive to Holsten from here?"

Tucker pocketed his pipe and stood up. "Now, why would you be wanting to visit Holsten? It's not like it's picturesque or anything."

Carina touched the old man's sleeve. "Mr. Tucker, I can't explain right now."

Tucker grinned. "You're quite a gal, ain't you? Anyhow, it's an easy five-hour drive. Pick up the trail that skirts the north side of Moose Mountain. It then angles down to the south-west. Plenty of watering spots along the way, even in this drought."

She thought for a moment then said, "Would you do me a big favor?"

"You're just like my granddaughter Ellie. She knows I'm a sucker for a pretty girl's smile. What d'you need?"

"Cyrus harnessed to the democrat and ready at dawn tomorrow. And please don't mention anything of this to my uncle. I'll explain when I return."

"You planning traveling on your own?"

"With Miss Vanderhagen."

Tucker nodded. "All right. I reckon this must be important to you, Miss Carina. Count on me. The buggy'll be waiting for you at first light."

Carina expressed her thanks and went in search of Millie.

Chapter 25

Much to Carina's relief, the torrid weather moderated by the planned departure time. The pre-dawn air was unusually crisp when she and Millie crept out of the house. Millie wore a long dustcoat over her muslin dress. She carried her floral hat in her hand and wore a silk scarf over her hair.

Tucker proved to be as good as his word. Carina found him adjusting the bridle of Cyrus, who was harnessed to the democrat, not in the stable yard but in the street, a few yards down from the house.

"Mr. Tucker, I can't thank you enough."

The old man grinned. "I'm willing to help in whatever it is you're up to. I brought the buggy out here so that people in the house would be less likely to see or hear anything. Not that there's much danger of that. Long after you went to bed, they were carousing in the dining room."

"Really?"

"Well, more like commiserating with the bride. Her new husband was called away on business leaving her on her lonesome on her wedding night, poor gal."

Carina took hold of the reins while Norman helped Millie onto the seat. She herself was about to climb up when she hesitated.

"I forgot to bring food. We'll be out a long time."

"Don't fret. The missus made up a basket of grub for you both. It's behind the seat, as well as water."

"Please thank Mrs. Tucker for me. Oh, yes, I need some matches."

Norman raised one craggy eyebrow. "Matches? Taken up smoking, have you?" He pulled a box from his top pocket and offered it her. "Here you are."

"Bye, Mr. Tucker. If anyone asks, we'll be back later this evening. I'm showing Miss Vanderhagen the countryside."

Norman winked at her. "Yes, of course. Holsten is a real mecca for tourists."

He stepped back and waved farewell. To minimize the sound of hoof beats, Carina let the gelding take his own pace along the empty street. The rubber-tired wheels rolled noiselessly over the dirt surface. Only when they were beyond the tennis courts and cricket ground at the western edge of the settlement did she encourage the horse to quicken his pace.

Millie turned her dark eyes on Carina. "Now, can you tell me what it is we're doing?"

Over the next several minutes, Carina explained how Julian was in trouble and would be in even more trouble if he followed Niven DeQuincy's orders. Although she made no mention of it to Millie, she had read in the newspapers that the unrest to the north was worsening. To throw several wagonloads of potent whiskey into the mix might be enough to precipitate the uprising the Regina paper was warning against.

Millie wrinkled her nose. "I understand but I fail to see how two girls like us can do anything to stop a wagon train that is protected by armed guards."

"We'll have to see about that once we arrive."

Carina had no difficulty finding the trail. From the lack of wheel marks, she guessed it was not heavily traveled. There was one steep rise close to Moose Mountain but afterwards the trail undulated over the prairie, no different from the arid regions to the north and south of Cannington.

They made periodic stops to rest and water the horse. The gelding grazed the grass on the side of the trail while Carina and Millie ate some of the food Mrs. Tucker had provided.

The air warmed up as the morning advanced but the sky remained overcast. Carina had the impression that for the first time in weeks it might rain, but she didn't share her thoughts with Millie. Although the democrat was equipped with a light canopy, Carina guessed it would afford scant protection in the event of a downpour. For the moment, the prospect of rain was not uppermost in her mind. After several hours of travel, she believed she could make out, in the far distance, buildings which marked their destination, the tiny hamlet of Holsten.

She remained silent until they got closer. "When we reach the town we have to figure out where the wagons are, which may not be too difficult. DeQuincy said they were on the north side."

Millie pointed to the settlement. "You call that a town?"

"It's what passes for one out here. Though, don't expect to find an opera house and a park with fountains. I just hope we're not too late. Julian has a head start on us and he rode through the night."

"We too could have left last evening."

"It wouldn't have been a good idea. Julian had someone to guide him, a man called Gibb. On our own, we might never have found our way in the dark."

They approached the town from the north-east on a gradual downward slope. The closer they came the more desolate was the scene. Many of the houses and businesses were boarded up or abandoned, giving settlement the appearance of a ghost town in the making. Only a smattering of pedestrians and carts in the main street showed it was inhabited.

"Look over there." Carina pointed to the right, through a gap between two derelict houses. "That's what we've come for."

Close to a weathered barn that had seen better days, extended a yard bordered by a wooden fence. Looming above the fence were the bulky shapes of heavy wagons laden with oaken casks, some of which were sheeted over with tarpaulins.

"How many wagons do you think there are?" Millie asked.

"At least a dozen, maybe more."

Millie straightened on the seat. "Don't look now but there are a couple of men carrying guns standing by the gate. This is not going to be easy. I can tell."

"First we leave the horse and buggy at the livery stable. That is, if there is one."

"Then what?"

"We make a detour on foot to get back to the enclosure. If we keep this line of buildings between us and them, we'll be out of sight of the guards."

Carina swung the democrat into the main street. Half way down on the left a sagging sign advertised a livery stable. A sullen-faced young man came out as the democrat drew up.

Carina climbed down. "We're not staying long. I'd like to be on my way in under an hour."

The youth nodded but his expression didn't change. "Anything you say, ma'am. The price is the same whether it's thirty minutes or three hours."

"You can park the buggy on the street. It doesn't appear to be very busy."

"You ain't kidding. Place is near dead." He gave a mirthless laugh and spat a stream of tobacco juice into the dust. "It's time I moved on, but my paw's sick."

"I'm sorry to hear that."

The stable man looked at her closely, then at Millie still on the seat. His face became animated. "Hey, we don't get many folk passing through no more, 'specially classy-lookin' wimmin on their own."

Carina thought it best to head off any probing questions. She asked the livery charge and paid him in advance. "Let's go, Millie."

The young man's eyes bulged from his head as he watched Millie step down, exposing in the process a shapely ankle clad in silk stocking. He looked even more dumbstruck when she removed the dustcoat, threw it onto the seat of the democrat and smoothed out her dress.

On another occasion, Carina might have been repelled by the man's vulgar manner. Yet, the way he ogled Millie gave her an idea of how to go about sabotaging the whiskey wagons.

She handed the stable man the reins. With a spring in his step, he began to unhitch the horse. Carina linked arms with Millie. "All right, let's start our work. Take your parasol. I know there's no sun but it looks good."

The two young women walked back up the street. They hadn't taken more than a dozen steps when Carina stopped and swung Millie around. "Look at that."

Millie stared blankly. "A blacksmith's shop. What's special about that?"

"Tools, we need a tool to get through the wooden fence."

"Can't we squeeze through the gaps?"

"Only one of us is going inside and, no, the boards appear too close for that."

"No one's about. Help yourself."

Carina entered the open-front shop and picked up an iron pry-bar from the anvil. It was some eighteen inches long and used, she guessed, to remove horseshoe nails. She tucked the bar into the folds of her skirt to be less conspicuous. They reached the corner and, shielded by the row of buildings, reached the side fence of the wagon compound without being seen.

The harness poles and axle trees of the wagons were lashed with ropes in an upright position to enable the wagons to be drawn closer together in serried ranks. Carina studied the layout through a knothole in one of the boards. After determining that it would be difficult but not impossible to pass down the lines of wagons, she took Millie's hand and led the way to the corner of the compound. From behind a scrawny hawthorn bush, she took a quick look and saw two guards talking to each other in front of the entrance gate.

She and Millie retreated some thirty feet back from the corner, where Carina found a fence board hanging by a couple of rusty nails. It scarcely made a sound when she levered it free. The resulting gap was wide enough for her to squeeze through.

Carina whispered in Millie's ear. "It looks like there are just two guards at the gate. There might be others out of sight. This is what we do. I want you to walk out onto the side road, then turn the corner and pass in front of the entrance. I'll leave it up to you how you attract the attention of the guards and keep them distracted long enough for me to slip inside and deal with the wagons. Have you got that?"

"You mean all I have to do is keep those two men occupied?"

"Can you devise a way to do that?"

A smile formed on Millie's lips. "I'll do my best."

"Good."

"How will I know when you've got back out?"

"Don't worry. That will be made plain enough. We'll meet back on the road out of sight of the entrance. From there we return to the livery stable. Ready?"

Millie snapped open her parasol. "Yes, ma'am!"

"Just a moment, I need your petticoat. I'm not wearing one."

Millie's face went blank. "My petticoat?"

"It's for a good cause. You'll learn all about it afterwards. Hurry, take it off."

"Hold this." Millie handed Carina her parasol. Then, supporting herself with one hand on the fence, she pulled her embroidered cotton petticoat from under her dress. "This cost me all of two weeks' allowance."

Carina took the petticoat and handed back the parasol. She sent her friend on her way with a gentle push in the small of her back and waited until she walked out onto the road. Millie waved to show that she was about to begin. Taking care to make no noise, Carina crept up to the corner and watched Millie saunter in front of the compound as casually as if she were out for a Sunday stroll.

There was now only one guard at the gate. Carina saw that he was hunched over lighting a cigarette, oblivious to the advance of the girl in the white dress. When he straightened and saw Millie, the cigarette fell from his lips. His expression was of a man who doesn't believe what he's seeing.

After a moment he recovered from his stupefaction. "Hello, l'l miss, what brings you here?"

Millie feigned surprise at seeing the man. "Oh, you startled me! There's so few people around. I came to visit my auntie but I've forgotten where her house is."

By now the other sentry, who was at the far corner of the compound saw what was happening and hurried to join his fellow guard at the entrance.

Carina guessed that her friend had inherited some of her actress-mother's talent, for she let out a shriek and pretended to twist her ankle.

The first guard propped his rifle against the gate and rushed to her aid. "Honey, are you okay?"

Millie clutched the man's arm. "I wasn't watching where I was going and hurt my ankle. And I think I've broken the heel of my shoe." Millie gave a heart-wrenching wail. "And they're a brand new pair."

"Here, sweetie, I'll hold you while you take your shoe off. Maybe I can fix it for you."

Millie rewarded him with a smile. "Oh, thank you, sir. You're such a kind man."

Satisfied that the guards would be preoccupied for some minutes, Carina retreated to the gap in the fence. As she was about to step through, her toe snagged a heap of dry tumbleweed at the base of the boards. She tucked Millie's petticoat under her arm and scooped up an armful of the tumbleweed and dry grass to use as tinder.

Once inside the compound, she was able pass down the narrow space between the back of one row of wagons and the front of the next. A few of the casks were leaking and the smell of whiskey was overpowering. At what she guessed must be the center of the group of wagons she came to a passage between the lines that led to the main gate. At this point the sentries had set one of the smaller casks on its side. A wooden spigot allowed them to sample the contents, liberally judging by the mess of spilt liquor.

Without wasting a moment, Carina threw down her bundle of dry vegetation and opened the tap. The amber spirit gushed out, spilling over the wagon wheel and soaking the tumbleweed and grass. Next, she tore Millie's precious petticoat into strips. These she tied together to form a long rope. If what DeQuincy had said was true and the whiskey was of high quality, her fuse would ignite and burn easily.

With the fuse now completely drenched, she fastened one end of it to a wheel spoke and paid it out as she crept back the way she had come. Along the way she used her pry-bar to smash open the bung of as many of the casks as she could. By the time she reached the end of the fuse, a veritable cascade of whiskey was emptying itself into the gap between the wagons.

Her breath came in short gasps when she straightened to survey her handiwork. Now came the moment of truth. She carefully dried her hands on her skirt and pulled Tucker's box of matches from her pocket. With trembling fingers, she grasped half a dozen matches and raked them along the side of the box. They immediately burst into flame. After counting to five, she threw them onto the alcohol-impregnated fuse.

The sudden ignition of the spirits threw her back against a wagon. A hot, blue-tinged flame danced in the air. She spun on her heel and made her escape. Only when she reached the fence did she look back. The entire alley was engulfed in flame. Acrid smoke swirled up from the pile of tumbleweed that she had used as an accelerant.

She gave a tight smile of satisfaction and squirmed through the gap in the fence. As fast as she could she ran to the corner. From her vantage point, she saw Millie balancing on one foot, with one of the two guards holding her raised leg. The other man had his arms around her waist and was trying to kiss her.

The sentry broke off his amorous advances jerked back his head. "What in hell's name is that?"

The second man pointed to the smoke rising from the compound. "Holy shit, the wagons are on fire!"

At that moment, the first cask exploded. A ball of flame mushroomed into the sky. The guard dropped Millie's leg and he and his companion rushed to the gate.

Millie staggered back but kept her balance. She bent down, picked up her shoe and lifted it above her head. "Hey! What about me?"

"Millie, over here!"

Millie saw Carina waving. She jammed her foot back into her shoe, picked up her skirts and ran to Carina. She pointed to the cloud of flame and smoke. "You did that?"

"With the help of your underwear. Now, let's get out of here."

By the time they had put the line of houses between them and the enclosure, the entire compound was engulfed in flames. The smoke from burning wood carried with it the sweet odor of whiskey. Amid the din of bursting casks came another sound, a series of sharp cracks like that of exploding fireworks.

Breathless with excitement, Carina and Millie reached the main street. The previously-empty street now was alive with men running toward the fire. No one paid attention to the two women on the boardwalk walking in the opposite direction.

When they passed the blacksmith's shop, Carina replaced the borrowed iron bar where she had found it on the anvil. At the livery stable, the attendant balanced on one foot, torn between wanting to investigate the cause of the commotion, yet fearing to leave his post.

Carina motioned to the column of smoke spiralling into the gray sky and, with false naivety, said, "Someone must have been careless with matches."

"You can say that again."

"I'm sure the fire department will quickly extinguish the flames."

The young man gave an incredulous laugh. "Fire department? This one-horse town ain't got no fire department."

"That's too bad. Could I trouble you to harness my buggy? This frightful smoke is soiling our clothes."

The man glanced at Mille and back to Carina. "Sure, ma'am. You got the right idea to git out of town. Nothing good ever happens here."

Ten minutes later, Carina and Millie were on the trail, with the town behind them. Carina reined in the horse when they reached the top of the incline. By now the flames had engulfed the entire compound. A column of smoke rose from the burning whiskey wagons.

"Do you think Julian is down there?" Millie asked.

"If he was, I hope he had the sense to get away as fast as he could."

Millie stretched out her palm. "Do you feel that? It's starting to rain. That would be the first rain since I arrived here."

"From the look of those clouds, we may be in for quite a storm."

Chapter 26

Had a hardy reveller been leaving the Mitre Inn in the early hours of the morning, he would have seen an exhausted gelding pulling a mud-splattered democrat up the street. In it sat two shivering young women, drenched to the skin from the slanting rain. They, however, didn't mind being soaked in the least. The rain had washed off the smell of smoke and the soot that clung to their clothes. Carina in particular was glad that there was no longer any trace of the whiskey that had splashed on her skirt.

She half-expected to see Norman Tucker waiting for them at the stable door and was thankful when he wasn't. The obliging old man deserved his rest on such a foul night. Millie stood by while Carina unhitched the horse from the shafts and stripped off the harness. Normally, she would have turned Cyrus into the paddock. On this occasion, she led him into the stable, where Tucker had left a generous portion of oats, as well as hay and water in one of the stalls. She brushed her horse's rain-soaked flank and even pressed Millie into grooming the other side. Only then did the pair creep into the house by the kitchen door.

An oil lamp burned low. Its soft light fell on the sleeping figure of Ellie, her head resting on the table, one end which was covered by a gingham cloth with two place settings.

Carina accidently knocked a chair leg. The noise woke the girl.

"Ellie, what are you doing up at this hour?"

Ellie got to her feet and brushed her hair out of her eyes. "Waiting for you, miss. I was worried. My grandpa, too. When we saw the rain come on, we thought of you and Miss Millie out on that trail in the dark. Bad things can happen when it rains. The creeks rise quickly. It took me a long time to persuade my grandpa to go to bed."

Carina hugged the girl. "That was very thoughtful of you, Ellie, of you and your grandfather."

Ellie's eyes lit up. "I made you some supper. It's still warm on the stove."

"We'd both welcome something to eat, but first we have to change out of these wet clothes."

She and Millie took care not to disturb the rest of the house and went up to their rooms. A short while later they were seated at the kitchen table in front of steaming plates of Ellie's stew.

Cannington, Tuesday, August 5, 1884

A couple of days have elapsed since our return from our wild adventure in Holsten. Although the journey back was arduous in the extreme, I am glad of the rain because it would have prevented the fire from spreading to the town. With the tinder-dry conditions that was a real possibility. Holsten is not an imposing settlement but I wouldn't want to be the one who burned it to the ground.

I'm sorry to record that Millie came down with a severe chill and I do feel guilty about that. She seems cheerful enough and is enjoying being pampered in bed. Yesterday, Sybil came over from the hotel and sat with her during the morning.

The whole whiskey incident has an unreal air about it, as though it exists only in my imagination. Uncle Alfred breezily asked how we had enjoyed our outing, with as much interest as if we had simply driven out to Fish Lake and back. Julian hasn't come back, much to poor Maud's distress. Yesterday afternoon, I saw Mr. DeQuincy walking along the street with Sybil on his arm. So it's evident he hasn't yet received the news about his whiskey consignment. Or perhaps he has and doesn't consider it much of setback.

This may be the lull before the storm. Talking of which, the weather has worsened. It is now hot and heavy again and the rain comes down in buckets. Right now, a thunderstorm is rattling our windows.

Rain was still falling on Wednesday morning when Carina came downstairs. No one else was was about, save Mrs. Tucker in the kitchen.

"Good morning, Miss Carina, did you sleep well in spite of the storm?"

"Yes, thank you, Mrs. Tucker. Is the rest of the family still in bed?"

"No, quite the contrary. The master and Mrs. Addersley, along with the new Mrs. Chesterman have gone the Beresford mansion to talk to Mr. DeQuincy. He's lodging there."

"I suppose they're anxious about Julian."

"Since young Mr. Julian works for Mr. DeQuincy, they figured he might know what has become of him. Fancy a man taking off like that on his wedding night!"

"I agree, very unusual."

The conversation with Mrs. Tucker was interrupted by the entrance of Ellie. She wore a yellow rain slicker which dripped water onto the floor.

Mrs. Tucker took the canvas bag her granddaughter was carrying. "Ellie, go and shake your raincoat outside. You're wetting my nice clean floor."

The girl looked down at the puddle at her feet. "Sorry, grandma. I've been to the post office. There's a letter in the bag for Miss Carina."

Mrs. Tucker reached into the bag and handed Carina an official-looking envelope, postmarked Montreal. Carina stared at it for several moments. She shuddered, knowing full well the news it contained. The return address indicated it was from Mendelssohn, Mendelssohn and Chabot, attorneys at law, and that could mean only one thing. Carina went into the breakfast room and used a table knife to slit open the envelope. Inside was single sheet of heavy vellum notepaper bearing the law firm's letterhead. It began:

```
Dear Madam,

    It is my solemn duty to notify you of
the death on July 14, 1884 of your great-
aunt, Mrs. Louise Cornelia Willis, widow of
the late Frederick H. Willis, and formerly of
Number 3, Sycamore Drive, Westmount, in the
province of Quebec. As executor of Mrs.
Willis' estate, I have carried out the wishes
of the deceased and I am much obliged to
inform you that Mrs. Louise Cornelia Willis
has bequeathed to you an annuity based on
interest earned from shares invested in la
Companie maritime de Trois-Rivières, in the
province of Quebec. The exact figure for the
annual revenue from this source will be
tabulated once all matters relating to the
estate have been finalized. The annuity will
be made payable to you yearly in four
quarterly installments.
```

The remainder of the letter detailed how the money would be transferred to her and included a surprisingly personal intimation that the sum would be 'quite considerable.'

Carina sank onto a chair, her eyes fixed unseeingly on the plate of toast Mrs. Tucker had put in front of her. In her last letter, Aunt Louise wrote to say that she didn't expect to live much longer. Nonetheless, news of her demise still came as a shock, especially receiving it through the dry formality of a lawyer's letter. Carina knew that her aunt had no family members living close, only a few friends of her own age. She was filled with remorse for not being with her at the end, despite her aunt expressly forbidding her to consider returning. Her death severed Carina's last remaining link to Westmount and eastern Canada. More than that, it underlined the transitory nature of existence. When her mother was alive and the house buzzed with activity, Carina never imagined anything would change. She was filled with the assurance that the life she led was how it would always be. Even after her mother's death, there remained a sense of permanence about the gracious Westmount mansion and the tight social network that went with it. To add to the sense of permanence was the bank her father directed, with its imposing Corinthian columns. Yet, within the space of a few of months the whole façade had come crashing down. Her father was disgraced and had been sent into exile. The Westmount house sold, the furniture dispersed, the loyal servants dismissed.

She was reminded of Shelley's poem *Ozymandias* and the words: *Look on my works, ye Mighty, and despair!* / *Nothing beside remains: round the decay/ of that colossal wreck, boundless and bare, / The lone and level sands stretch far away.*

Shelley was writing about the Egyptian pharaohs of thirteenth century B.C., but his sentiments rang true for late nineteenth century Canada. Carina could imagine her father looking out, not over lone and level sands but the endless expanse of prairie grassland.

True, Millie and her mother still lived in Montreal, the larger city to which Westmount was attached. Millie was a friend, a good friend, but nothing more. A few days ago Millie had given hints that she may not return East, although she gave no indication of what she might do instead.

Carina forced herself to eat breakfast, after which she went to her room and put on stout shoes and the raincoat she had brought with her but never had the occasion to use. The only hat she possessed capable of keeping off the rain was her riding hat. Downstairs, she studied her reflection in the hallstand mirror and laughed. Although, were she to meet some of the Cannington ladies, their appearance in the downpour would probably be no less incongruous than her own.

She plucked one of the umbrellas from the stand and left the house. Outside, the street lay empty. So used was she to a sky of intense blue that the scudding dark clouds and driving rain gave the settlement a completely different aspect, one of somber gloom. Ogden Fenn, doubtless, would have reminded her that the precipitation was welcomed by the parched earth and dry vegetation just as much as the hot sunshine.

The desire to walk overrode any inconvenience of weather. Carina took the boardwalk in the direction of the west side of Cannington, past the steepled church, the inn and the general store, out toward the playing fields and racecourse, now eerily deserted.

By way of sublime catharsis, the sensation of raindrops wetting her cheeks soothed the grief over her loss. She remembered what her aunt had said about having lived a rich and rewarding life, together with the injunction not to grieve for her. Carina resolved to live up to her beloved aunt's example. Already, the decision to leave Cannington had been made. How she would have managed to do so with no income and no help from her father had been a major obstacle, but one she was prepared to overcome. Now, thanks to Aunt Louise's generosity, she had been granted a large measure of independence. It was up to her to use it responsibly.

By the time she reached the edge of the settlement her mood lightened. She knew what she had to do. First, she would wait until Millie returned to Montreal. Return she would, for Millie possessed few options. Once on her own, she, Carina, would carry out her plan to bid farewell to the English colony.

She paused where the settlement land gave way to wild prairie. In the distance, now veiled by curtains of rain, she could see the trees which encircled the Beresford house. For some reason she thought of Sybil Halliday. With the arrival of Niven DeQuincy, the yellow curricle no longer made its run to collect its daily passengers. Carina mentally shook off the thought. What Mrs.

Sybil Halliday did or didn't do was of no concern to her and she'd prefer to keep it that way.

For the return walk she took the boardwalk on the north side of the street. Close to the assembly hall but set back farther on the lot stood the North-West Mounted Police detachment. In contrast to a typical Cannington building, the police post was a small, unpretentious log building extended in front by a covered veranda. A sodden Union Jack flapped against the white flagpole.

As she drew level, a figure in a long coat came out of the door and cut across the grass toward her. She recognized Sergeant Granger.

"Miss Chesterman, may I have a word with you?"

Chapter 27

Carina waited in the rain for him to join her on the boardwalk. "Sergeant, you wanted to see me?"

"I'd like to talk to you."

"What about, may I ask?"

Dillon tilted his head to look at the sky. In doing so a small tidal wave of rainwater sluiced off his hat brim. "Maybe you'd be so kind as to step into the detachment? Inside is more conducive to talk than out here in this deluge."

"Certainly." She walked beside him up the gravel path to the police building. On the porch she folded her umbrella and shook it. "Nature never does anything in half measures in the West, does it?"

"This rainstorm sure is making travel a tad difficult." He held the door open for her and she stepped into the office.

The interior of the police detachment struck her as an exercise in male-inspired simplicity. One potbellied stove, one plain oak desk, one spindle-backed chair behind it and a matching chair against the wall, these few items, together with the file cabinet in the corner and the rifle rack next to it, comprised the sum total of the furnishings. That is, if one didn't include the line of brass coat hooks by the door. To one side a corridor led to what Carina assumed were the troopers' living quarters and the, probably never-used, holding cell. The modest office was immaculately clean. The wooden surfaces gleamed with polish.

She took off her hat and coat and hung them on one of the hooks, where they dripped water onto the floor.

Dillon pulled the spare chair to the front of the desk. "Please sit down." He took a seat behind the desk. "I have news of your brother, Mr. Julian Chesterman."

Carina leaned forward.

"He's under arrest at Mounted Police headquarters in Regina."

"Under arrest!"

"He turned Queen's evidence in the case against Mr. Niven DeQuincy for the latter's alleged involvement in importing illicit liquor, along with a quantity of firearms and ammunition."

"So, there were guns and ammunition in that wagon train!" Carina brought her hand to her mouth.

Dillon struggled to maintain a straight face. "For the moment, I'll gloss over the question of how you come to know about the shipment of whiskey and its fiery end a couple of days ago."

She now had the explanation for the firecracker-like detonations amid the exploding whiskey casks.

"What's going to happen next?"

Dillon gave a non-committal shrug. "That is up to the crown prosecutor to decide. My personal guess is that, considering the serious nature of the charges facing Mr. DeQuincy, and the unthinkable consequences had he succeeded, your brother's testimony has prevented a tragedy from occurring. In the light of that, Julian Chesterman is going to be treated with considerable leniency."

"Why was Mr. DeQuincy involved in whiskey and gun running, at all?"

"We haven't yet determined his precise motives but I believe it was connected with a desire to foment rebellion among the native population and the Métis, who, you must know, are already in a highly agitated state. If that can be proven, Mr. DeQuincy is open to a whole raft of charges, including conspiracy to commit treason. But I am getting ahead of myself and this conversation is strictly off the record."

"Has he been charged?"

"Not yet, because we have not apprehended the gentleman."

"But Mr. DeQuincy is right here in Cannington. My aunt and uncle have gone to talk to him about Julian. Why don't you go and arrest him?"

Dillon gave a tight grin. "Your aunt and uncle by now have found out that Mr. DeQuincy is no longer in the settlement, though he was here until quite recently. We have good reason to believe he may be on his way either to Regina or he may have decided to travel across the border to the United States. Either way, we are eager to question him."

"Thank you, sergeant, for telling me this. I am ashamed that my brother is mixed up in this horrible affair. Has your inquiry made any progress in linking Mr. DeQuincy with the murder of Mr. Ogden Fenn?"

"Unfortunately, no. Although some of the circumstantial evidence certainly does point to his involvement, we have no definite proof he did it. And as you are doubtless aware, without concrete evidence, the police are powerless to act. These are still early days and the patience of the police is boundless. We're hoping for a breakthrough."

She stood up and Dillon helped her on with her coat.

"May I tell my cousin Maud what has happened to her new husband?"

"I called at the house and have already informed her of the developments and that if she cares to go to the capital, she can pay the prisoner a visit. She'll find he's being treated well. Although the accommodation isn't ideal, it isn't that much different from what our average police trooper enjoys every day of the year."

Carina left the police detachment and walked home in a pensive mood. As she was hanging her wet coat and hat on the hallstand she heard the sound of music coming from the parlor. Through the open door she saw Maud at the piano, her back to Carina. Carina entered and stood beside her but remained silent.

Maud didn't lift her eyes from the keys. "Do you know this tune, Carina?"

"Isn't it *Simple Gifts*?"

"Yes, such a beautiful old Shaker hymn, so simple yet so profound." She began singing in a soft voice. "*'Tis the gift to be simple, 'tis the gift to be free, 'tis the gift to come down where we*

258 - Michael Montcombroux

ought to be. And when we find ourselves in the place just right, 'Twill be in the valley of joy and delight'... I can't remember the rest of the words."

"I do. Keep playing." Carina sang, echoing the same gentle tone Maud had used. "*When true simplicity is gained, to bow and to bend we shan't be ashamed. To turn, turn will be our delight. Till by turning, turning, we come 'round right.*"

"Yes, of course, how could I have forgotten? You have a lovely voice. To be candid, just lately, I've been doing quite a lot of *coming down*, haven't I?" She lifted her face and smiled at Carina, a smile tinged with sadness.

Carina smiled back. "You heard about Julian."

"Yes, just now, from Sergeant Granger. Despite everything, Julian did the best thing by turning himself in."

"Are you planning to go to see him in Regina?"

"Papa says we'll leave the day after tomorrow, that's Saturday."

Carina cupped Maud's hand with her own. "I'm so sorry all this happened to you. I tried to warn you against Julian."

"You did. You didn't know then that he was involved in criminal activities, did you?"

"No, but my brother has always had a wild streak in him. When I heard he was working for Niven DeQuincy, I feared something bad would come of it. Perhaps you ought to have married the minister, Mr. Featherstonehaugh, after all."

Maud swivelled on the stool and looked fiercely at Carina. "That sanctimonious prig! Before you came and gave me pointers on how to dress, he treated me as though I was invisible. Then, later, when he noticed a real woman existed under my formerly dowdy exterior, he got all hot under the dog collar. Since I didn't immediately swoon in his arms, he took to criticizing my appearance." Maud mimicked the clergyman's voice. "'Miss Addersley, your skirt is...ahem, showing too much ankle. Miss Addersley, that blouse you have on is – dare I say – cut too daringly?' That sort of thing. At least your brother is a red-blooded gentleman who admires me for what I am."

"Yet he's made you unhappy."

"I must confess I'm not thrilled at having a husband about to face a prison term. But I married him for better or for worse. I'll wait for him no matter how long it takes. Then we'll try to build a life together. I know it's not quite what father and mother would have wanted, and I feel sorry for having let them down."

Carina squeezed Maud's fingers. "If anyone can save Julian, it's you. You have my full admiration. I am confident things will turn out well."

With a laugh, Maud replayed, with more vigor this time, the final few bars of the Shaker hymn. "You see, just as you reminded me, by turning, turning, we come 'round right. I know things will work out."

Carina left Maud to her music and went up to her room to change into dry clothes.

The rain continued unabated throughout the day and the next, limiting outdoor activity to the occasional walk. Carina used the time to help Maud prepare for her trip to the capital. To fill the rest of the hours, she, Maud and Millie – when Millie was not with Sybil at the Beresford mansion – played cards, sang and conversed about nothing in particular.

When Carina awoke at dawn on Saturday morning and saw the first rays of the sun, her heart bounded for joy. She had dreaded the thought of Maud and her uncle having to make their journey in the rain. She knew from personal experience what misery it was to travel for hours in an open carriage in heavy rain. Her uncle had chosen to drive to Broadview not Moosomin, because he said the Broadview trail crossed only one small creek, which would certainly be in flood, but he was confident he could drive across it.

Cannington, Monday, August 11, 1884

Early on Saturday morning I waved goodbye to Maud as she and her father set off to catch the train to

Regina to visit Julian. When they had gone the house seemed strangely quiet and desolate. Of course, Millie is still here, and Sybil is across the street at the hotel, though I'd love to see the back of her. Buoyed by the change in the weather, Millie went shopping with Sybil, though in Cannington, shopping means visiting Mrs. Ripley the dressmaker. The Cannington general store carries an assortment of luxury goods, but not the kind sought after by Sybil and Millie.

Since I had had enough of being confined indoors, I saddled Morgana and went for a two-hour ride. The changes brought about by the rain took my breath away. As if overnight, verdant green had replaced the prevailing arid brown. Prairie wildflowers are in bloom everywhere. Nature is surprising in the way she can shed one coat and quickly put on another. Moose Mountain's previously gentle springs and brooks are now gushing torrents of white water.

Thus passed Saturday. On Sunday, Mrs. Tucker and Ellie were given the day off.

My aunt readied herself as usual for the eleven o' clock service at All Saints' and while she was pulling on her white kid gloves, gave me an imploring look. "Are you quite sure you won't join us, my dear? Mrs. Pierce has extended a luncheon invitation. I am positive she wouldn't mind in the least if you came along."

"That's very kind of you, Aunt Rosalind. I think I'll stay here. My head is fragile this morning and I don't think I'd be the best of company for you and Mrs. Pierce."

In truth, there was nothing the matter with my head. I just didn't want to suffer through another of Mr. Featherstonehaugh's interminable sermons (really, the man is completely oblivious to the fact that the congregation's patience does have its limits!). The notion of lunching at Mrs. Pierce's didn't appeal to me, either. If anything, Mrs. P is even more outspoken in her disdain for Canadians than her husband, Captain Pierce. I was surprised to find Millie, usually not an ardent churchgoer, dressed in her finest and searching everywhere for a prayer book. Knowing Millie, I guessed the reason for the sudden burst of enthusiasm for churchgoing had less to do with a desire to commune with her Creator and more with wanting to show off the splendid new hat she bought yesterday. Just days before the creeks rose and made the trail from Moosomin impassable Mrs. Ripley received a new shipment of summer hats and gloves.

Since I had the house to myself, I decided to practice my flute. The Blavet piece is proving more difficult than expected. I brought the music stand from the parlor into the drawing room. Like that I could look out of the open French doors at the shrubbery and the paddock with the horses beyond while I played.

I'm not sure how long I had been concentrating on the music when I became aware that I was not alone. I stopped playing and lifted my eyes from the sheet music.

"Mr. DeQuincy! I thought you had left Cannington."

"Well, you thought wrong. I am leaving but first I have to talk to you."

"About what?" I became nervous. DeQuincy had an even more unpleasant air about him than usual. For one thing, his appearance. He lacked a collar and tie, something I had never seen before. The buttons of his jacket and vest were undone. Worse, he had a nasty look in his eye. I took a step back but came up short against the arm of the sofa.

"Your brother has caused me considerable inconvenience."

"What has that to do with me?"

DeQuincy closed the distance between us until he was no more than a few feet from me. His lips twisted into an ugly grin, which frightened me.

He cocked his head to one side and looked at me in an oddly quizzical manner. "Tell me, you didn't happen to have made a trip recently to a small place called Holsten?"

I was unprepared for his questioning but I was in no mood to lie. So I said, "What if I did?"

"Hah! I guessed as much. My guards reported a woman was involved, one with dark hair. That would have been your pretty friend Millie. The two of you set fire to the wagons loaded with my merchandise."

"You mean your illegal liquor?"

"The loss of the shipment has occasioned a serious setback for me." His mirthless grin broadened into an equally mirthless smile. "Only a real smart girl could have pulled off a stunt like that." His habitual polished speech changed abruptly to a vulgar American drawl. "I've got to hand it to you, honey. You're smart and good looking."

"You didn't come here to pay me compliments."

"You're right. Since I'm in a hurry, I'll skip the sweet talk. I'm heading to the States. I want you to come with me."

"You're insane if you think I'd want to go with you."

"You'd be insane not to accept my generous offer. It's about time you ask yourself some tough questions."

"Such as?"

"How far do you think you're going to get in your present situation?"

"I haven't a clue what you're talking about."

"Don't mess with me, girl. You are dirt poor. Your father hasn't two dimes to rub together and he's got one foot in the grave. You're living in this place on the charity of these English folk, snobs all of them. If you imagine you'll find a rich husband here, you're mistaken. The only thing that interests these English bastards is money with a name attached. And you don't have either money or a name."

"You have no understanding of me, whatsoever, Mr. DeQuincy. I haven't the slightest interest in finding a husband, here or anywhere else. You've offered marriage before and the idea repulses me."

"Okay, enough chitchat. I don't give a monkey's cuss what you think of me. You've got to recognize that I'm a man of wealth and power. Just think where you could be if you threw in your lot with me. I'm planning to re-establish myself south of the border in the Dakota Territory. Things are booming there and I've friends. With a woman like you at my side, I could make it big. Picture this. You'd have the finest dresses, a classy mansion on the hill, respect from everyone that matters, a passel of kids, if that's what you want. You're not going to get any of that if you bury yourself in this shithole."

While he ranted on like this, I watched his features become more and more distorted. I realized that this is what madness looks like. I struggled to keep my voice calm, though I'm not sure I succeeded. "Mr. DeQuincy, the answer is no and will always be no. Please go away and leave me alone."

He fell silent and dropped his gaze as if examining his boots. I thought for one moment that he was about to turn and walk out the way he must have come in, through the French doors. My spirits rose but were immediately dashed when he lifted his head to look at me. A chill came over me. I'll never forget the way his cold eyes focused on my face.

"You fucking bitch! You wrecked my business, and when I'm prepared to forgive you and offer you the world, you fling it back in my face." His voice dropped to a low growl. "Nobody, especially a woman, ever snubs Niven DeQuincy and gets away with it. I give you one more chance to reconsider."

By this time I was numb with fear. In a shaking voice, I replied. "What you're asking is impossible. Please, please leave me alone."

I could see him weighing my answer for a few seconds. "You stupid girl! You brought this down on yourself."

With a fluid movement of his right hand, he reached into the inner pocket of his jacket and pulled out a short-barreled revolver and pointed it at my head. It's impossible to describe what it's like to stare down the inky barrel of a loaded gun. The light reflected from the blued steel of the pistol. I wasn't so much afraid as completely drained of emotion. It all appeared as if happening to someone else and I was just looking on. That is, until he pulled back the hammer. I can still hear the metallic click.

I stood stock still in utter disbelief of what was happening. All this time, my arms hung limply at my sides, my right hand still gripped my flute, which pointed to the floor. With the pistol cocked and aimed at me, the seconds dragged on. I have no idea what he was waiting for.

At that moment I heard the sound of the front door open and close, followed by footsteps in the hallway. My eyes remained fixed on DeQuincy's. When he heard the noise, his gaze wavered. It must have been some basic survival instinct that took command, not any rational thought on my part. I took advantage of the momentary distraction to bring my flute up and swing it in a tight arc. With all my strength, I brought the wooden instrument down on the bony part of the wrist of the hand holding the revolver. Everything from that instant on melded into a blur. DeQuincy yelled in pain. The pistol went off with an ear-splitting crack. The bullet went wide and shattered the glass of the china cabinet behind me to my left. The pistol clattered to the floor. DeQuincy swore and clutched his injured wrist. He then spun on his heel and fled through the open French doors.

At that moment, the drawing room door burst open and my aunt rushed in. I was still rooted to the spot.

"What on earth was that? It sounded like a shot."

I was about to attempt an explanation of the events when Aunt Rosalind's eyes fell on the broken glass scattered over the polished wood floor. She put her hands to her face and brushed past me. I watched her reach through the broken glass.

Her voice rose in a strange cry. "My precious Meissen figurine, utterly ruined, utterly ruined!"

Still cupping the porcelain item in her hands, she sank to the edge of the sofa. I recognized the object as a porcelain shepherdess being wooed by a faun. Only, now the headless shepherdess and one tiny lamb were all that remained.

Tears streamed down the woman's cheeks. Her voice quavered. "This was given to me by my godmother for my twelfth birthday. I have kept it all this time, and brought it with me all the way from Devon, and now it's ruined beyond repair." She shifted on the sofa to hide her face, but I saw her body convulse with sobs.

That more than anything wrenched me out of my stupor. I was aghast that here was my aunt weeping her heart out over a broken china shepherdess, when, had she been one second later, she could well have found the blooded corpse of a real human being sprawled on her drawing room floor. I looked at the splintered remains of the flute in my right hand. Without saying a word, I tucked the remnant under my arm and was about to leave the room when my shoe brushed DeQuincy's fallen revolver. I picked it up and carried the pistol and the flute up to my room. I placed both on my writing table. I must have been in denial about what had happened. My thoughts were on Aunt Louise and what she would have said if she knew I had used her dear husband's precious flute to save my life.

I think I know.

Chapter 28

After half an hour spent aimlessly staring out of her bedroom window, Carina's nerves settled sufficiently to allow her to think straight and recognize what she had to do. She slipped the revolver into her skirt pocket and, without bothering to put on hat or gloves, left the house by the front door and headed straight to the mounted police detachment. No one answered her knock on the door. That didn't surprise her, as she imagined Dillon and his officers were out searching for DeQuincy to question him on the charge of whiskey – and possibly gun – running. Now they would be able to charge him with attempted murder. She tried the latch and found the door unlocked.

Ten minutes later she pulled the door shut behind her, having left a note to Dillon, along with the revolver, on his desk. It was only when she was writing the brief account of the confrontation with DeQuincy did it fully dawn on her that Aunt Rosalind must not have taken up Mrs. Pierce's luncheon invitation but come home directly after the church service. The initial shock of realizing that her aunt obviously misunderstood what had transpired when she heard the shot was tempered by the chilling realization of what would have happened had DeQuincy not been distracted by the sounds of movement in the entrance hall.

Aunt Rosalind was no longer at home. Carina took a dustpan and broom and swept up the broken glass, removed the jagged shards still hanging from the cabinet door and put the debris in the kitchen trash pail. The sight of a loaf of bread on a board on the kitchen table reminded her she hadn't eaten since breakfast. She found cheese and a crock of butter in the pantry. The ash in the cast iron cook stove was still warm from the morning, and it didn't take her long to kindle a fire and heat up the coffee left in the pot. The nourishment helped restore her confidence.

Later that afternoon, Rosalind Addersley came back. On meeting Carina in the hallway, she gave a polite smile and, without saying anything, went to her bureau in the corner of the living room and immersed herself in letter writing.

Carina wondered whether her aunt's singular lack of curiosity about the shot, who fired it and for what motive, was just one more example of the upper-class English idiosyncrasy of keeping a stiff upper lip. She couldn't imagine her uncle taking the matter as lightly and wished he was here. She had the need to talk about the episode. In the face of her aunt's cool indifference, she chose not to broach the matter with her.

Millie came back some time later, bubbling with excitement over the compliments she had received on her new hat and how she and Sybil had been offered luncheon by Mr. Rodney Beresford.

Carina assumed responsibility for preparing the evening meal, and the three women sat down together, with Rosalind Addersley unusually subdued and taciturn. Still exuberant, Millie filled the void with an endless stream of animated but trivial chatter.

The much-anticipated visit from Sergeant Granger did not happen that evening. Carina went to bed uncharacteristically depressed. She lay awake into the early hours, staring up at the darkened ceiling. Each time she closed her eyes, she saw herself standing in the drawing room with DeQuincy glaring at her over the barrel of his revolver. Sleep came at last but it was a sleep filled with anxious dreams that jolted her awake, bathed in perspiration.

Toward noon the following day, she was by the living room window watching the activity on the street when her heart leapt at the sight of Dillon striding down the boardwalk in the direction of the house. She ran out to meet him in front of the house.

"Sergeant, I've been waiting to speak to you." It was only then that she saw that his uniform and boots were caked with dried mud. He wore no hat and stubble darkened his chin.

He reached out and cupped her arm. "Are you all right? I've just come back and read your note and found the pistol."

"Can we talk somewhere?" She motioned to the house. "Not there. I find it oppressive."

"Let's go over to the detachment."

She fell into step beside him across the street and up the boardwalk to the police building. He held open the door and ushered her inside. She found herself seated in the same chair with the same plain surroundings as just a few days earlier. Only, now everything had changed.

Dillon sat at the desk and picked up the note she had written. "Before I tell you of the latest development, would you kindly go over what occurred when Mr. DeQuincy accosted you yesterday afternoon? You wrote a remarkably clear and concise account of it but I'd like to hear it from you, in more detail."

Carina related how the event unfolded from the moment she became conscious of DeQuincy's presence in the drawing room. She swore she detected a fleeting smile on Dillon's lips when she detailed how she took advantage of her aunt's arrival to bring the full force of her flute down on the man's wrist.

"You are quite sure he was about to fire the revolver, and not simply trying to frighten you?"

"He gave me the impression of being completely mad. Who can tell real the intentions of a madman? I am convinced that when the pistol went off it was not the result of me hitting him. He had the hammer cocked and was already squeezing the trigger. That and what he said when I refused to go with him, makes me convinced he intended to kill me."

"You're sure about that?" He picked up the revolver and held the checkered walnut butt between his forefinger and thumb, with the stubby barrel resting on the first knuckle of his left forefinger, as though giving her the opportunity to examine close up the instrument of the death she missed by a hair's breadth. "A Colt, single action, point three eighth of an inch caliber. It's known as a Banker's Special."

"A Banker's Special, really? My father's a banker but I don't think he owns one. Then again, he might and I don't know about it. What does single action mean?"

He swung open the cylinder and removed the remaining cartridges before again showing her the firearm. "Single action means the hammer must be pulled back before pulling the trigger. Like this." He used his thumb to cock the weapon. "That's why the hammer has this backward-facing spur. The reason I'm explaining this is because if he was merely blustering and attempting to intimidate you into accepting his proposal, he probably wouldn't have cocked the pistol. You only pull back the hammer when you mean business."

"He definitely meant business. He had the hammer back. I watched him do it."

"Yes, that's why it went off when you struck him on the wrist. You are an extremely lucky woman, Miss Chesterman. If I may say so, you're also an extremely plucky woman. I don't know if a man would have had the presence of mind to do what you did."

Carina lightened the conversation by saying, "Maybe, not many men would have been playing a flute in the drawing room. You said you were going to tell me about some new development. Have you been able to find Mr. DeQuincy?"

Dillon placed the pistol and cartridges in the drawer of his desk. His eyes held hers. "Yes, we caught up with Mr. Niven DeQuincy."

Carina leaned forward. "You did! Where?"

"A police patrol sighted him on the Moosomin Trail, traveling north. He was with another man and was driving a one-horse shay. The man he was with is known to police. His name is Kelman Gibb, a petty criminal with a long history of run-ins with the law, for theft and similar offences."

"The name Gibb sounds familiar. I overheard Mr. DeQuincy mention him to my brother in connection with the wagon train carrying the whiskey."

Dillon nodded. "Later, you can tell me all about your involvement with that shipment of illegal liquor."

"Why was he on the Moosomin trail? He said he was going to the United States."

"To reach U.S. territory by going south from here you have to cross some barren country, as you well know. That means carrying several days' worth of supplies. Mr. DeQuincy had no time to make the necessary preparations. He must have figured his best bet was to try and make it up to the Canadian Pacific line and catch a train going east. What he didn't take into account were the flooded creeks."

"Why, what happened?"

"When the gentleman realized he was being pursued, he attempted to cross Antler Creek. You will recall that's where you got stopped by the grass fire."

"Please don't remind me. It was just a dry creek then."

"Not now, not after all the rain. No one in their right mind would think of crossing it today."

"But he tried."

"Needless to say, he only got about half way across before the force of the water flipped over the buggy and swept it away."

"What became of the horse and passengers?"

"When my troopers arrived, the buggy was a mile downstream. Gibb managed to hang on. Fortunately for him, the horse was able to drag itself and the wreck of the shay onto a sandbar. "

"And, Mr. DeQuincy?"

"Gibb said DeQuincy, who had been driving, tried to swim to the bank."

"And..?"

"He didn't make it."

"We conducted a search but had to call it off at nightfall. At daybreak, we found Mr. DeQuincy's body snagged on a dead tree."

Carina fell silent for a moment. A chill settled over her. "I hate to say this but news of his death comes as a relief."

"He won't be bothering you any more. It's too bad we were unable to bring him to justice."

"You know, sergeant, I must be jinxed."

"In what way?"

"Many women my age have never even seen a dead body, but although I've been in the Northwest now just handful of months, in that space of time two men known to me have met unnatural deaths, one of them by murder."

"Death is unnerving in any form, no matter the circumstances."

"A person dying of old age or sickness is sad, but it's harder to deal with when the death is a product of violence."

"You are very perceptive, Miss Chesterman."

"Sergeant Granger."

"Yes?"

"Would you say we know each other reasonably well?"

He ran his fingers along his bristled jaw. "Fate has thrown us together in some weird and wonderful ways, I must admit."

"You have been a source of great comfort to me. I would like it if you'd address me simply as, Carina. May I call you Dillon?"

He extended his hand across the desk. "Certainly, Carina. I feel privileged to be considered your friend."

She offered her hand and he closed his strong fingers around it.

"You have obviously guessed I was responsible for the burning the whiskey wagons. By chance, at the wedding reception for Maud and Julian, I overheard DeQuincy order my brother to go to Holsten and see to the distribution of the cargo of whiskey. I knew what he was doing was illegal, I was motivated by wanting to spare my cousin Maud further heartache."

"That's what I figured."

"I understand DeQuincy's aim was to stir up unrest among the native people and the Métis. I fail so see how that would have benefitted him?"

"It appears, and this has been corroborated by your brother and Mr. Kelman Gibb, that DeQuincy wanted to force the

The Cannington Episode -273

government's hand. He never made any secret about what action he thought the government ought to take."

"You mean sending in a large military force?"

"DeQuincy was an American and contemptuous of the Canadian way of doing things. You will recall him expressing the opinion that the government in Ottawa should station cavalry and regular infantry units in the Northwest to nip in the bud the faintest whiff of unrest. He scorned the work of the North-West Mounted Police and feared the slightest instability would scare off would-be homesteaders and put him out of business. Unfortunately, the gentleman hadn't studied his own American history or he would have known that the presence of large numbers of troops doesn't automatically ensure peace and stability. Witness what happened at the Little Bighorn River just eight years ago."

Carina noticed the lines of fatigue on Dillon's face and guessed he had spent many sleepless hours in the saddle. After a short silence she said, "Now that DeQuincy is gone, I suppose the truth about Ogden Fenn's murder has gone with him."

Dillon pushed back his chair and got to his feet. "Not necessarily. The Mounted Police never give up on a case, no matter how scanty the evidence. We may not be much closer to knowing who actually pulled the trigger but I am becoming convinced it wasn't DeQuincy. Although the man made no secret of his poor opinion of Ogden Fenn, my investigation to date provides no grounds for believing he had anything to gain from killing the scientist."

"How can one explain finding cheroot that only he appeared to smoke?"

"At the moment, I can't. The cigar is only circumstantial evidence. Even if it had come from him that does not prove he was present at Fenn's campsite. Men who smoke cigars often hand them out as gifts. The finding only *suggests* that whoever dropped the cigar butt may have been in contact with DeQuincy. That could encompass a large number of people. Then again, there is nothing to say the cigar butt hadn't been dropped before the murder took place."

"When you showed it to me it looked very fresh."

"I agree, but proving it is linked to the murder is the hard part."

Chapter 29

Over the next few days Carina made sure she kept away from Sybil Halliday so as not to put herself in the paradoxical position of having to offer condolences over the death of a man who had tried to murder her. In a place as small as Cannington she knew it was only a matter of time before she and Sybil did meet. To prepare for this eventuality she asked Millie's about Sybil's reaction to the news of DeQuincy's demise.

"She's not gone into mourning. Just yesterday, we paid a visit to Mr. Rodney Beresford and she wore a beautiful canary yellow dress and matching hat. Over tea, she talked as though she hadn't a care in the world."

"Did she mention anything at all about Mr. DeQuincy?"

"Only that she thought it really bad luck he drowned in a flooded creek when all summer people have been complaining of drought. I had the impression she was more annoyed than grieved, which is odd. Why would anyone be annoyed at the death of someone near to you? That led me to think that, perhaps, she and Mr. DeQuincy were not as close as we'd been led to believe. When I first met them they acted like man and wife."

Carina observed that the Cannington community reacted to the drama on the Moosomin Trail in much the same way they received any outside news. The topic was acknowledged, barely, before conversation reverted to the ever-important cricket scores, tennis matches, and tea parties.

This bizarre air of normalcy was finally shattered by the return of Alfred Addersley.

He arrived, alone, having traveled over the Broadview trail. In answer to his wife's questioning he replied that Maud had decided to remain in the capital to be close to Julian.

"I found her lodgings with the Hilquist family. Nils Hilquist is the wholesale grocer our trading company does business with in the capital. He and his wife are a highly respectable couple."

"What about our son-in-law?" Rosalind uttered *son-in-law* as if referring to an outbreak of the plague.

"As regards to his health, he is both well and in good spirits. As for his legal situation, he's been before a magistrate who remanded him back into custody pending the outcome of the ongoing police investigation. I have retained a lawyer and we're hopeful that at his next hearing Julian will be granted bail. The fact that he's cooperating with the police is, I'm pleased to say, very much in his favor."

After reassuring his wife that everything that could be done was being done, Alfred's face took on a somber expression. "I have some other, extremely disturbing, news but I am reserving the announcement of it until dinner this evening when the leading members of the settlement will be present."

The guest list that evening consisted of Cannington's guiding lights, all of them male. Carina was acquainted with Mr. Seth Teague, Mr. Paul Fripp and Mr. Obadiah Featherstonehaugh. Mr. Percy Lansdowne-Coutts was there to represent the agricultural college. The others she knew only as occasional visitors to the house. Notably absent was Rodney Beresford, but no one expressed surprise. It was common knowledge that the Beresfords kept themselves to themselves and rarely accepted dinner invitations. Algernon, of course, was away with the Ottawa delegation. Rodney sent his regrets that he was unable to attend.

Rosalind Addersley sat to her husband's right at the head of the long dining table. Carina and Millie were relegated to the lower reaches of the seating arrangement, with Millie between the reverend gentleman and Mr. Teague, and Carina between Teague and Mr. Lansdowne-Coutts. The latter gentleman greeted her with a polite "Good evening, Miss Chesterman," after which, he ignored her.

Her uncle waited until after the main course had been served and eaten before making his announcement. While a dessert they called spotted dick, which consisted of a sticky steamed sponge pudding dotted with currents, together with a jug of thick yellow custard, was making the round of the table, Alfred rose to his feet. All conversation ceased.

"Ladies and gentlemen, I have two pieces of unpleasant news which will sadden everyone in the community. On the last day of my stay in Regina, I received a cablegram from Ottawa which appalled me with its contents. Whilst preparing to leave the dominion capital, our own Captain Pierce, I regret to report, suffered a seizure of the heart and died."

There came an audible inhalation of breath from those about the table. The stunned silence was broken by a spoon that clattered onto a plate.

The monocle fell from Seth Teague's right eye. "How can that be so, Alfred? The captain was in robust good health for a man of his age."

"The heart is a fickle organ," Alfred replied. "It could be that Captain Pierce was adversely affected by the stress caused by my second item of bad news. The government has denied our request for a spur line to the settlement. The delegation is on its way back, empty-handed and leaderless, as is the community of Cannington Manor."

A collective groan went up from the table.

Paul Fripp looked around at the solemn faces. "My God! That is bad news, dashed bad news. What the deuce are we to do now? That rail line was essential to assure the future of Cannington. It would have allowed us to get our commodities to market in a timely manner and be competitive with other producers. It would also have attracted visitors to the Fish Lake resort."

Carina sensed the palpable blanket of gloom that settled over the room. Each man in turn spoke of how the double blow of the founder's death and the loss of the rail link would affect life in the settlement.

Someone asked what would become of the captain's school.

Lansdowne-Coutts gave a more spirited response. "It will continue as before. That is what Captain Pierce would have wanted. Our young gentlemen scholars bring their vitality and culture to energize the town. And, it goes without saying that the fees their families pay are of unquestionable benefit to the community."

At the end of the dinner, Carina joined her aunt and Millie in the drawing room and left the gentlemen to their port wine and cigars.

Rosalind, who had not spoken at dining table, turned a resolute face to Carina and Millie. "The gentlemen in there were caught off their guard. Do not be misled by some of their pessimistic remarks. We English are a stalwart breed and are never crushed by adversity. Naturally, the death of Captain Pierce and the failure of the petition constitute a tragic and severe blow to us. The captain was both the founder and the head of the colony, an inspiration to us all. We are now without his firm hand on the tiller. But we will persevere, as he would have wanted us to do."

Carina spent a further twenty minutes seated next to Millie on the sofa, listening to her aunt expound on the importance of ensuring that the settlement prospers.

"Will some English families choose return to England?" Millie asked.

"No, of course not. Many of us made considerable sacrifices to come to this country and re-establish ourselves here. To contemplate a return to the Old Country borders on the unconscionable."

Eventually, Carina was able to excuse herself and go up to her room. Moments later, she heard footsteps and Millie pushed open the door.

"You're not in bed, are you?"

"No. Come in and sit down."

Millie dropped into the wicker armchair. "Phew! When I came out to visit you I thought I was in for a boring few weeks. I love your company but I imagined life in the Northwest would be tediously dull compared with Montreal. Instead, I feel like I've fallen into a madhouse."

"You're not alone. Before I came things were extremely placid."

"What's going to happen to the colony now?"

"It depends whom you choose to believe. As you heard for yourself, Aunt Rosalind considers the latest events a mere bump in the road. The gentlemen are less optimistic about the future." For reasons she could not explain, Carina decided, at least for the time being, not to share with Millie her plan to leave Cannington, just as she had kept silent about the attempt on her life.

Over the following days, she had the impression that her aunt's views would prevail. The community held a memorial service for the late Captain Edward Mitchell Pierce, for which the entire Cannington population crammed itself into the church. That out of the way, settlement life fell back into its time-honored routine. If anything, society exhibited even greater ebullience, though Carina thought it artificial and contrived. It was as if the Cannington citizens believed that scoring more runs at cricket, outdoing one's neighbor at hosting a tea party, and arranging for the dramatic society to put on a performance of *A Midsummer Night's Dream* would on their own help compensate for the latest setbacks.

About a week after receiving word of Captain Pierce's death, members of the Ottawa delegation returned home without the slightest fanfare. Carina only learned about it when her uncle called her into his study.

He motioned her to one of the dimpled leather armchairs in front of the desk. "Please sit down, dear girl. I have something important to say to you."

While he brought up the other chair, Carina wondered what else could have happened in this ongoing saga.

Alfred cleared his throat. "I thought you should hear this first from me before word gets around the community."

Carina nodded. "Yes, uncle."

"You may or may not be aware that the gentlemen who went with the captain to Ottawa arrived back late last evening. The creeks have gone down again and they made it from Moosomin station with no trouble."

"I'm glad of that."

"And as you know, Mr. Algernon Beresford was among the delegates."

"Yes, I knew that."

At this point, her uncle began to stumble over his words as though searching for an appropriate way to break his news. Carina watched him examine his fingernails for several moments.

"Mr. Algernon, you see, is the elder of the two brothers. It is common knowledge he is the one who sets the tone and makes the decisions regarding matters concerning running Inglesbury. Mr. Rodney is an excellent chap but plays what one might call a more secondary role."

"I see."

"It appears that when Mr. Algernon arrived back at his residence he was disturbed to find certain irregularities had been occurring during his absence."

"Irregularities, uncle?"

Alfred coughed into his closed fist. "Yes, irregular behavior, highly irregular. It transpires that his younger brother had taken to entertaining two ladies, namely, the American widow, Mrs. Sybil Halliday, and your young friend, Miss Millicent Vanderhagen."

"I am aware that Mr. Rodney Beresford invited them to the house on several occasions. The first time, I went with them for afternoon tea. Afterward, it was Sybil and Millie on their own. I do not have a great interest in drinking tea and eating cucumber sandwiches. Mr. Rodney used to send a curricle for them."

"Indeed?" Her uncle's voice drifted off and he stared out of the window. "Yes, well, you see, it turns out that the daily visits were not altogether innocent."

"No?"

"No, there was a lot more to the encounters than tea and cucumber sandwiches." Still with his eyes averted, her uncle ran a forefinger round the rim of his collar. "The trysts, for that is what they were, quickly developed a far different complexion."

Carina already guessed what her uncle was trying to say. She had long suspected there was a lascivious aspect to Sybil's relationship with the younger Beresford. Nor did it surprise her that Sybil had roped Millie into the game, though she regretted she had been unable to prevent it.

After a weighty pause, Alfred continued. "There was what one might call funny business going on between Rodney Beresford and Mrs. Halliday. I have no idea what young Millie's involvement was. Mr. Algernon didn't elaborate."

"And the precise nature of this *funny business*?"

Alfred cupped a knee with his hands, embarrassment written on his face. "It is extremely painful for a gentleman in my position to discuss this matter with a member of the fair sex, particularly one so young as yourself. Let it be said that the meetings involved activities of a highly intimate and lewd nature."

"Really?"

As if having overcome some inner hurdle, Alfred rushed through the remaining details. "Yes, seemingly involving the use of whips and leather restraints and the pursuit of all manner of bawdy activities, leading up to and including instances of carnal knowledge." Alfred raised his hands, palms outward. "And that's all I am prepared to say on the subject."

"Uncle, I'm shocked."

"So are we all, none more so than Mr. Algernon himself. The realization that his house was being used for dissolute activities during his absence by his weaker, libertine brother almost brought on a fit of apoplexy."

"My I ask whether Mr. Rodney Beresford volunteered this incriminating information about what happened?"

"Algernon found out when he checked the household account book. It seems that considerable sums of money changed hands between Rodney and Mrs. Halliday. When confronted, Rodney spilled the beans."

"Where is Mrs. Halliday now? And Millie?"

"That is what I wanted to inform you about. Mr. Algernon ordered the Halliday woman out of the settlement. He gave her just enough time to pack her things at the Mitre. Then, despite having just returned from a lengthy journey, he set off with her, driving his own rig to the station at Moosomin." Alfred glanced at the clock on the mantelpiece. "They'll arrive in time to catch the evening train. It transpires Mrs. Halliday intends to head west."

Carina made a move to stand up. "I have to talk to Millie."

Her uncle restrained her with a hand on her arm. "This is the part that concerns you directly, dear Carina. When Miss Millie received word that her friend and accomplice, Mrs. Halliday, was being expelled from the settlement, she begged to go with her."

"You mean Millie has left?"

Her uncle nodded. "She packed a light travel case and went with them to Moosomin. We will be forwarding the rest of her baggage to her later, when she notifies us of an address."

Carina leapt out of the armchair and ran upstairs. On opening the door to Millie's room, she saw clothes and other items strewn over the bed, proof that Millie had acted in haste. Beside the lamp on the night table, Carina found a note.

Carina darling,

I don't expect you to fully understand my actions. I have gone with Sybil. She decided on the spur of the moment to leave the settlement. I believe the sadness of losing her close friend, Mr. Niven DeQuincy, has taken a greater toll on her than any of us expected. Mr. Algernon Beresford kindly offered to drive us to the station. Sybil wants to go to San Francisco. She tells me she has connections there. But first we're visiting her old friend Lord Cottesmere. I'm unsure of the route we'll follow but Sybil is wonderful and arranges things so well. Isn't this all so exciting? I'm sorry I was unable to say goodbye in person but we left very early and in quite a rush. I'll write later.

Ever your dearest friend,

Millie

Chapter 30

Cannington, Monday, August 18, 1884

If I thought life was back to normal in Cannington, how wrong I was! But more about that later.

It has taken several days for me to even begin to come to terms with Millie's sudden departure. I feel so guilty over her going with Sybil. She is, after all, my friend and my guest and in a way I was responsible for her. My first thought was to go after her and persuade her to return, but how could I do that when I had no idea where to find her? She wrote of visiting Lord Whatever-his-name-is and later traveling to San Francisco, which is a long way away. Even if I did succeed in catching up to her, my mission might have been futile. There's no saying she would have changed her mind. On more than one occasion she stated she didn't want to return to live with her mother. The two of them no longer saw eye to eye on things.

There is no question now what kind of a woman Sybil is or what her motive for coming to Cannington was. I made a few inquiries about her so-called friend, Lord Cottesmere. No one I spoke to would even acknowledge having heard of the aristocratic gentleman. I was about to dismiss him as a figment of Sybil's imagination when I mentioned his name to Mrs. Ripley, the dressmaker. Although not a member of Cannington's moneyed elite, she has spent her life serving them and others of that ilk. The amiable woman told me that Cottesmere is an aging English roué with a reputation for debauchery that would make Nero look like St. Thomas Aquinas. His lordship fled England before he could be prosecuted for seducing young girls and is now in hiding on a ranch he owns in the Alberta District.

Having first met me in Regina, Sybil must have come to Cannington in the hope of recruiting me for some dubious purpose known only to her. I must have proved too difficult or perhaps I wasn't pretty enough or didn't wear the right style of frilly dresses, for she switched her attention to Maud. When Maud fell under Julian's spell, Sybil then went after Millie, who has by far the better figure of the three of us. I fear for poor Millie's virtue and I hate to think of what kind of a life she'll have with Sybil in San Francisco. Yet, there's still hope. On the surface, Millie may strike one as utterly charming but not too bright. Yet inside that pretty head of hers lies a brain capable of scheming along with the best of them. Sybil could soon find herself being out-manipulated by Millie, rather than the other way round. Whatever the outcome, I can't do much except wait and see.

As if to prove that life goes on no matter what, the good folk of Cannington held their Grand Summer Picnic today on the shore of Fish Lake at the foot of the slopes of Moose Mountain. Hectic preparations had been underway for days. Even the haughtiest of the English matrons donned aprons and applied themselves to baking bread, cakes and pastries and making candies. Countless bushels of lemons, along with similar quantities of sugar, were procured and converted into lemonade. An entire week's supply of cream was diverted from butter production to making the ice-cream no picnic can do without. The full tubs of that *frozen delight were stored in Cannington's ice-house until this morning.*

Not wishing to spend hours slaving in a hot kitchen, I made my contribution to the event by assisting. Norman Tucker to construct folding picnic tables from deal planks, with benches to match. I highly recommend pounding nails and screwing hinges as a splendid therapeutic solution for stress.

Before dawn, every freight wagon, farm cart and buckboard in the settlement was pressed into service to transport the impressive array of food and drink, portable furniture, tents, canopies, temporary toilets, baseball and cricket bats, badminton racquets and other equipment required for a successful picnic. The sun was barely up when the entire citizenry of Cannington Manor clambered aboard carriages, buggies of every description, set out on horseback or on foot (some even on bicycle!) to cover the eight-mile journey to the lake. As the procession set off, I was reminded of the description of the baggage train of Xenophon's army on its march to the Euphrates. Within less than half an hour the entire settlement emptied and assumed the appearance of an abandoned village.

I wasn't in any mood to picnic and spend the whole day beside the lake, pretending to enjoy games and eating ice cream and cake. Yet not to go would have shown disrespect. I compromised by saddling Morgana and riding there, with the intention of slipping away unnoticed at the earliest opportunity.

I have to admit the Cannington English certainly know how to enjoy themselves. The young men from the agricultural school took it upon themselves to organize the activities, from strenuous tug of war contests to dancing barefoot on the grass with music provided by fiddle and banjo. For an hour I helped out at the ice-cream stand. When the crowd drifted over to the hastily-marked out diamond to watch a baseball game between the school pups and a combined team of carpenters, flour mill employees and artisans, I mounted my horse and rode back home.

When I reached the house, I left Morgana saddled in the yard as I intended to pocket an apple and some cookies (I had refrained from sampling the treats at the picnic) and go for a ride. To my surprise, I found Ellie sitting at the kitchen table eating a cheese sandwich.

"Ellie, why aren't you at the picnic? Everyone's there."

The girl gave me a mournful look. "I just didn't feel like it, miss."

"You'd love it. You don't get many holidays."

"Miss Carina, just lately, I've not been feeling well."

"Are you sick?"

"Oh, no, not sick in my body. It's...I've been having these gloomy thoughts. Lately, they've gotten worse."

I sat at down opposite her. "Ellie, do you want to tell me about these gloomy thoughts? You know you can trust me."

Ellie smiled and nodded. "Some time ago I saw something I think may have had something to do with what happened to Mr. Fenn."

"Really?"

"After he was killed, everyone was saying the police suspected Mr. DeQuincy was responsible. Quite a few people saw him have that big argument with the scientific gentleman. And they had other rows as well."

"They now believe Mr. DeQuincy had nothing to do with it."

"That's what I heard. Then I got thinking, who else could have done it. And my mind kept going back to something that I saw the day before the murder."

"Tell me about it."

The girl swallowed the last of her sandwich and washed it down with a mouthful of tea. "As you know, to make some extra money I work at the Beresford place, doing floors, that kind of thing."

"Yes."

"When Mr. Fenn was last in Cannington, just before he died, he was staying at the Beresfords'. They always put him up there, as they do other gentlemen visitors, in Bachelor Hall. That's the wing on the east side of the house."

"Yes, I know."

"I was mopping the linoleum in the upstairs corridor of the bachelor quarters. It's a long corridor with rooms on either side. Mr. Fenn's door was fifth from the top of the stairs, on the left."

Ellie stopped speaking and I noticed she was breathing deeply, an indication she was troubled by what she was telling me, though up to then she had described nothing out of the ordinary.

I said, "Please, go on, Ellie. I want to hear this."

"Well, I was in the corridor and Mr. Fenn came up behind me on his way to his room."

"And?"

"Mr. Lansdowne-Coutts has the room next to the one Mr. Fenn was using."

"All right, I understand. What happened when you met Mr. Fenn?"

"Mr. Fenn stops to chat. He was always so friendly and treated everyone with respect. He made a joke about something and we both laughed. I guess he was a bit distracted and opened the door to Mr. Lansdowne-Coutts' room by mistake."

"Was the gentleman in his room?"

Ellie nodded. I saw a tear run down her cheek. She lowered her head. I reached across the table and covered her hand with mine.

"What is troubling you? Opening a wrong door can happen to anyone."

A tearful sob came from behind a curtain of glossy dark hair. Ellie sniffed. "I'm so confused I don't know how to begin describing what I saw."

I sensed that what the girl had to say was important. So I went to her side of the table and sat beside her.

"Miss Carina, what I saw was just horrible, horrible."

"Take your time, Ellie, but tell me everything. You'll feel better."

"It was so shameful. I've not been able to tell anyone about it. Usually, I can talk to my grandma but not about this."

I brushed back her hair. "You say you were in the corridor and Mr. Fenn entered the wrong door, correct?"

Ellie straightened on her chair. "That's right. I saw everything."

"What do you mean, everything?"

"I was standing directly behind Mr. Fenn and Mr. Lansdowne-Coutts was there."

"Where,"

"Standing beside the bed."

"Yes, go on."

"He had no clothes on."

"Is that what embarrassed you, seeing the gentleman unclothed?"

Ellie stared at me a moment before answering. "Oh, no. I'm used to seeing a man with no clothes on. Friday nights grandpa takes a bath in a tin tub in our kitchen. And my older brother, before he left to work up north in the lumber camps, often used to walk around stark naked, complaining he couldn't find his shirt and pants."

"Then, there was something more?"

Ellie nodded. "There was another gentleman in the room with Mr. Lansdowne-Coutts and he too was naked."

"Who was he?"

"One of the young gentlemen they call the pups."

"Do you know his name?"

"Mr. Bertrand Lee, the really good-looking one with the light-brown curly hair."

"And where was this Mr. Lee?"

"Right in front of Mr. Lansdowne-Coutts, bent forward over the bed."

I held off asking more questions as I could see the girl was having difficulty putting into words what she had seen. After a while, I said, "Can you tell what was happening?"

Ellie's face seemed to take on a maturity beyond her fourteen years. In a steady voice, she said. "Mr. Lansdowne-Coutts was doing to the other man what I've seen our stallion do to the mares when they are being bred."

"They were engaged in copulation."

"I've even seen a man do that to a woman. Last year when grandpa was sick for three weeks, Mr. Addersley hired Jake from the village to care for the horses. One evening I happened to go into the stable and found Jake in there with a servant girl. They were lying on a pile of hay. They didn't see me as they were so busy laughing and rolling about. I couldn't help watching because it looked like good fun. That was a boy with a girl. A man doing it to another man isn't natural, is it?"

"It's against the law and punished severely. What happened next?"

"Mr. Lansdowne-Coutts looked round and saw Mr. Fenn, who was standing in the doorway. Mr. Fenn mumbled a few words of apology before he backed out and shut the door. By then I'd moved away. Mr. Fenn shook his head and went into his own room."

"You saw all this. Did Mr. Lansdowne-Coutts see you?"

"I don't think so. It's a bit dark in the corridor. There aren't many windows. The next day, Mr. Fenn goes back to his camp and then we find out he's been murdered. I can't help wondering if what happened that day in Bachelor Hall had anything to do with it. Am I crazy?"

"No, Ellie you're not crazy and you were right to tell me about it." I grabbed Ellie and pulled her to her feet. "Ellie, would you come with me to the Beresford place and show me Mr. Lansdowne-Coutts' room?"

"Now?"

"Yes, while everyone is down at the lake. I want to see inside his room. Will you do that for me? This is really important."

"I'll do anything for you, Miss Carina."

"Morgana is still saddled. Are you able to climb up and ride behind me?"

"Sure."

We hurried out to the stable yard, where Morgana stood patiently waiting. I put my toe in the stirrup and swung into the saddle. Ellie hitched up her skirt, placed her shoe on my boot toe and, with impressive agility, levered herself up to straddle the horse's back behind me. She wrapped her arms around my waist and held on tight. I touched the mare's flanks and we set off at a brisk canter.

I approached the Beresford mansion with caution. First I had to reassure myself as best as I could that everyone was away attending the picnic. The normally busy courtyard sat deserted. Nothing stirred. Ellie jumped down. I dismounted and tied the horse to one of the hitching rails. I held Ellie by the hand and waited to see if anyone had heard us arrive and was coming to find out what we wanted. No one appeared.

Ellie pointed to a door. "That's where the stairs are."

Once inside, we took the stairs that led up to the corridor that runs the length of the upper floor. At the top of the stairs, we stopped and listened. There was still no sound other than our labored breathing.

Ellie advanced down the corridor. "This is Lansdowne-Coutts's room."

For several seconds I contemplated the closed door, hoping that the door was unlocked and the room empty. I slowly turned the knob and pushed the door open. The room was indeed empty (I'm not sure what I would have done had the occupant been there!). I stepped inside and looked around. Everything was neat and

tidy. *Boots and shoes were lined up against one wall,
and above them on hooks hung outdoor jackets and
coats. A game bag, a creel, a landing net and several fly
rods occupied one corner. The window stood open. A
gentle breeze billowed the chintz curtains.*

*I had a hunch that I might find the missing gun
from the rack in the house's gun room. My heart leapt
when my intuition proved correct. On a pine cabinet
beside the door, its muzzle leaning against the wall,
stood a rifle, which I immediately recognized as a
Sharps. There was no mistaking its long octagonal barrel
and curved brass breech lever that acted as a trigger
guard. I picked the gun up and my arms bowed under
its weight. I had forgotten just how heavy they were. I
now needed to find out if this gun was 'the gun' and I
pulled open the cabinet drawer. In it I found a tin box
containing several rounds of ammunition.*

*Ellie looked at me, wide-eyed. "What are you
going to do?"*

"Fire a shot from this rifle."

*Despite its considerable heft, I followed Rodney
Beresford's instructions on how to load it. First, bracing
the rifle's wooden butt against my thigh, I pushed down
the lever. The well-oiled falling block opened to expose
the mouth of the chamber. I inserted a round and
snapped the lever up to close the breech.*

"You're not going to fire that in here?"

*"Out of the window." The rifle was too unwieldly
for me to hold it steady. So, I brushed aside the curtain
and rested the end of the barrel on the window ledge.
This meant leaning forward at an awkward angle but
that didn't matter. Thankfully, the window looked out
over the rear of the house. My target was a large
haystack some distance away. I couldn't miss! I raised*

the rear leaf sight, adjusted it to the estimated range
and took aim by squinting along the length of the barrel
and lining up the metal tang at the end. Then, ensuring
the safety catch was disengaged, I cocked the hammer.

"Ellie, cover your ears. This'll make a loud bang."

I counted to ten and squeezed the rear trigger as
Beresford had demonstrated. There was a click to
indicate the weapon was now on hair-trigger. Then, I
held the firearm as steady as I could and pressed my
finger around the forward trigger. The rifle went off
with a detonation that set my ears ringing. Worse was
the vicious recoil that knocked me backward. The rifle
clattered to the plank floor and I fell on my back.

Ellie gave a squeal. "Miss Carina! Are you all
right?"

"Thanks, Ellie, yes, I'm fine."

The girl suddenly stiffened. "What if someone
heard the shot?"

"Let's get out of here as fast as we can." I reached
down and, without picking up the rifle, worked the
breech lever to eject the spent cartridge. I grimaced and
thrust the hot brass cartridge case into my skirt pocket,
where it scorched my leg through the fabric. Ellie was
already at the head of the stairs.

I paused to listen. "I don't hear anything. Do
you?"

"The house must be empty."

Nonetheless, Ellie and I bolted down the stairs
and ran out into the yard. As fast as I could I untied the
horse, mounted and hauled Ellie up behind me. I dug in
my heels. Morgana must have understood our need for
haste because she kicked up a spray of gravel as we set
off.

We maintained a fast pace until we were clear of the mansion and back on the road to the settlement. By then Morgana was more than willing to slacken her stride. Only when we were riding up Cannington's main street did I feel at ease enough to examine my trophy. I took the still warm casing from my pocket and flipped it over in my fingers. I almost uttered a whoop of excitement when I examined the base.

I couldn't wait to show Dillon my discovery.

"Ellie, if you want you can go home. I'll come and talk to you when I've finished here." I pointed to the Mounted Police detachment.

Ellie slid to the ground. "I'd much sooner stay with you."

"If you wish. Let's go and see if we can find Sergeant Granger."

Ellie and I burst through the door without knocking. Trooper Durkin looked up from the desk, surprise written on his rugged features. "Ladies, what has dragged you away from a lovely picnic?"

"Is Sergeant Granger available? I have something important to show him."

"Sarge is at the picnic." The trooper grinned. "He said he was going as official representative of the Force. He is, after all, the sergeant. Right now it's just me an' a couple of troopers keeping an eye on the town. With no one at home, we wouldn't want the burglars to have a picnic."

"Trooper Durkin, could someone go and fetch the sergeant? It's of great importance."

The officer stared at me for a moment, and then said, "From the look on your face, miss, I'd warrant the problem is more than just your pet cat stuck up a tree. I'll dispatch one of the men to get Sergeant Granger."

"I think I have found something that could be important for the Ogden Fenn murder investigation." To reinforce my message I held out the spent casing in the palm of my hand.

Durkin eyed it for a split second before heading for the door.

Ellie and I went back outside to wait. We saw a Mounted officer ride off hell for leather toward Moose Mountain. To keep Ellie amused and to prevent her from getting nervous, we scratched squares in the packed earth with a stick and played hopscotch, something I had not done since my early years at school. Ellie beat me, six games to four.

We were resting on the detachment's veranda steps when Dillon galloped up with the trooper at his side. Dillon dismounted and handed off the reins.

"You have some news for me, Miss Chesterman?"

I stood up. "Do you still have that cartridge casing we found at the campsite?"

Dillon motioned me to follow him inside, which I did. Like a shadow, Ellie kept one step behind me. Dillon opened the file cabinet and took out a small cardboard box. He opened it and placed the casing on the desk.

From my pocket, I produced the one I had fired and set it down beside the other. "Would you say the two match each other?"

"They are certainly the same caliber." He sat down to examine the two spent cartridges more closely. After a moment or two, he lifted his eyes. "Where did this one come from?"

"From a rifle at the Beresford house."

"They're fired from the same weapon. They both have the same irregular indentation from a faulty firing pin."

"*That's what I thought.*" *I then related as briefly as I could Ellie's story about Ogden Fenn mistakenly entering the room and finding Mr. Percy Lansdowne-Coutts in a compromising situation. I finished by saying how Ellie and I had gone to the mansion and found the incriminating weapon.*

"*What gave you the notion you'd find the rifle there?*"

I described Rodney Beresford's gun collection and how I had noticed one of the Sharps rifles missing. "*You told me it was a Sharps rifle that had killed Mr. Fenn. I just put two and two together.*"

After a moment's reflection, Dillon asked, "*Would you mind coming with me to the Beresford house?*"

A short time later we rode into the still empty courtyard. Needless to say, Ellie remained glued to me. I led the way up the stairs to Percy Lansdowne-Coutts' room. I stood to one side. Dillon opened the door and he and I went inside. I was about to exclaim "*There is your murder weapon,*" *when, to my astonishment, I saw the rifle was no longer on the floor. It was nowhere to be seen.*

He gave me a blank look. At that moment, Ellie, who was in the corridor, cried out, "*There's someone going down the other stairs.*"

We left the room and heard frantic footsteps descending the staircase at the far end of the corridor. Whoever it was reached the ground floor and a door slammed.

The three of us ran to the stairs and were half way down when there came the unmistakable sound of a gun being fired. Dillon took the remaining steps four at a time. He was in the front yard by the time Ellie and I caught up.

"The shot came from in there." He motioned to the stables. "You two get behind the house door. Don't move until I come for you."

I took Ellie by the arm and we retreated into the house. We stood with the door open just enough for us to watch Dillon pull his service revolver from its holster and advance across the yard. He positioned himself to one side of the closed stable door. No sound or movement came from within. With his pistol raised, he kicked open the door and rushed inside.

Ellie squeezed my arm. "What do you think's happening?"

"I've no idea, but it doesn't look good." I held the girl close.

It was several minutes before Dillon emerged. He holstered his pistol and came across to us. I knew from his grim expression that something unpleasant had occurred. Because he wasn't forthcoming with an explanation, I must have made a move as if to go and see for myself.

He gripped my arm. "No, I don't want you to go in there."

I touched his arm. "It's Mr. Lansdowne-Coutts, isn't it?"

Dillon nodded. "He used the Sharps you found in his room."

"The one he used to kill Mr. Fenn?"

"That's what it looks like."

"He's dead?"

"Yes. I would guess he found the gun on the floor of his room and saw it had been fired."

"What prompted him to leave the picnic?"

"The gentleman was standing not far away from me when my trooper galloped up and he would have

seen me mount up. It's my guess he remembered he still
had the murder weapon his room and figured that if he
could return the rifle to the gun room, it would then be
merely one rifle among many, with no link to him. He
probably waited until he could get away unnoticed,
came to the house with the intention of taking the rifle
back to the gun room. When he heard us arrive, he knew
the game was up."

Dillon went over and brought my horse. "You and
Ellie go back to the settlement. I have work to do here.
Tomorrow, I'll call at the Addersley residence and ask
you both for a formal statement."

I mounted Morgana. Dillon hoisted Ellie up
behind me.

He looked up at me and smiled. "I have to admit
that was clever reasoning on your part. I'm not sure my
superiors would have approved of you and young Miss
Ellie, here, putting yourselves in harm's way. As I said
before, pity the North-West Mounted doesn't recruit
women. We could use talent like yours."

Ellie and I rode home. Neither of us spoke. In my
mind I kept going over and over what had just
happened. I tried to fathom why Mr. Lansdowne-Coutts
would have been motivated to murder Ogden Fenn. I
was also in shock at being, once more, closely connected
to an unnatural death. More than anything I regretted
that young Ellie had to be there. I could see she was
frightened and I did my best to comfort her. I'm sure I'll
talk more to Dillon about Mr. Lansdowne-Coutts. Dillon
seems convinced that he committed the murder. I still
have a head full of questions, but if that man was guilty
of the crime, we can all take some satisfaction from
knowing that the murder has been solved.

Chapter 31

The self-inflicted death of Mr. Percy Lansdowne-Coutts sent a tsunami of shock waves through the closely-knit Cannington society that shook the famous English stoicism to its core. For a few days at least, the tragedy dominated conversation at every dinner table.

However, because of the sexual overtones to Fenn's murder and his killer's subsequent suicide, no one was disposed to delve too deeply into details or motives. At the Addersleys, Mr. Seth Teague summed up the consensus among the Cannington residents with, "The chap did the only honorable thing."

With those words all mention of the incident ceased. As if by mutual agreement, no one uttered the names Ogden Fenn or Percy Lansdowne-Coutts. The same indifference to the vicissitudes of fortune applied to the attempt on Carina's life, the drowning of Niven DeQuincy and the scandalous behavior of Maud Addersley, now Mrs. Julian Chesterman. Banned too, was all mention of the outrageous Mrs. Sybil Halliday. Word came that Mr. Rodney Beresford had left the settlement to travel to the spa at Baden-Baden in Germany for an extended course of balneotherapy to treat his arthritis. The dinner table discussion soon reverted to the perennially-vital topics that Carina had heard so often.

Carina, herself, advanced her departure plans. The impetus came after a late night talk with Alfred Addersley. She was preparing for bed when a knock came on her door. Puzzled that anyone would want to speak to her at that late hour, she pulled on her robe and opened the door to find her uncle pacing the landing carpet. "What is it, uncle? Is something wrong?"

er3013011301301301ode -301

"No, no, my dear, nothing grievous. I was wondering if it's possible to have a quiet chat with you."

"Yes, of course. Please come in."

Alfred, who was still wearing evening clothes, entered.

Carina pulled up the wicker armchair. "Would you care to sit down?"

"Thank you." Alfred sat and stared about the room, as if looking for a cue to begin speaking. "I'm terribly sorry to trouble you so late in the evening."

Carina sat facing him on the straight-backed chair. "That's perfectly all right, uncle. What is it you wanted to see me about?"

For another minute her uncle said nothing but sat with his head tilted forward. For a moment she wondered if he was unabashedly admiring her bare ankles and pink satin slippers exposed below the edge of the dressing gown. She tucked her feet under the chair. Since her uncle's gaze didn't alter, she had to assume he was gathering his thoughts. She waited for him to speak.

"Remind me how old you are," he said at last.

"I'll be nineteen in the fall."

Alfred eased his spectacles up the bridge of his nose and peered at her. "My, my, Carina, you are an extremely handsome young lady. I must say I have enjoyed the time you have spent with us. You certainly do bring a refreshing breath of modernity to our sometimes rather stuffy existence here in Cannington."

"Thank you for the compliment."

"Personally, nothing would give me greater pleasure than if you took up permanent residence among us."

"But..?"

"I'm afraid my unbounded admiration of you is not completely shared by my lady wife."

"I did have the impression that my presence in the house has placed something of a strain on Aunt Rosalind. Though, I don't know why. I've tried my best not to be a burden on anyone."

Alfred held up his hand. "No need for an apology. I recognize that you have, indeed, been exceptionally accommodating, always ready to assist in whatever needs to be done, always the epitome of discretion. I regret that dear Rosalind sees things differently. She broke down yesterday and declared that before you arrived, life was peaceful and uneventful. According to dear Rosalind, you came and brought in your train a veritable whirlwind of calamities. She asked me to come and talk to you."

"I agree there have been some awful happenings in the few months I've been in the settlement. Yet, the murder of Mr. Fenn and the death of Mr. Lansdowne-Coutts were quite independent of my being here."

"That's perfectly correct. What has severely afflicted my wife has to do with Maud. Rosalind was hoping Mr. Featherstonehaugh would eventually come round to making a proposal of marriage to the girl. I must say, the old duffer never seemed in any hurry to do so."

"I'll accept some responsibility for changing Maud's attitude, mostly in regards to clothes. Under my influence she adopted a fashion more fitting with her age and natural beauty. Before that, Maud complained that the reverend gentleman in question never paid her the slightest attention. That changed dramatically when she stepped out with a more stylish appearance."

Her words brought a smile to her uncle's lips. "Yes, I myself noticed the transformation. I hadn't before realized just how beautiful a daughter I had."

"When he saw the new Maud, Mr. Featherstonehaugh might well have intended to declare himself, but by then it was too late."

"Too late?"

"With her new outlook on life, Maud saw what kind of a man he was."

"Excuse me, I am not asking you to be indiscreet but what kind of a man is he, from a woman's point of view, that is?"

"I'm sure Mr. Featherstonehaugh has many redeeming qualities, but many women would find him haughty and overbearing."

"Haughty and overbearing, now that is interesting. Yes, I suppose, come to think of it, even I find him tedious to talk to. Some of today's churchmen are like that, you know."

"I'll admit that Maud acted in a rash manner in running off with my brother."

"Indeed, and that is at the heart of my wife's chagrin. She's highly sensitive to the opinions of others in society. Maud's taking off sent tremors through our ranks, much to my wife's annoyance. She also heaps blame on you for some of the other tumultuous events."

"You mean, those concerning Mr. DeQuincy?"

"I am sorry to say that dear Rosalind suffered a fit of hysteria and never fully comprehended the severity of that man's violence toward you. For that, I do humbly apologize."

Carina tugged her dressing gown around her. "That's all over now. The man's dead."

"Yes, indeed. It's curious how in a short space of time we've had three sudden deaths in Cannington. That's three more than during the whole period since its inception."

From the way the conversation was progressing, Carina could see herself spending the rest of the night dissecting everything that had offended Rosalind Addersley's sensibilities. After DeQuincy, there was Sybil. It was no understatement to say that that woman's sojourn in the settlement had ruffled many upper class feathers, not least those of Algernon Beresford upon his return from Ottawa. And after Sybil, Millie's short stay had not been without its drama. She wondered whether her uncle was prepared to discuss the reason why Percy Lansdowne-Coutts gunned down Ogden Fenn, but was not surprised when he glossed over the subject.

With the intention of bringing the conversation to a close, she said, "Uncle, I've decided to leave Cannington. That might go some way to easing the burden on your wife."

Alfred looked at her, expressionless. "Have you, now? I can appreciate your desire to put the unpleasantness you've experienced behind you, but you can't consider leaving just yet. Let me see, the cricket club dance is a week next Saturday. We wouldn't want you to miss that. Then, at the beginning of next month Cannington holds its harvest festival, a really jolly event accompanied by a splendid banquet and ball."

Carina smiled at the well-meaning Englishman. She didn't expect him to appreciate the ambivalent situation she would be in if she agreed to stay on as he suggested, when all the while, his wife was wishing to see the back of her. In spite of the pleas to stay, the urge to leave was stronger. The last tenuous threads holding her to this English outpost had fallen away. There was much she would regret leaving behind, above all, her beloved Morgana. The settlement's ordinary inhabitants, too, were kind and hospitable. She would miss the social life, particularly the tennis and other sports. She had also grown fond of young Ellie and her grandparents. Saying goodbye to them was going to be particularly heart-wrenching. As for Dillon Granger, her encounters with him would come to an end. Although, upon reflection, now that his murder investigation was all but wound up, he would be returning to his regular duties in the capital, which was where she was heading. So, their friendship might possibly continue there.

Before ending their midnight colloquy, Alfred made her promise to consider delaying her departure, at least for the time being. The impetus that clinched a more pressing date for her leave-taking came in the form of a letter from Maud to her parents. Along with the encouraging news that Julian might be free on bail in a matter of weeks was a note addressed to Carina. Maud wrote that Theodore Chesterman had taken seriously ill and was under the care of one the town's two doctors.

Her uncle promptly declared that she must hasten to her father's bedside. Her trunk and hatbox were brought down from the attic and she began sorting through her clothes and other belongings. Ellie volunteered to help her pack.

The girl was folding Carina's riding clothes when she said, "Life without you isn't going to be the same, Miss Carina."

"I'll write. And, perhaps, we can arrange for you to pay me a visit in Regina."

"Would you? That would make me very happy."

Carina begged her uncle to be excused from the customary round of farewell teas and dinners thrown for all departing long-term visitors. She wished to quit the settlement with the least amount of fanfare. He readily agreed, on account of the need for haste. In addition, she requested that she travel to the station in the same manner in which she arrived, that is, by the buckboard driven by Norman Tucker and accompanied by Ellie. Her uncle raised his eyebrows but said he would arrange for it to be ready early on the morning of her departure.

On her last day, she called on a few close acquaintances to bid an informal farewell. Her aunt was quick to point out that proper etiquette ruled out an unchaperoned visit to the police detachment, to which Carina reacted with amusement, thinking of the number of times she had been there alone. However, she was overjoyed when she met Dillon in the street.

He doffed his hat. "I hear you are leaving this fair town."

"Perhaps, it's for the better. As they say in French, I brought *malheur* in my wake. Quite a few unpleasant things occurred since I came."

"You can't blame yourself for any of that. It's the DeQuincys and the Lansdowne-Coutts of this world who carry misfortune with them."

Carina informed him of her father's condition and he expressed his regret. Their conversation lapsed into silence. She held out her hand. "Thank you, Dillon, for your support when I needed it most."

He pressed her fingers "It is I who must thank you. The Ogden Fenn murder could well have sat for a very long time in the unsolved crimes folder if it hadn't been for you."

"And Ellie."

"Yes, let's not forget Ellie. My work is complete, here. I, too, will be leaving soon. Trooper Durkin has been promoted corporal and will be in charge of this detachment. That means I will no longer be visiting Cannington with the same regularity as before. By the way, do you have somewhere to stay in Regina? What accommodation there's in the capital isn't really suitable for a woman on her own."

Carina shrugged. "My father was staying in the Empire Hotel. I suppose that's where I will put up until I can find something better."

"If I may make a suggestion, there's a lady, a widow by the name of Mrs. Faith Nesbitt, who has recently taken up residence in the city. Her late husband, Harold Nesbitt, was the dominion's chief surveyor for the territory. He died just under a year ago. Rather than return East, which is what many women in her situation would do, Mrs. Nesbitt decided to remain in the territorial capital. She had a fine house built on Victoria Avenue. I've had the pleasure of meeting her on a number of occasions and feel pretty sure she would welcome you to stay with her until you make your own arrangements."

"Thank you for that information. I look forward to meeting Mrs. Nesbitt. What number is her house on Victoria Avenue?"

Dillon grinned. "That I don't know. But since there are so few ladies in Regina and so few houses on Victoria Avenue, it won't be difficult to track her down. Ask someone and they'll point out where she lives."

Carina hesitated, then asked, "Are you busy, right now?"

"No, why?"

"Would you walk with me as far as the tennis courts and back? There's something I want to discuss with you."

"It will be my pleasure. Take my arm."

Oblivious to any stares she might receive, she slipped her arm into the crook of his.

Only when they reached a section of boardwalk with hardly any other pedestrians did Carina broach the subject that had been troubling her for some time. "Could you give me your professional opinion on why Mr. Lansdowne-Coutts felt the need to murder poor Mr. Fenn? I know what he was engaged in was unlawful. But why murder?"

"First, let me tell you what the law has to say. Until fairly recently, sexual relations between men, which is what we are talking about, was a capital offence."

"Punishable by death?"

"That changed to life imprisonment and in recent years the law has become somewhat more lenient. Offenders, however, can still expect long prison terms."

"Yet men take that risk. Why, when the penalty is so severe?"

"If I knew what drives men to have intimate relations with other men, I probably would be a college professor not a police officer. In spite of what many eminent religious leaders tell us to the contrary, it's my belief that some men are born that way. It's as natural for them to be attracted to a male partner as it is for other men to be attracted to women. Does that offend you?"

"Me? I've not given it much thought. If, as you say, some are born like that, then, as far as I'm concerned, it's all part of nature. Perhaps it explains why Mr. Lansdowne-Coutts was found doing what he was doing. It doesn't help to explain why he took a rifle and killed Mr. Fenn."

"That part is more difficult to understand. I don't much like the notion of two men being intimate with each other, but we have more serious matters to attend to than policing what goes on in people's bedrooms. Personally, what happens between two adult males, or females, for that matter, is their business not mine and ought not to concern the law. I hope I'm not speaking out of turn, here, but that activity..."

"Relations between men?"

"Correct. The practice is not uncommon among certain upper class Englishmen. I can offer no explanation why. It may have something to do with the way families raise their sons, sending them to all-male boarding schools at a very young age. In my police career I've had to deal with more than just the isolated case, but this is the first time it led to murder."

"Have you heard of a similar case?"

"Not in the territories. A few years ago there was a case in the province of Ontario. A young girl in her early teens was taking a shortcut across a stretch of rough grassland on her way home from school. It appears she stumbled across two men engaged in the kind of activity we've been discussing."

"How awful for her. What happened?"

"One or both of the men involved pursued her and stabbed her to death."

Carina gasped. "So that she couldn't report them to the police?"

"That was the only conceivable motive."

"Were the two men tried for murder?"

"One of them. The other fled to the United States, where he was killed in a saloon brawl."

"It's all so depressing. In the case of Mr. Fenn and Mr. Lansdowne-Coutts, we have one life wasted and another thrown away."

Carina and Dillon reached the tennis courts and took the opposite boardwalk for the return. They reached the police detachment and said their farewells. On her way to the house, her mood, whilst not joyous, was less somber than it had been.

The next morning, before it was fully light, she left Cannington Manor, riding on the high seat of the buckboard beside Norman Tucker. Ellie, having dropped back to sleep, lay under a blanket on a cushion of hay in the back. No one was abroad to see them go.

At the edge of the settlement, Carina took one last look behind her, sensing that it would be the last time she would set eyes on Cannington Manor.

Chapter 32

Regina, Monday, September 15, 1884

I've been in the territorial capital now just over three weeks and consider myself extremely lucky to have made the acquaintance (thanks to Sergeant Dillon Granger) of Faith Nesbitt. Immediately I got off the train I made inquiries and was directed to her house on Victoria Avenue. She received me graciously and, after a pleasant hour of conversation, asked if I'd like to board with her. She treats me more like a friend than a lodger and I feel quite at home. I believe she's happy to have a female companion to share this spacious house of hers.

Faith is a remarkable lady, in her mid-fifties, with a determined streak of independence about her, which I very much admire. After her husband's death, her family in Orangeville, southern Ontario urged her to move back there. Having accompanied her husband on a great many of his survey expeditions and living for months at a time in rough conditions under canvas, she was reluctant to return to eastern Canada and be obliged to reintegrate into a social structure every bit as claustrophobic as that of Cannington's. On that score, she and I are of one mind. She is a diminutive woman. The top of her head barely reaches my shoulder and I am average in height. What she lacks in stature she makes up in forcefulness of personality.

She obviously loved and admired her late
husband, Harold. Portraits of him adorn her
occasional tables and mantelpiece. There are
informal photographs, sometimes of him alone,
sometimes with his survey crews, surrounded by his
surveying paraphernalia. In one he stands, beardless
but heavily mustached, beside a tripod-mounted
theodolite. Behind him is a tent stretched over
spruce poles. The surrounding terrain is made up of
huge granite boulders and dense coniferous forest.
Interestingly, that same theodolite and tripod now
stands by Faith's drawing room window, an
invitation to peer through the lens at the level
prairie beyond. He surveyed thousands of square
miles of the Canadian West with the instrument.
When I remarked that it looked like new, she replied
that he had treated his beloved instruments like they
were babies, always keeping them safe from harm.
The tripod, however, shows signs of use. One can
make out stains and scratches on the wooden legs.

My arrival in the capital was none too soon as
far as my father was concerned. When I visited, the
poor man was bedridden. The community does not
yet have a proper civic hospital. A compassionate
woman by the name of Mrs. Mary Truesdell has
opened a private hospital in her house, with beds for
four men and two women. There are two doctors and
a handful of nurses in the community, but the health
services are woefully inadequate for a capital city
with a growing population. Because the water and
sewer system is still very primitive, the danger of a
typhoid outbreak is ever present. I was touched that
the police permitted Julian, under escort, to visit his

dying father. Poor papa scarcely recognized me, and I'm sad to record that he died three days later.

Father's death closes a chapter in my life, the most tumultuous part being my stay in Cannington.

My grandiose plan to come to Regina and set myself up as a music teacher has yet to get off the ground. I made inquiries and was shocked by what it would cost to ship a piano (even a modest upright) from Montreal. And to add insult to injury, I would have to pay excise duties on it when it came into the territories. The Regina Leader is highly critical of the government in Ottawa who treats the Northwest as though it is a foreign country, separate from Canada. The paper claims that the West was being exploited by the East. We are to Canada what India is to Britain.

The lack of a piano is but one impediment. The other is that, despite considerable growth, especially over the five months I've been away, Regina remains mostly a population of single men. To the best of my knowledge, single men are not disposed to wanting music lessons and, without a more balanced population, I would have difficulty recruiting pupils. Fortunately, thanks to my dear Aunt Louise's legacy, there is less urgency for me to find gainful employment right away.

Talking of Aunt Louise, I still have what is left of the beautiful flute she gave me, even though it is so badly damaged I doubt it could ever be repaired. Faith, who is herself quite musical, tells me that I would be better off with one of the newer silver flutes, and even hinted she might make me a present of one for my birthday in a month's time. I trust I'll never again have to use my flute to fight off an attacker.

I was firmly convinced I had severed my ties with the English colony when I boarded the train in Moosomin. I was wrong. Three days ago, I was in the kitchen preparing lunch, when Faith announced that a young person was at the door and wished to speak to me.

"I invited her to wait in the vestibule," Faith said.

To my surprise I found Ellie standing there. She looked quite grown up in a neat gray skirt and white shirtwaist blouse under a woolen coat. Her abundant dark hair was pinned up under a hat sporting a small spray of silk flowers.

The instant she saw me she rushed and gave me a hug. "Miss Carina, it's lovely to see you again!"

"Ellie, what brings you to Regina?" I cut short her reply as I sensed it would be a long story. Instead, I dragged her into the kitchen and introduced her to Faith.

Needless to say, Faith took to Ellie right away and insisted she stay for lunch. To avoid filling too much of this journal with the lengthy particulars, suffice to say Ellie had been sent to me by her grandparents. She produced from her pocket a rather crumpled letter written by Norman Tucker. In it he described how, since the death of Captain Mitchell Pierce and that of the agricultural college principal, Mr. Lansdowne-Coutts, discipline among the pups has deteriorated. The young gentlemen spend too many hours in the saloon bar of the Mitre Inn and conduct themselves in such a riotous manner that no woman, not even a married woman, feels safe. Tucker said they were casting lustful glances at Ellie, a girl of fourteen. He went on to express doubts on the very survival of the colony after the government's refusal to construct the spur line.

The letter ended with an apology for imposing on me and asked if I'd take the girl under my wing until things became more settled in Cannington, although he feared conditions in the settlement could get worse. He was prepared to send money to help toward her keep.

Of course, all this was discussed over lunch. When Faith grasped Ellie's predicament, she laid her open hand on the tablecloth and adamantly declared that Ellie was to stay here with us. She asked Ellie about her grandfather and, upon learning that he worked as a stableman, would not hear of him sending money. She instructed me to convey that to him. So, here Ellie is, and you've never seen a happier young lady. Faith, who never had children of her own, seems bent on virtually adopting the girl,

After Ellie settled in, she and I had a long conversation. I asked her what she'd like to do with her life when she gets older. She had no hesitation telling me her ambition was to become a teacher. Her own education is sorely lacking and she's the first to recognize that. She has, however, a thirst for knowledge. I, apparently, made a great impression on her with my books, my ability to speak French and play the flute and piano. Hmm!

A plan came to me. My father, in his will, left me a sum of money (it seems that papa managed to conceal some of his assets from his creditors). It's by

no means a fortune but a useful amount, all the
same. Julian received a larger portion of father's
estate. I don't begrudge him that as it'll enable him
to get back on his feet when he can finally put his
criminal past behind him. (I have met Maud and
discussed it with her). Personally, I am ambivalent
about this inheritance, because I have no assurance
that father made the money by honest means and
can't help thinking of it as tainted wealth. But one
cannot just throw it away. I then thought that if I
invested it wisely, in a few years time when Ellie is
of age, I can use the interest to send her to train as a
teacher. That way, my father's unscrupulous
conduct will be in part redeemed by Ellie's success.

There is no teacher training institution in
Regina, the nearest one being the normal school in
Brandon in Manitoba province (Brandon is a small
city on the transcontinental rail line). I cautiously
sounded Ellie out on the proposal and she was
ecstatic. I think she'd make an excellent teacher. She
has a quick mind, a sense of humor, endless patience
and a tough streak of character, just what is needed
to inspire and handle a class of rambunctious youth.
Until she can go and study, she'll remain here and
Faith and I will help rectify her inadequate
schooling by instructing her in mathematics,
history, languages and science and whatever else she
needs. She, in turn, wants to repay us by working as
she did in my uncle's house.

Faith agreed to the arrangement. She's
quickly realized that Ellie, although a simple, rustic
girl, possesses a strong sense of pride and self-worth.

Another reminder of the recent past arrived
in the mail this morning in the form of a letter from

Millie. It was addressed to me in Cannington but had been forwarded on. I saw by the postmark that the letter had been mailed fourteen days previously from Fort Benton in Montana Territory, in the United States. She writes:

My Dearest Carina,

Please don't judge me too harshly for leaving Cannington with only a hastily-written note of farewell and no proper explanation for my going. My impetuous action lies heavy on my conscience. Late in the evening before our departure the following morning, Sybil called at the house. I don't know where you were, possibly in bed already. Sybil had decided that the time had come for her to leave the settlement but declined to give a reason for it. As I said in my note, I imagine it was because of the tragic death of her close friend Mr. Niven DeQuincy.

I begged her to allow me to go with her. After some hesitation, she agreed. I was happy because I have no desire to return home and live with mother just yet.

Sybil plans to go to San Francisco but said we first travel to the Alberta District to take up the invitation to visit her old acquaintance Lord Cottesmere. Consequently, we took the train to Calgary and then the overland stage to a small town called Pincher Creek, which is the nearest settlement to his lordship's ranch. Unfortunately, whilst in the town we learned that the old gentleman had died just weeks before. Nonetheless, his nephew Toby, who had inherited his uncle's fortune, insisted we come to the ranch. During our week-long stay, Sybil and I were feted like royalty.

It appears to be the custom in the West that periods of mourning are kept short and that for his lordship was over by the time we arrived. Consequently, the evenings were given over to house parties, dances and musical recitals, with lots to eat and drink, especially the latter! Ranchers and several ladies from the surrounding area attended. We had some wonderful times. Everyone pressed us to remain longer but Sybil was anxious to be off.

We crossed the border into the United States and came down here to Fort Benton, situated on the Missouri River. The town itself is somewhat rough and tumble. The area is abuzz with gold mining. Day and night the streets are jammed with miners from the creeks and with men who work on the wharves, many of whom are exceedingly uncouth fellows. The main street is lined on both sides with saloons, dance halls and gambling joints. Bartenders come out and toss used decks of cards up in the air and the wind scatters them far and wide to be trodden into the dust by *the constant horse and wagon traffic. It is completely different to anything I've seen before.*

San Francisco is a city I've heard so much about, but this morning Sybil announced we were to spend the winter in Fort Benton and said she had rented a large furnished house for us both. Carina, I'm beginning to wonder if I haven't made a terrible mistake. I don't feel comfortable in discussing this with Sybil. She is always so enthusiastic and would only laugh at me. Yet, her behavior worries me, particularly regarding the many wealthy gentlemen she appears to have no trouble making friends with. For now, I suppose the old saying applies to me – I made my bed and now must sleep in it.

I long to hear from you and receive news of you and your peaceful life in beautiful Cannington Manor. Do write soon.

With all my love, your faithful friend,
Millie

Poor Millie! I'll write to her without delay to bring her up to date with my news and to hold out the hand of friendship. If she wants to come to Regina or return to Montreal, I'll do my best to help.

That evening, Carina took a solitary walk to the edge of town to watch the sunset. Even now in mid-September, a warm wind lifted her hair. The prairie vista here was not dissimilar to what she had grown accustomed to south of Cannington, the grass at her feet dry and brown from the hot summer sun. Several varieties of wild grasses grew on the stubborn soil. Yet it was the needle and thread grass that would forever remind her of her sojourn in the English colony and her talks with Ogden Fenn. She thought about him and wondered about the future of the empty land that stretched into the distance, now that his voice had been silenced. One thought led to another. About this hour, the genteel citizens of Cannington, dressed in their evening clothes, would be sitting down to dinner. Carina could not help imagining them as cabin-class passengers on some elegant ocean vessel, seated beneath crystal chandeliers at linen-covered tables, blissfully ignorant of the fact that their ship had struck a reef and was slowly sinking.

The five-month episode which constituted her stay in Cannington marked a turning point, not only in her life but in everything around her. Although many people, like those in the English colony, were as yet unaware of the changes to come.

The the sun sank below the horizon. Darkness began to creep over the land. Silhouetted against the afterglow in the western sky stood the buildings of the North-West Mounted Police headquarters that lay two miles from the town. She thought about Dillon. A smile came to her lips. In the gathering dusk she turned and walked home.

55434955R00180

Made in the USA
San Bernardino, CA
01 November 2017